KW-480-345

Praise for Deborah Swift

'This impeccably researched wartime thriller had me gripped from the opening pages – I loved it. My pulse was racing and at times my heart broke as Nancy's intelligence operation in The Hague grew more dangerous by the day'
Eliza Graham

'A fast-paced, exciting read ... kept me reading late on several nights. Will appeal to all lovers of both romance and wartime novels'
Kathleen McGurl

'Had me gripped from beginning to end ... Swift portrays the last desperate months of the war in Holland so vividly I found it hard to put *Operation Tulip* down'
Eva Glyn

'A nail-biting read from start to finish. Edge-of-your-seat action and a desperate romance make this a must for WW2 fiction fans'
Tessa Harris

'With real history in the raw, heart-pounding drama, bone-chilling cruelty, plot twists, and the sheer power of true love, this is a terrific finale to an unforgettable series.'
Yorkshire Post

DEBORAH SWIFT is a *USA TODAY* bestselling author of historical fiction, a genre she loves. As a child, she enjoyed reading the Victorian classics such as *Jane Eyre, Little Women, Lorna Doone* and *Wuthering Heights*. She has been reading historical novels ever since, though she's a bookaholic and reads widely – contemporary and classic fiction.

In the past, Deborah used to work as a set and costume designer for theatre and TV, so enjoys the research aspect of creating historical fiction, something she was familiar with as a scenographer. More details of her research and writing process can be found on her website www.deborahswift.com.

Deborah likes to write about extraordinary characters set against the background of real historical events.

Also by Deborah Swift

The Silk Code
The Shadow Network
Operation Tulip

Last Train to Freedom

DEBORAH SWIFT

ONE PLACE. MANY STORIES

HQ
An imprint of HarperCollins*Publishers* Ltd
1 London Bridge Street
London SE1 9GF

www.harpercollins.co.uk

HarperCollins*Publishers*
Macken House, 39/40 Mayor Street Upper,
Dublin 1 D01 C9W8

This edition 2025

1

First published in Great Britain by
HQ, an imprint of HarperCollins*Publishers* Ltd 2025

Printed and bound in the UK using 100% Renewable
Electricity by CPI Group (UK) Ltd

MIX
Paper | Supporting
responsible forestry
FSC™ C007454

This book contains FSC™ certified paper and other controlled
sources to ensure responsible forest management.

For more information visit: www.harpercollins.co.uk/green

Printed and bound in the UK using 100%
Renewable Electricity at CPI Group (UK) Ltd

'There are decades where nothing happens;
and there are weeks where decades happen.'
Vladimir Ilyich Lenin

'ichi-go ichi-e'
Japanese proverb,
literally one time, one meeting.
An encounter that happens only once in a lifetime,
and a reminder to treasure every moment.

Chapter 1

Kaunas, Lithuania

June 1940

Zofia stirred the pot in the airless heat. The stew would never be eaten, but Zofia didn't know that yet. Unfinished things were already a part of her life, as they were for so many in wartime. The book half-read where she would never know the ending, her best crepe dress left hanging in the wardrobe in Warsaw for the concert that would never happen.

She tugged open a shutter to let in some breeze and flapped a hand at the flies perched lazily on the sill. She paused to stare. There in the distance, movement caught her eye. Beyond the white church spire wavering in the heat, a cavalcade of ragged figures moved through a cloud of yellow dust. She swallowed, her stomach tightening. More refugees. Already there were too many sheltering from the sun on the steps of the library, and every day as she passed them on her way into work, she was glad to have been one of the early ones. How could there possibly be room for more?

She turned away and dabbed her forehead with a damp

dishcloth; the upstairs kitchen was stifling, with the sort of dry heat that made her neck run with sweat. She longed for the cleansing power of rain, for something to take the choke from her throat. Cooking for nine was no joke, but it was her turn, so she returned to the stove to stir the goulash.

Nine mouths: Uncle Tata, her twin brother Jacek, if he deigned to appear for dinner at all, and the people she called 'the Marks' – the Markunas family, Lithuanians who had taken them in when they'd fled Poland.

Right now, she could hear the bumps and thumps of the Marks in the downstairs shop, sorting and boxing their stock, the thick church candles and lamp oil that made the house always smell of beeswax and burning. A scrape of boxes being dragged below. They feared a Russian invasion and were getting ready to move out, all six of them, Mr and Mrs, the in-laws and the two sons.

Yesterday Zofia had been helping them too, but now the thought that she and Jacek would have to find new lodgings when the Marks moved out was hard to bear, and she refused to contemplate the prospect of being homeless again. She hoped Tata would have an answer.

Don't think of it. Salt the stew. She sprinkled in a liberal amount and stirred hard.

When this stove wasn't used for cooking, it was used for melting wax. Zofia ran a thumb along the edge of the hotplate to scrape up a curl of wax with her nail. It melted instantly into grease. They were all waiting for something. Everyone knew that the Russians were massed like a dark smudge just over the border, but no one knew what would happen, and the waiting made everyone brittle, ready to crack and break. The Marks – foolish or, who knows, wise – had unsettled everyone and decided to run.

Zofia had had enough of running. It hadn't even been a year since they'd fled Poland. When the Nazis invaded, they'd come here, to Lithuania. It would be safe, they'd thought. But now the influx of so many refugees from the border was a bad sign. People running away must be afraid of something.

Zofia put a spoon back into the goulash and brought it to her mouth, huffing over it to take away the heat. The meat had to be cooked and spiced because the sun had already turned their ration rancid, and there was only so much kosher meat available. The taste of old beef and cloves was sharp on her tongue, so she spat the undercooked gristle onto the spoon and tipped it in the bin.

She was glad when the Marks were downstairs in the shop. When they were up here, with a grand piano that took up half the space, there was no room to move. How in heaven's name they'd ever got it up here, she'd no idea.

Every house in Kaunas was the same, full to the brim of ragged Polish Jews like them, paying handsomely for the privilege. The three of them, the Kowalskis, were lucky to find a place, though the rent for such a tiny bedroom was exorbitant. Mrs Marks would shrug and apologize, as though to say, *not my fault*, but still insist on counting Uncle Tata's coins out right in front of him, as if she didn't trust him. Him, a teacher. It was humiliating.

Zofia helped herself to a few chunks of potato from the bottom of the stew and put them in her bowl. These days you had to see to yourself first. She'd had to fight Jacek for her share of everything ever since they were toddlers, and heaven forbid, she wasn't going to stop now.

Jacek was the first back. Impatient as always, these days he could never be still, prowling round the room like a lost wolf. 'Is it ready yet?'

'No. Meat's still tough. Another twenty minutes.'

'I'll have mine now.' He grinned and reached to take the spoon from her hand.

'You won't!' She whipped it out of his reach. 'Not until it's properly cooked. Anyway, what's the hurry?'

'I'm meeting Masha. We're going to the Romuva.'

Zofia turned her back on him. Jacek had found himself a sweetheart. Though some Jewish boys had shown an interest in her, nobody had asked her out, even though she was the eldest. By a whole two minutes. 'What's on?'

'A western.'

'You're going to see that rubbish?'

'I need a break. The office is full of bad news. Desperate calls from Poland about how the Jews that stayed are being rounded up by the SS and deported. The reports land on my desk and I have to decide what to do with them. Whether to publish or not.' He ran a hand through his hair, frustrated. 'We can't keep putting out these horror stories. People left family behind; they have to have some hope.'

Zofia batted him away again as he reached for the spoon. 'Hands off! We'll wait for Uncle and the Marks.'

'Come on, serve up. The film starts in an hour.' Jacek thrust a bowl towards her as footsteps hurried up the stairs.

'Here's Uncle now.'

As if he'd heard her, Tata stepped through the door. He hugged Zofia without looking at her, as he always did.

She pushed away his familiar figure in its worn-out suit. 'Tata, I'm cooking.'

Uncle Tata kept his teacher's briefcase tight to his chest with both hands.

'Why are you looking at us like that?' Jacek hacked a slice off the end of the loaf.

'We think the Russians will move over the border,' he said. 'If they decide to invade, they'll be after men like us, so best be prepared and pack up your things.'

'They won't,' Jacek replied, through a mouthful of bread. 'The Russians signed a peace pact. It's just posturing, that's what Ivan at the office says. Nothing will happen.'

Uncle Tata was sweating from the walk home, and he put down his briefcase and took off his spectacles to wipe his forehead on his sleeve.

Jacek towered over his uncle already. Tata was smaller and

older, and years of worry had taken their toll in his bent spine and papery skin. Jacek was broad-shouldered, with the solidity of a tree. His thick brown hair sprang straight up from his forehead.

'The head at the school says the Soviets have demanded that Lithuania form a friendly government and allow Soviet troops into our territory. And you know what the Russians do to teachers,' Tata said, still clinging to his briefcase. 'Send them to Siberia. Any kind of intellectual. Stalin fears anyone who questions authority, especially foreigners. The purging has already begun in Vilnius. So today we leave.'

'Huh!' Jacek's laugh was scathing. 'Where to? The Baltic Sea? You're overreacting. You think I don't know what's going on? No one else is going. It's just you, looking for trouble where none exists.'

'The Marks are packing up, you know they are.'

'All the more room for us. Look, if I thought there was going to be trouble, I'd know. I'm not a journalist for nothing.'

Zofia concentrated on the cooking. She didn't want to be caught between her uncle and Jacek. Lately Jacek always thought he knew best. Since working at the paper, he had a sort of arrogance that got under her skin. Where had he learned it, this *I'm always right* attitude?

And her uncle was just as bad. He thought that now their father was gone, he was in charge of them both. She shifted the pot aside and off the heat. 'Why now, Tata? What's changed?'

'We think the rumours are true. The line got thicker. Tanks. More troops. More activity. Mr Sovik's sister has binoculars. She can see it from the school windows.'

Jacek had helped himself to goulash and was now blowing over the bowl. 'So Mrs Sovik's sister is the expert now, is she? The troops have been there three weeks. It's just a training exercise, that's what Masha's father says. He's friends with the Russians at border control, and he says Lithuania's staying neutral. You're getting in a panic over nothing.' Jacek drew himself up, and his

5

body language told her he was not going to give in, no matter what Tata might say.

Tata could feel it too and his face turned tight and grim in a way that meant he was about to boil over. 'I'm not wasting breath arguing. Get your things together, Zofia, the things you can carry. Jacek, I'm serious. It's what your father would want. Do as I say.'

Jacek ignored him, until Tata came to stand over him at the table.

'Get ready—'

'You go,' Jacek said. 'I'm staying here.'

'We go together as a family. I promised your father we'd stick together.'

Zofia winced. Bringing up their father was always her uncle's trump card, but she knew it would only rile Jacek.

Jacek's expression was steely. 'You made plenty of other promises, and you broke every single one. I remember you promising to defend Poland with your last breath. And then what happened? You turned tail and ran. You and my father both. Only he got shot and you survived. Don't you lecture me on promises.'

A clatter on the stairs made them look to the door. Mrs Marks gripped the doorframe, panting. She was a thick-waisted woman in a floral apron, with eyebrows that were always up as if surprised. She took a moment to catch her breath before she could speak. 'The Russians. They're over the border. Truckloads of them. They're heading this way. Douse the fire.'

She blustered away downstairs with Tata running after her, full of questions. Jacek leapt up from the table to follow them both. Not to be left behind, Zofia threw water over the hot coals, shoved the spoon back into the pan and ran after them.

The downstairs shop was half-empty, the air floating with dust, and the dark mahogany shelves bare of stock. Zofia steered her way past the packing cases as the Marks's sons, Andrius and Darius, hustled back and forth shouting instructions to each other. She dodged past them to the open door, where Mr Marks was loading everything onto their delivery cart. It was already piled high with boxes, and Mrs Marks's pinch-faced parents were waiting to leave, perched amongst the furniture, like two crows.

Unthinkingly, she helped Mr Marks hoist a box onto the cart, seeing that the main road was queued with traffic. She skirted round the cart to look over towards the town, where a snaking line of vehicles with bundles strapped to their roofs was blocking the route. Coaches, cars, trucks, motorcycles. Anyone with petrol was heading away, out of town.

How had the roads filled so quickly?

'Holy Shabbat. What did I tell you?' Tata shouted to Jacek, who was on tiptoe, peering over the cars, staring west.

Mr Marks heaved up a dining chair, the back of his waistcoat patched dark with sweat. He barely paused in his loading to speak. 'We're heading for the Polish border. We'll be safer there. Because of Andrius and his music.'

Zofia was shocked. They'd go to Nazi-occupied Poland? 'What about the piano? Don't you want that?' She couldn't believe they'd just leave everything.

'No. If the Reds come, having such a thing is a death sentence. And anyway, how could we even move it? If they find Andrius, the Russians will separate us, send him to a camp in Siberia, make him do hard labour. At least the Germans have culture.'

Culture? So shooting Jews like her father was 'culture' now, was it?

'Jacek. Better pack,' Tata insisted.

Zofia left Tata arguing with her brother and went to look from the upstairs window. She passed the piano, its inky black hood serene. How could such a thing be a death sentence? It didn't make sense.

She didn't want to run again. She remembered the feeling of rootlessness, of having nowhere to go. But the view showed her that half of Kaunas was already on the move, and by the time she got back downstairs the pavement outside the house was empty except for a few boxes spilling their candles into the dirt.

A stationary queue of cars was honking and belching smoke into the dusty air, and further down the queue she saw that the Marks's horse and cart had joined it. She felt sorry for their thick-set pony, who was only used to light deliveries; the poor thing would find this load hard to pull.

Zofia stood on tiptoes and looked to where her brother had been standing but there was no sign of him. 'Where's Jacek?' she asked her uncle.

'Can you believe the Marks went without even asking me for the rent? That's a first.'

'Where is he?' she repeated.

'Gone to find Masha and go to the film,' her uncle said.

'What, now? When he can see everyone leaving?'

'He's making a point. He doesn't want me to tell him what to do.'

Zofia shook her head. She understood her brother. Knew that the idea of running again was too much to bear. 'We can't get out today anyway; look at the traffic.'

'I blame that Masha, she's got Jacek wrapped around her little finger. If they catch him, they'll arrest him because of that article he wrote – about Stalin. Never mind that it's a two-bit local rag; in their eyes, he'll be a journalist, and anti-Soviet.'

The grim expression in her uncle's eyes galvanized her. 'What shall we do?'

'Try the railway station, maybe, go south. But I promised your father I'd look after you both.'

'We're grown up, Tata. You don't need to do it any more.'

'We stick together,' he said. 'I won't leave without Jacek.'

Zofia turned and surveyed the desolation of the room. Jacek's bowl with the meat that still wasn't cooked properly, and her own bowl untouched. Eating seemed impossible. A moment where there was no option but to face it – they'd really have to leave. Anxiety gripped her like a wire. Jacek was already volatile and unpredictable, filled with anger and terror since the trauma of getting over the Polish border. What would this do to him now, to run away again?

But Uncle Tata was right. They should stick together. She handed her uncle his hat. 'Come on, we have to go to the Romuva and try to find him,' she said.

Every street was jammed with people on the move. The rumours had spread fast, folk scattering like ants from a fire. When they got to the cinema, it was almost empty, but Zofia spotted Jacek and Masha on the back row, and heard Jacek's hoarse whisper to Masha – something derogatory, she guessed – as she and her uncle passed by.

Their relationship was complex. Jacek still blamed Uncle Tata for being alive when Papa was not. Thought it was somehow Tata's fault that the Nazis had shot Papa and not him, although he'd never say that to their uncle's face. War left behind so many unsaid things, but Zofia could read her twin like a book, and felt his hurts as her own.

The film had begun so, guiding her uncle, she felt her way through the dim light of the projector to sit a few rows further down from Jacek and Masha. Tata went ahead meekly; he'd obviously decided to wait until the end of the film to try to talk to Jacek again.

The film was *Stagecoach* starring John Wayne, a gaudy American film subtitled in Lithuanian. Zofia could make out what was happening because as well as her native Polish, she also spoke English. She had hoped to work as a translator, for she had three Slavic languages as well as Russian and English, and now she had absorbed Lithuanian from working in the library. She loved to learn other tongues and was soon engrossed in the film.

After about a half-hour she realied her uncle was shifting uncomfortably in his seat. After what had happened to them in Poland, the subject matter – the way the Apaches, whose native land had been taken over, were portrayed simply as murdering savages – was just too close to home.

A noise like a deep rumble grew louder, vibrating through the floor of the cinema. Zofia turned to try to catch Jacek's eye, but he too was craning his neck to see if anyone else knew the cause of the disturbance.

The film stopped abruptly and the cinema was plunged into silence and darkness. A man near the front got up and fumbled his way to open the double doors. He was soon back. 'Tanks,' he said in an incredulous voice. 'Tanks rolling down the street.' He sat down heavily in his seat. Nobody moved. Nobody knew what to do.

Uncle Tata grasped Zofia's hand and squeezed it tight.

They were silent, hunched in the velvet seats, ready to duck or run. After about ten minutes the film cranked back into life with a spit of light and a flicker. Now it seemed to be full of some sort of meaning. They endured the gunfights, the stand-off and shoot-out and the deaths, and they did what everyone else did – watched the film to the end.

As the credits rolled they were all reluctant to get out into the light. What would be out there? In summer the light was unforgiving. There was no real night here yet at this time of the year, it was too far north. Just an intense twilight that seemed to pierce like a needle.

'Come with us,' her uncle said to Jacek as he passed.

Jacek stubbornly refused to reply; his leg was bouncing up and down, though, as if he wanted to run.

They waited by the cinema doors, a knot of about twenty hot and frightened people. Finally, Jacek braced himself, threw open the door and walked out like a gunslinger going into a saloon.

'There's nobody about,' he said. 'Guess they've passed through.'

Everyone exhaled. Jacek turned to Masha, who was waiting uncertainly, her heavily made-up eyes flicking side to side. 'I'll walk you home, you can't go on your own.'

'Jacek?' Tata tried to get his attention. 'We need to stick together.'

10

Jacek gave Zofia a mock salute. 'See you later, sis.'

Zofia watched him link arms with Masha as she tottered away on her high platform shoes. Masha was the kind of woman who always looked to be trying too hard. Jacek was, of course, taken in. What was it with men who were supposedly intelligent, yet seemed unable to tell the difference between real blonde and bottle blonde?

Zofia felt bad for her uncle, who was now being ignored by Jacek as if he didn't exist. But she took Tata's arm as they headed back down the main shopping street. 'He'll come round,' she said, more to reassure herself than him.

She pulled on her uncle's sleeve. He'd stopped and was staring into a shop window. She followed his gaze, then froze. The display was empty except for a red cloth covering the whole inside of the window, and suspended in front of the cloth was a portrait of Stalin in a gold frame.

The door had been broken and the lock forced, the panels splintered as if someone had hit it with a sledgehammer.

Across the road, the shop opposite was the same. The interior of the window draped in red crepe, a portrait of Lenin in a frame hanging there. Her uncle was trembling now, all at once shrivelled into an old man.

'It's all right, they've gone,' she said, urging him to move.

'Too much red,' her uncle said as they walked onwards. Every shop was the same. No longer were the windows full of clothing or haberdashery. The patisserie was gone and the post office. The milk bar and the greengrocer. All red. All the same. Stalin or Lenin. These portraits of the men with their thick black moustaches would dwarf any passer-by.

It shook her, this visual shouting. It was so much like the red banners and swastikas that had appeared draped all over public buildings in Poland, and she knew Uncle Tata would be seeing the same. In him too, the stark apparition of the past would be rising up like a tide of blood.

11

It had happened so quickly. What about the people's liveli-hoods, she wondered. Where had they all gone?

Her question was answered by a woman in a headscarf pacing distractedly in the street, staring up at the picture of Lenin and scrubbing her streaming eyes with a handkerchief.

Cobbler. Same-Day Shoe Repair said the shop sign. 'I didn't believe it was true so I had to come and see. How could they do this?' she said. 'They've taken everything. The tanks came, then the lorries. They stripped it all. The leather, the lasts, even the nails. Jonas worked his whole life building up his business, for what? To be stolen by the Russians in less than an hour?'

They had no comfort they could offer, except to say, 'It's the same all down the street.'

Zofia steered Uncle Tata away as she offered her sympathies. She was anxious to get him home, desperate for something safe and familiar. 'Come on, Uncle,' she coaxed. They'd go back to the Marks's house and make a hot drink, sit in their familiar kitchen, find some sort of normality.

Uncle Tata stumbled and tripped, and grabbed onto her arm, all semblance of being her protector gone. Looking down, she saw that the pavements at this end of the street were crumbling, their kerbs crushed by tank treads.

As they rounded the corner into their street, she was relieved to see the house intact. The hinge of the garden gate squeaked its mousey squeak just the same, though the shop echoed oddly as they walked through it. Fortunately, the Marks had fled in too much of a hurry to ask for the return of the key. Once inside, Uncle Tata locked the door after them and barred it.

Without the noisy presence of the Marks, the place was shab-bier. Most of the furniture had gone and the walls had blank spaces where pictures used to hang. As she boiled up water for coffee, Zofia couldn't help but notice the congealed stew in the pan, the scuffs on the skirting boards, the broken slats on the shutters.

All evening they waited for Jacek to return, but he didn't come.

Zofia pressed a finger down on the key of the piano, and a single plaintive note hung in the air. And it occurred to her that without the Marks, and Andrius who had loved to play, the instrument would be forever dumb.

When they finally went to bed, even the soft scrunch of her uncle's restless turning on his horsehair mattress seemed loud. Once this tiny cupboard had been a storeroom, but now it housed two makeshift bunks and a pull-out mattress on the floor. Tata usually slept on the mattress, with Jacek on the top bunk and Zofia on the bottom one. Although the Marks had left, neither she nor Uncle Tata could bring themselves to use their beds, and instead they crammed themselves into their familiar hole.

In the morning her uncle got up and got dressed as usual, as if he was going to teach at the school, and she watched him pore through his textbooks as if their pages might supply the answers he needed.

'Aren't we leaving today?' Zofia asked.

'We'll eat first, then we'll wait and see. We'll have that goulash.'

He was waiting for Jacek to come home, but he had probably spent the night at Masha's. Zofia's heart ached. And she knew they couldn't go back to Poland like the Marks. Jews were not welcome anywhere on German-occupied soil, and she still remembered the bone-aching misery of the winter exodus from Poland and leaving those they loved behind. Not to mention the horrifying scene at the border, which had sent Jacek over the edge, and from which he had never quite recovered.

She kindled a fire and got out the tail-end of the loaf to cut it while the stew heated.

'I'll get yesterday's laundry in,' she said, aiming for a cheerful tone. 'It's still on the line.'

She brushed the crumbs off the table and then went out of the back door.

The grating noise of engines in the street made her stop as if in suspension, listening, the pegs gripped in her hands and the coldness of the fresh sheets damp against her blouse. Shouts and running footsteps. She whipped round as two soldiers in khaki uniforms with the red flash on the collar staved in the front door with the butts of their rifles. They were inside before she could even put the sheets in the basket. Another four swarmed after them into the house, and she let the sheets drop, aghast at the sheer brutal speed of it all.

'Wait! Stop!' Her limbs had finally caught up with her eyes. She ran, tripping and stumbling up the stairs. At the top, she took in the scatter of books on the table and the floor.

Uncle Tata was white-faced with a cut across his forehead. While two of them held him, they ransacked the house like a tornado, throwing open the doors of the cupboards, smashing china, hurling books off the shelves to the floor like righteous zealots overturning the tables at the temple.

What was it all for? Against such a frenzy, all Zofia could do was press herself against the kitchen wall.

'Downstairs.' One of the soldiers, a youth of about seventeen, ordered her uncle to move with a jerk of his rifle.

'He's done nothing!' she shouted, putting herself in their way. 'Your parents would be ashamed of you!'

She saw a moment of doubt in his eyes as she confronted him, but he was swept up by the zeal of the other Russian boys as they pushed her aside and by sheer force of numbers dragged Uncle Tata downstairs.

'Intelligentsiya!' they yelled, like it was an insult. Children in grown-up bodies, they were acting like it was some sort of game, with all the cruelty and malice of the playground. Except they were young ruddy-faced men full of vigour and strength.

Uncle Tata could do nothing, and he knew it, so he went quietly, head bowed, his expression ashamed that his usual classroom authority had been turned against him. She hid her rage. She was young and strong, but what could she do against six men and their rifles with the bayonets already bared like teeth?

'Jacek Kowalski. Where is he?' another of them asked, as if she might actually tell them.

'Not here, gone,' Uncle Tata shouted.

Thank heaven Jacek wasn't home because he'd have swung for them and ended up dead. Jacek was a wild fighter, and these days his anger was like a volcano under a thin crust, ready to erupt and scorch everything it touched.

'Find him,' mouthed Uncle Tata as he was pulled away at rifle point. 'Get out of Lithuania.' The door was hanging off its hinges and impeded their stumbling exit. 'You're a good girl, Zofia,' he shouted. 'Don't hang around here. Go make something of yourself.'

But he didn't look back, and she felt his burning humiliation that he could do nothing but be dragged to heel like a dog.

One of the soldiers saw her stare and turned, pressing the cold tongue of his bayonet to her throat. 'Your house?' he said, his eyes boring into hers, 'is ours now.'

She nodded, but kept her head high.

'You too.' The smile was predatory.

She shook her head and glared back at him with more courage than she felt. Besides, she couldn't speak; her voice had got lost inside her throat.

She blinked back salt water as Tata was put onto the truck; all down the street men were being taken. Each truck was accompanied by one full of Russian soldiers. The young one who challenged her spat at her feet before they rumbled away.

What to do? Her mind wouldn't work.

She saw the woman from across the road drag her small daughter out of the house, a heavy suitcase in her other hand. Both were wearing thick winter coats despite the blazing sun. The mother's hand was clamped tight to the daughter so the little girl's face was screwed up with pain as she was hauled along.

'Where are you going?' Zofia shouted.

'The railway station. I can't stay here with no protection. They're savages. Just savages.'

Zofia wished she could go too. Should she go? She didn't want to be there when the soldiers came back. But there was Jacek. She couldn't go anywhere without him because she was tied to him by blood and a shared thread of history she could never explain to anyone else.

'Go make something of yourself.' What did Tata mean, and why wasn't she enough just as she was?

The woman was further down the road now. Zofia watched her in a panic of indecision. Another roar of engine noise and she ducked back inside the gate just as the truck full of helmeted soldiers stopped beside her neighbour and the little girl.

There was no noise, no shots, no fuss. They hoisted them up and the truck drove off.

Their suitcase was left standing forlornly by the side of the road. Zofia's legs began to shake. Her first crazy thought was *it was a good thing they took their coats.*

Her second thought was *I've got to find Jacek.*

Chapter 2

Zofia rifled through the bags in their tiny room.

Think, Zofia, think.

Her canvas bag was packed, it always was. Experience had told her to be ready to leave at a moment's notice, because time had a habit of running out when you least expected it. But Jacek had nothing with him. Where was he? She reckoned he wouldn't be so foolish as to go to work, so he had to be at Masha's. She'd try there first.

Masha worked at the hairdresser's and with all this upheaval she probably wasn't at work either. A moment of impatience while she wondered what Jacek saw in her. Masha shared none of his interests, and Zofia was faintly afraid of Masha's parents, who always looked down on her, as if being educated was a personal insult against them. Still, she'd have to go to her house and try to find him.

Zofia dragged her only winter coat, a blueish tweed, over her print dress and cardigan before filling a side pocket with matches. Thinking fast, she stuffed a knapsack with Jacek's underwear, vest, trousers, a few other shirts, passport, and paper qualifications. As an afterthought she shoved in the enamelled cigarette tin where he kept his favourite photographs of the other girls he'd dated, none of them remotely like Masha. His best fountain pen was there on the dining table, and this she slipped into her coat pocket.

She grabbed a fork, a small sharp one, for a weapon. They might need protection. Not that she couldn't cope in a fist fight – as a child Jacek had taught her a wrestling game called *biadować*. At home in Poland it was fought usually by village boys and young men. Jacek had always been bigger and heavier, but she had learned to hold her own mostly by dint of quick reactions and playing dirty.

Still, the Russian men were like dogs on heat. The fork might be useful, and she could say it was for eating. She thrust it down into her bag.

Uncle Tata's best black suit hung on the back of the door and hurriedly she picked through the pockets, her blood still fizzing with adrenaline. No money, but an old string of pearls with a diamond clasp that used to belong to her mother. Uncle Tata had treasured these pearls as a kind of insurance when they fled Poland, and she clutched their cool weight for a moment before adding them to her bulging pocket.

There was already a collection of small objects there, what she called her 'souvenirs', small things that would never be missed, lost things that had been left behind. A past she could cling to.

What else? Her mind was racing and she threw open drawers, looking for anything useful. A ball of string. Might she need that? She raided the Marks's rooms and came out with a selection of dog-eared maps of Lithuania and Russia, and a Russian phrase book.

Finally, she could fit no more in her bag and had to admit that she really had no idea what would be useful and what wouldn't; she could only guess. As she left, feet crunching on broken china, she made an attempt to prop up the door, though she was certain this wouldn't stop the Russians if they decided to return.

The streets were quiet, and the fact they were so still and silent made the birdsong seem even louder. Her senses prickled, alert for any kind of noise, in case more soldiers should come and pick her up the way they had taken her neighbour.

She passed the primary school at the end of the street but it was closed. No children were playing outside, the playground deserted.

A young woman in her slippers was staring at a notice on the door. '*Closed until further notice*, that's what it says,' she yelled at Zofia. 'Bloody stupid! I've two children causing merry hell. How am I supposed to run my laundry business with those two under my feet all day?'

'Why's it closed?' Zofia called.

'Don't you know? They took the teachers, every last one. Even Mrs Kalicinski who runs the kindergarten. Anyone they suspect might spread ideas that are Lithuanian and not Russian.'

Zofia left the woman still staring at the notice, her arms folded in disgust. Zofia's footsteps rang loud on the broken paving slabs as she lugged the two bags down the street, one on her back, the other weighing down her arm. *Please let Jacek be all right.*

To get to Masha's she had to cross the park by Perkūno alėja. Masha's house was in a poor area of town. She'd always thought Masha a sly weasel of a girl, not good enough for her brother, but she'd guessed he'd tire of her pretty soon and find someone else. But he'd sensed Zofia's disapproval, which had made him even more determined to stick with Masha, and at the same time she'd felt sorry for Masha, in case she thought Jacek really cared for her.

She avoided the narrow alley alongside the park and started to cross by the central path, but felt too exposed. She'd go around the edge rather than across the middle. As she walked, close to the hedge, the shadows of the trees by the path, all in full leaf, were moving strangely, swaying the way they shouldn't, and it took her a moment to recognize what the shadows were. The trees had been used to hang people. The bodies were turning in the slight breeze.

They must all be dead. This she understood suddenly, like a punch. They'd been left dangling all night. Her stomach clenched, but the further she walked on trembling legs, the more corpses she saw, until she was no longer surprised to see them.

She had to pass close to one of the bodies as she went out of the gate. And though she warned herself not to, she couldn't help but look. A woman, one cream leather shoe lying on the grass under her bare foot, her coat half off her shoulders. The clothes were familiar. That brown tweed skirt and pink knitted cardigan. An involuntary sound came out of Zofia's mouth and she pressed one hand over it to silence herself. The woman was her supervisor at the library, Mrs Wozniak.

The flies were gathering already around her body. She couldn't be dead, couldn't be.

The thought made Zofia so dizzy she had to stop and put down her bags so she could bend double and rub her fists against her eyes. She turned to look again. Definitely Mrs Wozniak. They'd been filing the stock cards together only yesterday and talking of her daughter's school lunch and how it was always beef, beets and barley on Tuesdays.

Where was the daughter? Who was caring for her now? Zofia felt bile rise as if she was about to vomit. She grabbed her bag and stumbled as fast as she could down the side of the park, terrified someone would see her and consign her to the same fate.

As she got to the end of the path she stopped and dropped to a crouch. Down the street a group of soldiers were shooting at the door of the church. Their talk was in Russian dialect and the accent thick, but it was the language of violence that she understood immediately. She retreated back into the hedge until they'd bludgeoned the door open and gone inside.

She waited, unsure whether to go forward or back, her breath shallow in her throat, until the Jesuit priest in his black robes was dragged out by his underarms and loaded into a truck. His usually florid face was the colour of white porcelain, but at least he was alive, unlike the others.

She felt the aura of the hangings like a deep buzz inside her ears. Zofia licked her dry lips and crawled back against the shadow of the hedge, praying for the Russian truck to drive away and wondering if the families of the hanged people would come to cut them down, or whether they were too afraid to even do that.

When the Russians drove off in a cloud of exhaust fumes, she exhaled and ran in a half-crouch all the way to Masha's house. Parched weeds grew in the paving stones by their front door. Her hammering brought no one until the curtain next to the door twitched. Zofia banged on the window. 'It's me, Zofia! Open the door.'

Masha's father opened it and grabbed an arm to haul her inside. Zofia's bag wedged tight against the door jamb and she had to yell to stop him wrenching her arm from its socket.

'Stop shouting,' he said, gripping her arm with bruising fingers.

She almost fell into the dark hall. Jacek and Masha came out to stare.

'They took Uncle Tata,' was all she could manage. 'The Russians. They took him.'

'When?' Jacek was on his feet. 'Where?'

'How the hell do I know? They just came with guns and put him in a truck. He left everything behind, even his best suit.'

'But where've they taken him?'

'I keep telling you, I don't know. The door's broken and there's no one left at the Marks's house.' She paused, afraid her voice would turn into a sob. 'They said ... they said they'll come back later. The Russians, I mean.' She was incoherent, trying to get the words out.

'Bastards. Why have they taken him?' Jacek's gaze searched hers wildly now, hoping for a different answer, one that would change everything back.

'They were yelling *Intelligentsiya*.'

'Get inside,' Mr Romaska said. 'Out of the hall. I need to lock the door.'

They went into the tiny parlour, where Masha's mother was

21

pounding mashed potatoes in a pan, and Masha's younger sister, Mariya, was colouring a picture with the wax crayons laid out on the table.

'Why didn't you come home?' Zofia asked Jacek, unable to keep the blame from her voice. 'You should've been there.'

'And that would have been a fine thing, to have Jacek taken too,' Masha said. 'He slept here in the parlour, if that's what you're thinking.'

'I don't care about you and your sleeping arrangements! What does it matter when you can be arrested for nothing at all!'

'Who d'you think you are? Don't you speak to Masha like that.' Masha's father stuck out his chin and took a threatening step towards her. 'Jan Edelmann came to tell us they were rounding up any men on the streets. We thought it was safer for Masha and Jacek indoors.'

'Well, it's not,' Zofia said. 'They just broke in our door like it was matchwood. And they did the same to the Church of St Mary Magdalene. I saw them take Father Damian.'

'Best stay indoors, then,' Masha's father said. 'And give them time. I know how these things work. There'll be a bit of fuss, then it will all go back to business as usual.'

'Tata was right,' Zofia said. 'We need to get out of Lithuania.'

Masha exchanged a look with Jacek and went to perch on the arm of the sofa, where Jacek grabbed hold of her hand.

'You needn't think you're going anywhere.' Mrs Romaska slammed down the potato pan. A large woman with hair bleached blonde as straw and an indomitable expression, she was the person Masha would become in another twenty years.

'You can't stop me,' Masha said. Her voice held a challenge that made everyone silent.

The father, who had been watching this play out with narrowed eyes, turned to Jacek. 'Enough argy-bargy. I think it best if you and your sister go home. We never promised you more than one night, and you have to see it's dangerous for us to have you here.

If they took your uncle, they could be after you too. Or any one of us. We didn't think, see? Putting up someone from the paper is too risky. Hell, it's not safe now to have anti-Soviet opinions.'

'Anti-Soviet opinions?' Zofia asked. 'So we're supposed to just let people be taken and say nothing about it?'

Jacek glared at her. 'Shut up, sis. I can speak for myself.' He stood to square off against Masha's father. 'You didn't feel that way last June when I spoke up for the workers at your factory, though, did you? Remember? When head office in Russia wanted to offer less pay for the same job and I wrote an opinion piece in the paper, saying it was a shoddy trick to play on working men. I don't remember you complaining about my opinions then.'

Zofia put a restraining hand on Jacek's shoulder but he slapped it away. Antagonizing Masha's father would do them no good.

'My Masha's not getting mixed up in this. Not with people like you – people who can't see which way things are going. Even if you do work for the paper or the bloody library. It's time for the common people to have some say. That's what the Russians believe.'

'The library's gone,' Masha's mother said flatly. 'The Russkies emptied it yesterday and burned all the books. They started with the Yiddish ones, then got excited by the flames and burned the rest.' Her eyes took on a gleam, and Zofia tried not to let her words hurt. 'Eloise came to tell me,' Mrs Romaska said with satisfaction. 'She saw the bonfire from her doorstep.'

'And she didn't do anything? Didn't try to stop them?'

Mrs Romaska rolled her eyes. 'What do you think? Did you try to stop them when they took your uncle?'

Zofia clamped her fingers into the folds of her dress, as if holding on to something would anchor her to reality. The picture of Mrs Wozniak hanging from the tree kept appearing in front of her eyes, so vivid it could never be erased.

Her uncle was gone, the last proper adult of her life. She couldn't take it in, the enormity of it. It was as if Uncle Tata somehow bore all the memories that tied her to her parents and her Polish childhood.

'Didn't they tell you where they were taking him?' Jacek said.

'No. They don't talk, do they? Just shove their bayonets in your face.' Why did he keep asking? 'We can't go back there to the Marks's. The Russians will come. They said so, and I believe them. I brought your things.' She dumped his bag on the rug next to him. 'We have to get out, like Tata said.'

'You're going nowhere, my girl.' Mr Romaska fixed Masha with an intimidating look. Masha was strangely silent. Her face was without expression. When she saw them all looking at her, she just shook her head.

'See.' Mrs Romaska was adamant. 'Like he says, we don't want no risks. So I'm sorry, but we're asking you to go.' She picked up Jacek's bag and thrust it towards him.

His face incredulous, Jacek took it. He turned to Masha. 'You said if it ever happened then we'd stick by one another.'

'I need to think,' Masha said. 'It's all happened quicker than I thought.'

'If we go together, I'll take care of you,' pleaded Jacek. 'I promise. We always said that no matter the differences between us … won't you come with me?'

Zofia gripped her skirt tighter. *I'll take care of you.* That was what Jacek had said to her at school, because he was the bigger one. And he'd sworn they'd never be separated. But since they came to Lithuania he'd sometimes pushed her away, called her 'kid', even though they were twenty-two years old. And though she knew he loved her underneath, since meeting Masha he'd grown to be a stranger. She couldn't decide if she was glad or sorry that Masha was now shaking her head.

'She's not Jewish like us. And you can't blame her if she's scared,' Zofia said.

Masha cast her a look of such derision it almost scorched. It brought Zofia up short, showed her a Masha she didn't know

24

existed. Zofia took hold of Jacek by the arm. 'Come on.'

'We can go together.' Jacek was still looking at Masha for some sort of reply, but Masha was looking stubbornly at the floor and wouldn't meet his gaze. Jacek drew himself up with effort, trying not to show how much the rejection hurt. 'I see. Well, I guess that's goodbye.'

Zofia felt the tension in his stomach as if it were her own. Then, in a brief flurry of movement, Jacek shouldered his pack and shot out of the house like a tiger let loose from a cage.

Zofia hoisted up her own bag and blundered after him, letting the door slam behind her, and he was twenty yards ahead of her already, striding up the road towards the park.

'Jacek! Wait.' She didn't want him to see those people hanging from the trees.

But he didn't stop and she had to run, panting, up behind him to grab his arm.

'Let go.' He shook her off and kept walking.

'Where are you going?'

'To the offices. The paper.'

'No.' She was at his shoulder. 'The Russians'll go there. I know they will.'

'There's nowhere else. I need to speak to my boss, find out what's going on.'

'Uncle Tata said we need to leave Lithuania. He made me promise.'

'I'm not leaving. It's all messed up. I was all right at Masha's until you ruined it all.'

'It's not my fault. I had to come. I didn't want you going back to the Marks's house and getting rounded up as well.'

He ignored her, loping forward, his knapsack bumping against his back. At the park gates he took two steps forward but then stopped. He was still a moment. She saw his shoulders' rapid rise and fall, as if he couldn't suck in enough air.

Then he turned. 'We'll go another way,' he said, pulling her by the arm.

'I know,' she said, resisting his pull. 'I saw it earlier. It's why we have to leave.'

'I can't do it again,' he said, his voice choked. 'I'm not going over a border and having to do all that again.'

He meant kill someone. He hadn't been able to let go of it, even after all these months. It still haunted him, as if he would run away from himself if he could.

He was already walking away, hurrying towards the offices of his paper, *The Kaunas Star*, a square art deco building, all curved concrete and glass, just off the main square. The place was deserted, with nobody passing on the pavements, no cars parked at the kerb. The empty street made Zofia's stomach contract in warning. A sudden distant rattle of gunfire caused her to recoil and duck, but Jacek kept on hurrying forward, intent.

As they approached the front of the building, Jacek slowed to look up. Now they were nearer, it was obvious that many of the windows on the second floor were broken, leaving jagged black holes. A red banner had been nailed across the door, and a notice affixed to it.

There was something daubed in red on the white stucco. It was the sign of the hammer and sickle. If they'd done this to the main paper, what would they do to the Jewish ones? In his spare time Jacek was an editor for the Jewish weekly *Apzvalga* – for members of the Jewish Fighters' Association, a Lithuanian paper campaigning against the increasing anti-Semitism.

She went to touch Jacek on the shoulder. 'Let's go.'

He pushed her off. 'I need to read the notice.'

She let him stride away, helpless, and watched as he scrutinized it.

He returned towards her, his expression dark, and in answer to her questioning look recited: '*These premises have been closed down and will be repurposed for the State*. It's written in both Lithuanian and Russian. D'you think they've taken Mr Vilkas?

He's an old man, he worked there more than twenty years.'

Zofia tried to haul him away. 'Come on, let's get out of here. It's too exposed on the street. Besides, we have to think what to do if you're not going to work tomorrow.'

He stopped short and looked at her with a realization in his eyes that made her catch her breath. He reached out his arms to grab her in a tight hug. It was a moment before she realized that his shaking chest meant he was trying to hold back his sobs.

The world had changed and there was nothing on earth they could do to change it back.

Chapter 3

Otto Wulfsson gathered together his paperwork on the desk into a neat pile and put the cap back on his pen. It had been a trying day, full of the sort of confusion he hated. Urgent messages coming in on the teleprinter and two messages from panicked staff at the German embassy in Vilnius with instructions they couldn't possibly follow. The Russians had already arrived in Vilnius, and Kaunas would no doubt be next.

It appeared Kaunas was no longer to be the diplomatic centre of Lithuania. It was to be renamed Kovno, and they'd had a memo that all consulates would soon be closing. This was bad news and the thought of it had hit him like a stomach punch. He glanced at his boss, the Consul General Sugihara Chiune, and saw that he had taken it hard too.

Sugihara had known it was coming. He'd been put here in this consulate on purpose to send information back to Japan. To make life even more unstable, the Germans, not content with Poland, were getting closer and closer to the Russian borders. It was like being caught between the jaws of two lions. That was why Sugihara drove out to the borders most days on his little trips of

28

reconnaissance, and why he was constantly wiring messages back to his bosses in Tokyo about what the Russians were doing, and about a possible German invasion.

What did it all mean for their little world inside this well-appointed house on the outskirts of the town? Sugihara was also pondering what to do; he said little but was constantly pacing the floor, back and forth, back and forth, under the red sun of the flag that hung behind his desk. Otto couldn't help but be aware of his boss's hushed conversations with his wife Yukiko, just out of his earshot.

Otto massaged his chest to try to relieve the tension. For more than a year he had done daily battle with the diplomatic mail in the quiet hush of this office. He'd watched spies and diplomats from every country come and go, and all had been received by Sugihara with a polite smile.

He suspected the time for smiling was over.

Sugihara's diplomatic immunity would cease. Where would he, Otto, go then? He had a doctorate in East Asian languages and civilizations from Harvard but, still, this was his home. And if they had to move, what could he do about his mother? She wouldn't want to leave. She barely went out of the front door now as it was.

He tidied the pens on his desk back into their pots, stacked his papers into a neat pile again, aware he was procrastinating. How he loved the painting above his desk! The vista of misty sky with a lone tiny figure set against milky half-hidden mountains. He liked the row of minute jade *netsuke* precisely arranged on the shelf above his desk, the little fox curled around its own tail, the jade frog, the little waterlily that opened to reveal a dragonfly, each one perfect, the size of a single typewriter key.

His eyes grew wet. It seemed strange to carry on as normal when it was all about to end. *No, that would never do.* He swallowed and stood up, turning to where Sugihara had returned to his desk to ask him if it was okay for him to go home.

Sugihara looked up at the scrape of Otto's chair and gave him a nod. It was the same routine every day, and Otto was used to his employer's manner of dismissal. Automatically, he shrugged on his jacket, despite the suffocating temperature, and headed for the door.

Voices beyond the window made him pause to look out and he stopped, a frown on his face. 'What's going on outside?' he asked.

Sugihara came to stand beside him. Below the window a restless queue had formed, despite the late afternoon heat. A crowd dressed for winter, all with anxious faces, shuffling from foot to foot in the wash of low sun. Some carried luggage with them, and one old woman, her head bowed under a scarf, was sitting on her bags, obviously intent on being there for some time.

Sugihara's eyes remained fixed on them. Without turning he said, 'Would you mind going out there and asking them who they're waiting for?'

Otto wasn't keen on tackling this disturbance, but he could hardly refuse. His leather heels tapped briskly on the stairs as he descended and creaked open the wrought-iron gate at the front of the consulate. At his arrival, the crowd clustered like flies, but Otto closed the gate again and stayed firmly on his side of the barrier. The number of people made him uneasy, and he guessed they must be Jewish because one of the elderly men had the long sideburns, and most were talking in Yiddish. Jews were nothing new in Kaunas, about a quarter of the city's total population was Jewish and they ran many of the city's businesses with good-natured efficiency.

'What is it? What do you want?' Sweat formed around his collar.

Several men tried to answer all at once and he couldn't make out what they were saying. Many seemed to be Poles or from other parts whose languages he couldn't immediately grasp.

'Slowly!' he shouted. 'One at a time.'

'The Japanese consul is our last hope,' yelled a wiry youth, gripping on to the metal railings.

'We want the ambassador to issue transit visas to get us out of

Lithuania.' This older man was clearer and his Lithuanian better. The word 'visas' echoed through the crowd.

Otto held up a hand for quiet. 'Why? What makes you think we can help?'

'There's a route to an island – Curaçao, somewhere in the Indies. A Dutch colony.'

It was a name he'd never heard of.

His blank look brought another tumble of words: 'Vladivostok.' 'Shanghai.' 'Trans-Siberian Railway.'

'We can pay,' shouted a well-dressed woman in a dusty hat, two small children clamped to her skirts. 'Please. We have to get out, or the Germans will kill us.'

Otto blinked. *The Germans.* Surely it was the Russians who were the problem right now. A burst of outrage in his chest at the insult to his father and his country of birth. 'I don't think we can help.' He turned to go back inside but caught a glimpse of two men trying to climb, monkey-like, over the fence, and others pulling them back. If he didn't do something, the whole building might be overwhelmed.

'All right,' he said, shouting over the hubbub in Lithuanian. 'All right! Choose people to represent you. No more than five. Tomorrow five of you can have an appointment with Mr Sugihara to make your request. But only if the rest of you go away immediately.'

'If we go, more will come,' the young lad said morosely. 'And we'll lose our place in the queue. There are thousands on the way here.'

Thousands coming to queue. For what? Otto felt himself waver. He tried a shooing gesture with his hands. 'Move away from the fence!'

Nobody moved. They remained stubbornly where they were.

'We won't move until we've spoken to the consul.' This man in the grimy yellow cravat had steel in his eyes, and a belligerent tone. Otto took a step back. He felt like an exhibit in a zoo with

31

all these people staring in. He was reluctant to turn his back on them in case they swarmed over, but he mustered his dignity, braced himself, and returned upstairs.

Sugihara was still at the window, calmly looking out, one finger holding open the blind. 'They look tired, these people.'

'From what I can make out, they've heard we can issue visas to get them through Russia to Japan. They're fleeing the German army.'

'I feared this might happen. The Hitler–Stalin pact of non-aggression is breaking down. They're right to fear war. But there are too many. I can't issue visas to them all.'

'And more are coming. But I told them we'd meet representatives tomorrow. It was all I could do to placate them. We'll never get the Russian authorities to clear them, not so many.'

Sugihara pressed his lips together before speaking. 'We can't even ask. I have no official diplomatic relationship with the Russian regime yet, and I don't want to cause them to close this building any sooner than necessary.' He sat down at his desk. 'We are still awaiting instructions from Tokyo; they're deliberating about how to deal with the Russians. I'm hoping it will all quieten down and they'll still need a Japanese consulate in Kaunas. But if we start asking the authorities to intercede ...'

'The men were saying something about a Dutch island,' Otto said. 'I didn't understand what they meant. It sounds like some kind of crazy rumour.'

'Maybe I should contact the Dutch consulate.'

'Is Herr Zwartendijk still there?'

'I don't know. He'll have had the same orders as I have, I expect. Notice to close down the premises and leave.' Sugihara tapped his pen on the desk. 'You're right. Let's get a clear story from these people outside first.'

'Maybe they'll be gone in the morning.'

A patient smile. 'You go on home; there's nothing more to be done here.'

Otto passed Yukiko, Sugihara's wife, as he went out of the door. She was with her maid, and he overheard her tell Sugihara that the maid was too afraid to go out for provisions.

Me too, he thought as he opened the door, ready to face the waiting throng. It seemed a crowd drew a crowd, for now he was convinced there were even more waiting, and the sight of them made him feel unaccountably guilty. He had read that the current regime in Germany was persecuting the Jews, and felt responsible in a way he couldn't articulate, even though he hadn't been in Germany since he was a small boy.

He stuck out his chin and walked carefully, deliberately towards the crowd. They remained immoveable, like a breathing wall.

The man in the yellow cravat gave a hand signal, and to his relief they parted silently, reproachfully, to let him by. But as he walked away to catch the bus to the town, he felt their stares on the back of his neck, sensed the tautness in the air. He suppressed his outrage that having them milling there made the place look untidy. He'd never liked to see beggars on the pavement in any of the places he'd been posted. And here they seemed even more out of place, disrupting the orderliness and peace of Sugihara's house.

A man at the bus stop told him all buses were cancelled. Otto strode briskly away, his shoulders stiff and with that uncomfortable feeling still lodged like a stone in his throat.

The long walk gave him time to think. Of course he'd heard that Jews were being repatriated out of Germany, but that the German policy should reach as far as here filled him with conflicting feelings. He should have paid more attention to the newspapers from Germany. He had always privately thought that the Germans were a well-organized nation, and if the Germans came here to Lithuania, there would be an orderly transition of power and he, Otto, would be given an even larger diplomatic role.

But now these refugees had washed up on the shore of his life like unwanted flotsam and he was having to rearrange all his certainties.

33

Chapter 4

In the basement of the Alexander restaurant in the poorer area of town, Zofia and Jacek huddled in the smoke and the pungent smell of cooking fish. Alexander's was a Jewish haunt and they'd ordered traditional Jewish fare – herring and stuffed cabbage rolls, counting out the few coins in their pockets.

'I think we should go back to the Marks's,' Jacek said. 'If there's no one there, we can at least get some more of our things.'

'No. Please don't, Jacek. It's too dangerous.'

He didn't reply, and she didn't put it past him to try, which caused adrenaline to shoot through her veins again. She glanced around the room, taking in the hollow-faced crowd that had gathered. Everyone was jumpy, and all had one eye on the door in case the Russians should come, but it was reassuring to be with other people, and she was grateful.

The room was shabby, with mismatched tables, the benches crammed with other Jews who, like them, were using it as a hub for getting more information about the Russian invasion. Zofia and Jacek were jammed up at a table with another five people, all of whom had been thrown out of their homes.

'There's no shelter at the railway station,' said Rudi, the restaurant owner, in his food-stained apron. 'More folk every day.

They've come from Vilnius and they don't know where to go, poor buggers, so everyone's rammed up there like cows in a pen. They've shut the synagogues. The Russians keep sweeping the Poles out, but more keep arriving. No one has anywhere to go.'

'At least Lithuania's neutral,' said another young man.

'Wrong,' Rudi said. 'Not any more. Now it's Stalin's law. Communism. The Party and all that. They're looking at people's papers. Say you're anything other than farmer or labourer, and it's goodbye *schlemiel*. You're shipped straight off to a gulag for hard labour. Breaking stones, building roads.'

'Or bang. A quick gunshot to the head,' another man said, miming it with a finger to the temple.

Jacek turned to Zofia and put his hand on her sleeve in a brief gesture of comfort. 'Don't worry, sis. He's exaggerating.'

Zofia didn't want to believe it, but with Uncle Tata taken so suddenly, a cold dread that he too might be forced into such back-breaking labour brought a prick of tears to her eyes. Uncle Tata was the least hardy man she knew, only used to wielding a pen, not a pick. At the same time she held a visceral fear that they might yet take Jacek too.

Rudi was enjoying reporting his bad news. 'They've closed down every meeting place. Nailed them all up. The choir, the art club. Anywhere people meet.'

'If they won't help us, then we have to get out before the Nazis get over the border.'

'They won't. Sit tight. The Germans made a pact with the Russians,' Jacek said.

'That? Pah. It's already crumbling. Lithuania used to be German. Now it's Russian. And I bet you the Germans are after invading all the Russian territories. Look at Poland.'

A young man with an eager face leant forward. 'Then we should get out of here now. There's chaos already and if the Germans do come over the border, there'll be too much panic to leave. We were in Poland before the Nazis came and saw it happen there.

Every road clogged, every train full. We were the lucky ones, we got out by the skin of our teeth.'

'Nothing's going to happen,' Zofia said, though underneath she felt the fear creep into her bones. 'We'll stay. Besides, where could we go? There's nowhere.'

A quiet man in a trilby hat who'd been listening to their conversation leant over to talk to them. 'The lad's right. The NKVD here are as bad as the Germans. Think you'll be safe? Polish Jews have already been executed by the Russians if there's a whiff of them being against the Kremlin. Think you will be different? The NKVD arrested most of the Polish officer corps and shipped them off to camps. Lawyers, university professors, physicians; engineers and teachers; and journalists too. And no one's heard of them since.'

'It's war,' Jacek snapped. 'News is slow. We should wait, let things settle.'

'If you think that, you're naive. Our underground sources say that Polish men in officers' uniforms were taken from the Kozelsk camp to the Katyn Forest and executed. Truckloads of bodies, according to a local logger. He saw it all and was so terrified he shat himself. Had to hide under brushwood until he could run away.'

The door opened and another young man came in, a man in a tattered overcoat and black wool cap. He didn't sit but called out, 'Hey, listen everyone; good news. There's a way out of here if we want it.' Briefly, he explained about the possibility of onward travel from Lithuania to the ports in Japan and from there to the rest of the world. 'Japan's neutral. There's a delegation going to the Japanese consul. If we can get him to issue travel visas, we might have a chance to get out.'

'No. He'll never do it.' The people were sceptical.

'We can ask, though, can't we? There's already a big queue forming outside his house. My brother's there, keeping my place.'

'And travelling through Russia?' Jacek asked. 'It's a crazy idea.'

'Rumour is, they'll turn a blind eye if we pay.'

'It's a racket, you mean.'

People soon gathered to hear what the young man in the cap had to say, but Zofia hung back. She looked at Jacek. 'What do you think?' she asked. 'It sounds possible.'

He rubbed a hand impatiently through his thick dark hair. 'Don't look at me like I should know the answers. Sounds like a trick to me. Why would this Japanese man do it? What's in it for him? We need more information. We could end up worse off than we already are.'

'We could get out.' Zofia leant forwards, voice alight with possibility. 'Think! We could go to America. The free world. Hollywood, like those films Masha watches.'

She watched his face fall at the sound of Masha's name. 'No. What's she got to do with it?' A pause. 'Let's give it a few more days. There's talk of an underground paper starting up, and then I'll be busy. Rudi won't mind if we bunk down here.'

Zofia knew he was hoping that if they waited, he might be able to make it up with Masha, but she worried that if they didn't seize their chance now, it would be too late. 'I might walk over there in the morning, see what's going on. D'you want to come?'

Jacek tapped a fist on the table. He didn't want to, she could see that. He was resistant to the idea of leaving. At the same time, he couldn't refuse to accompany his own sister, not now it was dangerous for a girl to be out on her own. She watched him wrestle with it.

'I think I'd better stay here in case there's news of Uncle Tata,' he said. 'They'd come here to tell us.'

She shrugged. 'I'll go on my own, then.'

'Damn it, Zofia. Stop rushing me.'

A pause while she waited for him to relent. But he didn't speak. Before, Jacek would never have let her go out there alone. The devil-may-care boy she'd grown up with had gone, evaporated on their flight from Poland, and now he was a man wrestling with nightmares and demons she couldn't see. It fuelled his writing, so he wrote feverishly at night when he thought she was sleeping.

Columns and columns, trying to get the memories out of his head and onto paper. In the mornings she heard the rip of paper and knew none of it would ever see print.

She was still waiting for him to agree, but his head was in his hands and he refused to look up. She shook her head with a sad sort of impatience and put a hand on his shoulder. His hand came up to cover her own in a wordless kind of comfort, but he didn't speak.

She sighed and made her way up into the light without him. She peered out into the street, alert for Russian vehicles or soldiers. Every move now had to be carefully considered. To stay or to go? Both prospects were equally frightening: to remain at the mercy of the Russians or to try to get out on some dubious Japanese visa. But at least making a plan was doing something, and if she could go to the consulate and find out more, then maybe Jacek would come round.

Chapter 5

Masha glanced behind as she walked down the street, handbag under her arm, listening out for the car. She was jubilant because the coup had fallen out exactly as Illeyvich had predicted; the Russian takeover had been swift, efficient, and thorough, and the main Kaunas institutions had already crumbled into chaos as the Reds swept by in their cleansing tide.

Though the sun was hot, it was sultry; a stormy wind had blown up, and a few heavy drops of rain threatened to ruin her carefully set hair. Her skirt flapped against her legs, and her loud-patterned blouse stuck to her back. She wished Illeyvich would hurry. There were too many soldiers around, more than they needed to keep the population under control, and she feared boredom might make them a danger. She often drew male attention, and the atmosphere in the town, now the actual revolution was happening, was febrile.

Another glance behind. Illeyvich would spot her easily. In plain sight was the best cover – the more obvious the better, because aristocrats and the intelligentsia never dressed this way. Of course she wasn't stupid, but she was careful to let people think so; she pretended not to understand anything about how the world worked. She'd been the brightest at school, with a mind calibrated like a finely tuned clock, but she'd quickly learnt that to draw attention to her cleverness only caused trouble at home. Her father had to be top dog. Nobody was allowed to get the better of him.

When people looked at her cheap clothes, they didn't see what was inside. To them she'd always just be Masha from the slum. Jacek thought of her that way, she knew, with a slight superciliousness that made her want to find a long slow way to hurt him.

Masha walked impatiently up and down the deserted street several times before the shiny Russian sedan drew up alongside her. The car was kerb-crawling and she slowed as the door was pushed open from the inside. Vladimir Illeyvich moved over so she could swing herself in. She got into the back, where he was leaning against the leather upholstery, the faint smell of cigar smoke and hair oil still hanging on his suit. His cigar smouldered in the ash tray, giving off a noxious smell, and she wished he'd put it out.

He said nothing. Illeyvich was born in Siberia and others in the NKVD joked that he was frozen from the inside out. Stiff in bearing and with a face that hardly moved, he was chief of the Russian Secret Service in Kaunas and never wasted words.

'Kowalski's in hiding with his sister.' Masha answered the unasked question. 'She came to tell him about the round-ups.'

He glanced sideways at her. 'You couldn't go with him?'

'Not without blowing cover or making trouble with my father. It would look odd to go on the run with him.'

'Your father doesn't suspect?'

A shake of her head.

'Sure about Kowalski?'

'Kowalski thinks he's attractive and intelligent and that a girl like me should be grateful. He pretends not to care about what he thinks is my lack of education, while simultaneously trying to educate me. He insults me without having the slightest inkling that's what he does.'

Illeyvich gave a small suggestion of a frown. 'Don't get too angry Masha. It might cause you to slip up. You have the names and addresses?'

'Yes. All Kowalski's contacts from the press office are in here.' She patted her bag. The smoke from the cigar was making her eyes water, but she dared not touch it; it would be presumptuous.

'Good. Most were taken in the first swoop. But if they run, we'll track them down before they can print anything. It's vital to close down all media outlets in the first days. Gag anyone involved in the press or the news. Then, the more confusion the better.'

'Got it.'

'We rounded up everyone from the *Kaunas Star*, except your man Kowalski,' he said. 'Keep tailing him and get details of any other contacts he has, especially in the Jewish press. Kovno must be picked clean of anti-Soviet risks.'

So quick. Her excitement mounted. It was already Kovno and not Kaunas. 'Your men know who I am?' She needed reassurance she wouldn't be taken with them.

'You're not exactly easy to miss. And they've been briefed.'

'Kowalski's sister is a problem. She doesn't like me flirting with her precious brother and is looking for any excuse for him to ditch me.'

'Then don't give him any. By the way, sorry about your job.' The hairdresser's was closed now and under Soviet control.

She shrugged. It had been a useful listening post to feed information back to Illeyvich and the NKVD, but the loss of it meant she'd be short of cash, and this she resented.

'You'll be deployed in a better role from now on,' he said, as if reading her mind. 'Intelligence. More pay. It's all gone quicker than we hoped. We expected more resistance. But then the Lithuanian men are weaklings who'd rather bleat than fight.'

The car was moving slowly down the main street with its red flags. The sight of them gave her a thrill, the feeling that at last things were changing. She hadn't thought the revolution, when it came, would be so bloody or so final. It had given her immense pleasure to see the people who had previously controlled the power and the money in the town, all the old tsarists, strung up by their necks.

In the end it had been easy, the liberation of the proletariat; the many versus the few. It was either the dictatorship of the landowners or the dictatorship of the common people, and she knew whose side she was on. It still riled her how her father and her mother had nothing and expected even less. Thirty years of night shifts, of heavy, dirty engineering for her father, and what had he to show for it? Injured hands and an empty bank balance. Her mother – toiling all hours, sweating in the stink of sheepskin at the glove factory. From now on, under Stalin's guiding hand, it would be different. She was working for a world where everyone would have an equal chance, where no one would have to escape the grind of their work through vodka and using a woman as a punchbag.

At last, Illeyvich opened the window to flick out his cigar butt. 'You'll alert us if Kowalski decides to leave?'

She nodded.

'The usual number.'

He wound up the window and tapped the chauffeur on the shoulder. She sat back as the car did another slow circle of the block before she unclipped her handbag and passed over the handwritten list of Jacek's contacts.

Moments later, Illeyvich opened the door again to let Masha out, and the car eased away in a stench of petrol fumes. The rain was pelting down now, splatting in the dust in dark splodges. She watched the car go before holding her bag above her head and running for home.

A few streets from her front door, she slowed, putting on her sulky persona, the one she used at home, the one guaranteed to make her parents leave her alone and not ask questions. Jacek Kowalski would come to her, she knew, because he couldn't help himself. She had him in a snare, convinced he was 'in love' with her. The love was all in his pants.

Not like Illeyvich of the NKVD. There was something about Illeyvich that appealed to her; his ruthlessness, the crocodile eyes that were always assessing you. Like her, he'd learnt to be detached, to be on the outside always looking in. Last year there'd been a treaty to compensate the Russians for the Polish land stolen from them by the Germans. The so-called Boundary and Friendship Treaty decreed that Germany would transfer Lithuania to the Soviets. As if they, the Lithuanian people who lived there, were simply dolls to be moved around in some huge doll's house. The treaty gave the Russians control of Vilnius, the capital of Lithuania. Masha had decided there and then she was more Russian than Lithuanian. She was tired of being the underdog, always downtrodden by the Poles or the Germans, and always under someone's boot. She'd joined the clandestine *Lietuvos komunistų partija* – the Lithuanian Communist Party.

She strode onwards through the rain, wondering how many of the men on the list she'd given Illeyvich would be alive tomorrow. When she'd first met him at one of their secret Communist meetings in Kaunas, she'd watched how the men deferred to him, seeing instantly he was a man with power. She wanted a share of it, and it wasn't long before he'd noticed her, she'd made sure of that. They recognized each other's intelligence, buried beneath the outside appearance, things that could never be spoken of but drew them together like two fingers of the same hand.

There was something of a victory each time she had a meeting with him. A feeling of euphoria that she'd arrived; arrived at a place where she could have control, where the whole unequal mess of life could be redistributed more fairly.

The NKVD recruited agents from all walks of life, from unemployed intellectuals to bona fide aristocrats. All were involved in what Illeyvich called the 'wet business', where enemies of the USSR either quietly disappeared or were openly liquidated. Masha had worked her way up the ranks to be his chief informant, and it gave her great pride that she was trusted by him to deliver the goods.

At her front door, she paused under the porch before going in, preparing herself for the mundane. She shook water off her bag and opened the front door to the usual smell of cooking cabbage and resentment.

On the other side of town, three Germans were sitting in the Kaunas Hotel, now hurriedly renamed the Kovno Hotel, in the same bar that the Russian Secret Service men often used. Soviet soldiers were in the other bar, and their noise and laughter could be heard through the adjoining door.

The room was cool in comparison with the sweaty heat outdoors, and better appointed than almost every other hotel in Kovno. In the corner a radio was playing balalaika and the notes drifted over to where the men sat, huddled together, smoking and talking in low voices. Though there was every luxury – leather chairs, cut flowers in vases, liqueurs in buckets of ice – Friedrich Zeitel was uncomfortable, and he wiped his damp palms down his trousers. His role in the propaganda ministry's press division was to report back to Germany what the Russian press was saying about Hitler, and of course it was never anything good. Today, as every day, he lived in constant fear they would shoot the messenger.

He was outclassed by the other two men, Brandt and Reinhart, and he knew it. Brandt, formerly of the *Kriminalpolizei*, was an individual who by the look of him spent too much time behind a desk. His overblown face was pale as blotting paper, and his expression dour. Brandt's family had come from Germany way back in the eighteenth century, when Catherine the Great, a former German princess, promised Germans free farmland should they choose to immigrate, and Brandt still thought of himself as some kind of royalty.

Reinhart was his shorter, younger sidekick, over-anxious to

please. Both were from the Reich Security Main Office under Heydrich. With this new situation with Russia, Zeitel wondered if this was it, and he was going to be sacked.

'It's chaos out there,' Brandt said. 'We came as soon as we heard. What can you tell us? Are they still letting Jews cross the border from Poland?'

'It's all unclear. People are on the move everywhere. There are so many rumours and all former lines of communication are down or under Russian control.' What he didn't say was that he'd been hiding in his apartment for two days, waiting for it all to die down.

'Has anyone managed to track down the Jew, August Bronovski?' By 'anyone', Brandt clearly meant him, Zeitel, because he was looking straight at him. The conversation was stilted because it was in Russian, not their native German.

Zeitel let himself relax slightly; they weren't going to sack him. 'You were right. Bronovski's been seen here in Kaunas – sorry, Kovno – at the synagogue and at the Jewish bank,' Zeitel said. 'Though of course now they're shut. Same old game. Smuggling photographs and trying to get refugees to write testimonies for him, but somehow he always manages to evade our men.'

'Who's on it?' Reinhart asked, leaning forward eagerly.

'Klein,' Zeitel replied. 'Ex Polizei. Now SS undercover. But Bronovski's wily and knows we're after him. We haven't managed to find an address yet, but Klein should be on it as we speak.'

'So what's the problem?' Brandt kept up the pressure.

'Ach, too many Jews in Kovno, all with similar names. We might just have to wait until we have more support.' Zeitel meant from the German army, though of course he couldn't mention those words, as the proposed invasion of Russian territory was still only a whisper.

'Have you checked Bronovski's address? Found out what he intends to do?' Reinhart, slim and edgy in an immaculately cut suit, pulled on his silk tie and fixed his intense eyes on Zeitel.

'We guess he'll go to the press,' Zeitel said. 'Aim to cause a stir with the photographs. Not here, though, somewhere in the West. America?'

'Yes, yes.' Brandt shook his head impatiently. 'I didn't come all the way from Moscow for you to tell me that. It's been months and you can't even tell me where Bronovski lives.'

'We want him dead,' Reinhart said. 'Soon as we find him. Bullet through the brain, that's what I'd do.'

'Oh, for God's sake, use some sense, Reinhart,' Brandt said. 'We don't want to alert the Russians to our presence here. We're businessmen, got it?' He turned back to Zeitel. 'The priority is to get hold of his material. If these sob stories get out, or the photographs of Warsaw, it could cause no end of political difficulties. More resistance, more fuel on pro-Jewish flames, undermine what the Führer is trying to do, his soft approach.'

Zeitel raised his eyebrows. Nothing about Hitler was ever a soft approach. 'I told you, I'm onto it. But is Bronovski that important? He's just one man, just a rag trader. He hasn't got that much clout, has he?'

'So you think it's wasting your time?' Brandt said.

'No, no, I didn't mean that.'

'Bronovski's well known as an activist. Our department's had tabs on him and collated hundreds of reports. He smuggled dozens of original photographs out of Poland. We don't know what's in them, we've only heard they're bad. He knows his fate if we get hold of him, and yet it still hasn't stopped him.'

Zeitel didn't want to spend his life chasing errant Jews around the countryside and being questioned by the NKVD. 'If he was going to squeak, why hasn't he done it already?'

'He tried,' Reinhart said. 'Some of his articles have appeared in the Jewish papers here, but then the Russian sympathizers clamped down on them, the way they do. Least whiff of anti-communism and they're on it like a pack of dogs. They accused the Jews of supporting capitalism. Which of course they do.

Moneylenders, goldsmiths, you get the drift.'

Brandt gave Reinhardt a disparaging look. 'The real story is that the Russians don't want to publish Bronovski's stories for fear that when war comes, and it will, it would put the shits up them and demoralize their troops. Bronovski's promising these displaced Jews that he'll tell their story all over the world.'

'He needs to be stopped,' Reinhart said. 'A takedown job.'

Brandt sighed and closed his eyes, but then said to Zeitel, 'Find Bronovski and find the material he's trying to sell. You're the man in town, so we expect you to deal with it. But that doesn't mean there aren't other people who could do your job if you can't.' A pause while he stared at Zeitel to check he'd understood.

'I'll see to it.'

'Don't forget, you know a lot, Zeitel. Enough to hang a man. And these days in Lithuania, people go missing all the time.'

'All the time,' echoed Reinhart.

Zeitel swallowed, recognizing the sting of the threat under Brandt's polite manner. 'I understand it's a priority,' he said. He stood up, but neither of the others did. Feeling awkward, he mumbled a brief goodbye and took his leave, glad to get out of there.

When he'd gone, Reinhart looked to Brandt. 'What do you think, boss? Think he'll get our man?'

'Zeitel's a slimy bastard, and lazy. But he'll do it to save his own skin. He's a man who'd swear black was white if it paid him a salary. And as for scruples, he wouldn't recognize one if it hit him over the head.'

Chapter 6

Zofia walked the few miles over to the Japanese consulate and was shocked to see the length of the queue outside. So many people, and so many of them Jewish. Some had brought chairs with them, others had fashioned makeshift shelters of canvas and rope to shield them from the sun, though now these had been battered by the flash storm. The impression was that they'd been there a while already and were prepared to wait even longer. Everything was steaming now in the heat, and there was a pungent smell of damp bodies and clothing.

She wound her way down towards the front of the line, with several people shouting at her to get to the back. The consulate was in a large, white-painted house that looked more suburban than grand, with large square gateposts and steps twisting up to a front door. At the gate there were two tall men who seemed to have appointed themselves as guards, one of them in a grimy yellow cravat.

Zofia approached a woman near the front whose skirt was covered in mud. 'Is it true, that he'll issue a visa to get us out of here?'

The woman huffed at her as if she was a nuisance. 'No, we're just sitting out here for the fun of it. What d'you think?'

'And where can it take you, the visa?'

'Vladivostok. Then on to Japan. From there to the United States, or to anywhere else in the world.' She thumbed to indicate the listless man and his son just behind her. 'We're going to New York.'

Zofia was astounded. It was surely a fairy tale. 'And you believe it?'

A shrug. 'We're here, aren't we? Stop with all the questions. You're making my head hurt. If you want a visa, just get to the back of the queue.'

Zofia walked back up the line, her heart fluttering with a kind of anticipation. America! The land of the free. Images sprang to mind from the movies before the war: elegant women on New York sidewalks, laughing gaily, always carrying hatboxes, or wearing furs, slender women in heels, smiling and tap-dancing in *Footlight Parade* or *Top Hat*.

The images faded as she came to a whole party of yeshiva students who were standing or squatting in the dirt with their harassed, black-hatted teachers. Fifteen or so young men, all in their obligatory caps, shuffling their feet and jostling each other. Most looked to be between sixteen and twenty years old. Their Talmud school was one of the most respected in the city. If these were waiting too, then there must be a grain of truth in the story.

The sight of this growing exodus fuelled her excitement. But then the reality of crossing the wastelands of Russia began to bite. Now, even in this heat, it solidified in her bones into cold fear. She took one more look at the queue before hurrying away. She'd have to talk to Jacek.

Back at Alexander's, she pushed her way through the tables that now had every seat occupied. Jacek was tapping a spoon in an empty coffee cup. Beside him lay a heap of damp belongings tied up in two bundles with string. Zofia recognised the flowery fabric of one of her own dresses and her father's suit jacket.

'What's all this?' She elbowed her way to sit on the bench next to him, persuading another woman to move up.

'You were right,' he said. 'I went over to scout out the Marks's house. It's been taken over by the Russians. Rough louts full of bravado and the stink of victory. I could hear one of them thumping out "Barynya" on the piano. Drunk as lords and they'd thrown all our things out onto the path. Of course, it would bloody rain, wouldn't it?'

'You shouldn't have gone. What if they'd seen you?'

'I made sure I was out of sight of the house, down behind the trees by the bottom gate, and waited until there was no one around – then gathered up as much as I could.'

'You fool. They could have caught you.'

'I was quick. It was odd, like being a kid again, all that sneaking around someone's back garden. I searched for money in every one of Uncle's pockets, but no. If there was any, the Russians have it.'

She didn't tell him it was she who'd emptied them. Instead, she said, 'What will we do with all this stuff?'

'Sell it? I don't know. It just seemed stupid to leave it there. It's our stuff, isn't it?'

She told Jacek what she'd seen at the embassy. 'It doesn't look good, not if men from the yeshivas are leaving. But just imagine if we could get to America.'

'Why? We always said we'd go back home to Poland, didn't we?'

'What, when we're old? The Nazis have a grip on it now. And even before that, Papa had to struggle against the Austrians, then the Prussians – one dictator after another. Don't you want to live in a place where you can breathe? Don't tell me you want to go back to Poland. Poland's like a rag torn apart by dogs.'

Jacek stuck out his chin. 'And it's a better idea to travel across Russia, right into the teeth of the Siberian gulags? Let alone get on a ship to America? Come off it, sis. It's madness.'

'I bet if Masha said she was going, you would.' It was an underhand dig, but it hit home.

Jacek's eyes sparked. 'You don't know what you're talking about.'

She couldn't go without him, but equally she was scared to

stay. They had no home, just these two bundles, her own canvas bag and Jacek's knapsack. Not much money either, only the loose change and the pearls.

'We've got a chance,' she said, 'And yet you won't take it.'

He sighed and turned away.

Frustrated, she burst out, 'You're all talk. Writing everything in the paper and calling for change and yet you never do anything; nothing to change it all but hide behind your pen. That's all it is, you're just scared.'

'Who was it that got us here to Lithuania? If I hadn't, if I hadn't ...' He paused, took a halting breath. 'You had the easy part. All you had to do was run. You can just ...' He didn't finish, just let out a heavy sigh and returned his attention to the table.

She watched the back of his head for a moment, her stomach in knots. She both loved him and hated him and the two things were tangled together like twisted wire. Though she knew in her heart that life was never as straightforward as it seemed, the dream of America was intoxicating. Baseball and rodeos. Gary Cooper and Jean Harlow. The Empire State Building and Manhattan Island. She'd have to persuade Jacek some other way. Arguing over it just hurt and made everything worse.

Chapter 7

The next day, in the Japanese consulate, Otto helped Sugihara to clear the mahogany table under the Japanese flag in preparation for receiving the refugee visitors from the queue. When they'd opened up the leaves and dusted it down, Otto stood by the window, chewing his thumbnail, watching to see which men had been chosen for their meeting. He hoped it wasn't the man in the yellow cravat who'd been so aggressive.

The crowd had thickened further overnight, and he'd had to walk the length of the queue, pretending they were invisible, like ghosts, existing in another dimension from his reality. They were silent, eyes following him with intense stares as if they might suck the marrow from him. He dreaded them finding out he was German.

Did these people really think Sugihara could do anything to save them? Otto knew about the route across Russia via the Trans-Siberian railway, but thought it was unlikely the Russians would ever let these Jewish refugees use it. The earlier civil war in Russia had decimated the Russian economy and now vast areas of the interior were crippled by famine and poverty. Russian autocrats, instead of choosing to fund aid for the destitute, had chosen to mend the railway track. But not for people, for goods.

Otto left the window and turned to deal with the pile of routine correspondence on his desk while Sugihara moved his chair to the head of the table so there would be room for them all to sit. Sugihara was dressed neatly in the Western style, unlike his wife, who almost always wore the traditional kimono and drifted through the rooms in a whiff of jasmine perfume.

When the grandfather clock pinged the hour, Sugihara gestured to Otto. 'Bring them up,' he said. 'I'll get Yukiko to bring tea.'

The chosen men were already waiting just outside the gate as Otto unlocked it. Damn. The man with the yellow cravat was there, first in the queue. Otto put him in his fifties, his lowered eyebrows were turning grey, his cheeks sunken and lined. He seemed to be the leader and the rest were a motley bunch of beggars. All had holed shoes as if they had walked a long way, some were even tied on with string. One man had no socks or hat either, but a grimy bandage wrapped around his head. Another was carrying a decrepit carpet bag.

Shouts came from the crowd wishing them luck as Otto let them in and relocked the gate. He gestured them forward, wincing at the idea of these dirty men sitting on Sugihara's velvet upholstered chairs. He said nothing, though, and followed them up.

Sugihara welcomed them all as if they were diplomats and bade them sit. For a moment, Otto saw the man in the yellow cravat stare at Sugihara's neat suit and then take a long, slow look at their surroundings – it made him instantly aware of the gleaming electric chandelier and the polished walnut furniture, the paintings and the *netsuke*, and it filled him with embarrassment.

Yukiko brought a tray of Japanese tea and Sugihara took his time to pour the small cups of fragrant liquid and offer a cup to each man. It seemed strange to see their big hands wrapped around these tiny cups. One poor fellow's hand was shaking so much he couldn't even pick it up.

'Tell me what you want,' Sugihara said, 'your names, and why you wait out there.'

The man with the yellow cravat answered in broken Lithuanian, but his voice was firm. 'August Bronovski. We are refugees. Have nowhere to go. The Russians, the Germans, nobody want us. If the Germans come to Kaunas, and believe it, they will, then they kill us.'

'What makes you think that?'

'They think the Jews are an enemy. And we know it, they will come. Like in Poland, like in Czechoslovakia. And if not the Nazis, then the Russians they deport us to Siberia. Why? Because we think for ourselves.' Bronovski gestured to his companion, who delved in his carpet bag and pulled out a thick bundle of scruffy papers. Bronovski placed them on the table and spread them out. 'Here – testimonies of my people. Eyewitness accounts, you see? And here – photo.' He placed a small thin envelope on top. 'You want know why we run? This is why.' He thumped his palm down on the heap. 'How we driven from our homes, beaten, tortured, seen our sons and daughters killed.'

Otto swallowed. He'd heard of his homeland's rampage into its neighbours, but had been able to ignore it – until now.

Sugihara said nothing, just stared, leaning his head towards the table. Even from where he stood, Otto saw the documents were originals, not copies, with all different handwriting and paper. He shifted from foot to foot, uncomfortable, wishing he was somewhere else.

'Mr Sugihara,' said Bronovski, 'if you read, you will see same story, over and over. Always the same. Families divided. Men to one camp, women to another. Looting and stealing of our property. Rape and execution on the street. Or camps. No one ever return. Look at the photographs. Just one will tell you our suffering. You speak Polish?'

Sugihara gave a nod.

'Then read.' He shot a glance towards Otto, continuing in broken Lithuanian. 'We are the survivors. You think we are too many? There should have been a thousand more of us. So now we need your help to get out of here before more of us die.'

A quiet then as Sugihara began to sift through the papers, reading first one, then the next. The men drank their tea in silence, eyes fixed on his face over the rims of their teacups. Otto could hear his own breath, ragged, as if he'd run a long way.

Sugihara took his time. He opened the envelope and took out a faint grainy photograph. Then he stood and walked to the window, and stared out for a long time. He turned back. 'I will need to ask if it's possible by asking my counterpart in Tokyo,' he said. 'I can send a letter.'

'A letter?' Bronovski asked. The refugees looked at each other, despair written in their faces. 'You don't understand. Too slow. We don't have that time. We've nowhere to go now. Today. And I must take these papers to America.'

The man with the bandage leapt up and loomed over Sugihara, his one visible eye wild as he threatened him with a stream of angry Yiddish.

Otto, taken aback by the sudden change in atmosphere, restrained the angry man by the sleeve, but the man writhed and continued to yell until he was hoarse and tears streamed down his thin cheeks.

'Sorry, but I can't make out what he's saying,' Otto said desperately to Bronovski, as he took hold of the man's other arm in a futile attempt to calm him.

'He say Nazis came to his shop. Dragged his mother from her chair, shot in face. They rape his sister and take her away, then beat him half-dead with the butts of their rifles.'

Otto heard the words detonate inside him, like a series of shocks.

There was a thick silence then in the room, except for the bandaged man's sobs. He seemed to have understood that his story had been told and now he was flaccid, quiet.

Otto dropped him like he was a hot potato. He didn't want to even be near the smell of such violence.

Bronovski pointed to the papers. Quietly he said to Otto, 'Read, sir, please. It's all there.'

Otto backed away, but Sugihara brushed down his sleeve, outwardly calm. 'Thank you, gentlemen. I'll see what I can do. I'll send my aide with a message when I receive a reply from my home country.' He held out a hand for it to be shaken, but the bandaged man began shouting again.

One of the other men put an arm around his shoulder to placate him. 'All right, my friend, all right.'

Bronovski turned to Sugihara. 'Begging your pardon. We go now. Gustav's not been the same since that day. The broken head make his mind bad. Tomorrow, I will return for my papers. I trust you are good man. When you read them, you will know what to do.'

Otto escorted them out, shoulders stiff with tension. That his countrymen could do such things had punctured his pride, left him feeling like he'd lost something he never knew was a part of him. He firmly locked the gate.

When he returned, he spent a good few minutes tidying his desk, putting everything in order again, trying to quieten his stricken conscience. He didn't want to read the documents or look at the pictures. He wanted to shut his ears to it all. Sugihara, meanwhile, was poring over them, his forehead screwed up in concentration.

'They may be all lies,' Otto said. But he knew they were not.

'I don't think so,' Sugihara said as he turned over another page. 'They seem too ... too real. And the photographs. Bodies piled on carts. Something is rotten in Germany.' Finally, Sugihara said, 'I will cable Tokyo. Take down this message.'

Otto went for his pad and pencil, unable to rid himself of his discomfort.

'I request permission to issue visas to hundreds of Jewish people who have come to the consulate here in Kaunas seeking transit.' He paused as Otto scribbled it all down. 'This request is a humanitarian plea. The refugees' request for visas should not be denied.'

Otto typed up three copies, one for the Japanese ambassador in Germany, one to the envoy in Latvia and one to the foreign minister of Japan.

'They said more people were coming,' Sugihara said. 'Given we already have our notice, maybe it would have been wiser to just shut the consulate early. But—'

'No,' Otto interrupted. He had no answer yet as to where he would go if he couldn't be Sugihara's aide. 'But if we can find a solution to the Jewish problem, we should do so.'

Sugihara raised his head. 'It's not a Jewish problem,' he said. 'It seems to me it's a German and a Russian problem.'

A German problem. Somehow his problem. 'And now a Japanese one.'

'Then let's hope Tokyo approves the visas,' Sugihara said.

Otto couldn't agree more. He couldn't bear to look at them. How many more had stories like the ones they'd just heard? It was unthinkable.

Chapter 8

A week later

Zeitel usually slept well. The jobs that would cause him heartache were easily passed on to someone else, and Kaunas was a long way from *Kriminalkommissar* Brandt and the Nazi head office in Vilnius. So he was snoring in his apartment when the doorbell rang. He groaned and glanced at his watch. Two in the morning. He threw on a robe, went to the door and, mindful of his neighbours, hissed, 'Who is it?'

'Klein.'

He opened the door warily. 'Shh,' he chided the burly figure standing there. 'What the hell time is this?'

'It's done,' Klein said.

'Come in.' Zeitel held the door open wide, 'and keep your voice down.' Not a conversation he wanted to have on the doorstep. 'I guess I can find us a drink.'

'Bronovski's dead?' he asked as soon as the door was closed.

'He was living with an elderly couple on the south side of town.'

'And you got the papers?' He got out brandy from the sideboard.

'We shot all three. Left a Soviet military cap there. They'll just assume it was Russians.'

'And what did he tell you?'

Klein looked blank. 'Nothing. He refused to say anything.'

'But didn't you threaten him? Did you search the house?'

'Yeah. Couldn't find those papers or photographs you were after. The house was full of junk. Took me and Helmut ages to sort through it. That couple must have kept every newspaper and every receipt they ever got. Even found magazines dating back twenty years or more. But we found nothing in Polish, it was all Lithuanian stuff.'

'What about his room? Bronovski's?'

'He didn't seem to have one. Extra bed cordoned off with a blanket on a string.'

'You mean he was sleeping in the same room as the old folks?' He didn't hand Klein the second glass.

'Looks like it. There was just a bag with a few bits of old clothing and dog-eared ration books from the Jewish Fund. Nothing important. Anyway, they're still sleeping in the same room, if you get my meaning.' He grinned.

'You went through everything?'

'Anything that could move, boss, we shifted it. Under the carpets, the cushions. Everywhere. Just dust and crap.'

Zeitel paced, thinking. Brandt wouldn't be pleased at that news. 'And there's no clue as to where he might have left this dossier of documents?'

'No idea. Asked him, of course, beat him up before we shot him, but no go.'

'The couple?'

'Pathetic pair. They'd have confessed to anything if they thought it would save them. They were shaking in their shoes – or they would have been if they'd been wearing any. They were no use to us once Bronovski was dead, so we just despatched them with minimum fuss.'

'So now we've got no intelligence from Bronovski, and none

of his papers. That about it?'

Klein started to look uncomfortable. 'Like I said, we smashed him up. He was in a pretty bad way. He wasn't about to talk.'

Zeitel drained his brandy. 'I don't pay you to come back empty-handed. You'd better keep watch on the house. If he's missed, his friends might go there to see what's happened to him. Or the Russian police. You wouldn't last long with them.'

Klein shifted and his face took on a mutinous expression. 'Lost a good pair of trousers and a shirt to that job. Never easy, taking someone out. Nobody could have done better than us.'

'Then next time I'll employ Mr Nobody, and let the Russians deal with you.' He paused and then let out a sigh. 'All right, follow up any other leads you can. I want results, mind. Am I clear?'

'We'd need extra.'

Why did it always come down to this? Zeitel paced a bit to keep him waiting, but being in his dressing gown didn't exactly give him the edge, and in the end he agreed to pay Klein and his friend Helmut for anything else they could discover.

When he'd gone, Zeitel couldn't sleep. He went back through to the bedroom, where the whole of one side was taken up with a model railway track, lovingly laid out and accessorized. He set one of the engines going from the tinplate station and listened to the whirr as the Bing loco buzzed around the track. He always found this calming.

His wife Halle had left him because of these trains, said he cared more for them than for her. She was probably right; he'd spent hours building the layout. He pressed the button to slow the train at the crossing before pulling a tiny lever to make the electrical signal lift. Without it the train couldn't continue. In his little world, everything was a perfect miniature version of pre-war life. The boats sailed on the painted blue lake, while the top halves of little tin people bathed in the 'water'. The shops still had smiling people under flowering window boxes. None of the buildings had been bombed like at home. His were the best, the most expensive, the most lifelike trains available, and he cursed the fact that the Bing Works no longer existed, liquidated in 1932 because the owners were Jews. The Bings were good Jews, he was sure. Not like Bronovski, who'd been intent on making trouble.

Klein had messed up, but Zeitel knew it wouldn't be Klein but him who would be the one to blame as far as Brandt was concerned. Brandt would want to know why Klein hadn't brought Bronovski in for grilling, and there was no real answer except incompetence. Having that conversation with his Nazi friends wouldn't be a pleasant experience. Zeitel set another loco going past his plaster of Paris mountains, the noise of its tiny load of freight drowning out his thoughts.

Chapter 9

'*Permission denied.*'

Otto put the cable carefully on Sugihara's desk. This was the reply to the third cable they had sent. There it was again, in black and white. Along with a load of explanatory nonsense from Tokyo about issuing visas being against the interests of public security. A quick look through the blind at the window showed the crowd at the gates had grown denser. The rumour about the faint possibility of visas had spread.

The actual Russians seemed to be leaving them alone for the moment. They were too busy raiding businesses in the centre of the city and policing the railway station. That didn't mean they never would interfere in this strange crowd that had sprung up outside their door, and indeed Otto half-hoped they would. It would be much tidier and less risky that way, and might get rid of the needling guilt.

The July heat was oppressive and Otto was forced to take off his jacket and work in his shirtsleeves, something that made him feel unaccountably vulnerable.

Sugihara came in from lunching with his wife and their three sons and immediately saw the cable on his desk. He stood looking at it from a distance.

Otto tried not to look too interested.

Finally, Sugihara said, 'A young man stopped me as I got out of my car. He was a few years older than my eldest son, but skin and bone and in a terrible state of exhaustion. He was begging me for a visa. In a few years' time, my son could be standing on someone's doorstep asking for help.'

Otto straightened his tie, though it didn't need straightening. He felt suddenly German again, in a way he hadn't before, and responsible.

Sugihara gave him an intense stare and said, 'We will issue the visas.'

Otto let out his breath. Thank God. 'But won't we need permission from the Dutch consulate to send people to this Dutch colony, Curaçao, whatever it's called?'

'I called the Dutch ambassador, Herr Zwartendijk, last night. He agrees.'

Otto blinked. It meant Sugihara had already decided yesterday without consulting him. Perhaps because he was German. It stung, but he replied politely, 'As you wish, sir.'

'Sit down, Otto.' Sugihara leant forward and fixed him with slate-black eyes. You realize that if I sign this many, we must all be prepared to be dismissed by the foreign ministry. After all, it's against their express orders.'

'You mean, doing it will ruin my career?'

'Probably. Until a few years ago, Jews who owned German passports didn't need entry visas to Japan because the two countries had a treaty. But now it's a mess. The German authorities have begun revoking citizenship from Jews they've driven out of Germany, making Jews, to all intents and purposes, stateless. Fortunately, Kōki is a pragmatist. It doesn't matter to him whether they're Jews or non-Jews, if their trade will benefit Japan. Of course, being German, you might see it differently.'

Otto dropped his gaze. Hirota Kōki was the Japanese foreign minister, and he'd spoken to him often on the telephone, a most polite and pleasant man. Otto longed for those conversations again; he was beginning to feel more of a rapport with Japan than Germany. He didn't feel German but he didn't want to lose the protection of the consulate. The Russians he knew had no love for the Germans, yet he'd hardly noticed that until now. He had the distinct feeling of being in the wrong place at the wrong time. But if he could keep favour with Sugihara it would count for something, surely? 'I still think we should do it.'

'I don't understand this ill-feeling towards the Jews,' Sugihara went on. 'It seems senseless. Why are the Germans expelling their best scientists, their best academic brains, their best businessmen? And why are the other nations doing nothing? Jewish skills would be assets in Japan.'

'But sir, the people outside aren't scientists or anyone special, they're just poor people on the run – women, children, old men.'

'I daresay all the Lithuanian intellectuals in gulags look like poor specimens by now.' Sugihara let that sink in, and Otto immediately flushed.

'No, Japan should welcome them,' Sugihara continued. 'Everyone – women, children, old people. It would strengthen Japan's economy against the Chinese, especially in Manchukuo, though I don't think my superiors in Tokyo see it that way. They're too afraid to land on one side or the other.'

'Those people are not going to stay in Japan, though, are they? Most want to go to America, or they've got transit papers from Zwartendijk to get to Curaçao, wherever that is.'

'The Dutch Indies. Some may stay, though, when they see the beauty of Japan.'

'If we do issue visas, would it involve staying on here longer? I mean, keeping the consulate open?' Otto was hopeful. Sugihara hadn't told him where he'd be posted, and obviously it would be unsafe for him to remain in Lithuania as a regular citizen now it was Russian. He would be classed as an intellectual and have no diplomatic protection.

'Until they post us somewhere else, yes. You agree, then?'

'I'll do whatever you think necessary, sir.' It was his standard diplomatic answer.

'No, Otto. Not "what I think". What do you think? You've a brain, haven't you?'

He swallowed. 'I agree, sir. Let's give them a chance.'

Sugihara nodded. 'Wise choice. When it is over, you will have friends all over the world. What are we here for, unless it's to do the right thing?'

Was it wise or stupid? These visas were going expressly against government orders. He might never work anywhere else again.

We're mad, to do it, thought Otto, *quite mad.* But the weight that lifted from his shoulders made him almost euphoric.

Chapter 10

It had taken Zofia a week of reconnaissance of the queue outside the consulate to pluck up the courage to go to speak to Masha. In this time, she'd tried every way she could to persuade Jacek to leave Lithuania, but nothing had worked. He was scared, but of course he couldn't admit it. Now, as a last resort, she was going to Masha's house. She went early, hoping to catch her in, and that there'd be fewer soldiers on the streets. After a hair-raising journey dodging down back alleys, in which she expected to be stopped at any moment by Russian soldiers, she was outside Masha's door. The noise of raised voices came from inside. Masha and her father, arguing.

She hammered rather too loudly and saw the curtain twitch. The door opened a crack and Mr Romaska was there, filling the doorway with his bristling presence.

'You,' he said. Then he yelled, 'Masha! For you.'

He stomped away from the door.

'What's going on?' Zofia asked Masha when she came. 'What was all that shouting?'

'Nothing. Just an argument, that's all. About me being out too late. Where's Jacek?'

'At Alexander's.'

'Oh. I thought you were him. He's okay, isn't he?'

'Yes. We're going to apply for visas and get out of Lithuania. He sent me to ask if you'd come with us.'

Her eyes changed, losing their guarded quality, and she gave Zofia a sharp look. 'Why didn't he come himself?'

'He's busy, making plans.'

She seemed to consider this a moment and then stepped out into the thundery heat and closed the door behind her. She folded her arms. 'What d'you mean? What did he say?'

'Just that he wanted you to come with us. To a new life in America.'

'America?' Her expression was sceptical.

'Where there's no war. Where we'll be able to speak our own minds, earn our own money and buy a big house that won't be taken over by the state.'

Masha suppressed a smile. 'You do talk shit. They'd never let us go.' She sighed. 'Anyway, my father would stop me.'

'That's what Jacek said. But you're not a kid any more, even if they treat you like one. You're old enough to go without them, aren't you?'

This was a challenge and Masha smiled for a moment as if Zofia had said something ridiculous, but then she replied, 'I suppose.'

'Are you in?'

'Might be. Where did you say you got these visas from?'

'We have to queue at the Japanese consulate.'

'Where's that?'

Zofia explained. 'We'll be there first thing in the morning. Once we get our visas, that will be us – gone.'

Masha stared a moment as if she couldn't believe what she was hearing. 'Are you out of your minds? How many are going? Ordinary Lithuanians, or will it just be a load of Jews?'

Zofia winced, but stood firm. 'Some will be refugees like us, yes. But there'll be other people too. Folk looking for a new life and a future away from Communist oppression.'

Masha narrowed her eyes. 'Plenty of oppression in the United States too.'

Zofia stood her ground. 'You coming with us or not?'

'Maybe. What would I need to bring?'

Zofia's heart lifted. 'Travel light. You have to carry it all. We'll pass through Siberia, so warm clothes. As much money as you can.' She was making it up as she went along, but Masha nodded. Zofia felt they were playing a game, that none of this was real. Was she really planning on leaving? Even to her it sounded far-fetched. 'Shall I tell Jacek you'll meet us in the queue?'

A twist of the mouth. 'I'll need to think about it.'

'He loves you, you know. He really does.'

Masha's face didn't change, her expression studiedly nonchalant, but a flush spread from her neck to her cheeks.

Zofia pressed home this small advantage. 'We'll see you tomorrow, right?'

A gruff voice from the house calling her. 'Masha?'

Masha startled, but retreated back to the door. At the second call she lifted a hand in farewell and went back inside. The door shut unceremoniously in Zofia's face.

Later that day, after her father had gone to the factory, Masha walked down to the public call box in the new Soviet Postal Office. She closed the wooden doors around her and dialled, long fingernails scraping around the dial. Illeyvich's secretary answered and with a few clicks and whirrs of the switchboard, put her through to him.

She explained to him about the Japanese consul and the visas.

Illeyvich's voice came back as clearly as if he was in the next room. 'Yes, we know about it and we're turning a blind eye for now. There's no harm in it, because we want rid of these Jewish leeches, and if they want transit we'll make them pay. So we do nothing, just let them go.'

'What about Kowalski?'

A pause. 'He's another matter. We'll need to pick him up for interrogation before he has a chance to leave. Where's he staying?'

'Alexander's, the restaurant on Gruodžio Street. His old lodgings have already been requisitioned.'

'Then I'll get someone on to it and we'll catch him at the restaurant,' Illeyvich said. 'Keep with him, and make sure he stays there if you can.'

'I've to meet them in the morning at the Japanese consulate, but I'll try to make sure he goes back to Alexander's. Don't worry, I'll stick to him like flypaper.'

At Alexander's the electric had gone again, and the restaurant smelled of fish oil and kerosene from the lamps. The place was busy with sweating people dressed in several layers of clothes. Suits over pullovers, coats over suits. Whatever they could do to hang on to their possessions. Zofia crammed herself into the seat next to Jacek. 'I saw the Russian newspapers. The Lithuanian Air Force has been grounded. It's a coup, and things will only get worse for us if they discover we're anti-communist. Now will you believe we need to get out?'

'None of these people are going.' He gestured around.

'None of them work for the press.'

'So? You really think it's a good idea to go on a train where we know no one, where we could be picked up at any time? What would Tata think if he knew I'd let you get taken to a Russian camp? They'd split us up and there'd be no one there to look out for you.'

'I don't need you to look out for me. We're in this together.'

He leant back away from her. 'Look, sis, it's too risky. Let's just ride it out, okay?'

'If Masha said she was coming with me to try to get a visa,' she said, 'would you come?'

A puff of exasperation. 'Masha and I are finished. They threw me out of their house, remember? And she didn't exactly take my side, did she?'

'What if I told you I'd spoken to her and she thinks leaving Kaunas is a really good idea?'

Now she had his full attention, and his expression was thunderous. 'You didn't?'

'She's going to meet us tomorrow. I told her we'd be in the queue.'

'What the hell do you think you're doing, going to Masha behind my back? What did she say?' He stood up. 'You bloody idiot. You've just made me look stupid.'

He turned to go but there were too many chairs in his way. Zofia lurched to catch him by the arm. 'I just asked her if she wanted to come with us, that's all, and she said she would.'

He shot up the stairs out of the basement and she followed him. At the top he turned, eyes blazing. 'Oh yes, you think I have no voice of my own, do you? You with your ideas from books and films where nothing real ever happens, where everything always has a happy ending?' His words were full of venom. 'You'll make things worse! I never said I was going anywhere, did I? What did you tell her?'

'Just that we were going to queue for the visas and to meet us there.'

'You can't stop meddling, can you? I'm not allowed any life but you want to interfere in it.' He was panting now, on the pavement in the sultry heat. 'I can't go over a border again, like last time—'

'I'm not asking you to—'

'I'm done with it, hear me? We're not going, and there's an end to it. Go and harass someone else.'

He began to stride off down the street but Zofia pelted after him. 'Wait! Where are you going?'

'Away from you, where d'you think?'

She grabbed his arm, but he shoved her away. She wouldn't let him go, though. 'Masha and I are going, so you'd better bloody be there.' Her childhood wrestling instincts made her cling on, until finally he tore himself free with a volley of curses.

She ran after him but when she rounded the corner, he'd gone. There was just a street sweeper in a navy blue all-in-one duster suit with a red cap, moving the grit from one part of the pavement to the other, scraping with a broom that looked as if it was almost bald. More and more of these workmen had appeared as if by magic, manual workers for the Russian regime.

Shaken, Zofia retreated into the dim interior of the Alexander restaurant, where Rudi was regaling the remaining customers with bad news stories of deportations and executions. She ordered a cup of his terrible coffee and closed her ears. Maybe she had been a little pushy, but Jacek would turn up here again eventually. He had to; he had nowhere else to go.

But that night he didn't return, leaving Zofia with a gnawing sense of guilt and worry. She'd have to try for the visas without him, and the thought of it made her want to cry. She had pinned her hopes on this dream of a new life, one where she would be free, free to live without the crushing feeling of being marked out because of the accident of who her parents were.

Sometimes she wanted rid of the whole business of being Jewish, to spit it all out and be rid of the rules of Deuteronomy and Leviticus, to forget about guilt and atonement, the holy days of Rosh Hashanah and Yom Kippur.

Truth be told, she wanted it more for Jacek than herself. He was the one suffering most. Maybe he'd gone to Masha's. She hoped so. But if she couldn't take him with her, she'd just have to go alone. And what if he was right? What if she never made it out of Russia? The thought of having no one – of being suspended, rootless in the vast emptiness, filled her with trepidation.

Chapter 11

Zofia was one of the first to join the queue the next morning, dressed in her old print dress and blue coat, her canvas rucksack over her shoulders. It was hot wearing the coat, but it wouldn't fit in her bag, and she didn't like to leave her treasures at Alexander's. Even friends couldn't be trusted these days. A trickle of other refugees arrived after her, footsore and exhausted, and the queue had grown to about a quarter of a mile long. She peered over the heads of those in front; it moved so glacially slowly that it grew faster than it shrank.

Would Jacek come? She kept looking over her shoulder to see if he'd joined the line. She couldn't believe he'd let her do this, get a visa to sail halfway around the world alone.

The late-summer sun beat down on her shoulders and scorched the top of her head even though she'd tied a scarf around her dark hair, turban-style. When the couple next to her heard she was Polish, they passed the time sharing their own escape from Poland. Hollow-cheeked, they told her the rest of their family had been put on Nazi transport to camps.

Their conversation was interrupted by a lazy voice in Lithuanian. 'Hey, Zofia.'

Masha stood before her, carrying two big cardboard suitcases as if she was going on holiday. She was dressed up in a boxy floral dress and her face was stiff with powder and lipstick. The powder didn't quite hide the bluish stain of a black eye. But with her pin-curled blonde hair she stood out like a parrot among a bunch of crows. 'Where's Jacek?' she asked.

The Polish couple glared at her, uncomfortable, and another woman behind them with two small children said, 'No pushing in!'

'Sorry, I was saving her place,' Zofia said, as Masha didn't apologize, 'And one for my brother.'

Masha plonked the cases down at Zofia's feet.

'He'll be here any moment,' Zofia said, hoping that he would, or what would she do with Masha? Even standing here with her felt awkward. 'Are you okay? What happened to your face?'

'Walked into a lamp post.' A pause. 'Argument with my father.'

The queue slowly shuffled forward, with Masha craning her neck, looking behind for Jacek in just the way Zofia would if she didn't feel so embarrassed, and if her heart wasn't beating so fast.

The queue had slowed as it had reached midday, and the sun spiked mercilessly down on them, making everyone dab their foreheads and wipe their necks. Masha sank down on top of her suitcases. 'When's he coming?' she asked for the umpteenth time, her doll-like lips pouting. 'My father will kill me if he finds me here.'

'I don't know. Soon. He said he'd be here.' *Please, let him come.*

They shuffled forward inch by inch. Masha's floral dress was limp with sweat, and she kept pushing at the curls in her hair to keep them in place.

'Haven't you got a scarf?' Zofia asked her.

Reluctantly Masha knelt to open a suitcase and drew out a silk chiffon scarf in a bright orange. Zofia watched her tie it carefully over her hair.

It was late in the afternoon when Jacek came. Zofia spotted him straight away, striding up from the consul's house, and examining the queue, no doubt looking for her. She was glad to see he had his knapsack with him, fit for traveling. His gaze couldn't help but be drawn to Masha's scarf as it stuck out like a flaming beacon. Jacek's face lit up and then took on a more studied expression as he sauntered towards them.

'Jacek! Here! Over here.' Masha stood on tiptoe, waving.

He didn't hurry to embrace her, merely gave her a nod.

'All right, Zofia?' he asked.

'We thought you weren't coming,' Masha said.

'Spent the night at Rudi's house. I had a few things to do. Sold some stuff to get some cash. Someone told me it costs money for the train tickets.'

Zofia couldn't help but grin, the relief was so great.

Jacek was still talking. 'Even if we get visas, we still have to raise enough for the fare. And the Russians want it in dollars.'

'In dollars?' Zofia frowned. 'Why?'

'Guess it's so that if the Germans come, they can trade with the Yanks. Buy arms and supplies.'

'How much?' Masha asked.

'They say three hundred.'

'What? We'll never get that much,' Zofia said. 'How much have you got?'

'About a hundred and eighty and it's in Lithuanian *lit*. But I heard from Rudi that the Nazis are massing troops on the Russian border, and we all know what that means. So let's get the visas first. As soon as word spreads about that, more people will join this queue so we'll have to worry about money later.'

Zofia was vaguely annoyed at how Jacek had taken control, as if the whole idea of the visas belonged to him.

'Will the Japanese ask questions? D'you think he'll give visas to people who aren't refugees?' Masha asked.

Zofia looked to Jacek. She hadn't thought of that.

'Of course he will,' Jacek said, and he grasped Masha by the hand.

Chapter 12

Otto was on his way home after another uncertain day at the office. He walked morosely down the main street, now renamed in honour of Stalin, passing deserted shops and red flags. He kept on walking, deep in thought, but stopped to look as he passed the only shop with a window display – a new Russian *Intourist* travel shop that had just opened. Hanging from wires were garish photographs of Moscow, with smiling women and children in the foreground.

The Russians were obviously keen on encouraging people to have a family holiday in Russia. It made him want to laugh. Now the Russians had come, everybody just wanted to escape. Only the protection of the Japanese saved him from Russian rule and the fear of deportation to a gulag like other educated men.

Earlier, at the consulate, Sugihara had assigned him a 'helper' – a Polish youth from the queue, someone else who could speak the language to help him fill out forms and stamp visas. They had worked in the corridor, writing out the necessary records and paperwork and supplying Sugihara with the papers to sign, and the building was fusty with the smell of unwashed refugees shuffling up the stairs and along the corridor.

That man Bronovski hadn't been back for a visa, though. Otto frowned. He would have thought he would be first in the queue. And his scruffy bundle of papers was still on Sugihara's desk. Odd how he hadn't returned.

As he walked to work, Otto thought of the situation with frustration. He couldn't seem to order it all, and if there was one thing he liked, it was order. And he just knew that signing this many visas without permission from the big bosses in Japan was bound to lead to trouble in the end. Worse, the more they signed, the more of these poor people kept appearing.

Even away from the consulate, the atmosphere in Kaunas – he refused to call it Kovno – was tense. The 'Sovietization' process was being escalated. The military police and the so-called 'workers' militia' were actively rounding up anyone who was anti-Soviet. This included anyone Lithuanian trying to get out of Russia, as defecting from the supposed 'paradise' of Russia was in itself an insult to the Russian regime.

Thousands of Poles from Vilnius who'd been trying to leave had been rounded up and sent to gulags already – he knew this because of memos to Sugihara, and telegrams from the British government who had been protesting over their treatment.

What would his mother say when he confessed that he no longer had his job with Sugihara? He'd been putting off telling her, hoping it would never happen. She relied on him. Since his father's suicide, she'd made herself housebound in the evenings, refusing to go out. It was a kind of illness, like she was waiting for his father to come home from work, but of course he never came, just like on the day he died.

It gave him stomach cramps just thinking about it. He stepped past two Russian soldiers on the street who were dragging a man from his house by force. Otto blanked it out and kept his head high, trying not to look. *Nothing to do with me.*

At last his house was in sight – an apartment of two rooms in a big 1930s block. Kaunas had grown enormously after the civil war between the Red Army and the White Army, and this was one of the new builds. He trudged up the concrete stairs to the third floor and let himself in. His mother, brown eyes wide with alarm, came hobbling into the hall to waylay him.

'There's someone to see you,' she whispered, nodding back to the front room with wide eyes.

Otto stiffened. 'A Russian?'

'No. No, I don't think so.' She gestured again to the front room and Otto hurried in.

The visitor was sitting in one of the armchairs but didn't rise to greet him. Instead he said, 'Your mother gave me coffee. There's some left in the pot.' He indicated the side table. 'My name is Friedrich Zeitel. I wanted to discuss a few things with you. Diplomatic business. I wondered if your mother would like to take a walk, while we talk.' He gave her a meaningful look.

Ma hovered in the doorway. He might as well have asked her to go to the moon. 'A walk?'

'Yes, Ma, just go along to the market and back.'

He hustled her to the coat stand and whispered, 'Just half an hour, that's all.'

'But I—'

She took off her waist apron and, flustered, grabbed her coat. He bundled her into it and gave her a hat.

With a push, she was outside. The door banged shut behind her.

Otto came back and sat, but he was bolt upright in his chair. He recognized that Zeitel had a German name and it had put him on his guard, and not only that, but he also sensed that the visitor had something unpleasant to say. He looked like a policeman, with that too-tightly knotted tie, the bland but officious manner, and the way he bossed his mother about and expected her to jump.

'You work at the Japanese consulate, I believe, with Chiune Sugihara,' Zeitel said. 'And you are German-born, yes?'

Otto was wary. 'Yes, but I've lived here in Kaunas most of my life.'

'But your father was a wine merchant from Mosel.'

How did he know that? 'In the Twenties. Importing wine back then was profitable. He brought his business here when I was only a baby, but operated it from Germany.'

The man was staring at him. An awkward silence. Otto filled it. 'At the beginning he used an importer, a go-between, but finally he decided to do it himself and we actually moved here when I was eight. Wine by the barrel – a good business, until the Russian civil war came and transport dried up. That was what killed him, I think, the loss of his business. But I have never been back to Germany.'

'But you speak German?'

'*Ein bisschen.* We used to speak it at home for Father. My mother, well, she preferred to learn Lithuanian. To get along with the other mothers, see? But I speak Russian too. And a little Polish. It was all necessary for business here.' Where was this all leading? 'What is it you wanted to speak to me about?'

'We need information about your friend Sugihara. We need to know if the Japanese are really as friendly to the Reich as they pretend to be. You see, we've noticed that there seem to be a lot of Jewish people seeking help from Sugihara, and although it is in our interest for them to leave and go elsewhere, the ... how can I put it ... the over-zealousness of his help, the fact he is giving out so many visas, it gives us some cause for concern.'

'So this is about the visas?' *I knew it would bring trouble, I just knew it.*

'There are some people who we want to track down. Some friends of a Jew called Bronovski. I'll bring you a list, and you can let me know if any of them have asked for transit visas.'

Bronovski. The Jew with the yellow cravat, who hadn't collected his papers. 'I'm not quite clear what you're asking. Who is it that you represent? You didn't say.'

'I'm employed by the main office of the *Reichssicherheitdienst* – German security service.'

Even more worrying. 'I don't understand what you think I

have to do with any of this. I'm simply a secretary. I just do my job, do what he tells me. Nothing more, nothing less.'

Zeitel leant forward, hands on knees. 'Then we will pay you to do more. We want to know how Japan is viewing this exodus of Jews, and whether we can trust Sugihara's government. You see, when the agreement between Japan and Germany was first mooted, Tokyo was scared – thought it might disrupt Japan's relations with Britain and they'd lose their imperial trade, but in the end they saw the sense in it. Now we fear Japan will renege on that agreement.'

'But Japan doesn't want to go to war against the Russians. They signed a non-aggression pact with the Soviet Union, didn't they? Sugihara told me.'

'To break the plutocrats in the West, yes. But the Japanese are not fools. They also want to line their nests and defend themselves from Chinese or Russian communism.' He paused and gave a slight smile. 'You are seeing the unwelcome results of Russian communism here already, are you not?'

'Changes, yes. It's only to be expected.'

'So Sugihara's playing both sides. A friend to Russia and a friend to us. But soon he will have to make a choice. The Japanese government will have to make a choice. And we need to know what they are thinking. Which side they will jump.'

So war between Germany and Russia was coming. A sweat broke out on Otto's brow. 'Are you asking me to be a spy?'

'You have read too many novels. No. We are seeking a diplomatic relationship with you. One that will benefit us both. The pay is handsome and, once the consulate is closed, will enable you to settle back in Germany again, in a place free of communist dogma. Perhaps you will even have enough to restart your wine business.'

Otto was queasy at the idea of deceiving Sugihara. 'He keeps himself to himself. I don't know if I can be of much assistance. And the consulate will be closed down soon.'

'Exactly. We are hoping to make sure Sugihara is transferred to Berlin. Where we can keep an eye on him.'

Berlin? But what about Ma? She couldn't go to Berlin.

Zeitel was continuing. 'But while he is here, there is not much time for us to get the information we need. Weeks at the most. A few days' work is all we ask, and in exchange, free passage back to Germany and a generous payment.' A raise of the eyebrows. 'Be worth about four hundred in American dollars.'

The amount made Otto freeze. So much? It was tempting. The consulate would soon be closing, after all, and he had nowhere else to go. He should talk to his mother, but then again, she'd talk him out of leaving. It was what she always did, shut down the possibility of any change.

His silence went on long enough for Zeitel to sit back in his chair and ask, 'Well?'

'I'll need to think it over.'

'I don't think I was clear enough in my invitation. If you choose not to accept, then as a German-born citizen, you have a duty to the Reich to serve in the armed forces. Not to do so means a trial for anti-German activities.' He smiled and shrugged. 'Not my laws, I'm afraid. Herr Hitler is determined that every German should be part of his German revival.'

So there it was. The bald truth. There had never really been a choice. His mouth was dry as sand as he looked at Zeitel's well-polished brogues.

'I guess I can count on you to help us. And trust me, you'll be glad you did.' Zeitel placed a green dossier of documents on the table. 'Fill these in. Details of who Sugihara contacts, what he says to Tokyo. Any friends of August Bronovski. Be thorough. Take copies of any letters if you can. I'll collect each evening after you finish work.'

'Every night?'

Zeitel stood and held out his hand. 'You understand our time window is short. Once the consulate shuts there'll be no place here for a man like you – one who can speak several languages and is a German alien. Make no mistake, it would be the gulag for you unless you got out.'

Zeitel's hand was still waiting there, hovering in mid-air.

Otto grasped it and shook it. The other man's hand gripped his sweating palm firmly before letting go. Otto had the queasy feeling that he had unwittingly agreed to do something he didn't want to do.

Once Zeitel had left, Otto's mother came back, and he heard her banging about in the kitchen.

'Sorry, Ma,' he called.

She peered through the hatch from the kitchen. 'What's going on?'

'Just consulate business, nothing to worry about.' He was aware of his sweaty hands and wiped them down the sides of his trousers.

'That's right, keep me in the dark.' She shook her head at him. 'You think you're so clever. But you can't see what's right in front of your nose.' She disappeared from the kitchen and came into the living room. 'Two of us can have secrets,' she said. 'I was waiting until you looked less distracted. That appointment I had, last week? The doctor says I've got two years.'

The words reverberated round his head. 'Two years of what? What are you saying?'

'That lump under my arm. It's cancer and it's spread.'

She took off her apron. Her lower lip was trembling, and now he knew, it seemed obvious. She looked thinner and greyer. She was still young, yet she looked old. Why had he never noticed it before?

'But what are they going to do?' he asked. He hurried to throw his arms around her waist and press her to him.

She was stiff a moment before she yielded and allowed him to kiss her on her powdery cheek. 'It's a long time since you did that,' she said.

'You should've told me, Ma,' he said. 'Don't worry. I'll take care of you. Everything's going to be all right.' He pushed away the thought of Zeitel. 'Is it an operation? What?'

'We can't afford an operation.'

'We can. I'll make sure we can.' He thanked God, maybe the money from Zeitel would be useful after all. His mind was racing, trying to take it all in.

'How? Make money from thin air?'

'Don't you worry, I'll think of something. We'll get you that treatment. Now sit down, rest. I'll bring you some tea.'

Ma smiled, and something like her old vitality returned. 'I have to be at death's door, do I, before you offer to make me tea?'

'Just sit, Ma, okay?' He hurried into the kitchen and frantically searched for the tea caddy. *Death's door*. The words haunted him. He couldn't imagine life without his mother. Two years, she'd said. He spooned the tea into the pot, tears pricking behind his eyes. Mustn't cry. Without her, he didn't even know who he'd be; she was the one with all the ideas, all the opinions. She was the strong one, not like his father, who'd taken the coward's way out and gassed himself in the shop's garage.

Thank God for Zeitel and his cash. She'd have the best, only the best. The best treatment that money could buy.

Chapter 13

'Did you get them?' Zofia asked.

Earlier today Jacek had gone to try to get more dollars on the black market, and returned to the queue when the sun was low in the sky. He looked wan and there were dark circles under his eyes.

'Shh.' A whisper. 'Yes. I was lucky, I sold the pearls and got dollars in denominations of five – much easier to hide than single dollars. The Russians want to get hold of dollars so we must keep them hidden. They're under the inner sole of my shoe.'

'Have we enough yet?' Masha asked.

A sigh and a shake of the head. He turned to Zofia. 'I had news from a man at the Café Metropole. My old editor, Vilkas, has been shot. They didn't even bother to hide the body. He was found by a farmer in a copse of trees just outside the town, along with three other men from the *Kaunas Star*.'

Masha turned her head away, but Zofia grabbed Jacek by the arm. 'That could have been you.'

'We thought they'd been sent to a camp, but no. They didn't bother to put them on transport, just murdered them. Their hands were bound and they had their shoelaces tied together.'

Zofia felt her head swim. Had that happened to Uncle Tata? The thought made her nauseous. She tugged at Jacek's sleeve.

'Will they come here looking for you?'

'I doubt it,' Masha said. 'Why would they bother for one man?'

'Because of his anti-Soviet column in the Jewish paper, stupid,' Zofia said.

Masha glared. 'Don't call me stupid.'

Jacek stepped between them. 'I'm afraid my passport says I'm Jacek Kowalski, so I suspect it's only a matter of time before they catch up with me. They're in the city centre now, but the net is widening every day. I called at Alexander's and heard that another friend, Bronovski, has been killed by the Russians. Him and the old couple that were sheltering him. The place had been trashed and turned over, just like the Marks's.'

Masha sighed and looked at her shoes as if she was bored by all these tales of killings.

'I wish Uncle Tata was here,' Zofia said to Jacek. 'It doesn't seem right to go without him.'

'I just wish they'd hurry up,' said Masha. The queue had hardly moved.

Zofia saw that Jacek was fidgeting, and smoking heavily, his fingers stained yellow by nicotine. 'I'm sure going over the borders by train will be different to fighting through barbed wire,' she said to reassure him.

'I know that,' he said. 'Don't worry, sis. There's no future for any of us here. If they're shooting journalists, there's no way of reporting what's true any more. Vilkas was a good man, an honest man. He made the *Kaunas Star* what it was. Now he's gone, getting out of here can't come soon enough.'

'You're so clever to think of it,' Masha said.

He tucked Masha's arm in his and planted a kiss on the side of her neck. 'It was Zofia's idea,' he said.

Inside the consulate, Otto was in charge of preparing hundreds of visas. This process made him uneasy, not just because of Zeitel, but because he knew they shouldn't really be doing it, and up until now Sugihara had always paid lip service to doing things 'by the rules'. There were now so many people crushed up outside the building that it was like being under siege.

He'd worried about Zeitel all night, but decided to do nothing. If he could last a few more days, Sugihara would surely make provision for him to accompany him to his next posting. On several occasions he had heard Sugihara on the telephone to officials in Tokyo about where he, Sugihara would be sent next. Otto tried not to look as though he was listening too desperately as these calls went on.

But late that afternoon, he was asked to get General Miroyuki Sato, a diplomat in Tokyo, on the line. Sugihara was still in his shirtsleeves, signing off visas, his ink running low again in the pot.

Otto held out the receiver and Sugihara stretched his cramped hands by clasping them together before taking it from him.

'We have proof now,' Sugihara said into the mouthpiece. 'The Germans are intent on annihilating the Jews. It's a bad situation. We can't align ourselves with this and still keep our standing with the British. We have to get our men around the table again.'

From Sugihara's uncomfortable expression, there was obviously disagreement on the other end.

'But we have evidence of their atrocities—'A pause. 'No, it's not just rumour and propaganda.' Another pause. 'Yes, yes.'

Another longer pause and the chittering noise of someone talking at length while Sugihara sighed.

'To where?' His eyebrows shot up. 'You're sending me to Berlin?'

Otto paused in writing in the ledger, still as a statue. Berlin? No. So it was true. His stomach gave a lurch. Would he be going too?

'What about my staff? I have seven staff here as well as my family—'

More talk, followed by Sugihara's protestations. 'But what shall I tell them?'

Sugihara's face greyed as he took in what Otto assumed were

more instructions.

'I understand. But I'll be writing to the minister. We need assurances of—'

But the line had obviously been cut off. 'Hello …? Hello …? Damn them all.' Sugihara slammed the phone back into its cradle and then began pounding the powder he used to make ink.

Otto didn't dare ask anything. It was bad form to listen in to the consul's conversations, and considered best for him always to keep his mouth shut. But he'd gathered that Sugihara would be going to Berlin, and that he, Otto, an actual German citizen, wouldn't be going with him.

For the rest of the day Otto's nerves became worse and worse. Every conversation then became of intense interest. He scrutinized every letter. Finally he could bear it no longer.

'Mr Sugihara, sir,' he asked, 'what will happen to the diplomatic staff here when you are reposted?'

Sugihara looked up from the pile of visas. 'I was waiting to see if I could get better news, but you're right, you deserve to know. I asked the same question, and the answer was "we have no plans to redeploy your staff at present".'

'What does that mean?' His heart plummeted.

'It means what it says. You'll be left to fend for yourselves. They won't give you immunity or transfer you. You'll be subject to the laws of the government here.'

'You don't know what will happen to us, your staff, yet you're writing visas for these refugees?'

Sugihara opened a drawer in his desk and took out a neat pile of visas. 'These are the first ones I wrote. In case of this situation. There is one here for you and your mother. See?' He patted the pile.

'My mother? But she's ill. She's not well enough to leave. And where will we go? How can you be so calm? My mother has lived here for years!'

'That is something you must discuss with her. I'm sorry. I tried everything I could think of, but nothing moves them. It's the same for the cook, the children's nanny, for all our staff. I wish it were otherwise. But the visas will get you out of Russia at least. They are stamped as transit visas to Curaçao.'

The reality of it made Otto's head swim. Curaçao. The word echoed oddly in his head, a nonsense word. He was to be joining the ranks of the refugees outside. 'How long have we got?'

'Weeks at the most. I keep trying to extend our stay, but the Russians are getting harder to deal with, and I think we'll soon be out at gunpoint.'

'And you sit there writing visas for Jews?' The words were choked.

'Because each of them is just like you. A person with no place to go, and a death sentence on his head.'

Chapter 14

Zofia was alert for any movement from the consulate. It was the middle of the next day when the Japanese consul's aide ducked out of the door and stood beside the fence. He was a young man who looked uncomfortable in the heat, and seemed astounded by the sheer numbers waiting outside.

By then their little group was in sight of the curved front steps of the building. They pressed forwards when the aide called for quiet. He was hollow-cheeked and looked like he hadn't slept, though he was immaculately attired, his dark grey trousers neatly pressed to a knife-edge.

He cleared his throat and his hands twisted before him.

'This building will be closing today at five o'clock,' he said. 'We have received orders that no further visas will be issued. You must all leave immediately. There is nothing more Mr Sugihara can do to assist you.'

He turned to go just as the crowd erupted into a frenzy of outrage and desperation.

Behind Zofia and Jacek there was a family of a woman and two children. 'What did he say?' the mother asked. She had not understood the language.

'No more visas,' Zofia said. 'The consulate closes today.'

The word spread like a flame and the crowd began to crush towards the railings. Masha cannoned forwards into Żofia, who found herself squashed against the black-suited man in front.

Just when she thought the breath had completely left her lungs, a window opened in the house.

Mr Sugihara's head appeared. 'Move back,' he said. 'Do you want to kill your countrymen? My assistant will come later and issue tickets. Those who do not behave in an orderly way will not be given a ticket. I can make only one hundred visas today. Those with tickets will be given a visa. That is all.'

The window shut. People began to jostle for position, hauling at each other's sleeves to pull each other out of the queue.

Żofia clung on to Jacek. 'Stick together,' she said. 'We have to stick together.' She was frantically counting the number of the people in the queue.

'We aren't going to make it,' Masha said. 'We're number one hundred and twenty at least.' So she'd been doing the same. She wasn't as stupid as she made out. 'I think we should give up.'

Jacek ignored her and exchanged a look with Żofia.

'We'll wait,' she said firmly.

Masha sighed and played with the ends of her scarf. The queue had not shifted at all. The refugees had nowhere to go. Most had no shelter, and owned no documents, having fled Poland with nothing. Any document, however flimsy or forged, was a slim chance of protection against deportation to a gulag or concentration camp. Nobody wanted to leave. They had no money to bribe the Soviets and were thin and exhausted from foraging for food. The chance of life was all they wanted, and no one wanted to give up their shot at freedom. Too many remembered the escape from Poland and the fate of the Jews there. Fear hung over the queue in a black cloud.

What will happen to us if we can't get away? was the question on everyone's lips.

A few hours later, the aide came out with the tickets and

the crowd surged towards him until the window opened again. Sugihara looked out, and the crowd solidified again into an expectant mass. This was the man who held their lives in his hands.

His presence at the window was like the eye of the Almighty.

The aide warily went up the queue. One ticket per family with children. Zofia hadn't realized children could travel on a parent's visa. Would they count as a family?

'We're going to make it,' Jacek said to Masha, exultant. 'We're going to get out.'

The man approached with his batch of tickets. The family in front of them got a ticket, then finally it was their turn.

'Can we travel on the same ticket, me and my brother?' Zofia asked, sending up a silent prayer.

'No. Not adult siblings. Only families or husband and wife. Your papers will be checked.' He glanced between the three of them. 'Sorry, but this is the last ticket,' he said. He smiled shyly and handed it to Zofia.

Astonished, she found herself with the flimsy piece of card in her hands as he held up his empty palms, and flapped them at the queue. 'See? No more.' She saw him glance up at the window.

'I won't go without you,' she said to Jacek, as the aide hurried away, head down. 'We've always been together. Our whole lives.'

'Why did he give it to you?' Masha said, eyes flashing.

'It's not my fault,' Zofia said.

Jacek held up his hand for peace. 'We're not giving up, though. We'll stay here,' he said, 'and Zofia will get her visa, and we'll just have to hope the Japanese consul relents, and they don't shut up shop. We've got this far, we're not giving up now.'

'They should have given it to you,' Masha protested to Jacek. 'You're the one at risk.'

'They hanged her boss at the library,' Jacek said. 'I say she goes without us.'

'I don't want to go without you,' Zofia said. 'You're the only family I have left.'

Behind them the family of four were hugging each other tight. The mother had fallen to her knees wailing, and had pulled both children into her arms – the curly-haired boy and the girl with ragged pigtails. The woman was trying to stem her tears by pressing her face with her sleeve. The children looked up at her bemused, not understanding why their mother was so distraught.

Zofia took in the scene and imagined being in the woman's shoes, with those two little children to protect, and stepped towards the man, who was trying to pull up his wife from the dust. Something about the children's wide bewildered eyes got to her. She held out the ticket. 'Take it,' she said. 'One visa will take a whole family. We are grown-up. We have more chance, but your children cannot save themselves.'

The man looked down at her with wonder in his face. 'No. No? You are sure?'

She pressed it into his hand and covered it with hers. 'May good luck go with you all,' she said.

When she turned back Jacek glowered and grabbed her by the shoulder. 'What the hell?' His whisper was fierce in her ear. 'You should have got out while you could.'

'Didn't you see those children? This way four people can escape, not just one.'

She heard the slam of the window as Sugihara shut it at the same time as his aide closed the door.

A car was brought out of the drive, close to the door. A big black Buick, the one belonging to Sugihara. Two liveried men from inside the building began to place suitcases and attaché cases by the front door. It looked like it was true, and Sugihara was really going to leave. At this, one man tried to climb up the drainpipe at the back of the house, but he was spotted and the staff gardeners threw stones at him until he came down.

'You could have got out of here,' Jacek repeated. 'You could have been safe.'

Zofia closed her ears and stood stubbornly in the queue. She couldn't think what else to do. She'd just given away her hopes and dreams to someone else.

The crowd was restless, but no one gave up waiting. One by one in front of them the queue grew shorter as the people with tickets went inside and emerged kissing their precious piece of paper and tucking it safely into their pockets. Finally, the family of four went inside, and now there was nobody ahead of them in the queue and the heat of the sun dissolved into cloud.

The men from the consulate packed Sugihara's luggage into the trunk of the car and slammed it shut. A hubbub as people realized their chance of escape was slipping away.

'You.' Sugihara's young aide was back, and pointing at Zofia. 'He wants to see you.'

'I won't come without my brother,' she said.

'And me,' Masha said, grabbing tight to Jacek's wrist.

'No. He says no other people. Just you.'

She looked to Jacek, but he shooed her forwards. 'Go,' he said, his face red with emotion. 'I didn't believe you before, about the visas, it seemed too impossible. But go, see what the big man wants.'

'No, I don't want to—'

'Please, Zofia, see if you can get out. We'll be all right.'

She shook her head, still protesting, but Jacek grabbed her in a hug and whispered, 'What did Tata say? "Get out of Lithuania".'

'Are you coming?' The aide's mouth was set in a tense line, but he ushered Zofia forward, and then relocked the gates behind her. Inside the gate was an orderly garden that looked as though it needed watering. Rows of wilting greens. A child's swing hung from a tree.

The aide gave a deliberate cough to stop her dawdling. 'You want my advice? Hurry. Mr Sugihara will leave in fifteen minutes.'

Up the stairs to the first floor and into a large room lined with polished empty shelves. Mr Sugihara was there at the desk, a short man in a colourful silk tie who held a brush delicately in his hand. His shirt shone white in the gloom. A small pot of ink stood before him, next to a pile of papers – thin green paper printed with Japanese characters.

'Ah. Here you are. What is your name?' His expression was kind.

'Zofia Kowalski,' she said.

'You gave up your visa,' he said. 'I saw you. The family are very grateful and the father asked if there was anything I could do for you.'

'We wanted visas to go to America,' she said, 'but I won't go without Jacek. That's my brother, my twin brother. He used to work for the paper. But he won't go without Masha Romaska, his … his fiancée.'

'May I ask a few questions?' The Japanese consul pulled a piece of paper towards him and asked the assistant to write a record. 'You are from?'

'Poland originally.'

'City?'

'Warsaw.'

'Your passport?' She gave it to the aide, the tall thin man, presumably his secretary, who scratched down her particulars in a ledger before handing it back.

'So Polish Jews?'

'Yes, Jewish. We've been here a year, living with the Markunas family, who are Lithuanian, but they've just left. They feared for their son who is a musician. But then the Russians took over our house … and took my uncle away.'

At the choke in her voice, he looked up. 'I'm sorry to hear it.'

'My uncle … he told us to get out of the country if we could. My brother's a journalist, you see.'

'A journalist, you say.' He paused and ruminated a moment. 'Have you any relatives you are going to? Anyone who can vouch for you?'

'None. My mother's dead, she died when we were small. My father was taken by the Nazis in Poland. I had two aunts who looked after us but they stayed behind. Too scared to leave. Since then we've had no news and we don't know where they are now. We fear the worst.'

'I see. So where are you living?'

'Nowhere – that is, we're camping out at Alexander's restaurant. Rudi's very kind to us. There are about fifty of us there, all refugees. It's a roof over our heads, even if it's not really a restaurant any more and the coffee is awful.'

He smiled, then turned to his aide who Zofia sensed was watching without appearing to watch. 'Prepare a transit visa made out for Curaçao.'

'Where is Curaçao?' Zofia asked.

'A Dutch dominion in the Caribbean.'

'But we want to go to America.'

'America won't admit you unless you have a relative there. But Curaçao can be a destination at least. You don't have to actually go there, but you do need a destination. There is a large Jewish population in Shanghai. I suggest you try to head for there until … until the situation changes.'

She nodded. She had no choice but to accept any lifeline he could offer. 'We need three visas.'

'For your brother, yes, but this other person, your brother's fiancée? Who is she?'

'Masha? She's Lithuanian. Born and brought up here in Kaunas.'

A shake of the head. 'I can issue you and your brother with a visa, but not the other woman. The Russian authorities would regard that as anti-Soviet, to deport a native. She will have to follow him later.'

Zofia swallowed. 'Then I can't go. My brother and I were together since before we were born and I just can't go without him. And he won't go without Masha. They think they're in love.'

'In love?' Sugihara's mouth twitched as if suppressing a smile.

94

He seemed to think for a moment, and then closed his eyes and let out a sigh. 'Let's hope the Russians believe in love.'

He turned to his aide. 'Otto, bring up this young lady's brother and his fiancée. His name?'

'Jacek Kowalski.'

The aide frowned and strode away in a stiff kind of way.

Sugihara went into an adjoining room and while he was gone, Zofia sidled over to the aide's desk behind her. His shelves still had a few objects remaining, a row of miniature carvings. So delicate and beautiful. The little jade fox entranced her so, almost without thinking, she reached out to slip it into her pocket. The smooth weight of it and its coolness in her hand surprised her.

At the sound of footsteps, she leapt away from the shelf. Sugihara was back with a batch of scruffy papers in his hands. Zofia kept a grip on the little fox. After a short wait the aide was back with Jacek and Masha behind him.

The aide asked Masha to wait outside. She looked disgruntled but went to sit down on the hard chair he indicated in the corridor. The door clicked shut.

'Very pleased to meet you, sir,' said Jacek, for once on his best behaviour and holding out a hand to be shaken.

But the handshake was interrupted by the noise of a car drawing up outside.

'It's a Russian car,' his aide said, peering out of the window, agitated. 'Four soldiers. Armed. Looks like they've come to throw us out.'

'Quick, then, take their passports and prepare three transit visas in their names, please.'

'You will give us visas?' Zofia couldn't believe it.

'What's another few when I've written so many?' He beckoned Jacek closer. 'But if I do you this favour, will you do one for me? I need someone reliable with a kind heart.' He pushed the heap of scruffy papers across the desk towards him. 'And I cannot trust these to the post. They are too precious. So I need a courier.'

'What are they?' Jacek asked.

'Eye-witness accounts of what the Germans are doing in Poland. From a Jew called Bronovski. He didn't come back for them, but I can't leave them behind. I think they should be seen by my friend in Tokyo.'

'August Bronovski? I knew him,' Jacek said.

'He didn't come back for them because he was killed by the Russians,' Zofia added.

Sugihara frowned. 'I was impressed by him. His determination that these stories should be told. He gathered them together to try and convince me to grant these visas to anyone who came knocking. Witness accounts of Nazi atrocities. My instinct tells me you have a similar story.'

Zofia's eyes widened. She had never thought to write down her story.

She reached past Jacek for the top paper in front of her, written in a scrawling spidery handwriting, like that of an old man. She lifted it to see another beneath it scribbled in pencil as if in a hurry, and another in Yiddish that looked like an excerpt from a diary. She caught a few words of each and the cramp of fear returned to her belly.

'Yes,' she said. 'It was like they say.' She passed the document to Jacek.

Jacek scanned it and then handed it back to her as if it burned. His lips tightened and he shook his head as if to clear it. 'What do you want me to do with them?'

A blast on the horn from outside, and Yukiko, Sugihara's wife, appeared from the adjoining door, her eyes anxious. 'We're ready,' she said. 'Everything's packed.'

'Then take the children down and put them in the car. I'll be along shortly. Tell them five minutes.'

Her footsteps faded as Sugihara gave Jacek his full attention. 'This is important. You must deliver these to my friend General Miroyuki Sato in Tokyo. He is closing his eyes to what is happening in Germany and Poland. I will package them under my diplomatic seal and you will pretend they are a pair of gloves, a gift from me for his wife. When he opens them he will no longer be able to say he has heard nothing of these atrocities. He will no longer be able to ignore it while the government brokers another pact with Germany.'

Another blast of the horn outside that made her heart pound. She and Jacek exchanged glances. They needed the visas and she could see no harm in it. And being Polish nobody would be surprised to see that Jacek had such documents even if the package were opened. If it could inform the Japanese of what the Nazis were doing, and persuade them not to enter any kind of alliance with Hitler then that would be good, wouldn't it?

'What do you think?' Jacek turned to Zofia.

'Yes,' she said. It was the least they could do.

'You can trust me,' Jacek said to Sugihara. 'I'll deliver your parcel.'

'Please, can I add something?' Zofia asked. 'Have you paper?'

Sugihara pushed a sheet over. She picked up a fountain pen from his desk, uncapped it and began to write frantically in Polish. She couldn't do much for her father, but she could at least do this.

The Nazis came for my father, Jacob Aaron Kowalski, in broad daylight while he was reading a newspaper. When he heard the commotion and shots outside, he and his brother, my uncle Theodor who we call Tata, tried to escape through the back door, but they were waiting there too. One of them shot my father in the head. They killed him for no reason but that they were Jew-hunting for sport. My brother and I were at work, but my uncle, who escaped, came to tell us, and after he showed us my father's body, he showed us my father's shoes, which were still next to his armchair. We saw the blood in the garden where they shot him. Imagine having to run for your life wearing only your socks ...

She kept on writing furiously, head down, even though Jacek had put a hand on her shoulder to stop her. She'd got to the part about the border crossing, but her eyes had filled with hot tears and she didn't want to write that down. She scrubbed her eyes with her sleeve. She wasn't going to tell anyone what Jacek did.

'It's all right,' she said to him. 'I didn't tell.' She continued in her thin looping hand:

> *My father was an honourable man and a good father. I'm glad it was quick for him, for if he had survived, I think he would be one of the unlucky ones.*
> *Zofia Kowalski*

When she'd finished writing, she raised her eyes from the paper, shocked to see the tidy interior of the room once more.

The aide, who Sugihara had called Otto, was staring at her, and she wiped her wet cheeks again.

Sugihara took up a piece of blotting paper and very carefully pressed it down onto the paper. 'So now I have one more. I will get my wife to package them for you. Wait a moment.'

Sugihara stood then, and she heard his feet trot down the corridor. 'Yukiko,' he called. The sound of children's voices and doors opening and closing.

'What about Masha?' Jacek said urgently. 'Will you give her a visa too?'

The aide looked uncomfortable. 'I don't know.'

'Well, I won't go without her.' He opened the door to the corridor and beckoned her in.

'What's going on?' Masha asked Jacek. 'Did you get visas?'

'We hope so.' He took hold of her hand and squeezed it.

Zofia watched Otto walk over and place three sheets of paper down on the consul's desk. Three pieces of paper. Their visas! But they were still unsigned. She was terrified Sugihara would drive off without signing them. *Please, come back.*

She looked up at Otto, the skinny young man with the long nose, and he wouldn't meet her eyes.

Feeling awkward standing in the middle of the room, she turned her face away until she heard him stride back to his desk, and the scrape of his chair and the rustle of papers. Moments later she glanced to see him bent over in the other corner of the room, emptying the contents of his drawer into a briefcase. He was searching for the fox on the shelf, but she kept the cold nub of jade tightly pressed to her palm, her face hot.

Otto fascinated her, because she had thought him to be about her own age, but now she realized he was probably older, immaculately dressed, his hair cut very short. The sun shone down on the shoulders of his jacket, which was surely too hot for this weather. It made her curious, how someone could have come to be working in such a place. He wasn't Japanese, but Mr Sugihara had employed him as his aide. He was good-looking in a pale kind of way, with the kind of skin to flush easily.

Jacek was pacing the floor but Masha had wandered behind Sugihara's desk and was openly staring at the flag hanging there.

'Masha!' Jacek gave her a warning look.

A horn sounded outside and they all startled.

Then Sugihara was back, springing towards them with a brown paper package in his hands. It was neatly taped, sealed with red wax, and well tied with string.

Masha's face was blank, her head to one side, her eyes curiously assessing, as if trying to work out what it all meant.

Sugihara took a rubber stamp and rolled it back and forth over the ink pad before stamping it with an official-looking stamp, the Japanese imperial emblem of the chrysanthemum that she'd seen on the gatepost outside. Then he signed across it with three or four quick dabs of his brush. When he handed it to Jacek, she saw that the stamp was also made up of the words 'Consulat du Japon, Kaunas, Lithuanie' and a mass of Japanese kanji scrolling around it.

'Tell nobody what's in it. Or it could be dangerous for you, especially if the Germans come over the border. It's only gloves, you understand? Do I have your word?'

'Yes, sir, you do,' said Jacek.

'Splendid. So now,' he said, 'your visas.'

Jacek sat with the package on his lap as Sugihara filled them out. 'Jacek Kowalski. Zofia Kowalski ... and ...' A moment's hesitation. 'Masha Romaska.'

The door flew open as Sugihara was signing the last one. A Russian was there in military uniform, his red hat on the side of his head. The sight of him made Zofia rigid with fear.

'You must come now. It is time,' the Russian said to Sugihara.

Otto was already walking towards the door, but Sugihara completed his brushstrokes. 'All done,' he said, handing the visas over. Zofia took hold of her visa, seeing the same chrysanthemum stamp. Her sleeve brushed over the ink, making it blur. She gasped.

He took it back out of her hand to blow on it. 'Don't worry,' he said, 'it is fine. Good luck, Miss Kowalski, and I hope you too will find love like your brother.' His eyes twinkled.

Masha simpered and said, 'Thank you, Mr Sugihara.'

Sugihara nodded back to her but Otto was waiting, his face blotched red, as Sugihara picked up his briefcase and gave him a handshake. 'Good luck, Otto. Stay under cover and I will do my best to get you a posting once I'm installed,' he said. 'Keep your visa safe. I'm sorry I cannot do more.'

'Come now,' called the Russian from the door. He held the door open for Masha, who gave him a dazzling smile, and they all followed the Russian man out.

Zofia prayed the soldier would not ask for their papers, but they seemed more intent on Sugihara and the consulate. Otto was balancing a cardboard box of files in his arms as he went down ahead of her. She hurried after them in time to see Sugihara lock the door and get into his big black Buick. With a roar it drove away, followed by the Russian and his comrades in their army truck.

Ahead of them, Otto walked away, shoulders bowed, balancing a cardboard box against his chest, his briefcase dangling forlornly from one hand. It gave her a pang to see him suddenly as just another young man on the move.

Vaizgantas Street was emptying now the consul had gone. Many tried to stop Sugihara's car by standing in the road, but it just nosed its way through, leaving a trail of disappointment in its wake.

'Three visas!' Jacek said, tucking the parcel under his arm. 'I told you it was worth the wait.'

Masha leapt to give Jacek a hug, and he embraced her awkwardly with one arm.

'Put the visas out of sight,' Zofia said. 'We'll never get another.'

'What did he give you?' Masha asked pointing to the parcel. 'What was it about? I didn't catch what he said.'

'It's nothing,' Jacek said. He flicked a warning glance to Zofia. 'Gloves to deliver to a friend of Mr Sugihara – the wife of someone he knows in Tokyo. When we get out.'

'What sort of gloves? Are they silk? Why is he sending her gloves in the summer? They must be evening gloves. I'd love a pair of evening gloves, I saw some once with little pearl buttons all up the—'

'We've to take the package to Japan,' Jacek said, interrupting. All of a sudden it seemed to dawn on him that they'd actually be leaving. 'We'll need to get train tickets, then. Will the Russkies even let us buy tickets or give us a permit to cross Siberia?' His face creased in worry again.

'With these transit visas, perhaps.' Zofia tucked hers safely in her bag. 'We'll have to be careful, though. They won't like Masha trying to leave. They want us all to be good Russian citizens.'

'Or slaves in a gulag,' Jacek said. 'Did you know they take them by train? Rudi told me. They call the people "white coal" and throw off corpses at every stop.'

'That's complete nonsense,' Masha said. 'Just a stupid rumour.'

'Where can we buy our tickets?'

'I don't know,' Jacek said. 'We'll ask at the Café Metropole. Someone there will know what we have to do next.'

When they got to the Café Metropole they found out that if you had a transit visa you could apply to the NKVD for a permit to cross Siberia. Lists of names were posted up regularly but it could take a couple of months before their names were listed.

'I think we should take a chance,' Jacek said on their way back to Alexander's. 'Having our names on any list means they can trace us. Besides which, they'll try to persuade Masha to stay. Lithuanians have always been Russian according to them.'

It was a conundrum, and one they couldn't solve.

Masha was surly and kept looking at the door of the café as if expecting her father to appear at any moment to drag her home. At one point she disappeared and said she had to make a telephone call, to tell the owner of the hair salon where she used to work that she would be leaving.

When she got back, Jacek arrived shortly afterwards, looking pleased with himself. 'All sorted,' he said. 'I was talking to someone at the Metropole and he knows a forger who can get us the permits for a price within a couple of days.'

'So soon? That's wonderful.'

'I don't want to travel on a forged permit,' said Masha. 'I vote we wait.'

'Well, you're outvoted,' said Zofia, 'Two to one.'

Chapter 15

The consulate was closed. It was the last time Otto would walk down those stairs or through those gates. Three years of his life, he thought, and it was all finished in an afternoon, with jobs half-done, letters half-typed, and no time for real goodbyes. He strode home, anxious to put space between him and the consulate.

Now Sugihara was gone, Otto felt peculiarly on edge, as if the Russians might come for him at any moment. Already, his favourite *netsuke* was gone, and he was convinced the Russian must have snaffled it when he wasn't looking. He was lugging a box of files from the consulate and they were pressed to his chest; it made him walk awkwardly, his briefcase handle biting into his hand. The briefcase was full of his other *netsuke* and illegal copies of the letters Sugihara had asked him to type.

Insurance, he called it to himself. It had been no trouble to put in extra sheets of carbon paper. He had worked with Sugihara long enough that his boss never questioned his loyalty, and this made Otto feel both guilty and a mite resentful to be so much taken for granted. Otto sighed. He supposed Sugihara had a lot to do, what with the children and everything, but still.

He'd hoped Sugihara might promise him work at his next position, but any conversation had been made impossible by that last girl who had come for a visa for her family. There was something about her that stuck in his mind. Her brother couldn't keep still, nor could that other girl, the blonde one. Her eyes roamed everywhere. Maybe it was her, not the soldier, who took his little fox. That blonde girl had that furtive look they had when they came from the wrong side of town.

But the Jewish girl, she was attractive with her wide eyes and shiny dark hair like a raven's wing. But it was more than that. Her clarity. Yes, that was it, as if she knew what she wanted and was determined to get it.

Zofia Kowalski. He'd noted her name as he stamped her visa. It had given him a tight feeling in the throat to watch her grab Sugihara's pen and write as if she couldn't get the words out quick enough. Like grief was stuck in her throat, choking her, and she just had to get it out. She'd shielded the paper from them all, the way he used to do when he took his examinations.

He was sure Zeitel would want to see what was in that letter, but it was bundled up with the others and taken away before Otto could see it. Her letter had been put amongst Bronovski's papers, and Bronovski was a man in whom Brandt, Zeitel's boss at the *Kriminalpolizei*, had a special interest. The thought niggled him like toothache.

There was no way he'd tell Zeitel that Zofia Kowalski was one of Bronovski's friends.

A cart nearly mowed him down as he crossed the road – he'd been so deep in thought. Horses and carts had appeared from nowhere now the Russians had commandeered all private cars.

When he got home, he batted away his mother's questions about why he'd brought home so many files. 'Just a bit of overtime.'

She was knitting, but her hands looked like a collection of bones, and her cardigan gaped loose over her emaciated chest.

'You feeling all right?' he asked.

She stood up shakily. 'Got to get on. Need to peel the beets.'

While she was in the kitchen, he got out the copies of Sugihara's files for Zeitel, and filled in his report about the wires sent from the office, and the calls to Zwartendijk in the Dutch consulate – the man who was helping Sugihara with the Jewish exit visas by stamping them for Curaçao.

After a while, the unmistakeable smell of borscht cooking wafted from the kitchen. Food had been less certain since the Russians took over, but his mother, never the best of cooks, did her best with the meagre rations she could purchase. He'd have to tell her today that he'd lost his job. But not yet. The thought was like a weight.

A buzz of the doorbell. He closed the file and hid it under the chair. His mother limped to answer the door. She knew, of course, by some sort of sixth sense, that her son was up to something, but had decided to turn a blind eye. Her silent looks of recrimination made him miserable. He knew that he was making decisions that would affect them both, and yet he could not tell her about the German threats.

Zeitel clumped up the stairs, and his mother opened the door for him to enter. Her eyes met Otto's with a look of faint disgust.

'I suppose you want me to take a walk,' she said pointedly.

'No hurry,' Zeitel said. 'We'll have some tea first.' He came in and took off his hat and placed it on the arm of the chair before wiping the sweat from his forehead with a sleeve.

'Glad to be out of the sun,' he said. 'Sugihara has gone, I take it.'

'The gates of the consulate are locked and the Russian military are on guard now, to stop looters. The woman who lives upstairs is not happy.'

'Oh? I didn't know it was a shared occupancy building.'

'She refused to leave when the consul arrived, and so Sugihara accommodated her. She was no trouble.'

'And Sugihara's off to Berlin.' He smiled in a satisfied sort of way. 'That'll sort him out.'

'It will be quite a shock for his family after being out here in the sticks.'

'Yes, but better there, where he'll have to stop this business with the Jews. So tell me who he called, and how he spent his last day.'

'He didn't call anyone. There was no time. When they rang to say they were closing us down today, he just started to issue more visas. He wrote like a demon. We all did. The crowd outside got wind of it, and started kicking up a fuss. Sugihara got me and a Polish youth to sit in the corridor. We had to write up the records as fast as we could, and prepare the documents for his brush. He kept asking us to hurry it up. We couldn't work fast enough for him.'

His mother bustled in with a pot of tea as usual, and conversation stopped. She attempted small talk. 'Lovely weather today, isn't it?'

'Thank you for the tea. You can leave us to talk now.' Zeitel's attention turned to the hot water in the jug, but the way he helped himself to tea did nothing to make him feel like a friend. Otto tried to behave normally but found his throat already tight. He didn't like the way Zeitel had dismissed his mother so rudely.

When she had gone and the door to the outside had made a definite disgruntled slam, Zeitel spoke. 'None of those people have valid papers, you know. Sugihara was acting strictly outside international law. He and all those who worked for him could be prosecuted for that. The Reich does not look so kindly on those who break the law.'

Otto felt under pressure. The other man's relaxed demeanour, the way he assumed the upper hand, made Otto fearful. What if Zeitel refused to pay him, or wouldn't let him travel out of Lithuania?

'I don't suppose you have records of these people?' Zeitel asked.

A shake of the head. 'Sugihara's documents went with him.'

'Were all of these people Jewish?'

'Most, yes. But there was one young woman who was not. A Lithuanian, with her fiancé and his sister. Sugihara gave the brother a package to take to General Miroyuki Sato in Japan.'

He'd said too much, but he couldn't take it back now. He needed to prove he was on Zeitel's side or they'd never get out of Russia.

Zeitel fixed him with a look that meant 'go on'.

'From Poland. Papers detailing what's going on.'

'About what?'

Surely he knew. He swallowed the lump in his throat. 'People complaining of beatings, of being taken to camps and never coming back. Of …' he hesitated, '… gas vans. Mass graves.'

'Untrue, of course.' Zeitel narrowed his eyes. 'What these people will make up.' He put down his cup. Something seemed to have suddenly struck him. 'How many papers were there in this package?'

'About thirty … fifty? From all over Poland and Czechoslovakia. Sugihara asked Kowalski to take them to Tokyo.'

Zeitel froze in his chair. His eyes took on an intent look. 'Describe these papers. Describe them exactly.'

'Just a pile of papers. All different handwriting.'

'Could they have come from Bronovski? Jewish testimonies?'

'I don't know.' He bottled his reaction. Best to play innocent.

Zeitel leant forward, fixing him with snake-like eyes. 'You're telling me you didn't think to intercept them?'

'I couldn't. It would have looked odd to interfere. Sugihara got his wife to wrap them personally. And the sister was so grateful for her visa and—'

A commotion as Zeitel got to his feet and towered over him. 'So we don't know what else went in the package?'

'Gloves. They were supposed to be a gift for someone's wife. Just a box of gloves.'

'But it could be anything?'

'I don't know … It could be, or it could be nothing.'

'Their names. You'd recognize these people again?'

'I don't know—'

'But you wrote out their address, didn't you?'

Zeitel stepped forward and Otto stepped back until he was

almost pressed against the door. 'I may have done, I mean, I can't remember.' He was panicking now. 'Yes, they had lodgings with some Lithuanians.' He didn't say he knew they were at the restaurant.

'His name again?'

'Kowalski.'

'You need to find Kowalski. I won't issue your transit papers out of Russia unless you find this package and deliver it to me. It sounds like Sugihara is playing both sides, trying to discredit the Reich, and if that's the case, we need to know. It's the last thing we want floating around the Japanese offices.'

'But I can't possibly—'

'You were Sugihara's aide, weren't you? They'll know you. Go to Kowalski's house, make some excuse, say Sugihara wants the package back for some reason.' He stood then, ready to leave. 'I'll be here tomorrow to collect it.'

Chapter 16

Sitting at the battered deal-wood table at Alexander's, Zofia nursed her cup of cold coffee and each time the door opened she looked up, as did Masha. Jacek had gone to fetch the forged train permits and tickets from the Café Metropole.

'He's been gone a long time,' Masha said. She was restless, sitting beside Zofia examining her nails. She was wearing red lipstick, applied with rather too much enthusiasm.

'He'll be back soon.'

'And then I suppose we'll be on our way.' Masha sounded resigned, not enthusiastic. 'What's the first thing you'll do when you get to America?'

'Look for work, I suppose. What about you?'

She shrugged as if she couldn't care. 'Find some big hotel where I can have a long, luxurious bath. And after that find a restaurant and order steak and potatoes.' She glanced at the door again. Summer seemed to have ended, and every time it opened there was a cold draught.

'You'd need money first. Jacek will have to get a job.'

'Maybe we'll get married and live in one of those big houses with green lawns and a shiny automobile parked outside.'

'More likely to be a one-room hovel in a tenement block.' Zofia didn't say that she had the same dream, but feared she'd end up poor again. After all, she'd be alone, and Masha would have Jacek. 'You'll have to work too.'

Masha tilted her head to one side and looked at her. 'I'm not afraid of hard work. I haven't spent my whole life in an ivory tower like some I could mention. Real work, on my feet all day, not pushing a pen. And life's for living, isn't it? Stop trying to work everything out in advance. You never know what might happen. Maybe we'll end up staying here. You can't control everything, so stop trying.'

Why was she so belligerent? To Zofia's relief, at that moment Jacek arrived, hurrying down the steps, his expression tense.

'Did you get everything?' Zofia asked.

'Quick, get your things.' He pulled Masha by the arm. 'We need to leave. There's a group of Russian soldiers heading this way. They're armed.'

'They won't come here,' Masha said, but Zofia was already bundling her things together, closing her rucksack.

'We have to go. Now.' Jacek tried to hoist Masha up out of her seat, but she was resisting.

As if to reiterate his words, there was a scuffle at the door.

Two young Russians in army fatigues, rifles ready, rushed down the stairs and gestured to them all to get up. When no one complied, they grabbed hold of the nearest people by the arms and hustled them at gunpoint towards the door.

'Quick, outside. That way, through the back.' Jacek turned over a table as a distraction. Crockery crashed to the floor.

Zofia grasped Masha's arm and dragged her to the swing door to the kitchen. Masha was dragging her back the other way. It was like hauling a dead weight, and her suitcases bashed against the door jamb. They swung into the bins as Zofia struggled to get to the stairs at the back.

Zofia glanced back to see Jacek bursting through the swing door after them. He winced and ducked at the sudden crack of gunfire and the crash of tables being overturned, shouts and screams.

Jacek put a hand on Masha's back to push her forward, and grabbing the handrail on the stairs, Zofia hauled her way up and into the light. Masha was on her heels, but was slow, struggling with her big cases.

'Leave one,' Jacek shouted.

'I can't, I can't,' Masha wailed. 'Stay and help me!'

Jacek yanked one of them from her hands and hurled it back down the stairs, where it exploded into a heap of gaudy coloured clothes. Zofia caught a snapshot of it as she blinked. White leather shoes, a flowered skirt, a bundle of stockings.

Masha couldn't seem to speak, outraged, her mouth open, until Jacek pulled her into a run. Still she resisted, but he dragged her with an arm around her neck.

Around the back of the restaurant an alley linked to another longer one across the street. This longer alley was where people put their bins and rubbish, but Zofia didn't slow, she dodged down it on nimble feet, her heart thudding, her one thought to get as far away as possible from the soldiers at Alexander's.

Behind her, shouts and the pepper of gunfire set off small explosions of fear in her chest. Zofia crushed herself into a crouch behind a bin. Next to her, Jacek pressed himself to the wall, shielding Masha with an arm over her head. 'Shh.' He put a restraining hand over her mouth.

Masha tried to get up, but Zofia pulled her down by her skirt. 'Do you want to get us all arrested?' she hissed.

'We can't stay at Alexander's,' Jacek whispered, once the noise had stopped.

'Then we'll have to sleep at the station while we wait for a train,' Zofia said.

'At the station?' Masha looked horrified.

'You might as well get used to it,' Zofia said. 'We'll be spending the next few weeks in stations or trains.'

Chapter 17

Zeitel turned up on Otto's doorstep every day, and Otto always dreaded the visits. There was something unwholesome about Zeitel, the way sleep grits gathered in the corners of his eyes and spittle at the corners of his lips. His shoes always needed a polish and his coat was creased as if he spent too much time sitting down.

'So the Russians closed the restaurant?' Zeitel asked him, lounging in his best armchair, the one Otto's mother usually sat in with her crocheted blanket. 'Bloody inconvenient timing.'

'They accused them of illegal meetings – it's against Russian regulations. But I asked around and one of the barmen told me Kowalski and his sister had fled – scarpered out of the back. No one's seen them since. The NKVD are after all the Jews for anti-Soviet activities.'

'And? What other leads have you got?'

Otto tried to hide his nerves by lighting a cigarette, but as he didn't usually smoke, it made him cough. 'I went to his girlfriend's house. Masha Romaska. But her father's a proper bruiser. Said he'd no idea where his daughter was and nor did he care, that she never took any notice of him, her father, anyway.'

'So you've no idea where they are now?'

'When I was at the consulate, I heard the sister tell Sugihara her brother was a journalist. With the *Kaunas Star*.'

'So where are they? Those offices are closed.'

The pressure made Otto twine his hands in discomfort and swallow to relieve the choking feeling at the base of his throat. 'They seemed pretty desperate to get out of Kaunas … I reckoned they wouldn't wait for official permits to travel. So I rang up the Trans-Siberian booking office.' He paused, guilt getting the better of him, before he spoke. 'They're booked on the Wednesday train.'

'Shit.' Zeitel thumped a palm down on the arm of the chair, releasing a cloud of dust. He fished in his pocket and brought out a timetable. He thumbed through the small booklet, then stabbed a finger at it. 'Kaunas to Moscow. You'll have to leave tomorrow if you want to connect with the Trans-Siberian.'

'Me?'

'You know what they look like, so it has to be you. Track them down, get hold of those documents of Bronovski's. It's your fault they've got this far, and they'll be ahead of you. You should have intercepted the thing at the consulate.'

'I can't just—'

'Tell your mother you'll be away. Just for a few days.'

'I keep telling you, my mother's not well. She needs me at home.'

But his words fell on deaf ears. Zeitel rose to his feet, his presence threatening. 'Get the package from Kowalski as soon as you can, then stay on the train until we can get to you at Omsk. That should give me time to send a car and one of my men to the station there to collect it.'

'What about tickets?' Otto threw out every excuse he could.

'Easy. I've got friends in *Intourist*. I'll send the tickets with a courier, they'll be with you tonight.'

'What if Kowalski won't hand it over?'

Zeitel withdrew a pistol and bullets from inside his coat and placed them on the table. 'I've found this very persuasive.'

Otto blinked. The sight of the gun in his apartment made him reel. 'Oh no, I'm not experienced with firearms, I could never—'

'Take it.' Zeitel was casual. 'Nothing to it. A kid could do it. Just point and pull the trigger. Just get whatever's in that package. Someone will meet you in Omsk so you can hand it over.'

He must have looked shocked because Zeitel squinted at him. 'You won't be able to stay in Russia, you know that. You'll need to get back on the train after Omsk and go on to Vladivostok so you can make your way to Japan and from there to Germany.'

'But what about my mother? I can't leave her here all alone. She needs hospital care, she has cancer.'

Zeitel brushed it off with two words. 'That's rough. But you can make arrangements for her afterwards. War is war. We all have to do unpleasant things. You will be paid and no doubt the money can be used for hospital bills.'

He was right. Otto gripped the edge of the chair. He'd been worrying about how to pay for treatment now the consulate was closed. 'But I'll have to tell her, or she will wonder where I am. Can't she come with me?'

The look Zeitel gave him made him feel foolish. No, of course she couldn't.

'When can I send for her?'

'Once you reach Germany, I suppose. Of course, it could always be made known to the Russians your mother is anti-Soviet, so don't think of using your transit pass for going somewhere else. We will always find you.'

These words struck him like stones.

When Zeitel had left, Otto hid the gun and the bullets in the bottom of his underwear drawer. His hands were shaking. He couldn't leave his mother, or go on the run. Let alone shoot anyone. How could Zeitel even think that? No one had ever told him that working in a consulate might open him up to this kind of blackmail, and it still didn't feel real.

His mother returned and stripped off her coat and gloves. 'Has he gone?' She took in the room as she rubbed her blue hands. It had turned cold for September. Her skin was papery and she seemed more frail now he thought he'd be leaving. 'It smells of him in here.' She wrinkled her nose. 'What does he want? You'd better tell me, you always look like a dog without a bone when he's gone.'

'Consulate business,' he said, aiming for a natural manner. 'They want me to go to Omsk for a few days to collect some papers.' The lies made his face hot.

'Because you've lost your job, eh? Margit at the market told me the Japanese consulate shut down. Why didn't you tell me?' Her eyes, which always saw the child in him, bored into his.

'Because I didn't want to worry you.'

'It worries me more when you hide things. Like when you failed a test at school. I can always tell.' Under the broken body, she was still as strong as a carthorse.

'It's Russian orders.'

'But he's German, huh? Don't think you can fool me.'

'It's just business, Ma. Stop making a fuss.'

'What will you do for money if the consulate's closed?'

'Something's being sorted about that. Sugihara promised me.'

She stared at him, then with a gesture of impatience went into the kitchen to unpack the vegetables. He heard them thud one by one onto the counter.

'Sons. Sometimes I despair,' she said in a whisper designed to be heard. Then she called, 'What's this about, this sudden hurry to send you to Omsk?'

'I told you. It's just to collect some papers.'

Her head appeared at the hatch. 'Who for, then? Sugihara has gone. They saw his car, getting the hell out of here. It was flanked by Russian troop cars, heading towards Moscow.'

'I've to send the papers on to him. Then, no doubt he'll tell me where I'm to be posted next. Where we're to be living.'

'Just like that. You tell me nothing about all of this and then just expect me to up and move? Like a tail being wagged by a dog? I can't go. Not now. I haven't got the energy.'

'I didn't mean it to happen this way, Ma; I thought there'd be more time.'

'Well, where's Sugihara going? Moscow?'

His voice came out small. 'Berlin.'

Silence. Before the outcry. 'No. You promised me! Is that what this is about? I'm not going back to Berlin. Not after the way they abandoned your father, ruined his business, and left him to rot. How can you think I will?'

'Calm down. We don't know what's happening yet. I might get posted somewhere else.' He floundered, knowing he was lying. Lying for her life, as well as his own. 'We just have to wait until Sugihara pulls a few strings. Meanwhile, I've got this little job to do. I'll only be away a couple of days.' He went over to the hatch and leant through, tried to take one of her hands. 'Have I ever let you down before?'

She pulled her hand away. 'You're not telling me everything, I can feel it. A mother knows her son.'

'Just a few days, Ma, then I'll be back. And I'll call you. Promise I'll call.' If he kept saying it, it would have to be true, wouldn't it? But he knew he was fooling himself, and it tore at his heart.

He must get the papers from the Kowalskis and deliver them to Zeitel as soon as he could. Then try to persuade Sugihara that he needed an aide in Berlin. His mother would come around to the idea of Germany. He could send for her straight away. They had good hospitals there, hadn't they? Better than here in Kaunas. And by then, he'd have been paid. Enough, surely, for the operation Ma needed.

His mind ran through the possibilities, like a rat in a maze. He could befriend Jacek Kowalski, then say that as a friend of Sugihara, he'd be happy and honoured to take the parcel in his stead. He'd be nice and reasonable, and the whole thing would be over.

Chapter 18

The baroque-style station in front of them dwarfed the black silhouettes of the passengers who milled about its archways and colonnades. Zofia dodged the traffic at the kerb as they pushed through the crowd, Jacek dragging Masha forward by the arm, and Zofia scurrying behind. A line of people confronted them, and Zofia realized that this was just the queue to get through the barrier to the platform for the first leg of their journey.

Kaunas to Moscow. A small train. Then the mighty Trans-Siberian express – Moscow to Omsk, Irkutsk, Vladivostok.

Six thousand miles across the heartland of Russia.

Zofia wiped a hand across her gritty forehead where the dust had clung to her skin. A fine drizzle made everything damp, and she couldn't dispel the fear that even now Jacek might be picked up by Russian army patrols and deported to the middle of nowhere. She watched him, and how Masha fawned on him. She was anxious about Sugihara's parcel, unsure whether he might forget it, or lose it on the train. Now it had their story in it, she felt attached to it; there was something about seeing her father's experience in black and white that had brought the whole reality of it into sharper focus.

She scanned the others in the queue. That group from the

yeshiva school – they'd been ahead of her outside the Japanese embassy. Their old long-faced teacher, all greying whiskers and wrinkles, looked hot and bothered and was flapping his hand in front of his face to cool himself. His assistant, younger and harassed-looking, was trying to round up the students and keep them together. It looked like they were all to travel on the same train. Seeing someone she recognized eased the fluttering in Zofia's stomach.

As a child, she had heard about the myth of Siberia – a threat, not a promise. The vast cold land where the Russians sent people to work in inhumane conditions, in temperatures that could drop as low as minus ninety degrees Fahrenheit. Siberia was a wasteland of ice, stiff-cold forests, drifting flecks of snow; a place so remote it was almost out of mind. Was Uncle Tata out there somewhere?

She turned to Jacek. 'You realize the irony of it; that we're going through Siberia on a railway built by prisoners and political internees like Uncle Tata?'

Jacek wouldn't entertain the thought. 'They won't have sent him there.'

'We might be travelling right past him.'

'Then he'd be glad to see us get out of Russia.' But the set of his jaw told her that her words had hit home.

They were both quiet then, lost in thought about their uncle – taken God knows where – and the stab of guilt that came with the thought. That they were going to be leaving him behind. Zofia took a long shuddering breath and swallowed. Jacek put an arm around her shoulder to comfort her, and her eyes filled.

It was their turn to show their visas. And it would do no good to cry. Damned if she'd fertilize their soil. She'd learnt that much from Poland.

To her relief, they were let through, and she turned to look at Jacek in jubilation.

Like her, he seemed poleaxed. But he embraced her in another quick tight hug. From him, that meant a lot. He hadn't done that of his own accord since Poland. She squeezed him back, feeling the tension in his body, the tension that meant he was always ready to run.

They were on their way. They were actually going to do it, get on the Trans-Siberian to Vladivostok. She couldn't help but remember Father's childhood stories of hungry bears, ogres that lived under bridges, and the howl of wolves, and she wondered if Jacek remembered them too. The only person who seemed unmoved was Masha.

The journey to Moscow was crowded and they had to change at Vilnius and Minsk, travelling third class on hard wooden benches. On the last leg, Zofia was so tired after the terror of waiting to get away – the fear of being caught and ending up dangling on a tree like Mrs Wozniak – that to be in this box on wheels, in its own self-contained world, lulled her into slumber. The light dimmed and she slept through until morning.

She awoke to find they were already clanking, moving into a grey suburb. Moscow. She rubbed her eyes and face to bring herself back to life. She put a hand out to wake Jacek, who was slumped against the window with Masha lolling on his shoulder. 'Looks like we're here,' she said. 'Best get our papers ready.'

Even now she feared that the papers would not be enough to protect them, but having any kind of papers was insurance. Many had no formal papers at all. She hoped Sugihara's chrysanthemum seal and signature would be enough. Her bowels were cramping at the simple thought, that a word from someone who didn't like the look of them could mean the difference between life and death.

Jacek was chivvying Masha to get out her passport and travel visa. She was rifling through her suitcase with her bright ragbag of clothes, while beyond the window the station was dreary and grey. A belch of steam and they dismounted onto the platform. A scatter of skinny-looking pigeons flapped away into the girders above.

There were men in dark coats watching them all disembark. Their intense watchfulness made Zofia think *Secret Service*.

Zofia ignored them, her head down, following the rest of the people elbowing each other up the platform, all in a tearing hurry.

Moscow. A place she had never been to in her life.

Masha was bashing at her skirt to brush out the creases, and, realizing she must look equally crumpled, Zofia ran a hand through her hair and straightened her knitted hat. Unlike Masha, her minimal luggage had few changes of clothes. She buttoned up her coat as a kind of armour as she approached the turnstile where a Russian soldier in green uniform was examining passports and papers.

'Miss Kowalski?'

The voice made her turn in panic. At first she didn't recognize the tall, skinny man standing behind her.

'We met in Kaunas, at the consulate.'

Ah, now it all clicked into place. Mr Sugihara's aide, Otto, the man with the long nose and intense look. 'I remember! You helped us with our visas. We're so grateful. Are you staying in Moscow too?'

'Yes, the consulate closing has meant I must look for work elsewhere.' He leant in to whisper, 'And a man who speaks six languages is not welcome any more in today's Lithuania.'

'Are you travelling on the Trans-Siberian?'

'Yes. Eastwards. My experience with Sugihara might give me work in Japan. I will travel there first to get settled and then afterwards send for my mother.'

A mother. She'd wondered if he was married. She somehow hadn't seen him as the marrying type, and now she looked at him more closely she could see he was not as confident as he appeared. She liked the way he spoke of his mother so deferentially, though his manners were somewhat stiff. As the queue shifted forwards, she caught him staring at her again. They shuffled closer to the gate, each trying to avoid the embarrassment of touching, as she struggled to get out her ticket and pass.

'Let me hold your bag for you,' Otto said to Jacek, seeing him struggling with bag, his papers and Masha's suitcase.

'It's all right, I can manage,' Jacek said.

Zofia snatched her own canvas bag to her chest. Though Otto seemed pleasant enough, she had lost too many possessions in her life to ever let go of it. Her thoughts went to the little collection of objects in her coat pocket, and with a tinge of guilty pleasure she was glad Otto would never know her souvenir from the consulate, his little fox, was one of them.

At the turnstile, Jacek and Masha had managed to get through and were waiting on the other side a little further into the concourse. Otto stepped ahead of her, and the soldier flipped open his passport and nodded him straight through.

Zofia held out her pass and tried to look calm. The soldier took a long time examining it, but finally let her by. Full of relief, she hurried towards Jacek and Masha.

Otto waited to talk to her. 'Will you stay overnight in Moscow?'

'Just one night. My brother booked us a room at the Moskva Hotel. It was what we were told to do if travelling this route. The people at *Intourist* were insistent on it, and took our dollars to pay for it.'

'How fortunate! That's exactly where I'm staying. I guess they want our cash before we leave the country. And for control. So they can keep us all together and not have us wandering loose around the city.'

Just as she was agreeing, she saw a moustachioed official in a Russian-type soft hat holding up a cardboard placard. It had the words 'Hotel Moskva' written on it in Lithuanian in big, roughly painted letters. A group of other passengers was waiting expectantly, flanked by two armed men in military-style uniform. The name of the hotel was embroidered on their caps.

'You are for the Hotel Moskva?' asked the Russian official.

Jacek told him they were, shepherding the women close to him

'And me,' said Otto.

'This way,' the Russian said. 'Before we take you to the hotel, we will take you on a tour of Moscow, to see our history, to help you get your orientation. Follow me.' He set off striding towards the exit.

Jacek turned to Zofia and lowered his voice, 'I don't like the sound of it. Stay close by my side. I don't know what's going on, why they won't take us direct to the hotel, and we need to stick together.' He grabbed Zofia's arm and pulled Masha closer.

A bus was waiting outside. It looked like an ordinary passenger bus, but with '*Intourist*' written on the front in both Russian and English.

They were guided towards it, with the two military men behind them. Even Sugihara's man, Otto, looked nervous about boarding. An *Intourist* representative checked their train tickets. There was silence as they all climbed up the metal steps and scrambled to their seats. Everyone on the bus probably had the same unspoken thought: that they were going to be taken somewhere they didn't want to go – a prison, or worse.

The official guide sat at the front of the bus along with what Zofia thought of as his guards. Masha and Jacek sat together, and Zofia in front near a window, but she was rather disconcerted when Otto slid in next to her.

'It's Otto, isn't it?' she said.

He smiled, revealing small white teeth. 'That's right.'

'Zofia,' she said.

'I remember. I had to write it down on the records, and I thought it sounded a pretty name. Shall I put your bag in the rack?' He pointed to the net luggage rack above.

'I'll keep it with me,' she said, holding it on her lap. 'I might need something out of it.'

He nodded but, though he was only being helpful, there was a certain strain about him that she could feel in the pit of her stomach. By now the bus had set off and their guide had grabbed a small white megaphone and was booming out in fluent Lithuanian, gesturing to the windows with his stubby hands. No one wanted to be on this bus, but there was no point in objecting, not here in the middle of Moscow where the grey-green uniforms of the state police were on every corner. After Kaunas, the magnificent pale domes made the city feel like a scene misplaced from a fairy tale.

'Shortly we will be arriving at Gorky Street, the most famous street in Moscow,' the guide said. 'We can drive a short way down it, but it is being widened, and you will see the works going on ahead of you.'

She peered out of the window, but was too tense to take in much of what she was seeing. It seemed to be a mass of concrete dust and men in overalls and caps.

'Stalin's "phase one" is almost complete,' the guide said, 'and it will transform the centre of Moscow for the twentieth century. Here they are creating a new boulevard, so its historic buildings have been shunted back intact. A massive undertaking. See there, the electricians working?'

'They actually moved a whole building?' one of the other passengers asked.

She rubbed the window pane and looked out. Men in workers' overalls, coiling lengths of black rubber tube, then trailing them over gaping holes where buildings had once stood.

'Incredible, hey?' The guide was enthusiastic. 'And over there, just up the street, the Moscow Central Eye Hospital was dismantled from its foundation, hoisted up and turned on its axis on special rails. They pushed it back a whole twenty yards. Twenty yards! Can you imagine? And the medics still operating during all of this! Such a feat of engineering, and with no disruption to the hospital.'

'Propaganda,' whispered Otto.

'We are now passing the Aragvi Restaurant. You will dine there tonight.'

'Don't we have a choice?' Zofia asked Otto.

Otto whispered, 'Obviously not. I take it they'll bring us by bus.'

The bus continued at a stately pace with the tour guide pointing out places of interest. Finally, it stopped. 'The Eliseevksy Store. We will stop here for you to purchase souvenirs or food for your onward journey.'

Everyone had to get off the bus and Zofia found herself looking up at an impressive stone facade of pale stone and shining windows. The group of refugees was led inside and Zofia was immediately dazzled by the brightness. She tilted her head back to see three vast chandeliers the size of wagon wheels, great glittering glass confections, lit with dozens of bulbs even in the daytime. It was breathtaking, and Zofia couldn't help loving it. Her second feeling was guilt at being seduced by its beauty. She reminded herself of how the Russian guard took Tata away.

Surrounding a central alabaster column were trestles laden with fruit and vegetables and all manner of delicacies.

'The Eliseevsky Store is famous throughout Russia,' the guide said.

Masha turned to the guide. 'This is an actual store?' she asked, her mascara-ed eyes wide.

'The biggest in Moscow,' he replied, puffing out his chest, pleased. 'We will wait by the door until you have made your purchases.'

One of the group of yeshiva students said politely, 'I don't think I need anything, so I'll just get back on the bus, if that's all right.'

'Make purchases, and then we will take you to your hotel. If, of course, you prefer to walk and find another hotel then …' A shrug.

The message was clear. They must buy something, or the hotel they had already paid for would not be accommodating them. All at once, the palace did not seem so glamorous and the light not so shimmering.

'Have you any money?' Zofia whispered to Jacek.

'Not much, and we'll need it.' His brown eyes were worried.

'Just buying the tickets almost wiped us out.'

'I have money,' Otto said, overhearing, 'If there's anything you'd like?'

'No, no,' Zofia said. 'We couldn't possibly …' It had offended her pride that he should offer her charity.

Masha, who had picked up a shiny red apple from a stand, waved it in front of their faces and hissed, 'I worked it out – it's fourteen *lit*! It's robbery. All the prices are the same, everything's overpriced. I would never have believed Stalin's People's Party would allow such corruption.'

Zofia looked at her. She hadn't thought Masha knew anything about politics or the new regime.

'Well, it seems expensive to me,' Masha added, as Otto walked away towards the rear of the shop.

'We'll have to buy something, though,' Zofia said, 'unless we want to end up on the streets of Moscow. And let's think sensibly. Let's get bread, something sustaining that will last.'

They headed over to the bread and pastry section, which was displayed before a wall of gilded wallpaper and fluted stucco columns. Above them soared a Baroque painted ceiling in cream and gold. Before they got to the counter and display, Zofia could already smell the sweetness of almond paste and sugar and the yeasty aroma of the bread.

The glass cabinet was full of delicacies in golden pastry, *vatrushki* with a filling of soft cheese, and *kartoshki* shaped like little sweet potatoes. Even a chocolate and nut confection. Zofia swallowed back water.

'Oh please, Jacek, can't we have one?' Masha pointed to the chocolate nut balls.

'We can't afford it,' Jacek said. 'And if we are forced to go to the restaurant tonight, we'll need money for that. He led them to the bread counter. 'Let's try to get away with a loaf.'

Even the loaves were the cost of a whole meal, but they pointed to the biggest, cheapest loaf, and soon a queue of other refugees was behind them.

Zofia saw that one of the tables was laid out with piles of sweetmeats, and ornamental enamelled spoons. As she passed, her hand accidentally brushed the table and then closed around one of the spoons. In a trice it was in her pocket.

Almost immediately a hot fever enveloped her. What was she doing? She could get them all arrested.

Jacek was paying and, as he did so, Zofia scanned the room. Nobody had seen. But she noticed that the local customers, all women, were smartly dressed in shiny leather shoes with matching handbags. None of them looked as ragged as the group queuing at the bread counter. Only Masha would pass, and even she looked bedraggled now.

At the door she came across Otto again. He had several packages with him.

'Did you know that a hundred years ago the building was owned by a princess?' he said, his eyes lighting up with enthusiasm. 'I came here once with Sugihara. Apparently she was a patron of Russian literary life and supported a salon that included poets like Pushkin. Unpopular now, of course, because he was too much the libertine.'

'How interesting,' Jacek said. 'What a shame it's turned into this.'

'Oh Otto,' Zofia said, 'you remember my brother, Jacek. And Masha, his fiancée.'

'Ah yes, from the consulate.' They shook hands.

Masha smiled but couldn't take her eyes off Otto's purchases.

'Jacek's a journalist,' Zofia added.

Jacek made a face. 'I was, you mean. Was a journalist. Literary life has been stamped out now in Lithuania.'

'Not too loud,' Otto warned. 'They're not above arresting us if we don't toe the line.' He smiled at Jacek. 'I believe Sugihara gave you a parcel to deliver to the naval offices in Tokyo. I find I will be going there on business shortly after our arrival, so I'll happily take it for you, if you like. Save you a journey.'

126

'Oh, that's good of you,' said Jacek. 'We don't speak Japa—'

'It's all right,' Zofia interrupted. 'We are looking forward to seeing a bit of Japan and exploring Tokyo. We can deliver it ourselves.'

Otto nodded but she could see he was put out. An awkward silence ensued.

'What did you buy?' Masha said. Somehow from her it didn't seem too nosy.

'Oh, just a few pastries for the journey,' Otto said.

Nobody replied, because it was what they all had wanted to buy. Zofia's shoulders tightened. Otto had good manners, but he seemed to have attached himself to them for no reason, and she didn't know how to get rid of him without looking impolite. Something about the fact that he was so tidy and well dressed, when they were not, felt awkward.

Again when they got back on the bus, he naturally assumed he could take the seat next to her, without an invitation. The bus set off again with their guide commentating all the way about the expansion of Moscow and the reunification of Russian land that he called the 'Patriot's War'.

Otto began to explain in a low voice, about how the guide meant the Russian Civil War, but that the Russians refused to acknowledge now that there had ever been division. Soon Masha was craning over her seat from behind, listening intently, hanging on his every word. Zofia found herself warming to his enthusiasm, though inside there was a niggle of discomfort, which meant she kept her bag clenched between her feet and sat as far away from Otto as she could sit. She wasn't prepared to trust anyone, not until they were safely out of Russia.

At the desk of the Hotel Moskva there was a representative of *Intourist*. They were told to meet there again for dinner at six thirty and had to hand over their paperwork before they were given keys to the rooms. It made Zofia nervous to be without her passport, this small token of validation. Without papers, it would be too easy to get lost in this vast Russian state.

Zofia was to share with Masha, while Jacek was given his own room. Surprisingly, as they walked by with the keys to their rooms to go to the lift, Zofia heard Otto asking if they had any vacancies. She stopped short because he'd definitely given her the impression that he'd already been booked into the hotel.

The *Intourist* receptionist asked to see his train ticket, flipped through a ledger and said they did have a vacancy, on the second floor, Zofia heard Otto agree to take it before she hurried to catch up with the others. A uniformed security guard, who looked about seventeen years old, stood at the end of the corridor, next to an internal wall-telephone, but Zofia ignored him as they unlocked the door. Watching eyes were everywhere in Russia.

The hotel room was bare but functional, with a telephone on the bedside table, though when Masha picked it up, there was no dialling tone. There was no one to ring anyway. Masha explored the room in a business-like way, opening the wardrobe and all the drawers in the chest, as if she was searching for something.

Masha seemed satisfied and Zofia read the card in Russian on the back of the door – everything had a price tag. Laundry five roubles, breakfast five roubles, use of bathtub two roubles. Everything was expensive and everything was designed to separate them from their money.

'Don't use the bathroom down the corridor,' she said to Masha. 'They'll charge us.'

'What?'

She explained.

Masha pouted. 'And I was looking forward to getting all cleaned up.' Already her suitcase was on the bed and she was shaking out her dresses and hanging them in the wardrobe. 'They can't stop us washing, though, can they?'

'Maybe they charge the water by the pint; wouldn't put it past them.'

There was a sink in the room, so they both made use of it to wash their hair and freshen up after the journey. Zofia unpacked her few possessions and reorganized them more tidily in her knapsack, all except for her 'souvenirs', which she kept always in her pockets. She took out the *netsuke* – the jade fox curled up to sleep – and marvelled that anyone could have carved such detail on something so small. She let it drop back into her coat pocket with Jacek's pen, the enamelled spoon, and the rest.

A sudden waft of perfume as Masha spritzed herself with something from her case. 'They'd better give us our passes back and let us go on the train tomorrow,' Masha said.

It was the thought on Zofia's mind too. 'Our tickets are only valid for tomorrow's train. So we have to hope so.'

'I bet the shops in America will all be like Eliseevsky's. All glamour and no real food. The cost of those pastries! You could feed a family for that.'

'Maybe. Will you stop complaining; it's time to go for dinner.'

Masha gave her a look that she could have sworn was one of amusement and it made her feel uncomfortable.

Zofia went to fetch Jacek. 'Bring Sugihara's parcel with you,' she said.

'It'll be all right here.'

'Just bring a bag. I don't trust the floor attendant.'

'Stop nagging me. You should have let Otto take it. He was already going to Tokyo.'

'But you promised Mr Sugihara you'd deliver it personally.' That innocent-looking parcel held the pain of too many people. She imagined all those words like birds trapped inside a cage, and how glad she'd be when he could finally set them free.

'Don't fuss, sis,' he said. But he did as she asked.

When they were ready to go, Masha saw that Jacek had the bag with him. 'What's in there? You won't need a bag.'

'The package from Sugihara.'

'You're not taking those gloves with you? They must be one expensive pair of gloves. We might need to sell them. We're going to be short of money by the time we get out of here.'

'No.' Zofia's answer was too vehement. 'He'll deliver it unopened like he promised.'

'There could be anything in there. Did you see him wrap it up? I say we should open it and look. He'll never know.'

'Don't be silly. It'll just be the gloves like he said.' But Masha was right. She had no idea if there were actually gloves in the parcel as well as the papers. The slim wrapped box could contain anything. But she trusted Sugihara. Something about his calm demeanour had reassured her.

Masha pouted. 'I could wear them, if they're fashionable.'

'We're not opening it. It was our bargain, so he'd give us three visas instead of only one,' she snapped. 'Without him, you'd still be in Kaunas.'

'Kovno,' she said. 'The Russians call it called Kovno now.'

They travelled down in the lift together. Back in the lobby, Zofia was relieved to find there was no sign of Otto.

'I see you ditched your admirer,' Jacek said.

'Ha ha. He's not my admirer. He's a confirmed bachelor. Lives at home with his mother.'

'So what? Counts for nothing.'

'Lay off. It's thanks to Otto we're here at all. Our passes were prepared by him before Sugihara signed them.'

'So why didn't Sugihara give him the gloves to take to his friend?' Masha asked sharply. 'Why give them to you?'

It was a good question, and one she didn't know the answer to. 'I got the impression that Otto's decision to travel was made at the last minute. He didn't have a reservation at the hotel.'

'That's because he's sweet on you,' Jacek said. 'Must be.'

Zofia brushed it off with a roll of her eyes. But underneath she was uneasy. There was something strange about the way Otto had just appeared and followed her. But then she put the thought aside – she was being paranoid. The flight from Poland had made them all jumpy and suspicious of perfectly innocent things. Otto had signed their visas, hadn't he?

Masha was paying needle-sharp attention, noting what Zofia and Jacek bought, and their developing friendship with the man Otto. She'd noted Otto's expensive shoes and cultured voice with grim resentment. After they were dropped off for dinner, Masha persuaded Jacek and Zofia to wait, saying she had to call her father. The call to Illeyvich done, she came out of the telephone box near the Aragvi Restaurant with her story ready.

'Did you get through? What did your father say?' Jacek asked.

'Oh, the usual,' Masha replied. 'It took a while for the woman in the office to put me through and there was a lot of factory noise, always is on night shift, so it wasn't exactly easy.' She was casual, knowing they'd swallow it. 'He threatened me, told me he'd come and fetch me home. Same old story.'

Jacek made a sympathetic face. 'Forget him. Let's go.'

As they walked towards the corner of the street with Zofia following, Masha breathed out. She'd got away with it. She hadn't spoken to her father; after their last fight she had no wish to see him ever again, but Illeyvich now knew her whereabouts; that she was still shadowing Jacek Kowalski, was now in Moscow, and she had no option but to go along with travelling on the Trans-Siberian Express or blow her cover. She asked Illeyvich whether she should go, or abandon shadowing him. She also told him her fears that the man Otto was also some sort of German agent.

After his initial annoyance, Illeyvich had been pragmatic. 'I suppose now you're there, you're best to keep an eye on him and stick with the Kowalskis,' he answered. 'There's no time now to get word to the next checkpoint.' A silence while he thought. 'We'll arrange for someone to pick up Kowalski the day after, in Sverdlovsk. Stay on the train, and travel with the sister. You're to dump her later at the Jewish settlement in Birobidzhan. She'll be no trouble there, it's a mosquito-infested hole in the middle of nowhere. I'll wire the NKVD offices to expect you.'

'Can't I get rid of her sooner?' She didn't fancy such a long trip, not away from Illeyvich and Kovno, the centre of the action.

'There are no women's camps any sooner. And anyway, that's the best place for her. It's where we're sending all the Jewish troublemakers that can't work. Nice of her to buy a ticket, we can save ourselves the trouble of transporting her.'

Masha wasn't keen, but she had her instructions and it was her chance to impress Illeyvich with her efficiency. Her boss was a bully, of course; she'd recognized that straight away, but she knew how to handle bullies. She'd lived with her father long enough, and Illeyvich was a man worth cultivating, a man of influence.

She glanced up at Jacek, who had taken her arm like he thought a proper gentleman should and was striding along towards the restaurant, and thinking he was the one in control. She gave a secret smile and played along. What a good thing he didn't know about the Nagant revolver in her handbag.

Dinner had been yet another attempt to separate them from their money, thought Zofia. The only good thing about it was that they had got to sit with a Lithuanian grandmother called Irina and her daughter, and another Jewish family, and the sense of friendly camaraderie in this hostile metropolis had been reassuring. There'd been no sign of Otto, and she wondered how he'd escaped coming here – but then again he wasn't a Jewish refugee like they were.

When the coach brought them back, they departed wearily for their rooms. What a day. Zofia opened the door with their room key and flung herself down on the nearest bed as Masha switched on a lamp.

'Hey. Someone's moved my suitcase,' Masha said as she put her handbag away. 'I put it over there near the wardrobe and now it's further over.' She pointed to where her tattered suitcase lay open next to the bed.

'Looks the same to me,' Zofia said.

'No, I swear it's been moved.'

'D'you think someone's been in here?' Zofia said, a chill enveloping her.

Masha was methodically putting her clothes onto the bed, searching her suitcase.

'Is anything missing?'

'I don't know.' She was intent on it, focused, not like the usual scatter-brained Masha. Zofia saw her put out a nightdress, and a fancy camisole. 'Good thing I had my handbag with me. I'm trying to remember what was in here because I had two cases and I had to leave one at Alexander's, remember? You'd better search your bag too.'

Zofia opened it up and knew immediately it had been tampered with. 'Shit. It's been searched. I told Jacek our things wouldn't be safe with these Russians.' She'd repacked it earlier, and now everything was back, but not as neat as before. 'It's a good thing Jacek had most of our money,' she said as she searched the side pockets. 'There was a fork here. It was at the bottom under a pair of stockings. Now it's gone.'

'A fork? What did you want with a fork?'

Zofia didn't want to explain, it would sound foolish. 'It's gone.' She searched again, emptying it all out.

'My jewellery's gone too,' Masha said. 'It wasn't much. Just an amber bracelet and a necklace from my grandmother. Not even gold, but it's gone.' She hovered for a moment, uncertain, her eyes scanning the room, before she went to look in the wardrobes, under the beds, under the telephone, in the lamp socket.

'What are you doing?'

'It could be bugged.'

'Bugged? Why? What for?'

A shrug. 'I don't know. The NKVD. If they've been in here, well, who knows? Best to report it. And we'd better tell Jacek.'

They hurried to knock on his door. He opened it looking rumpled, like he'd been asleep in his clothes.

'We've been robbed,' Zofia said. 'Has anyone been in your room?'

'I don't think so,' he said. 'It's all exactly as I left it.'

Zofia explained what had happened. 'Should we report it?'

'We should get the police.' Masha was adamant.

'I don't fancy an encounter with the Russian police,' said Zofia.

'Let's think it through,' Jacek said, pacing in the small space between the bed and wardrobe. 'They didn't come in here, so it might just be petty thieving – after all, women are much more likely to own jewellery, things that can be sold on.'

'But what shall we do?' Zofia asked.

'Nothing.' Jacek said. 'Look – if we open up an investigation or get the police or authorities involved in any way, then it's asking for trouble. They'd make us delay our trip, question us about everything, or worse, we could be arrested for false accusations. Both ways they win, whether we report it or not. They know this, and so they put us here, where the Moskva Hotel staff know they can pilfer from us and we can't do anything about it.'

'That necklace was the last thing I owned of my grandmother's,' insisted Masha. 'It had sentimental value. We should consult the authorities, surely?'

Jacek put a hand on Masha's shoulder. 'If we want to leave in the morning, best keep our heads down.'

'But I think we—'

'We just need to get out of Russia.' Zofia cut off Masha's objections. 'And tomorrow we'll be on our way. Let's not make a fuss.'

In his room, Otto couldn't sleep, but tossed in his pyjamas under the thin floral bedcover. He couldn't believe he was in Moscow with a gun in his suitcase, like in some cheap American movie. Earlier, with some of Zeitel's dollars, he'd bribed the floor attendant, an acne-ridden youth, to let him go into Zofia and Jacek's rooms, and this had made him squirm even more. He'd searched Jacek's room first and deduced that he had taken his bag with him. There was no sign of the package. He'd hoped he could do this thing quickly and without even having to get on the train. Already he was worrying about Ma and how she'd be managing without him. He'd left a note, of course, telling her not to worry and that he'd call her from Omsk.

After relocking Jacek's room, he'd searched Zofia's room too, the one she shared with Jacek's girl, Masha. He'd found nothing except a few trinkets, which the floor attendant was glad to pocket in recompense for giving him the key. It made him queasy to go through Zofia's things, like an intrusion and a betrayal of trust. And she had so little, not like the other girl who had a whole suitcase that seemed to be full of shoes. That's what struck him too, that Zofia Kowalski was travelling all that way with only a scruffy canvas bag and hardly a rag to her back.

When he pulled out a silver fork, it puzzled him. Had she stolen it? It struck him as strange, and he almost left it there, but decided as she had little else, no jewellery or trinkets, he'd better take it to make it look like petty thieving. The floor attendant seemed pleased with it.

Later, he'd watched for their return from the restaurant. As the coach disgorged its occupants, he stepped back out of view behind the curtain. Jacek Kowalski had his rucksack over his shoulder, and presumably the package was in there. He was taking care not to leave it unattended – bad news.

In one way Otto admired Kowalski. He was obviously intelligent and loyal enough to keep his word to Sugihara. And his sister was delightful. He watched her lithe figure run lightly up the steps until she disappeared from view. He couldn't imagine threatening her the way Zeitel wanted, it would be outlandish.

The brother's girlfriend, Masha, was striding after them, glancing side to side as if expecting trouble. She looked brittle and easily distracted, but there was something calm and Madonna-like about Zofia Kowalski.

Otto took the gun from his case and the bullets to figure

out how they worked. They seemed incongruous, lying on the flower-patterned bedcover. He couldn't imagine even loading it, let alone firing it. And at someone like Jacek Kowalski or his sister? Unthinkable.

The thought struck him that he was a coward. Just like his father.

Yet he would have to wrestle the package away from them somehow, and he had to do it before he reached Omsk, or Zeitel would get his mother arrested. The worry of what might happen to Ma if he failed weighed like dough in his chest. Yet here he was, doing things Ma would think unspeakable. Bribing someone, intruding in someone else's room. She would be disappointed in him. He was disappointed in himself.

And now he realized he had to actually get on the train, which opened up a whole new bunch of dilemmas, not least of which was how he was supposed to follow the Kowalskis without being obtrusive. He hurried down to reception and asked the *Intourist* representative if he could choose a seat. Of course, but for a price. He enquired which carriage and compartment his friends the Kowalskis were booked into. Then he booked the last place in carriage C, compartment two. A stamp on his ticket confirmed his reservation.

Chapter 19

The Trans-Siberian Express ran only twice a week, and the refugees left early, chivvied out into the chill dawn while Moscow was still slumbering under its blanket of construction dust. Zofia peered out from the bus to see Otto hurrying towards them with his polished leather suitcase. She quickly looked away from the window. One of the other women, the solid-looking Irina, was sitting next to her, thank goodness, with her daughter on the other side of the aisle, so Otto couldn't sit beside her. Instead, he sat in the seat behind. Jacek's words about him being sweet on her made her neck flush, just knowing he was so close.

At the station turnstile, the Japanese visas in their passports were examined closely, but after the first few yeshiva students from the coach passed through, they were all waved onwards. Dr Rabinowitz punched his fist in the air and the students gripped each other's arms in excitement. Zofia began to feel that their escape might even be possible. She turned to Jacek and risked a smile.

The scale of the journey ahead hit home as soon as she saw the Trans-Siberian Express. A great beast of a locomotive, tall as a house and black as tar, pulling a long line of iron-grey coal wagons and goods cars as well as passenger cars. This was it. They were to be on this train for fifteen long days. Jacek rushed towards it, looking for their carriage, dragging Masha by the arm. A stench of engine oil and steam made Zofia cough as she blinked through the thick coal smoke from the stoves that heated the carriages.

She glanced back to see Otto in conversation with the guards at the checkpoint, and that he gestured towards her and Jacek as he was talking. By now Jacek was further down the train, helping the yeshiva students aboard, offering to heave some of their luggage up. Dr Rabinowitz and his assistant Rabbi Nowak had trunks of books and scrolls with them, ready to set up a school wherever they should end up.

The train was full, and most of the passengers were Jews. Rich ones in first class with mounds of luggage, and poor ones wearing shoes held together with wire. She noticed two Chinese businessmen in perfectly pressed suits with a whole trolley of luggage. They must be important because the porters were scurrying around them, helping them into the best first-class carriage.

The younger of the two, a handsome well-dressed man, smiled at her as she passed and, startled, she smiled back before she was distracted by a goods train departing in a gush of steam from the opposite platform.

'Rubber,' said Otto, rushing up to her from behind.

His voice, close to her ear, made her jump.

'It's a rubber transport to Germany,' he said. 'Since the war, Germany's ports have been blockaded and the merchant shipping shut down. This line links Germany and Japan, especially for rubber. It's gone ahead of us. Hundreds of tons go on this route every day. So it's not just people on the Trans-Siberian Express.'

'How interesting.' She hadn't asked, but he was intent on explaining anyway. She wasn't sure if she found it endearing or annoying that he was trying to make conversation.

Jacek and Masha had disappeared on board and they had to search further down the train for the second-class carriage for which they had designated tickets.

A few moments later Jacek stuck his head out and waved at her and with relief she hurried to join him.

The yeshiva students were booked in the 'hard' class further down than their carriage, known as the *Platzkart,* where the bunks were all in one compartment. Zofia was glad because she knew they might be noisy and all she wanted now was peace.

Down the narrow corridor to their carriage, which had six compartments. Theirs was number two, and it had four sleeping places and a cramped cupboard space for luggage. There was an adjoining washroom and a toilet shared with numbers one and three. Zofia was disconcerted to see that Otto was now hovering just outside their compartment.

Like children, Masha and Jacek had already staked their claim to the top bunks, where there was more storage because of the luggage racks above.

'Oh, that's lucky. We're in the same compartment.' Otto waved his reservation. 'D'you mind if I take this one?' Otto pointed to the bunk below Jacek's.

'Be my guest,' Jacek said, giving Zofia a wink.

Zofia was furious with Jacek and felt herself flush.

'There are no curtains on the beds,' Masha said with horror. She was right. There was nothing to give anyone privacy, to keep people from each other; the only more private areas were the toilet compartment halfway down the corridor and the samovar compartment at the end for hot water.

Zofia folded her arms, aghast at the lack of privacy. She cursed Jacek for welcoming Otto in, though it wasn't exactly his fault about the reservations. But she'd been looking forward to anonymity, to just being the three of them. Now she would have to sleep right next to a stranger. She couldn't help watching Otto, how he unpacked a freshly ironed shirt and hung it on the side of the bunk, how he took out a newspaper in Russian and began to read, sitting less than four feet from where she was to sleep.

Every now and then Otto would look over to her and their

eyes would clash. Zofia hurriedly looked away, all too aware of him in the confined space.

They all went to bed early, for there was nothing to do but sit and read or drink tea. Otto went to fetch tea from the coal-fired samovar and came back with a steaming glass in a metal holder.

'The restaurant's further up, too,' he said. 'The timetable for meals is just outside.'

That night, Zofia didn't undress but, using a piece of string from her coat pocket, she rigged up a kind of screen across her bunk with one of the sheets. Then she pulled the other sheet and thin blanket over her and turned her back on the rest of the compartment. Above her, Masha and Jacek held hands and whispered across the gap between the bunks.

It was going to be a long journey.

In the morning, Zofia walked down the corridor to the third-class compartments to see where Dr Rabinowitz and the yeshiva students were staying. Their situation was even worse. They were all crammed together in an open carriage with hard seats, and no separate compartments, where the smell of other people, their food, their sweat, and their cigarettes was already unbearable.

'We're on our way,' Dr Rabinowitz said, not in the least put out by his surroundings. 'New York, here we come!'

His zest for the journey made her smile.

On her return, she shared out the bread for breakfast and followed Otto's example to make tea in the charcoal-fired samovar at the end of the carriage. Having Otto there was like having an uninvited guest, though he was polite and did offer her one of his pastries, which she refused, though Masha was cheeky enough to say, 'I'll take it, if she doesn't want it.'

Jacek and Otto soon got into a conversation about Japanese culture and Russian books. Although she knew Otto spoke fluent Russian, she was surprised to learn that he was keen on some of the Russian literature she loved. When they were children, Jacek loved to spar in an argument, and she'd seen far too little of that side of him recently. Otto was a match for him, though, and she watched Otto and her brother vie good-naturedly over who could remember the most quotations from the Russian classics, and she began to enjoy their conversation. When he was passionate about books Otto looked handsome in a classical, understated way, and a different light shone in his eyes.

'"The mystery of human existence lies not in just staying alive, but—"'

'"In finding something to live for."' Jacek completed the Dostoevsky quotation.

Above her, Masha's feet swung back and forth. 'Staying alive'll do me,' she said. 'I just want to get to America as quick as we can. Yee ha!' She mimed throwing a lasso.

Jacek grinned up at her. 'Only a few thousand more miles to go!'

They passed the first checkpoint at night, and the train rattled on for two more days, while they were awake and while they slept, cutting its long line past deserted stations and into a featureless flat lowland, a thousand miles from Moscow. To give him his due, Otto was a quiet companion, spending most of the time reading or staring out of the dirt-crusted window. Sleety rain came and went. She hoped the weather wasn't going to be like last year, when the winter started early and seemed to last for months.

On the third day, when they awoke they were emerging from a different landscape, a thickly forested area of tall spruce and pine. The temperature had turned gradually colder and the landscape more inhospitable, and Zofia was glad they were to approach their first major stop, the city of Sverdlovsk, in the daytime. They were skirting a low stretch of the Ural mountains, and small flurries of snow were in the air, melting into glistening droplets on the train windows. Box-like buildings could be seen in the distance, grey and grimy, smoke hanging over them in a dense pall.

'It used to be called Yekaterinburg after Catherine the First, wife of Peter the Great,' Otto said. He seemed to like explaining things to them, especially to Masha and she lapped it up. Zofia was amused by the way he'd taken on the role of a glorified tour guide but she couldn't object; after all, without him they'd still be in Kaunas.

Something caught his eye and he stopped talking to stand and peer out of the corridor window, one hand shielding his eyes against the low light. His expression had changed to a tense watchfulness. She rubbed the window to see what had caught his attention. A road ran alongside the railway track, and a row of sand-coloured Russian trucks were keeping pace with them as the train slowed, preparing to pull into the station.

'Jacek, there are Russian army trucks coming,' Otto said. He straightened his collar and tie.

Masha went out into the corridor to look. 'He's right.' Her eyes were curiously sparked with excitement.

Jacek leant half out of the bunk to look out of the window. 'We're not at another state checkpoint yet, are we?'

'No, just Sverdlovsk,' said Otto.

Zofia had hoped to get out, to get a brief snatch of fresh air and stretch her legs, but the sight of the trucks and the armed soldiers' rifles made her wary. The train took a few more minutes to creak and clank to a halt, eventually juddering into the station amid a squeal of brakes and a hiss of steam. Zofia tied back her make-shift curtain, pulled back the sliding door and stuck her head into the corridor.

Shouts and the thump of men's boots on the concrete platform, and suddenly the door into the corridor opened and a crowd of men in khaki uniform and blue-banded caps pushed themselves aboard.

Zofia hurriedly withdrew. 'They're coming on board,' she said.

Otto peered out of the door into the corridor. 'NKVD,' he whispered. 'Russians. The People's Commissariat. Have your papers ready.'

Zofia fumbled to get them from her pocket as she heard the men moving down the carriage.

When they got to their compartment, she saw they wore thick leather belts stuck with short-barrelled revolvers. The guns rattled her. Any armed man in uniform now made her breath come quicker as she tried to suppress the panic inside.

It will be all right. We have Sugihara's visas.

Despite the draught, her hands were clammy with sweat as she held out the passport and visa. The two men seemed older than the previous Russian soldiers she'd seen. The one in charge had a growth of stubble and the kind of expressionless blue eyes that were almost transparent.

She and Masha handed their passports and visas over and waited silently as the NKVD man flipped open the passports with his mouth in a hard line. Masha smiled at him but he didn't smile back. Finally with a curt nod, he returned their papers, and Zofia let out her breath. Masha was staring openly at the Russians as they turned to Otto and Jacek on the opposite bunk.

Otto was the first to hand over his papers and the men spoke to him politely, and asked him a few questions in Russian. He answered them calmly and told them he was headed for Vladivostok with a stopover in Omsk.

Jacek was on the top bunk, his legs dangling over the edge, but the men gestured for him to come down. He sprang down, ready with his papers, but as soon as the man in charge had them in his hand, he whispered to the other soldier.

'This is the one,' he said in Russian.

The Russians scrutinized the papers together, until the younger one drew his revolver in one quick flourish, and pressed it to Jacek's chest.

Jacek's eyes flared in shock.

'Jacek Kowalski? You will come with us.'

Zofia's heart leapt like a hare. She grabbed Jacek's arm, horrified. At the same time, Jacek grew taller, trying to regain composure.

He smiled at the soldiers, though suppressed panic made his voice waver. 'There must be some mistake, I have a valid visa to go to Vladivostok and from there to Japan and to Curaçao, just like my fiancée and the others in this compartment. See? Signed by Chiune Sugihara, from the Japanese consulate.'

'Perhaps. But we have a warrant for your arrest. Anti-communist activities. You're a journalist and not to leave Russian soil. We have orders to arrest you before you leave.'

'Why? He's done nothing wrong!' Zofia stood up to protest, as Masha jumped up too to catch hold of his sleeve. 'We're together,' Masha said.

The man with the cold eyes smiled at her, but pushed her away.

'I'll come with him,' Zofia said, standing up again and seizing his arm in a panic. 'We're family, we stick together.'

'Let go.' Jacek turned and shook her off. His eyes were enormous in his white face. 'This is my trouble, not yours.' He faced up to the NKVD man in charge. 'You can't arrest me. I demand to see a lawyer.'

He let out a laugh, a harsh uncompromising sound. 'You're welcome. If you can find one where you're going.'

'Out. Now.' The other soldier jabbed Jacek with the gun.

Jacek's expression compressed into rage and he tried to slap the gun away.

Zofia could see where this was heading, and she leapt in. 'It's a mistake,' Zofia said desperately. 'You've got the wrong man. He's not a journalist! You've got it all wrong. He's a mechanic—'

'Don't hurt him!' Masha cried.

Jacek shouted, 'Stay the hell out of it, Masha,' as he reached for Zofia's bag.

'That's m—'

He shook his head violently, fixing Zofia with a meaningful look. She realized all at once what he was doing. He was leaving her with his rucksack, and Sugihara's package, entrusting it to her.

'No,' she whispered. 'I can't.'

'You can,' he said, eyes full of fire. 'You're the best person I know. It's not for me, is it? It's for all of us.'

The Russians shouted, 'Hands up!'

'No! Wait!' Their protests were battered down. The younger soldier pushed Masha out of the way with a hard shove.

'No luggage.' The soldier jabbed his revolver in Jacek's stomach. Jacek reluctantly dropped the bag. His eyes bored into Zofia's again.

She knew what he was asking, but it burned a hole in her heart.

'I'm sorry,' Jacek touched Zofia's cheek with his hand. 'This is it. This is my retribution coming. I knew it would come,' he said bitterly, 'but I just didn't know when. Remember me,' he whispered. 'Don't forget me, will you?'

'Never,' she said, clawing at his chest. She tried to cling to his arm but he was being dragged away as he spoke. 'Jacek!'

Masha tried to go after him too, but Otto thrust himself in their way, blocking the corridor, his hands up. 'Better not. He's right. Making a fuss will lead only to trouble for you both.' It was the first time he'd spoken during the whole exchange.

'Get out of my way!' Zofia tried to push by, screaming at him in frustration.

But Otto remained unmoved, legs wide, his arms against the walls. 'It's better if you don't ...'

Zofia fought, shoving and kicking, to get past Otto but, though skinny, he had a bigger reach and her wrestling skills were useless when she couldn't get past his long arms.

No sooner did the door thud shut than the whistle blew, a long piercing whine.

The platform seethed with Russian troops and two other men had also been dragged from the train. They were being forced at gunpoint, hands behind their backs, to the waiting line of vehicles.

Zofia made a renewed effort to get past Otto as the locomotive ahead of them began to shift and gather up steam ready to depart.

A jolt. She fell back as the carriages stuttered and stalled.

The train began to move and at last Otto stood aside.

Both the women dashed to the window as the train lurched away. Zofia leant out and yelled, 'Meet me in Japan, you hear me? I'll wait for you in Kobe.' She was shouting into the wind, but her voice was carried away and Jacek didn't react. He was already being bullied towards the trucks.

The sight of his strong back in his dark overcoat, the way he walked so proudly, made her chest contract and her fist come to her mouth.

Otto pulled Masha away from the window. She was crying noisily. 'Where will they take him?'

Otto was silent except for a shake of the head. This deliberate silence was the answer Zofia didn't want to hear. He calmly picked up Jacek's rucksack and put it on his bunk, but Zofia immediately snatched it back. 'I'll take that,' she said.

A moment's tussle, but seeing her ferocious expression, he let go.

The train picked up speed but all Zofia could think of was that empty railway station and those trucks. *We'll find you*, she thought. *We'll wait in Kobe. Keep believing.*

Masha turned away from them both. Her face was blotched red, as if she was angry, but her eyes were dry. Shock, Zofia supposed. She put her arm around her and hugged her wordlessly. When she looked up, Otto was still looking at them.

'What d'you think you're looking at?' Zofia snapped. 'You did nothing! You could have helped us and you just stood by.'

Otto turned away, climbed onto his bed and faced the wall.

Now the train felt like a prison. Somewhere they couldn't escape. *Too fast – we're leaving Jacek behind and it's going too fast.*

She couldn't even take it in, and when eventually she spoke, her voice was ragged, as if she couldn't find how words worked any more. 'I'm sorry.' She reached to tap Otto on the back.

He turned and sat up, but his gaze didn't connect with hers.

'It's not your fault,' she said. 'I know you couldn't do anything.

We always knew there was a risk, but we'd pretended the train was safe, that they couldn't find us here.'

'They would have taken you too, if you'd given them trouble.'

'I know. But we should have gone with him.'

'He didn't want us to,' Masha said.

'He hasn't got his gloves.' Zofia pointed to where they were still lying on the table by the window. 'And his bag's still here,' she gestured to her bunk. 'All his clothes, everything. What will he do without them?'

She gathered the gloves up and put them in his rucksack. After that, she couldn't talk of Jacek, it hurt too much. They stared out of the window and watched the barren landscape unfurl. Now, unbelievably, there were thin patches of snow amid the forest and the carriages were getting colder. How quickly the weather could change. How quickly life could.

Zofia wrapped herself in the bedclothes and hid away behind her curtain.

After a few more hours, Masha pulled it aside with a finger and held out a steaming tin cup. 'It's tea,' she said.

'That's kind.' Zofia spoke the words, but her thoughts were still with Jacek. How could Masha be so calm? But then again, she hadn't persuaded him to come on this damn train. Her own eyes were itchy and swollen from crying behind the curtain where no one could see.

'If you'll permit me, I have some vodka,' Otto said from the opposite bunk. 'I think we all need some.'

He took out a small glass bottle and without even asking, leant over and emptied some of it into her tea. Zofia took a sip and it made her throat burn, but the warmth helped to bring some semblance of feeling back, though she was still seized by the unreality of the fact that Jacek was gone, and that Sverdlovsk was getting further away by the second.

Masha thanked Otto and he offered her the bottle. She took a large swig, like a hardened drinker, and then passed it back.

The next half-hour was filled with the passing of the bottle. Zofia wondered how Masha could drink that much without getting drunk.

'What did Jacek mean,' Masha asked, 'about it being, what did he call it? Retribution for something?'

It was a relief to talk of him, to bring Jacek's presence back into their compartment. 'When we left Poland … so my uncle and I could cross the border, Jacek had to kill someone. He's had nightmares about it ever since. One of the border guards was a young Nazi, who looked about sixteen. Why do they take them so young? Almost a child. But he had a gun and Jacek had to creep up on him to kill him so we could pass through.'

'Jacek did that?' Otto was wide-eyed.

'He caught him by surprise and stabbed him first in the chest, but he wouldn't die. So Jacek had to cut the young man's throat. He was scared if he didn't, he'd shout for help and we'd all get caught by the Nazis. But the knife was blunt and the business brutal, and Jacek told me he never wanted to see that look again, the silent pleading where the boy begged him for mercy as he bled to death.'

'Jacek never told me that,' Masha said.

'He won't speak of it. He told me something else. Something that haunted me. It was that in the same moment he killed him, he loved him more intensely than he had ever loved anyone in his life. Can you imagine that? He said it was the worst thing, leaving him there, a corpse, while knowing the boy's family, maybe his mother and father, were waiting for him at home.'

The train rattled its *rackety-clack* down the track, but nobody spoke.

Otto's face was a mask. Silence was the only fitting reply.

Finally, Zofia turned to Otto. 'How long until the next stop?' she asked.

He seemed to gather himself together. 'Tyumen, then Omsk. A day and a half away. Omsk's a major city on our route but we won't get there until the middle of the night.'

'Do you think we should get off there?' Zofia asked. 'Try to find Jacek?'

'No. How could you do that? We don't even know where he's been taken. And hunting for him is too risky. Go on to Japan. Your brother will meet you there if he can.' Otto was definite. 'I'll stay with you until then, and make sure you're okay.'

Zofia smiled politely, the way she knew she should, but she didn't want his protection. Maybe he was trying to help, but she didn't want anyone else interfering in her life, and the raw thought of Jacek made her chest ache. She shuffled to the back of her bunk and wrapped her arms around his bag.

'Thank you,' Masha was saying to Otto. 'I don't know what I'll do now, but it feels good not to be two women on our own.'

Zofia stuck her head back out of the curtain and glowered at her.

Later, when Otto went to buy food from the dining car, she took Masha to task over it. 'Look, I don't want you making eyes at Otto. I didn't invite him to join us, and I don't know why he keeps hanging around us.'

'Maybe he's lonely. After all, he was on his own and the three of us were all together ... and besides, where else could he go now? This is his bunk.' She paused and looked over at where Jacek had slept. 'My father will kill Jacek when they find out he left me on my own.'

'Don't be stupid. It's not his fault. Jacek couldn't do anything about it, and anyway he told me your father hits you. I wondered why you put up with it.'

'Because he's not all bad. Nobody's all bad.' She swallowed. 'My father never stood a chance in life. Nobody gave him any education, nobody thought he could learn anything. The Tsars treated them all as factory fodder, slaves to their regime. You can't blame him for being angry. But what he does at home is none of your business. He's my father and I miss him.'

Her belligerent face dared Zofia to disagree. Zofia thought of her own family, now all split up into different parts of Russia, and her heart heaved.

Otto came back from the dining car with a plate of grey-looking goulash and slurped it in noisy gulps. He seemed to shrink because of the atmosphere in the carriage.

'Look,' whispered Zofia to Masha. 'Let's not argue. He wouldn't want it.'

Masha started to sob noisily. 'It's not fair. I only came because of Jacek,' she said. 'I thought if I didn't, he'd find some other girl. Someone smarter. And now he's gone, I've got no one and I can't go home.' Her lower lip quavered.

Zofia couldn't help but be moved.

'It's all right,' Otto said, embarrassed, putting down his spoon. 'We'll stick together.'

'Jacek will find us,' Zofia said. 'Or we'll find him when the war's over.'

Masha sniffed and looked at her sideways. 'I thought you hated me. Because I'm stupid and not like you. But Jacek understood me, he talked to me like I knew stuff. About films and Hollywood. Like I wasn't any different.'

'I never hated you.' It was a lie, but Zofia felt a squirming in her stomach because Masha had spoken the truth and it shamed her. 'We just never got to know each other, that's all.'

Masha appeared mollified, though Otto looked distinctly uncomfortable and turned away to finish his stew.

Zofia watched the trees flash by. Masha was all contradictions; one minute angry, the next petulant, the next bitter. Zofia reminded herself that, like her, Masha had just lost the man she loved in the most shocking way, and she should make allowances. No matter what she thought of Masha, Jacek had loved her and that had to count for something.

Chapter 20

Grief came in waves; at times overwhelming, at times a quiet agony of loss. They grew used to Otto sitting opposite them, his long spidery legs crossed at the ankle as he reclined on his bunk. Masha seemed to have befriended him, and he was encouraging it, she could see, though his eyes would slide often towards her. Zofia didn't understand what he found so fascinating and would turn her head away whenever he did it.

Otto shared his pastries and his vodka, and kept up stories of his childhood in the wine business. Zofia tried to ignore it and kept to herself, wrapped around her bags and wondering all the while if Jacek had been taken to a camp.

He wasn't dead, at least. She was sure she'd know by instinct if he was.

She knew, though, that Jacek had entrusted Sugihara's package to her, and she never let it out of her sight. Coming into Tyumen, they passed great slabs of factories and the smoking chimneys of heavy industry. The people on the platform, scurrying to and fro like cockroaches, were hunched in winter coats and fur hats; already in Siberia, in this unseasonal cold, the temperature at night was dropping below freezing.

As the train creaked into the station, a crowd of waiting

babushkas was huddled there with items to sell – baskets of nuts and dried fruit, hard dry sausage and bread rolls. A train guard came along the carriage and told them they'd be stopping for fifteen minutes.

'Thank God,' Masha said. 'The dining car's rubbish and too expensive. We'll be able to buy supplies.'

'I'll try to find a paper,' Zofia said. 'I'd like to know what's going on in Lithuania.'

'You won't find anything useful from the Russians,' Otto said. 'It will all be propaganda. But do go and see what you can get. I'll look after your things.'

'Aren't you getting off?' Masha asked Otto. 'Just to get a stretch?'

'No, we haven't got very long, so I'm staying aboard.'

Dr Rabinowitz, the yeshiva teacher, bustled by in his wide-brimmed black hat, followed by a group of students. 'The train attendant just told me, don't leave anything on the train, my dear,' he warned her. 'Thieves get on at these smaller stops and take anything they can if it's not attended.'

'Surely not,' Otto said. 'I'm sure you can leave your things here. After all, I'll be here to watch everything.'

'I'm taking no chances,' Zofia said, and began emptying everything from her own bag into Jacek's rucksack, stuffing it down. She eased the precious parcel into the space at the back. 'We were robbed in Moscow, even in a secure hotel room.'

Otto looked away.

'Mr Wulfsson?' A sing-song female voice calling. A green-uniformed train attendant, the *provodnitsa*, peered through into their carriage. She had a badge with 'Tonya' written on it in Russian.

'Mr Otto Wulfsson?' Her eyes searched the carriage for a response.

'Oh! That's me.' Otto startled and stood up.

'There's a call for you in the station office. Hurry now.' She gestured to him. 'You have fifteen minutes.'

He grabbed his coat, scarf and hat. Zofia wondered who could be calling him out here in the middle of nowhere. He hadn't said where his family wine business was, and it was a German name, Wulfsson, she was certain. Yet he had worked with Sugihara. An enigma.

She had some sympathy, though. Many refugees had fled Germany before the war. Maybe he was Jewish, or Catholic. Who knew what his story was? They all had stories.

'Come on!' Masha said, interrupting her thoughts. 'Only fifteen minutes.'

Ahead of them they saw Otto's long loping figure hurrying behind the train attendant, towards the door to the station offices.

Otto rushed past the hawkers selling smoked fish and dodgy cigarettes, to the only public telephone, where the receiver was already dangling from the machine by its brown cord. He dived into the box-like cubicle to pick it up, his immediate thought that something had happened to Ma.

His breath clouded before him as he said, 'Hello? Hello? Who is it?'

'Zeitel. Which carriage are the Kowalskis in?'

'Second class. Compartment two, coach C.'

'Only four bunks?'

'Yes. She and the brother's fiancée on one side, me and the brother on the other. Only the brother got arrested by the Russians – some sort of tip-off that he worked as a journalist.'

'Shit. Did they get the package?'

'No. They didn't take the girl and they didn't seem to know about the package. He wasn't allowed to take luggage. Now Zofia Kowalski has it and she won't let go of it. She even sleeps with it.'

'What does it look like?'

'Just a brown paper-wrapped parcel. About the length of a shoebox but flatter. Sugihara's official consulate stamp on it and it's sealed. I'm telling you, the NKVD seemed intent on arresting the brother, but if they raid us again, I'll be at risk. My papers

153

say I work as a translator, and the Russians hate us all. And I've no idea why they didn't take me or the sister or the other girl. Seemed like they were just intent on Kowalski.'

'Then you need to move fast. Get that package as soon as you can and if you can't persuade her to give it up, then you need to ...'

The line clicked and went dead. Otto hammered on the steel cradle to try to get it to revive. He paced, hoping Zeitel would call back. The fact he'd rung him at all made his legs shaky. He remembered again how Jacek was taken. It unleashed a kind of horror in him. He'd liked Jacek; he'd been friendly, and they'd struck up a rapport.

The phone suddenly gave a shrill ring and before it could even ring again the receiver was clamped to Otto's ear. 'Yes? Zeitel?'

'We got cut off. Damned Russian telephone system. At least we know it's not bugged. I was telling you we have to speed up. If she won't cooperate you must take it by force. The next station is Omsk. Got it? Omsk. A car will be waiting to take you and the package back to Kaunas.' The line crackled, but he caught the rest of the instructions. 'There's pressure from my side. Another conference is scheduled in three weeks' time between Goering, the Italians, and the Japanese Foreign Minister. We need to make sure nothing in the pipeline will foul it up. You've got the where-withal. Use it.'

'I'll try, but it's such a confined space and there are so many people about that—'

'You're playing with fire, my friend. If we don't get that package, someone may denounce your mother to the Soviet authorities for anti-Soviet behaviour and—'

Abruptly the line went dead again. Otto slapped the receiver back and braved the wind on the platform, waiting for it to ring again. The cold flags ate into his shoes. *Ring, damn you.*

'Mr Wulfsson?' It was Tonya the *provodnitsa* for their carriage. 'Train leaves in two minutes.'

'Yes, yes, I'm coming.'

He went and stood right next to the phone, willing it to ring. It remained silent. Oh God, Zeitel had spoken of his mother. Ma's face, full of that mother bear look, loomed in his imagination.

You bastard. If anything happens to her, I'll kill you. He felt the irony of this thought, that he was too much of a coward to use the gun he'd been issued, even to save her.

A choking groan came from his lips. He picked up the phone and shouted down it, 'Ring! Why won't you bloody ring?'

'Sir, you must come now,' Tonya shouted from the door.

Still he hesitated, until the train began a slow shunt and he had to run like crazy to get aboard, hauling himself up the steps, his hands burning on the icy metal handrail. He staggered down the carriage past the yeshiva students, who had managed to buy packs of cards and were dealing them out to play 'Durak'.

In his compartment he saw that Masha was chomping at a packet of sunflower seeds and Zofia was quietly reading a Russian newspaper, though her eyes were mournful and several times he caught her staring into space. The rucksack was right there next to her and one arm was wrapped protectively around it. She looked up when he returned, and gave him a wan smile.

'I keep expecting you to be Jacek,' she said.

His heart twisted at her pain, and the fact her eyes were so glassy. He clutched his stomach – a churned-up mess of guilt and fear.

'You all right?' she asked.

'Just tired,' he said.

'Who was calling you?'

'Just my mother's doctor. To say he checked on her.'

'Is she okay?'

'Yes, she's good.' He couldn't tell her of the fear that she was already struggling, even though he'd asked a neighbour to look in on her. He couldn't tell her he feared she'd get the NKVD knock on the door. And he definitely couldn't tell Zofia he'd orders to shoot her.

155

Chapter 21

The track cut through the landscape like a scar. Zofia walked up and down the carriage, unable to stay still. Siberia, seen from the window of a train, was numbing – the mile after mile of brown grass sticking up through a thin layer of snow, the sparse trees in the mist. The bleak emptiness echoed the hollow in Zofia's chest, the space for her missing twin, and the forced inactivity made her want to scream. Several times a day she strode from carriage to carriage, just to be on the move.

To do nothing seemed too painful and felt as though she'd accepted it, that she wasn't still screaming inside for them to bring Jacek back. She always wore her blue coat with its pocketful of treasures and took Jacek's rucksack with her. It had become like a talisman, something to cling to in this single-track world between worlds. She pressed her hands against the cold window to watch the ground near the track go by, to stare mesmerized into the deep depressions of icy water stained brown by rust.

Eleven more days to go. She'd get to the promised land, to America, and then she'd be free. And she'd never give up hope for her brother. *I'll wait for you in Kobe, Jacek, leave messages for you everywhere I go.*

She must try to sleep. Time had lost its meaning – they were travelling across time zones and now it seemed night was day and day was night.

Hours passed, and she saw that Masha and Otto had begun to talk to while away the time. Masha was telling him about a school play she'd taken part in, and they were laughing. She was acting parts and flirting a little too, tossing back her blonde curls and looking up at him under her eyelashes. The blonde was growing out now, and it gave Zofia a strange satisfaction, but Masha looked flushed, two spots of red in her cheeks. How dare they laugh when Jacek was missing? Had they no feeling?

Otto seemed to sense her disapproval. 'He would want us to laugh,' he said.

The view had changed in the last hour to the occasional straggling village of rotting timber houses, black against the grey mist, but it was still a few more hours before they were due to arrive at Omsk. Otto began to open up more, to tell her about how much he loved working for Sugihara, and how he was dreading having to work for someone else. *He's a nice man*, she thought. *The war isn't his fault.*

Though it was evening, the temperature had dropped again and Masha was now complaining about being too cold. Zofia hoped she wasn't sickening for something and rushed to the tea compartment to fetch them all a hot drink before turning in. This time, she left the rucksack behind with Masha and Otto. She'd only be gone a few minutes and there was no station in sight.

As she got to the compartment door she almost collided with a man coming in the opposite direction; he wasn't looking where he was going. She leapt back, full of apology.

It was the young man from first class; the Chinese man she'd seen on the platform. 'Oh, I beg your pardon!' he said. 'My fault.' His gaze was all apology under his fashionable wire-rimmed glasses and his smile genuine under the slim ghost of a moustache. 'So sorry. You first.' He spoke in perfect Russian.

She unscrewed her flask, aware all the time of him waiting in the doorway, watching. The hot water spluttered out and a few drops spilled on her hand. 'Ouch.'

'Yes, an unpredictable dragon, that one,' he said.

She turned to smile at him. 'But only a baby compared with the steam engine pulling this train.'

He laughed. 'Are you okay? It didn't burn?'

'No, fine. It was just a splash.'

'You travelled from Moscow?' Again, the perfect Russian.

'Yes. You?' Although she knew he had.

'Uh huh. Is this your usual samovar?'

'Yes, we're just up there, in second class.' She was reluctant to mention anything about Jacek, though she couldn't help the sharp anguish she felt.

He was still talking. 'Ah. We are in first. I'm travelling with my boss, Tanaka-san. I am his Russian translator. When I am not his tea-maker.' He grinned.

'You speak it well. Do all Chinese learn it in school?'

He frowned. 'Chinese? I'm not Chinese. Japanese. From Yokohama, close to Tokyo.'

She was instantly abashed. 'Sorry, it's just that we're heading for the Chinese border and I assumed …' She tailed off and moved out of the way so he could get near to the urn.

She was about to go at the sound of the hiss of the water, but he carried on talking to her. 'You're not Russian either, though, are you?'

'No. Polish. We had to get out … well, it's a long story.' She was anxious to make amends for her gaffe about him being Chinese. 'I know another Japanese man who speaks Russian, though, Sugihara at the embassy in Lithuania.'

'I don't know him.' He had switched to Polish. Perfectly understandable Polish.

'You speak Polish!'

'Yes, I'm a translator. I like meeting people from other places.

Sugihara-san at the embassy, is he a friend of yours?'

'No. Yes. Well, it's complicated.' She tried to change the subject and reverted back to Russian. 'Is it usual to speak Russian and Polish in Japan?'

'No.' He laughed again. 'My parents tried to discourage it.'

'So what made you want to learn?'

'Foolishness. I tell you a secret – when I was about nine years old, the Bolshoi ballet came to Tokyo, part of the reparations after the war between Russia and Japan. My parents took me and my sister, and I've never forgotten it. The dancers, the women in their tutus, so frail, so ethereal. Their long legs! Not like the Japanese women in their clumping wooden *geta*. How the ballerinas soared and leapt! I was totally enchanted by it.'

She hung in the doorway, watching his animated face. 'Did you go to the ballet this time when you were in Moscow?'

'No. I've never seen them since. The political situation put paid to that, all the young dancers conscripted into the army. But all through my childhood I held the image of it. I imagined the whole of Russia was like that – a place white with glistening snow and swan feathers, and full of the beauty of the ballet. I decided to learn all I could about Russia and to study the language. But dreams are not reality, and that's why now I am stuck in a compartment with the most boring man on earth. He lectures me every day on why we failed to convince the Russians to sell us their oil.'

She smiled at his rueful expression. 'Oh dear. So not a good travelling companion, then.'

'Definitely no.' He leant towards her and whispered, 'And I'm sad to say I've lost all my childish ideas of Russia over the last few years. I'm glad to be on my way home.'

'You are going to Tsuruga?'

He nodded as he fastened the top on his flask. 'I'd better hurry. The *provodnitsa* normally brings the tea, but in this terrible weather she's caught the flu, the samovar is empty, and my boss likes hot water for his shaving. He'll give me a flea in the ear if I don't get back soon! It was nice to meet you.' He smiled and caught her eye, and his spark of humour was like a breath of fresh air.

'Nice to meet you too. I'm Zofia.'

'Haru. Haru Kimura.' He gave a small bow and then a jaunty wave as he went. It had been lovely to speak a little Polish, and he had made an impression on her. He was dressed like an American, and she liked the way his face was so open, and his eyes so warm and lively. She was so used to seeing people who were afraid, or people who were hiding something. She wished she had his openness, but she was wary, unsure who to trust and, even though Japan was supposed to be friendly towards the Jews, she knew it would be safer to avoid other people if she could.

He'd only just hurried away with his flask when Dr Rabinowitz, the teacher of the Yeshiva students, appeared at the samovar too. The *Platzkart* one was already empty because there were too many students using it.

'Not long now,' said Dr Rabinowitz. 'Sorry to hear of your trouble. I pray you'll be reunited with your brother before too long.' He smiled at her in a fatherly way, his eyes full of compassion. 'We're almost halfway there, thank heaven.'

Choked, and all at once guilty for enjoying her conversation with Haru, she began to make her way back to their carriage with their flask, sharing a few words as she passed with the other passengers, most of whom were dozing or playing cards in their compartments.

Otto and Masha were sitting close to one another, their heads bent over something.

They were opening the Sugihara parcel. Oh no. She'd been too long; she shouldn't have stayed talking. Alarmed, she broke into a staggering run as the train rounded a bend.

'No! What d'you think you're doing?' She slapped the flask down on the table and leapt to grab the parcel back.

Masha warded her off. 'Hey, it's okay. It's just my hands are cold,' she said. 'I just want the gloves.'

Otto had taken hold of it but she leapt on him like a tiger. 'Give that back. It's mine.'

He clung on, but she slapped him so hard in the face he gasped in shock.

'Whoa!' Masha tried to pull her away. 'What the blazes are you doing? Leave him alone. We looked. We can't see any gloves in here anyway, just the papers.'

'There are no gloves!' She was hot with righteous anger. 'There never were, it was just an excuse for Jacek to deliver it. It's mine. You've no right to go into my things.'

'It's Jacek's,' Masha said. 'Sugihara gave the parcel to Jacek, so I've as much right to it as you.'

'And I worked for Sugihara,' Otto said, holding on to the parcel. 'Just calm down.'

She managed to tug the parcel from Otto's grip. 'You'll tear it!'

The train was slowing now, coming into the station at Omsk, and the undercarriage made a metallic groan as a gust of steam blew past the window.

'Is this Omsk? Already?' Otto looked panicked. 'Give it to me, please.' He tried to snatch the parcel out of her hand again but she turned to cradle it against her chest.

The package had been torn open. 'What the hell?' She rounded on Masha. 'You stupid idiot. You've no idea what you've done, have you?'

Masha was silent, pouting.

Zofia pressed the papers to her heart until the train drew to a halt.

'Leave me alone,' she said to Otto, who was looming over her. 'Don't you dare touch me! These are mine.'

'I want those papers, that's all.' He was almost tearful, his face mottled and red. 'I worked for Sugihara. It won't matter if you never deliver them, but it matters to me. You have your visa already. You'll be safe with or without those papers. But I won't. If I don't have them it'll be a death sentence for me.'

'What the hell are you talking about? Leave me alone.'

Masha was standing now, holding up her hands between them, trying to stop the argument. 'What's in these papers that is so important?'

'Testimonies from the Polish people about the Nazis, and a letter from Sugihara,' Zofia said. 'But Jacek promised Sugihara he wouldn't open the package, and now look – the seal's broken. The embassy will think it's incomplete, or he's stolen something, or interfered with it. How could you? You've destroyed Sugihara's trust in us.'

'Please, just give me the package,' Otto said. His face looked stripped bare, his eyes pleading.

'Go to hell.' Zofia, tearful with rage, leapt away and staggered at full tilt down the moving train, bracing herself against the corridor wall with her free hand, heading for the hard third-class compartment where she prayed Dr Rabinowitz might help her. The yeshiva students were engaged in their card play and had a group of spectators around them, but they barely looked up. Zofia edged her way into the crowd watching the game, the package clutched to her chest with both arms.

Otto was not far behind her, but she refused to meet his eye, and she knew he wouldn't dare to steal it from her amongst all these people.

The tension between them was like electricity. The train was at the station, and she feared he'd try to grab it and get off. Five minutes. Ten. His eyes blazed at her, but she stared back at him defiant, her chin raised.

The train was shunting forward again now, chugging out of Omsk, away from the station. Otto gave a last desperate look outside at the station buildings sliding away.

Once the train was moving, she saw him cling to the side of the window and press his forehead hard against the glass. What was he up to? What did he want with the package from Sugihara, and what did he mean about it being a death sentence? What could it possibly matter to him?

Her senses were on fire; all her assumptions about Otto gone. She walked unsteadily back to their compartment.

When she got there, Masha beckoned her over with frantic gestures.

'While you were gone I looked in Otto's suitcase.'

Zofia sat down heavily on the bottom bunk. 'What? Why did you do that?'

'I'm just nosy. And I thought he was behaving a bit strangely, staring at you all the time. And there was a gun and bullets in his case.'

Zofia's stomach dropped. 'He's armed? D'you think he's a spy?'

'How the hell should I know?' Masha paused, her forehead furrowed in concentration. 'You're supposed to be the clever one. When I said my hands were cold he kept saying you wouldn't mind me going in your bag, that I should get out the gloves, and you know what happened next.'

'He's German. I think he's been after the package all along. How dare he? Act like he wanted to make friends, when all he wanted was—'

'I've got the gun. It was loaded, I could tell by the weight of it.'

'What? How could you tell?'

Masha tossed her head. She pointed to her suitcase. 'The gun's in there now.'

'Okay, Masha,' she whispered, horrified. She spoke slowly as if to a child. 'You've got to put it back, and we need to call someone.'

'Who? Who would help us? The NKVD police? You heard what he said, and I think he's right. If we draw attention to ourselves we could be sent to a camp. They'll use any excuse.'

'But what will Otto do when he finds out it's gone?'

'I don't know,' Masha said. 'Maybe we should just throw those papers out of the window, then he'll stop hounding us.'

'No. That's what he wants, to stop the evidence getting abroad. So I must deliver it. We must do it for Jacek. Sugihara trusted him.'

At the sound of Jacek's name Masha was suddenly quiet. 'I miss Jacek. I didn't think I would, but he was the best.'

'What do you mean, you didn't think you would?'

'Nothing, nothing. I don't know what I'm saying. It's the shock. It's just, Jacek would have known what to do.' She stopped speaking and pressed her lips together.

Otto strode towards them, pale-faced and looking at the ground.

'Get out. You're not coming in here,' Zofia said, closing the compartment door on him.

'Then pass me my things,' he said through the glass.

They heaved all his belongings out into the corridor, slid the door closed and pressed down the latch.

Otto knew he'd failed as soon as the train left Omsk station. He hadn't managed to get the package by persuasion, and as the train drew away he knew that if Zeitel's car was waiting for him, it would have had a fruitless journey. He had tried to be kind, to do this in a way that wouldn't hurt anyone, but he had failed. His hands were trembling and he gripped the frame of the corridor window harder. He wasn't cut out for this.

Now his mother would be in danger, and all because he wasn't brave enough to make the decision that had to be made. Though she was tough as iron inside, Ma was frail and ill and she hadn't done anything wrong. She didn't deserve trouble. He thought of all the soldiers caught up in this war, killing and thinking nothing of it, of Jacek killing the German guard, and he wished he was back in Sugihara's quiet office before all this had begun, polishing the *netsuke* and filing papers.

He would have to do it while they were asleep, while she was too sleepy to know what was happening. Oh God, he couldn't do it. Not a beautiful young woman like her. He'd have to load the gun and have it ready to threaten her. Would she scream? What would happen? He couldn't shoot her. Please God he wouldn't have to do that.

Would Zeitel's men still be waiting for him at the next station? The thought made him feel nauseous.

Too many questions. He looked at his watch and made calculations. There was a strangling feeling in his throat. They would arrive at Novosibirsk, a small stop, in a day's time, in the middle of the night. That would be the time. It wasn't too late, not if he could do it then.

He found a vacant compartment but he couldn't sleep. He dragged his brown suitcase up and down the corridor to the samovar station and the restaurant car. People stared at him curiously as he passed, as if they could see the turmoil in his face. Later, when everyone was asleep, he returned to the vacant compartment and slunk in there to load the gun. Perhaps the threat of it would be enough to make Zofia give up the package.

Otto clicked open the latches on the case and rummaged in the bottom. He took a while searching, but finally had to get everything out and line it up on the lower bunk. After fifteen minutes of searching frantically by the dim battery-operated reading light, there was no mistake. The gun and the bullets were gone.

With a growing unease, he realized the women must have taken them. And if they had, then they'd know exactly what kind of a man he was. The humiliation burned; that he'd been outwitted by them, and that they'd think the worst of him. It made the job harder because now he was pretty sure they wouldn't let him anywhere near them, and he couldn't blame them.

But what hurt most was that Zofia would think less of him.

He curled himself up on the unfamiliar bunk and watched night bleed into day and day darken into night. Outside, he saw not a single creature, neither bird nor man, not even tracks, just rivers glinting with specks of ice and grey clouds over grey forests. He stared out, feeling as if he were the last man on earth and wondering if the Nazis would come for him at Novosibirsk.

Chapter 22

The train creaked up a long gradient, crossing a timber bridge over a gully, threading through thick pine forests whose shadowy depths reminded Zofia of a childhood tale, the one where the shapeshifting witch lay in wait for unwary children. At the top of the hill they rounded a bend and picked up speed to hurtle down towards a long flat plain where the trees were stunted and thinly spread. Like something from pre-history, no habitation broke up the wild terrain. They had seen nothing of Otto the day before and there were another few hours before the train would arrive at Novosibirsk.

'Shall we get ready for bed?' Masha asked. 'We should sleep before we get to the next stop.'

'I don't think I can sleep. I'm too wound up about Otto and worried he'll try something at the next station.'

'Where do you think he is?'

Zofia shook her head. 'I don't know and I don't care. I can't believe he pretended to be a friend. He's just strange. I should never have trusted him. All Germans hate the Jews, and I should have known. I don't like to think of him still on here.'

'Do you think he'll try anything?'

'I don't know. But I'm going to stay dressed and keep my

shoes on anyway.'

'It's cold. I think I'll wear my coat,' Masha said. 'I wanted a hot drink, but I'll make do with the bottled water. I don't want to risk going out there again.' She swigged from the glass bottle on the table. 'Wish it was vodka.'

They got into bed fully dressed in coats, hats and shoes, just in case they needed to run, and Masha pulled down the blind on the door before climbing up to her bunk. Zofia switched off the light and dozed, but she was too full of adrenaline to sleep properly. For these few hours of darkness, the train was quiet, except for the constant rhythm and rocking of the train. Even in the third-class compartment, the yeshiva students, usually chattering and full of laughter, were sleeping.

When the train slowed, Zofia sat up and looked out of the nearside window. Pillars, many platforms with bridges and stairs. She pulled up the blind to the corridor to see the platform they were approaching was unlit, though Novosibirsk station seemed to be a big echoing place of concrete and glass. Even at this time of the night, a small crowd of hawkers was waiting, faces white in the dark, ready to hand goods through the windows in return for a few roubles.

Her first thought, as always, was of Jacek, and she found herself searching the crowd for his face. *Stupid*, she thought.

She checked the latch was down, and wondered if Otto would get off or whether he was asleep in third class with Dr Rabinowitz and the students. Not wanting to talk to anyone, she curled up again to try to sleep as the train slid to a halt.

She was dimly aware of the clank of train doors opening and slamming shut. Other people getting off to buy provisions, even in the dark. Russian voices and the hiss of steam. The noise of coal being emptied into the hopper and of water gurgling into the tanks. More people getting on and the thud of boots in the corridor.

Then, a glint of something at the edge of the door.

A flicker that came and went.

A long blade sliding up between the latch and the door.

For a moment she thought she was imagining it, that it was some sort of trick of the light.

It moved slowly as she watched, fascinated, until the latch began to ease upwards out of its housing. It took seconds but it felt like minutes.

Until with a gasp, the realization of what was happening hit her, and she kicked at the underside of Masha's bunk with her boot. 'Masha!'

Too late; in the last few seconds the latch gave, and it was so quick, the flick of the knife hardly had time to register before the door to the corridor slid open, and the bulky figure of a man in a padded overcoat filled the small space.

Not Otto. A stranger's face in a fur hat loomed over her, one hand grabbed a shoulder and something cold pressed against her throat. The knife. The smell of something sour on his breath. She contracted herself into a ball.

An accented voice, deep and coarse, but not Russian. 'Give me the papers, the parcel from Sugihara and all will be well.'

Act like an innocent passenger. 'What's Sugihara?'

'No games.' The knife flashed above her eyes. A threat.

She opened her mouth to yell for help but his hand, cold and stinking of leather, clamped down on it.

'Where is it? In your bag?'

He grabbed the back of her neck to pull her away, searching. The knife flashed past her face as he tried to yank the rucksack away from behind her, but she clung to it with all her strength. They tussled a moment until with a sharp twist she rolled away from the knife.

'Masha!' she yelled, and at the same time jabbed a knee hard upwards into his groin.

She felt it connect and he curled in on himself with a grunt of pain.

Now. She kicked out with the heel of her shoe to his forehead. The force of it jolted through her foot and he fell backwards onto the bunk behind him, losing his hat and cracking his head on the sharp edge.

His eyes glazed and his head swayed before he spluttered an expletive and lunged for her again. *Fingers in the eyes.* Jacek's lessons came back to her. A jab with all her strength into the soft wetness of his eyes.

Relief as he covered his face and doubled over again.

A noise above. Masha was already scrambling down the metal footholds. She grabbed the glass water bottle and with a grunt of effort slugged the man in the back of his balding head. The blow was surprisingly effective. Glass shattered and the intruder slumped forward onto the bunk beside her as water cascaded over her feet. Blood already dripped from a cut on the back of his head. The knife clattered to the floor.

By now the train was hissing steam, gathering power, but Masha slammed him again, still clinging to the broken bottle.

'Bastard. I hit him,' she said, dropping it.

The man struggled to get up but then fell back, losing consciousness. His eyes rolled back in his head.

'Shit. It's not Otto.' Masha turned to Zofia. 'Who the hell's he?'

'Don't know. He was after the package, though.'

'Shall I brain him again? We can't leave him here. He might get up.'

'We need to call someone, the *provodnitsa.*' Zofia charged into the corridor and almost cannoned into Otto.

'I heard someone shout,' he said. 'What's the matter?'

'Go to hell.'

'Are you all right?' His eyes were anxious.

'Are you spying on us?'

'No, just couldn't sleep. I heard shouting. What's going on?'

'A friend of yours,' she said. 'Broke into our compartment. Masha hit him with a bottle. He tried to rob me, at knifepoint.'

169

'Where did he go?'

'Nowhere. He's still there.' Her voice cracked.

Otto rushed past her towards their door. By the time she followed him in, Masha had Otto's gun pointed to the intruder's head. Zofia took a sharp breath.

'Good God.' Otto stared at Masha and then at the man who was face up on the ground now, his head a bloody mess. One eye was half-closed where her heel had struck him, and there was blood puddling onto the wet floor. 'What have you done?'

'He threatened me with this,' Zofia picked up the knife.

'Careful with that thing!' Otto took a step away.

Zofia held the knife out in front of her. 'Don't you dare come near me.'

Masha turned the gun towards him.

Otto backed away, hands up. 'All right, all right, calm down. Just put the gun away.'

'Calm down? It's your bloody gun. I found it in your luggage,' Masha said.

'Be careful! I mean it might—'

'Go off?' Masha said. 'I know what I'm doing.'

She wasn't serious, was she? Did she know how to use it? Zofia was still too shocked to think.

'Who is he?' Otto gestured at the man on the floor who was sprawled face up between the two bunks.

'Don't you know him? He was after the Sugihara papers,' Masha said.

'Never seen him before.'

'Then why was he after the papers?' Zofia had recovered enough to speak, but shock meant she still clung to the knife, a heavy-handled thing with a long blade.

Otto's expression was drawn. 'I've told you. I don't know who he is, I swear. We should fetch someone, the police, anybody.'

'And then what d'you think would happen?' Masha snapped. 'They'd arrest us all.'

'No. Search him first, see if you can find out who he is,' Zofia said. 'What shall I do with this?' She waved the knife.

Otto winced. 'Get rid of it. Masha, go and check there's no one in the corridor.'

Otto tried to shake the man awake, but got no response except a groan and then another lapse into silence. Zofia rummaged through the man's pockets. He was still breathing. She searched gingerly, heart hammering, afraid he'd suddenly jump up. 'No papers.'

'Then he's too clean,' Otto said. 'He doesn't want anyone to know who he is.' He sat back on his haunches.

Masha returned. 'There are cars parked by the station, even though it's the middle of the night. One of them must be his. What shall we do? We can't just leave him in here. He might wake up at any minute.' Masha was strangely calm. 'We need to get him out of here – off the train before he has a chance to come round.'

'Someone will see,' Zofia said in rising panic. 'Then they'll definitely arrest us all.'

'We have to do it as the train's leaving,' Masha said, matter of fact. 'Before it picks up speed. Try to drag him to the door, then throw him out.' She pointed the gun at Otto. 'And you're going to help us.'

'All right, all right!' Otto said. 'Give me that back. It could go off.'

'No chance.'

Zofia lurched and grabbed the side of the bunk. 'Oh hell, the train's moving.' A screech of metal as the train shunted again and jerked back before it began to chug slowly forwards.

The man on the ground groaned, semi-conscious.

'Drag him, hurry.' Masha seemed to have taken charge and she and Otto dragged him by the ankles to the door, his head bumping along the corridor. 'Help us, Zofia!'

Zofia was too dazed to think. His padded coat alone was a weight. The panic seemed to sap Zofia's strength, though Otto was stronger than he looked.

'Here, let me.' Masha shoved the gun into Zofia's hand, and told her to keep watch at the end of the corridor in case the train attendant was awake.

Thank God so many were still sleeping. The platform was sliding away and the train wheels gaining momentum.

No train attendant.

Zofia thrust the window down to open the train door from the outside. When she twisted the handle and kicked it open, it whipped back, clanging against the side of the carriage. A blast of icy air made her eyes fill with water. Masha and Otto bundled the man into the doorway. Masha moved like a man, all semblance of girly flightiness gone.

Zofia felt the cold weight of the gun and held it at arm's length, frightened it might go off.

'Not yet,' said Masha to Otto. The air rushed through the door. 'Now.'

They pushed. The cold air revived the man and his eyes filled with panic. He grappled for the doorway a moment before he teetered and dropped away. The sleepers and track whooshed past under Zofia's eyes.

Masha stood for a moment in the doorway, her flowered skirt blowing around her knees.

Otto turned away from the door, rushed into the toilet compartment and vomited.

Masha was about to try to close the door when Zofia pulled her away, 'No! Don't try to close it. You might get sucked out.'

Masha snatched the gun back from Zofia's hand and followed Otto, who was staggering back towards the compartment, wiping his mouth. Zofia followed, light-headed, feeling like she was looking at the train from a long way away.

'What the hell have you done?' Otto asked. 'He's got to be dead.'

'Don't blame me!' Masha said. 'He came into our carriage in the middle of the night and threatened to carve us up! What did you expect us to do?' She held her head high and waved the gun at Otto. 'And don't tell me you're not involved in this some way. This is yours.' She held the gun up in front of his eyes.

'You've really torn it now,' Otto said, a hysterical edge to his voice. 'If Zeitel sent him, when they find him, they'll definitely go to my house.' He was trembling all over.

Zofia sat on the edge of the lower bunk and leant towards him. 'You'd better tell us what's going on because you're making no sense. Who's Zeitel? Who's "they"? The Russians? Are you a refugee? Why didn't Sugihara give you his papers, and why do you want them now?'

'I didn't want to do it. But they threatened me.'

'Who?' Masha demanded.

'Just give me a minute.' He sat down next to Masha, panting, short of breath. 'The German Security Office. I'm German. I was born there. They don't want evidence of German atrocities to find its way to Japan.'

'I knew it,' Zofia said. 'You disgust me.'

'The Germans are negotiating a deal with the Japanese, and those papers of Bronovski's could stymie their plan. I was supposed to get the papers back, and if you wouldn't hand them over, I was supposed to kill you to get them. But I couldn't. I'm not brave enough.'

Masha let out a low hissing whistle. She barked out an amused laugh. 'That's bad.'

Zofia blinked. She couldn't believe what Otto was actually planning. And she'd trusted him when all the time ... 'So who was that man who got on at Novosibirsk?'

'I don't know. I was supposed to deliver to them at the previous stop, but I flunked it. I'm not cut out for this sort of thing. They picked the wrong man. I don't want to hurt anyone. I don't want any trouble.'

'Looks like it's found you anyway, kid,' said Masha.

'If they sent one man, they might send others after us,' Zofia said. 'Who are these people?'

Otto explained about a Nazi called Zeitel and how he'd made threats to him and his mother.

'So what will you do now?' asked Zofia.

'I don't know. After what we've just done, I can't even think straight.'

'Are you a Nazi? Whose side are you on?' Zofia asked.

'I'm not on any side. I got caught up in this somehow and I just want out.'

Masha smiled as if she was enjoying it all. 'Well, you're not getting your gun back, for a start.' She opened her handbag and dropped it inside.

A moment's hiatus amid the rattle of the train. Outside the black night roared past.

'We were well out of the station when he fell from the train,' Zofia said, her voice still shaky. 'It will just look like an accident, won't it? He hit his head as he fell, okay?'

'True. We did nothing,' Masha agreed. 'Just pretend it never happened.'

Otto shook his head. 'He might have survived.'

'No.' Masha was definite. 'Not out there. It must be below freezing.'

Zofia's voice shook. 'He could make it back to the station, couldn't he?'

It was a possibility none of them wanted to consider.

'We need to clear up,' said Masha.

'I've got a towel,' Otto said.

For the next forty minutes they scrubbed silently at the linoleum floors of the compartment and corridor in the howling draught from the open door. Otto too was on his hands and knees. 'Someone's coming!' he cried. They shot back into the compartment.

Outside, voices and then shortly after, the train slowed. They heard the clang as someone shut the flapping door. They stayed rigid, listening until the voices receded.

'Were you getting off the train?' Otto asked. 'What's with the outdoor clothes?'

'We were scared. We found out you had a gun. We wanted to get away from you.'

Otto stood up and looked Zofia in the eyes, contrite. 'I would never have done it,' he said. 'I swear it. I hoped … I hoped we were friends. And I'd never have had the nerve.' He sat on the edge of the bunk and pressed his shaking hands to his knees. 'That man – I think Zeitel must have sent him. When I didn't deliver at Omsk I guess they sent someone else. So the big question is: what will they do next? I'm guessing they're not going to give up. And even if he's dead, we have to assume they'll find a body.'

'We need to give them the papers,' Zofia said. 'So they stop going after us.' An idea struck her. After a moment she said, 'They don't know what the package looks like, okay? So what's to stop us making up a fake one, and you can deliver it?'

Otto seemed struck dumb.

'Neat,' Masha said. 'We should have thought of that before.'

'How about this?' Zofia was warming to the idea. 'We write out some fake testimonies, seal them up in some sort of package, with a forged seal and Japanese *kanji* copied from the real parcel. We need the real seal to show the people in Tokyo, but it might take the Nazis a while to figure out a fake. Otto will deliver the fake and pretend he did actually kill me. Meanwhile, I'll hide along with the real papers and keep them safe.'

'Hell, it might work,' Masha said. 'Worth a try.'

'You're not thinking straight. This isn't a child's game,' Otto said. 'These are not men to mess with. They'll be armed. And anyway, how do I get a message to them that I even have it?'

'You can't. But the next stop isn't until Krasnoyarsk. I memorized the timetable,' said Masha. 'We've got at least a day and a half before we get there, and meanwhile no one can get on or off. When we get there, we'll have to hope your Nazi friends are waiting.'

'Are you kidding? I hope to God no one is, and they'll have forgotten all about it,' said Otto.

'Ha!' Masha scoffed. 'Fat chance. We have to be ready.'

She's actually enjoying herself, thought Zofia. *She's not the woman I thought she was at all, or the woman Jacek thought he knew. And who would have thought she would think to memorize the timetable?*

Otto was twining his hands around each other. 'But what if there's trouble and the Nazis try to take me back to Kaunas?'

'Not our problem,' Masha said. 'You chicken?'

Zofia looked Otto hard in the eye. 'If the Nazis turn up, tell them you really did what Zeitel asked.'

Otto hunched his shoulders and lowered his eyes.

'Tell them I'm dead, hand the package over, and then get back on the train to travel on to Japan and Germany, just like Zeitel told you to do. As far as they're concerned, you just followed Zeitel's orders, but it's a chance for you to escape this whole thing.'

'Whoever they send, surely they'll sense something's wrong because I didn't deliver at Omsk.'

'Then you'll have to convince them all is well,' Masha said. 'Make an excuse and then hand over the package. You don't know exactly what's in it, remember. It will buy us time, that's all. With any luck, it'll take a few days for them to get the package to Zeitel, and maybe a few more hours before it dawns on him it's a fake. And the train will keep going all that time. They'll never catch us up.'

'I'm not sure I can do it. I'm no use at acting.'

'If you don't waylay them, I suspect they'll probably want to search the train, and I'll bet they'll not be as scared as you are of using a gun.'

Otto swallowed, and Zofia saw the small war go on in his eyes before he agreed. 'If I do it, it's for all the refugees still waiting to get out of Lithuania. And I'll do my damnedest to get back on the train.'

Chapter 23

Masha walked up and down the long, swaying corridor but didn't register the view. Illeyvich would never believe it. She was trying to work out the significance of it, the ramifications, and whether braining the bastard had been a good idea.

It felt good to move, although walking the wrong direction down the train was disconcerting. She'd been on edge all day because sitting in a carriage with Zofia and Otto was like walking a cliff edge; she never knew when she might fall. So far she'd kept up the pretence of grieving girlfriend, but it was getting harder all the time not to give herself away. Zofia Kowalski kept eyeing her as if she should be doing something else, when all she could do was copy her and hope it passed as grief. She was surprised how hard his loss had affected her, but she was trying her best to be Russian, to not let emotion get in the way of her job. She stepped aside to let a woman with a flask pass by on her way to the samovar.

She should never have signed up for this assignment. But then again, Illeyvich hadn't exactly given her a choice. Masha went into the toilet compartment and peered into the mirror, a mirror scratched and pocked with brown rust, and was glad to see her face looked the same as always. She got out her lipstick and slicked it on. *There. Better.*

She had to make sure that package stayed on the train. There was something about it that the Nazis were interested in, and she'd bet her life Illeyvich would want to get his hands on it too. Russian agents survived as long as they stayed on the right side of him, otherwise they just disappeared into a gulag somewhere.

There was just one problem. She'd no way to contact him to tell him what she'd found out. The train wasn't going to stop at a station until Krasnoyarsk.

Would Illeyvich be angry she'd killed a Nazi agent, or would he laugh when she told him Otto Wulfsson was supposed to kill Zofia Kowalski for the package but he hadn't the guts to do it? That they'd had to send someone else, and now the mystery Nazi was dead at the side of the track.

She smiled as she washed her hands. The part where they shoved the bastard off the train had been an unexpected treat. The only worrying thing was they might find the corpse and then the authorities would start to ask awkward questions, and Illeyvich would want to know why he hadn't been informed. He always had to know everything. She shook her hands dry because the towel provided was filthy.

Until Krasnoyarsk, she was trapped on here. This was supposed to be a simple journey to Birobidzhan, a simple babysitting job, but now it had turned into something else entirely. Zofia Kowalski was jumpy as hell and twice as suspicious of everyone and everything. From now on, Masha thought, she'd have to keep her head down and say as little as possible. Keep quiet and act dumb. Stick to the plan; that was safest. Get Zofia Kowalski to Birobidzhan. Obey the orders she'd been given.

She examined her lips and rolled them together, checked her teeth for lipstick stains and tilted her head down to see if her roots were growing out. Shit, they were too. And zero chance of getting peroxide on the train.

In Kaunas, Zeitel leant out of his car window and watched the apartment as the soldiers in the truck flooded out and across the road. The road was already pot-holed from Russian tanks, and weeds sprouted in the cracks. The whole city was looking poorer, more decrepit. He sat in his car and ate a bar of Austrian chocolate as he watched Frau Wulfsson being brought downstairs and hustled into the truck. Her face was as pale as raw pastry, and she was still in her nightdress and some sort of housecoat.

A neighbour came running after her, trying to pass her a bag of clothes, but she looked blankly at her as if she had no idea what was going on. It served her right, thought Zeitel. So far, her useless son had failed to deliver the package he was after. He knew it was petty, this revenge, but Otto Wulfsson had been warned, after all.

Zeitel munched his way through the bar and ran his tongue over his clagged teeth. Brandt had called him yesterday at home, tightening the screws, putting pressure on him and giving him more unwelcome news.

'How many second-rate men do you employ, Zeitel?' he'd asked.

There was no answer to that, so he said nothing.

Turned out, Klein had somehow fallen from the train at Novosibirsk and died of a head wound and hypothermia. The call had come this morning. When Wulfsson failed to come up with the goods, naturally he'd sent Klein to get the package back. Paid for him to fly by private airplane to get on at Novosibirsk, and do it quietly, no gunshots, no fuss. Now his best fixer was dead and Brandt hadn't been impressed.

Klein might have had his faults, but Zeitel had been surprised by his death; he was a big man and fit, and a useful man in a fight. So how come he was lying on a cinder track as food for the bears? He could have been left there for weeks. He'd only been found that morning because a farmer had been out to collect coal chippings for his fire. They'd identified him by a tattoo on his neck.

'Accidental death' they were calling it – but he knew the thing stank and so did Brandt.

Even if it had been an accident, it still made him look like an amateur, the fact he'd sent someone who couldn't survive. It would go on his record as a failure. Not that there was such a record, except in Brandt's head, but he was fairly sure Brandt had it all logged as if the record was real.

'How are you going to fix it?' Brandt had asked.

Zeitel was agitated because he had no immediate answers. There was no way to catch up with the train, and Brandt was a man with a reputation. People disappeared on his watch if they didn't pull their weight, and a worm of fear was uncoiling in Zeitel's belly.

The truck was driving off now, Wulfsson's mother hidden by the men in the back, their guns bristling. Zeitel scrunched up the chocolate wrapper and threw it out of the window. Getting old Frau Wulfsson arrested was the only thing he could do today, and it was futile, he knew. But it eased his fear to pass it on to someone else. He'd gone to the Soviet office and told them the woman had been heard praising the old regime and calling Stalin a filthy pig, and that flimsy scrap of hearsay had been enough to get her arrested. He was well aware that it was that easy – if he didn't deliver, then Brandt would arrange for him to be on a truck just like that one.

It made him feel helpless, that whatever he did, he couldn't stop the train. It was like life, it was still escaping, moving further away, and he couldn't keep up with it. Not like the train at home, going round its fixed little circuit, always coming back to the tin guard with his little red flag.

The next chance to do something was Krasnoyarsk.

He'd already wired his contacts there for reinforcements. He'd had to raid his savings to pay for mercenaries – SS men, hardened operatives. Four of them. Maybe that was too many, but he wasn't taking any chances this time.

He got through to his SS contact Fischer at Krasnoyarsk, and explained the importance of the parcel. After Zeitel had agreed to wire him the money, Fischer agreed to search the train, arrest Otto Wulfsson and bring in the woman.

Wulfsson should be a pushover, and the other was just a woman. How hard could it be?

Chapter 24

Otto slept badly. His heart was stuttering, as if it couldn't keep up, and at every footfall he kept thinking someone was coming after him. The pale dawn came too soon, to reveal a landscape devoid of anything except a prairie of bog and thinly spread snow. The windows were so steamed that rivulets of water ran down the inside.

Across from him, he could hear the women's breathing. But they too were restless, tossing and turning as the train rumbled on. He was back in his old bunk, the one he used to have under Jacek. Thoughts of how the NKVD just bundled Jacek away still gave him feelings of panic, though now he felt he was not so alone.

The two women weren't exactly friends now, but they weren't enemies either and there was some solidarity in that. He was supposed to help if anyone came into their compartment again, but these women were terrifying in their capability. They'd killed the last man, good as.

They hadn't threatened him again with the gun, and he hadn't insisted they give it back. He supposed that keeping it made them feel more secure, though he worried that Masha might fire it by accident. She was an odd character, one minute cold and belligerent, the other charming and naive. Sometimes he caught her looking at him in a strange, calculating way that unnerved him.

Women. They were all a mystery. And he hardly dared admit it to himself but every time he caught the sparkle in Zofia's eyes, his chest ached with longing.

Otto dozed as the sun came up. When he finally sat up and looked across, they were both busy writing. They'd got pieces of paper from the students further down the train and Dr Rabinowitz's assistant had loaned them pens and ink, so there was quite a pile of papers already on the table by the window.

Masha was copying carefully, letter for letter.

'Can you read Polish?' he asked her, propping himself up on an elbow.

Masha shook her head. 'Only Lithuanian and Russian. These are such long words and such a strange writing.'

'Come on, Otto,' Zofia said. 'We need some different handwriting. Can you do one in like a cursive, and one in block print?'

'What shall I write?'

'Just copy the Polish. You can speak Polish, can't you?'

'A little. Enough to copy. You don't mind me reading them?'

'No. But just be careful not to damage them.'

The papers were fragile, dog-eared, sometimes stained. At first, he treated the testimonies gently as though they might bite, because men were prepared to kill for them, but then, once he began reading, he couldn't stop. He hadn't understood before what the Nazis were doing in Poland. The cruelty, the beatings, the rape. The smell of burning buildings, the broken glass, the pitiful attempts to save the family dog. He'd seen the effect the papers had on Sugihara, and now he realized why he had not entrusted him, a German, with this evidence. It hurt, but he could understand it.

He was sceptical of the reports at first, thinking them exaggerated, but the more papers he read, the more a cold wash seemed to flow over him, and the more he was both disgusted and ashamed, full of hate for his countrymen.

The photographs made him almost choke. It felt indecent to even look at them. He pushed them back inside their flimsy envelope.

At the very bottom of the pile he came across Zofia's own testimony. He recognized it, for he'd seen her writing it on embassy paper in Sugihara's office, but had no idea what it contained. He'd closed himself off from it, he realized. He'd shut his ears to the people's stories of brutality, thinking of them all as just an inconvenience, as 'trouble' he could do without.

A lump of gristle seemed to form in his throat as he read what she had already lost. Her family and her homeland, her father's terrible uncalled-for death. And then her brother, taken from the train.

He looked up and caught her gaze. 'I'm sorry,' he said. 'I can't copy this.'

She looked up, her mouth pressed together.

'I just didn't know any of it,' he said. 'Or rather I knew, but somehow it hadn't penetrated, what it actually meant.'

Masha looked up from where she was painstakingly copying a letter. 'People are devils, aren't they,' she said. 'What makes people think they can do it, ride over folk like they're horse shit? The bosses treated the workers like they were worth nothing. But then my father was the same. He'd get angry and then want to hit someone smaller. Beat the shit out of me sometimes with his belt. Just because he was bigger, I think. Went on all the time in our house. Guess it's the same with countries – the bigger ones just want to beat up the smaller ones because they can.'

He looked up, surprised. Masha's words were bitter but had the ring of truth about them.

'Sounds tough, Masha. It must have been hard to live with,' Zofia said.

A shrug. 'You get used to it. It's what you're brought up to.' Masha wafted the paper she was copying in the air and the moment vanished. She took on a more lively tone. 'My handwriting

184

is godawful. Didn't have much education, see. Hope it will do.'

Zofia picked it up. She wondered what it must be like to copy and not understand a word. 'It's good. People wrote these in a hurry.'

For the next few hours there was simply the sound of pens scratching on paper, as the three of them wrote out letters in different styles of handwriting.

'That should be enough,' Otto said. 'As long as it looks convincing from a quick glance. By the time they open it, fingers crossed we'll be in Vladivostok. I just have to hope they think I don't know about the switch, that I appear blameless. That way, they won't take it out on my mother.'

Zofia's throat tightened. She knew the Nazis to be ruthless. 'We have no photographs,' she said.

Otto shrugged. 'They won't know that until they open it.'

'Eight more days,' Masha said. 'Let's hope they don't open it immediately.'

'What about the packaging? We'll need brown paper and string.'

Zofia said, 'Maybe we could ask the *provodnitsa*? I'll go and see if I can find her.'

'No, best not to let anyone know what we're doing. Leave it to me. I'll get us some.' Masha was out of the compartment before they could stop her.

'She will too,' Zofia said to him. 'She's totally brazen. She'd convince you to give her the buttons off your coat if she thought she could get away with it.'

'I feel sorry for her. She had a rough kind of upbringing.'

'You're really on our side, aren't you?' Zofia looked up at him with her clear brown eyes.

Otto swallowed. 'I'm just on the side of what's right. I just want everything to go back to how it was before – before the war. People just living their lives.'

Zofia held his gaze, and he had to look away for fear she'd see his attraction for her. 'The genie back in the bottle,' she said. 'But it's not up to us. All we can do is play our part, and Jacek made a promise to Sugihara in exchange for our escape. He couldn't have known what it would lead to. But it's our promise, not yours. It was bad of us to push you into taking risks for us. Especially if you think it might affect your mother. If you feel you can't do it, you have to tell me.'

Otto thought about it a moment. 'It's the same risk I agreed to with Zeitel. The only thing is, I'm doing it for you and not for him, and it feels better this way. To choose rather than be threatened.'

'Is that why you decided to help us?'

'I suppose. I kind of liked you. I admired the way you fought off that intruder. I couldn't imagine doing it, that's why. How you could decide things, like the cold courage it took to take the decision to drop him from the train.'

'There wasn't a choice. Masha was right.'

'I guess not. The train does something too – it's the constant movement.' He felt like they were bound together by it. The everyday routine of it. How he'd watched her brush her hair, seen the way she pushed out her lips to blow on her tea, and how before bed she carefully put her scuffed shoes side by side. 'What I worry about most is whether there'll be time to call Ma,' he said. 'She'll be worried. I told her it would be a short trip. I'm going to tell her to stay with a friend, somewhere out of Kaunas where it's safer.'

'Good idea. You know it'll come out sooner or later that the documents are copies and the real ones are in Japan with General Sato.' Her voice was gentle.

He shook his head as if ridding himself of a fly. 'I can't think about the ifs or I'd never do anything. I realize now that that's what I've done all my life. Worry about the ifs and be afraid of the future. Yesterday I saw all at once that a five foot tall woman was fiercer and braver than I was. It shocked me. I've sat out the war and hoped it would just go away, but now I have to do my bit. For you, and for all the others waiting to get out of Lithuania.'

'Friends, then?' She held out a hand to Otto, and he took it in his and clasped it in a tight squeeze.

'Friends,' he said, feeling heat rise to his face. 'Look, once we've done these papers, I think you and Masha should move compartments. In case they jump you again. There's a vacant compartment at the end of the corridor. Number six. They must have got off at the last stop. If you move down there, it might be safer. I'm sorry, but Zeitel's men know which one you're in.'

She watched him squirm before she glanced at the passing landscape of flat snow-crusted marsh. 'There are no stops between here and Krasnoyarsk.'

'I know. But there could be a fuel stop, and I'm only trying to keep you out of danger. I don't know what will happen at Krasnoyarsk, or who will be waiting. Maybe they won't believe me, won't believe you're dead, and still search the train.'

'I could conceal the package somewhere.'

'They'd still threaten you, pressure you to find out where it is.' He didn't want to use the word 'torture'.

'I hadn't thought of that.' Zofia thought for a moment. 'What about if I have a disguise?'

'I suppose. It'd be better than nothing. Masha might help. She was in a lot of plays at school, she says. Maybe she'll have some ideas. The main thing is to try to blend in with other people or find somewhere to hide.'

'Hide? Where? There's nowhere on this train. But I'll ask Masha. She's got a few more clothes in her luggage than I do, at least.'

Otto helped the women move their luggage and belongings into the other compartment. He had to hope no one had booked that compartment at Krasnoyarsk, but then again they could always move back once they'd got out of the station.

His stomach was already roiling at just the thought of it. He had no idea who or what would be waiting for him, but he tried his best to hide his fears from the women.

187

The fake package had been wrapped in brown paper and string that Masha, who was being ultra-helpful, had stolen from a different parcel in the luggage compartment. Zofia had written the *kanji*, even though it was something he felt he could have done better. She wanted to practise writing Japanese and, to his surprise, she had done a very good forgery for one who didn't speak the language.

He'd enjoyed watching her concentration and the way she copied so carefully. He couldn't help looking at her long, slender neck and her dark eyelashes. He had never seen a girl so beautiful.

She had a quiet kind of authority; it had been her idea to use beetroot juice for the ink, by saving bits of borscht from the restaurant car, and to make a passable-looking seal from a stub of candle wax. Masha flirted with him at every opportunity, avid for details of his life with Sugihara, but he had no interest in her at all. It was Zofia who had captured his heart.

When the package was done, they toasted it with hot black tea from the samovar.

It would have to do. No one knew what the real package looked like, after all.

Afterwards Zofia insisted on mending and resealing the real package. 'It makes me feel better to have it secure again,' she said to him. 'Like putting the world to rights.'

He looked at her white face; the pale porcelain skin, the way her hair grew in a widow's peak, and it made him shiver. He could never tell her, though, that he had fallen for her. He feared she might laugh at him, and there'd be no taking it back once it was out.

'You'll come back to our compartment to tell us once you've delivered it, won't you?' Masha asked.

He reassured them, though he was almost sick with nerves.

Now he was alone in the empty compartment as the train rumbled through the early hours, eating up the miles. The fake package was there on the table next to his bunk and he had to face what was coming at Krasnoyarsk, even though he knew it might not be good. In some dim way, he knew Ma would be proud of him. But he was ready to use his wits, and to try to convince whoever came that Zofia was dead and this was the real Sugihara package.

Chapter 25

When Zofia suggested it, Masha was not very encouraging about the disguise. 'We can't do much. I haven't anything except what's in my suitcase, and a different dress will hardly make you disappear. You'll still look the same but in more fashionable clothes. I suppose one of us could dress in Jacek's clothes from his bag so we look like a couple, but I can't see either of us getting away with being a man.'

'Especially not you,' Zofia said.

Masha smiled as if this was a compliment.

A knock at their door, which made them both jump. Thinking it might be Otto, Zofia put her ear to the door, 'Who is it?'

'*Provodnitsa*.' A female voice. Zofia opened the door. Tonya was outside, an armful of bedding in her hands. 'You need clean sheets?' she asked. 'More soap?'

'Thank you,' said Masha, standing aside to allow her to pass.

They watched, moving their belongings as Tonya whipped off the old sheets and flapped out new ones, tucking them in with brisk efficiency.

'Have you moved?' Tonya said, frowning. 'I thought you were further down.'

'No, this is ours,' Masha said, brazening it out.

Tonya seemed to accept it as she busied herself winding the dirty sheets into a ball. 'All done. We'll be in Krasnoyarsk soon.'

'How much longer?' asked Zofia.

'An hour or so, that's all.' Tonya bundled up the old bedding in a business-like manner and took it away.

'That's it,' Zofia said, once she'd gone. 'That's how I can disguise myself and hide the parcel. Dress like a *provodnitsa*, and carry around a load of sheets.'

Masha's eyes took on a glint as she leant forward in her seat. 'You know what? It might work. If only we could get hold of a uniform.'

'They'll probably be in the linen stores next to first class,' Zofia said, 'but the door's kept locked. I passed one of the other attendants the other day, you know, when I went the wrong way to the toilet near the dining car. They were opening it with a key.'

'Then we'll have to break in. You can keep watch.'

Zofia felt doubt creep in. 'Is there time? What if someone sees us? We could get caught.'

'And it's worse than being caught by the Nazis?' Masha seemed amused.

Zofia didn't like being laughed at by Masha. 'All right. But we'll have to do it now.'

'I'll need to look at the lock,' Masha said without missing a beat. 'But a hairpin or a penknife should do it.'

A few minutes later they were navigating their way down the train towards first class, Masha in the lead, and Zofia behind, her knapsack on her back, not only to hold the parcel, but also the uniform if they could get one.

The train was long and they had to sway through more second-class corridors and finally the dining car adjacent to first class. In the dining car a few passengers were reading the papers or drinking glasses of tea in metal holders.

As they passed, one of the men near the end of the car looked up from his newspaper. Haru. He was smiling at her now, in an open friendly way, but she knew she couldn't stop to talk to him. He leapt up to open the door for them at the end of the carriage where the kitchen corridor was. Masha ignored him, but Zofia, suddenly hot and embarrassed, thanked him politely in Russian, hoping he couldn't see her nerves written on her face. What if he came along while they were breaking in? They were obviously not first-class passengers. Wouldn't he wonder where they were going?

She had no time to consider him more because Masha was striding ahead, past the polished wood doors in the first-class corridor, until they came to the row of store cupboards located just before the guard's van. Thankfully, the corridor was empty.

'Stay over there by the door to first class,' Masha said. 'Call out if you see anyone. It's more likely to be a *provodnitsa* from that side than a conductor from the front.'

'Okay, but be quick.' Zofia stood by the door, looking through the glass window to the corridor as behind her, Masha fiddled with the cupboard door. Somehow it didn't surprise her in the least that Masha knew how to pick a lock.

While she was there, she saw Haru approach the first-class compartment and open it for his companion, a shorter fatter Japanese man with a balding head. As she watched he glanced up to see her looking, and hurriedly she dodged out of the way of the door. When she looked back, he'd gone and the corridor was empty.

Masha, meanwhile, had got the cupboard open and was rummaging inside.

A glance back showed her one of the waiters, a blond-haired man in a green waistcoat, striding up towards them.

'Someone's coming!'

Masha pushed the door shut and hurried towards her, carrying a bundle of green. She thrust it into Zofia's hands and Zofia began shoving it down into her bag. Behind Masha she saw the cupboard door swing open again as the train rounded a bend, but there was no time to go back because the door to the dining car opened and the waiter was there. They were blocking his path.

'Can I help you?' he asked.

'I thought there might be toilets this way,' Zofia said, hiding the bag behind her.

'You're at the wrong end of the dining car. It's back the other way.'

'Oh, thank you,' Masha said, simpering at him. 'Being on a moving train is so confusing.'

They hurried away. Now the dining car was empty, but they passed Tonya pushing a trolley full of sheets as they went down the train. When she went into another compartment, Masha grabbed a few folded sheets from the trolley. Zofia hoped Tonya wouldn't notice the linen had gone. It made Zofia anxious to think she might.

In their compartment, Masha pulled down the blinds so no one could see in while Zofia changed. The unfamiliar green jacket and skirt smelt of dry-cleaning fluid, but she fastened up the brass buttons and tied back her hair into a tight knot in the style of the other *provodnitsas*. Shame she had the wrong shoes – Tonya had ankle boots so she could get out in the snow, but Zofia hoped no one would notice her feet.

'Does it look convincing?' Zofia adjusted the little green hat and smoothed down the uniform skirt.

'The jacket's too big,' Masha said. 'You're too skinny. Here, put this belt on to pull it in.' She handed her one of her belts.

'How long now until the station?'

Masha looked at her wristwatch. 'I reckon about half an hour.'

'I wonder what Otto's doing.'

'Well, you can't go out and look. You might bump into Tonya, and then we really would be in trouble.'

Zofia tried not to think of Otto and what might be waiting for them at Krasnoyarsk. Maybe there'd be no one and all this dressing-up and stealing sheets would be for nothing. She folded all the bedding on her bed and piled it up, storing the package between the layers.

Although her Russian was good, Zofia knew she'd never been any good at play-acting. She had always been 'the servant' in school plays, too self-conscious to act a bigger part. So her mouth was dry and she kept playing with the scarf she was supposed to wear. She wasn't sure she could do this.

Masha seemed taken by the idea and had relished dressing up as an older woman with a scarf wrapped around her brassy hair like a *babushka*, and a shapeless old jacket of Jacek's buttoned up over her clothes. They'd agreed the Nazis would be looking for young women, so she should try to appear older.

She hunched over and scowled. 'Do I look like I could be someone's mother?'

Zofia was surprised to find Masha's body language was actually convincing. Masha had rubbed off her lipstick and sucked in her lips so she looked old, and her frown scored lines down her cheeks. But would it be enough? 'I don't know. It's dark, so maybe. But not close up.'

Masha shrugged. 'Well, it's the best I can do. We'll have to hope that if anyone comes, they don't look too closely.'

Zofia wondered why it was that she never felt really close to Masha, even when they were doing something together like this. When it was just the two of them, Zofia realized she knew hardly anything about her. After Jacek had been arrested, she'd assumed Masha would get off the train and go straight back home, yet here she was. What did she plan to do when they got to Vladivostok without Jacek? Jacek was never far from her own thoughts, yet Masha rarely spoke of him. It was as if to her, he'd never existed.

'I hope Otto manages to pass the package over,' Zofia said.

'Why don't you just get rid of it? Jacek wouldn't blame you. It's causing us all sorts of trouble.'

It was tempting. Once Otto had delivered the fake papers, what was to stop her simply throwing Sugihara's package away? Then, even if she was searched, the Germans would find nothing. But it was too late for that; Otto had told her Zeitel knew she had it, and he wasn't going to give up looking for her.

'Because I can't forget Jacek's face when the Russians took him,' she said. She and Jacek had always been able to guess each other's thoughts, and she remembered the insistence that she should take his rucksack, the very last time she had the chance to look into his eyes and know what he was thinking. He had trusted her to take the package and the only thing she could do now to bring him close was send him her thoughts. *Stay strong. Survive.*

Masha had lost her frown and was looking thoughtful. 'I think it must be the photographs they're after, they could be worth something to the press.'

Zofia dragged her mind back to the conversation. 'I hope so. As long as we can get them to General Sato, he'll know what to do.'

Zofia gazed from the window. She felt self-conscious in this green wool uniform that itched around the neck.

The battery lights had come on in their carriage. Outside, the yellowish lamps of the city glimmered on the horizon as the train curved around the bend. Boxy silhouettes of factory buildings and a grey ghost of snow on the ground. Masha seemed curiously calm, but Zofia couldn't stop fidgeting.

Was she a fool to trust Otto? What if he didn't hand over the package but instead told the waiting Nazis where to find her? She was relying on a man who'd been asked to kill her, and she'd no idea what he was thinking at this very moment.

She brushed down the unfamiliar uniform for the twentieth time and wondered how she'd come to this. Why kindness in the world seemed to have vanished, like a sun setting.

Slowly the train eased into the station and lights began to shine through the windows and into the carriage.

'Krasnoyarsk.' She read the Russian sign aloud. 'This is it.'

Masha pulled her scarf lower over her forehead, and glanced at Zofia's taut features under the green hat. She remembered the thrill of waiting in the wings for the play to begin, that flush of nerves and the heat of excitement that seemed to fizz in her veins. The expectant noise of an audience rustling in their seats, and the smell of the heavy velvet drapes as she waited for them to swish back.

But here there was no audience and there'd be no applause. If their disguises failed, they'd be in trouble. Getting dressed up like this was an amateur solution for a problem that needed a professional one, but it was the best they could do, hurtling through the Siberian *taiga* with no access to a telephone.

If she was arrested, Illeyvich would have to vouch for her.

The other possibility, that they might be assassinated, she deliberately put to one side. Masha knew how it worked; she needed to prove her allegiance to the Party if she wanted to advance. She was used to the cut-throat competitiveness that lay hidden beneath the idea of communism, the unswerving loyalty to Mother Russia that made the Russians who they were. It was the thing that inspired her, the feeling of being a part of something so vast.

She was armed under her coat – not that Zofia needed to know that. If the Germans killed Otto at Krasnoyarsk, then that would be of little account, but she was determined to fulfil her patriotic duty and make sure that Zofia Kowalski and her precious parcel made it to Birobidzhan, where Illeyvich's comrades would be meeting her.

Chapter 26

Otto wiped his forehead with his free hand, wishing the cold sweat was not so obvious. He had his overcoat over his suit and tie, and it was buttoned up right to the collar. He hadn't expected the weather to turn so bitterly cold. Dusk turned the approaching platform grey and grainy and the wind was already piercing as he pressed down the window so he could reach out to open the door. A milling crowd of people five deep ranged along the length of the train; anxious passengers, all different face shapes, rich fur-clad Russians, the colourful flat-faced Kazakhs and the dark-eyed Tatars, all waiting under the sulphurous gas lamps of the station.

Servants wheeling trolleys piled high with luggage yelled at passengers to make way, and hawkers crowded forward with wheedling cries, pushing their baskets and trays at the windows.

Just outside the station doors, armed Russian soldiers stood stamping their boots and smoking, rifles slung over their grey greatcoats. They were half-hidden from view and paying no attention to the train. Otto searched for people who looked German, like they might be waiting for him, and glimpsed two burly men approaching the door.

Both over six feet tall. One with a moustache, one without. Men in big overcoats and fur hats with earmuffs. No luggage.

Instinct told him they'd come for him.

Zeitel's men. It was them, had to be.

He swept his eyes left to right, to where two other men, dressed almost identically, were waiting further along the platform and scanning the carriages. His stomach turned to water.

The train was gliding the last few feet along the platform edge and the crowd jostled towards it. The waiting passengers left a gap for people to dismount from the train, and behind him other travellers pushed him forwards.

I am a German agent like them, he said to himself, trying to bolster his confidence. *We are Nazi colleagues. There is nothing to fear.*

The iron wheels creaked and the train jerked to a halt. Before he could even think, he was jumping down the steps, holding the forged parcel up over his head as he wended his way through the crowd. They must have had a description because all four men closed in on him.

'You are Otto Wulfsson?' demanded the man who had grabbed him by the elbow.

Otto shrank back. The German language disconcerted him. His voice came out high-pitched and breathy in reply. 'Did Zeitel send you?'

'Yes. I'm Fischer. You have something for us?'

He tried to calm his voice and take on the persona of a Nazi agent. 'Good evening, gentlemen.' He held out the parcel. 'The package from the Jew Bronovski. See, it is still sealed.' He stumbled over the German, and the knife-like wind made his eyes water.

His attempt at politeness was futile. The package had already been snatched from his grip and though he tried to pause on the platform, Fischer propelled him towards the station exit. On his left was the other man with the moustache, flanking him, and the other two behind.

'What about the girl, Zofia Kowalski?' asked Fischer, still gripping his arm, his breath a cloud of steam in the cold night air.

'Where is she?'

'Dead. I ditched her just after Novosibirsk. Threw her off the train.'

Now Fischer stopped. 'Like Klein, our man at Sverdlovsk? He was a good man. A personal friend of mine.'

Otto found himself looking into a craggy face and eyes sharp with enmity.

'Who's Klein?' It was surprisingly easy to lie. 'I've never met anyone called Klein.'

Fischer turned to the two behind. 'Check he's telling the truth. Search the train for the Kowalski woman. Start at Carriage C. You've got twelve minutes before it departs.'

'You won't find her. She's dead, I tell you.' But the men behind him had turned and were already striding towards the train. He tried another polite request, 'Now if you'll release my arm, I'm to travel on to Vladivostok and from there to Berlin.'

The grip tightened. 'Zeitel wants you brought in,' said Fischer. 'You have a few questions to answer.'

Meanwhile the other man holding the package turned it over to examine it. 'It's unopened and looks like it's got Sugihara's seal,' he said. 'Let's see what Hauptscharführer Wagner in Krasnoyarsk has to say. Zeitel's sent him instructions.'

Fischer nodded. 'Okay, Siegel, move it.'

The other man grasped him by the sleeve.

Otto's heart seemed to tighten into a knot. The last thing he needed; interrogation by the SS. 'There's been a miscommunication,' he said desperately. 'Zeitel gave me strict instructions to go on to Vladivostok and from there to Berlin.'

'Nice try, but those orders have been superseded,' said Fischer.

Otto resisted as Siegel and Fischer began to steer him towards the exit. Eager hawkers stepped in front of them, brandishing cheap keyrings and cigarettes, but the men were unstoppable and just barged past. Ahead of them people with bundles and cases were crowding through the narrow exit to the road outside.

'What about my luggage?' Otto shouted to Fischer over the station announcements and the hubbub. He was still trying to reason with him. 'I need to go back for my suitcase.'

No answer. Each man had a grasp on one arm as they hustled him along. Fischer was heavier and determined, and Otto's struggles were like waves hitting a sea wall. He thought of Zofia and of the other men searching the train, and prayed they would not find her.

Through the narrow archway under the streetlights, hazy in the half-light, he glimpsed a string of parked cars, and it set off a jangle of terror. If he didn't act now, he'd be driven away, and then the chances of any kind of escape would be nil. The words of the testimonies of the Polish Jews echoed in his head.

There were steps down to the exit. Fischer's sidekick had one hand holding the package. Knowing this, Otto summoned all his strength and as he was mid-step he barrelled sideways so his captor lost his balance. With a desperate wrench he broke free. A sharp pain in his shoulder muscle as he tore his arm from Fischer's grip and shot back up the steps. Dodging past other passengers, he sprinted away.

He heard Fischer's voice shout, 'Siegel! Stop him.'

Feet pounding, Otto blundered down the platform with no sense of direction, he was just running to get away from those men. He was aware of passengers separating, curious faces staring as he shot past, and the huge flank of the train towering alongside him.

A dry crack. And then screaming. People running for cover.

A wild-eyed woman dragged her toddler out of his path. Otto glanced behind and Fischer's friend Siegel was strolling towards him, a pistol smoking in his hand. In an instant he took in that Siegel must have passed the package to Fischer, and that he couldn't have seen the soldiers by the doors. Siegel was a man so solid, he didn't look like he could run. He raised the gun again, in an almost leisurely way.

Otto ducked and ran.

Another crack and something hit the side of the train with a sharp metallic clang.

Otto thrashed his way up the platform, the rectangles of the illuminated windows of first class flashing by.

The train seemed to go on forever. Past the coal wagon, past the locomotive.

Surprisingly, frighteningly, despite appearing leisurely, Siegel's shadow covered a lot of ground. Otto took his chance to put the locomotive between them and, running ahead of the huge engine, jumped down onto the track.

He landed awkwardly, jarring an ankle on the cinders, but scrambled along the track, round the back of the engine, skirting the coal tender and the first few carriages and aiming for the shadow of the train.

Another sharp crack as his pursuer took another shot between the couplings, but it ricocheted off the coal wagon. From the other side of the train Otto heard Siegel's feet land and the crunch of gravel as the man followed him.

'Stop!' A shout in Russian.

Shit. The shots and commotion must have drawn the attention of the soldiers.

A quick glance between the carriages made him stumble as NKVD soldiers rushed towards the train, rifles ready and excited for trouble.

'Hands up!' A volley of shouts.

Otto peered around the edge of the first carriage, his legs shaking so much he could barely stand. Siegel was surrounded and had dropped his gun, his hands clasped above his head, but to his horror, one of the soldiers jumped down onto the track to see what Siegel had been firing at.

Otto let out a whimper of despair, quickly suppressed. If they caught him, it would be the gulag for sure. His chest heaved and his breath came in hoarse puffs of steam. He put his hand over his nose to try to quiet himself. Adrenaline coursed through his veins like fire. It made him alert and gave him enough muscle for a sudden spurt of speed.

He dashed alongside the train and jumped up onto the coupling between a carriage and what looked to be a luggage van, where he clung to a narrow housing around the closed door and flattened himself out of sight.

Footsteps came towards him, crunching on the frozen cinders. He stared out into the dwindling light, hardly daring to blink.

Meanwhile, on board the women waited. They heard the clang of doors and the noise of passengers getting on, the thuds of luggage being thrown into overhead nets, the shuffle of feet along the corridor, along with the familiar smell of iron, coal and steam.

'Otto hasn't come back yet,' Zofia said.

'I'll go into the corridor,' Masha said. 'See if I can see him on the platform.'

She eased herself up like an old woman and peered out. A few moments later she was back in and closing the door with a bang. 'There are two men searching the compartments. They're throwing open every door. They're already at number three.'

'Shit. This is it. Dim the lights.'

She grabbed the pile of sheets and tried to look busy. Just in time, for the door opened and two big men were suddenly in their space. She turned to greet them.

'Can I help you?' She tried for a pleasant manner, despite the fact they were crowding her.

'We're looking for a woman called Zofia Kowalski. We were told this carriage.'

The uniform was working. They just assumed she was the train attendant.

'Miss Kowalski?' Zofia shook her head. 'Sorry, sir, but I think she got off at Novosibirsk. Is there a problem?'

'Which was her bed?'

Masha pointed to the one behind Zofia.

Zofia stood aside, clutching the pile of sheets within which the parcel was hiding.

Rigid, she watched them search under the mattress and all around the bed. *Please don't search me,* she thought.

Finding nothing, the men exchanged glances. 'Did she leave anything behind?'

'I don't think so,' said Masha in an old person's voice.

'The compartment has been emptied and cleaned since then,' said Zofia putting on an indignant expression. 'If she's left anything, it will be in the luggage wagon with the other lost property. It's the third carriage down from the engine, before first class.' Thank goodness she'd noticed that.

One of the men turned to the other. 'Have we got time?'

'If we hurry.' And as suddenly as they came, they were gone.

A metallic clang of the door as they went through to the next carriage. Outside, the last-minute slamming of doors as the train prepared to depart.

Zofia held her breath until the whistle blew, and then slowly, the train began to slide forwards. She didn't move but was aware of the shift of gravity as the wheels turned on the tracks. Had the men gone or would they come back?

Zofia slumped onto her bunk, drained.

Masha shot into the corridor, where she was silent, staring out of the train window, unbuttoning her coat and pulling the scarf from her hair. 'The men got off,' she said, jubilant, as she came back in. 'I saw them on the platform.'

The train was just easing its way out from under the dim station canopy. Outside, a sharp crack like a gunshot. Then more. Men shouting in Russian.

'What the hell?'

'Soldiers, they're firing at something.' Masha pushed her back inside. 'Best stay away from the doors.'

Otto held his breath as he waited, clamped against the icy body-work of the train. The engine began to fire up, building a head of steam. A hiss as the expansion of steam pushed the pistons into motion. The metal rod connected to the wheels creaked. Shouts and the shrill pierce of the whistle in the damp misty air. He risked a peek around the corner. The Russian soldier was still creeping towards him, rifle ready, his figure just a moving black shape barely visible in the increasing darkness.

At the train whistle, the soldier stopped, then obviously fearing he'd be in the path of the engine, turned and began to run back the way he'd come. Otto's heart thumped loud in his chest.

No time for him to run back or follow. The train would depart any moment.

The carriages shunted together and he winced at the grind of iron against iron on the coupler. A sudden shunt under his feet and the jolt rippled up his spine. He was caught between the luggage van and the carriage. He tugged frantically at the door at this end of the carriage but it was locked. He had seconds to get himself aboard.

There was no choice except to take the shortcut.

The train began to move and he clung to the edge of the carriage as he tried to reach one of his legs around the edge. He had to get to the steps into the luggage van. But the thin metal ledge he was standing on was slippery with ice, and the train was moving, unbalancing him.

He gripped the lip of the steel housing with his fingers as the train lurched and shuddered.

Behind him the station platform was slowly moving away, and he was aware that a single shot from an NKVD soldier could just pick him off like a fly on a wall. A light was on inside the train and he saw a ledge under the window he could cling on to. He reached a leg round to it, and let go with one arm, gasping as he grabbed for the next handhold. The tips of his toes barely gave purchase on the narrow metal lip around the edge of the carriage.

The length of the carriage seemed interminable, and he was like a spider, inching his way, terrified he'd drop any moment. The train whistle blew another deafening hoot and the shock caused him to wobble until his fingers burned, but finally he was perched on a step beneath a door and he grappled frantically at the handle while his fingers strained to keep hold.

Open, damn you. The train was moving slowly, gathering momentum, but the brass handle clunked open and he had to force the door open against the wind pressure. His muscles strained to keep the gap open as he got his shoulder in.

Shouts from behind him and another shot.

His arm muscles were on fire. He let them relax an instant and then made one last push against the pressure of the door. A small gap of a second. He threw himself bodily into the empty opening, landing on his hands and knees. Behind him, the door blew shut with a bang exactly like another gunshot.

Otto rolled over, eyes watering, wondering if he was still alive. His knuckles were red and bleeding and his fingertips too, but apart from that it seemed to just be the throb of his knees. And the fact he was so out of breath and wheezing that all he could do was lie there amidst piles of teetering suitcases and sacks of mail, as his heart seemed to ricochet in his chest.

'I guess he didn't make it,' Masha said, as the train left the lights of Krasnoyarsk behind. They'd both heard shots being fired but Masha was the first to voice her worry.

'Maybe he's further down the train.'

'Or maybe he's dead.'

'Don't,' Zofia snapped.

'You never liked him anyway. The way he made eyes at you.'

'I did. I just didn't know him well enough before.' Zofia closed her eyes to shut out the nightmare that Otto might be gone.

So when the carriage door opened and Otto peered in, at first she couldn't believe it, but then she burst into tears.

Otto came in and sat down on the edge of the bunk opposite. 'I nearly didn't come in. I didn't recognize you. I thought you were Tonya.' He tried to take her hand but then he hurriedly withdrew it. 'Don't cry.'

Zofia scrubbed at her eyes with her sleeve, angry at herself. She hadn't wept since they took Jacek, all her tears were exhausted, so why was she crying over Otto now? It didn't make sense. Perhaps it was the shock. Otto had a big bruise on the side of his face and his hands, usually so white and clean, were filthy and covered in blood. He looked like a wreck.

'Did they take the parcel? What happened? Did they shoot at you?' Masha asked.

'Yes, they took it. But I don't want to talk about it,' he said. 'Except I need to get cleaned up. I hate having dirty hands.'

He went into the adjoining washroom and she heard the spurt of water and the sound of him washing in the sink. When he came back, he said, 'It's not good. Not good news. I don't think they'll give up.'

Zofia slumped. 'Shit. What do you think they'll do next?'

'I don't know. But the SS is involved. High-up Nazis. They wanted to interrogate me.'

'They came here too, looking for me,' Zofia said. 'Two of them. But we kept up the pretence, said I must have got off the train.'

'I told them you were dead.'

Zofia stared at him. The idea gave her a strange sense of dislocation.

The engine was going at full rattle now, but the tension wouldn't leave Zofia's shoulders. The fact that the Nazis were so keen to get the papers only made her more desperate to hang on to them. She suspected they wanted to destroy them, and she couldn't bear it. They contained the ghosts of so many people. At the same time, she knew that to keep them would be risking the lives of her two travelling companions.

'It's not fair to you, I brought you all this trouble.'

'Fair?' Masha said. 'Since when has life been fair?'

Otto's legs were shaking and he had his head in his hands. 'When's the next stop?'

'Irkutsk,' Masha said. 'Two days from here.'

Chapter 27

Two more days of rattling through the *taiga*. Zofia travelled quietly, avoiding the other passengers as much as she could. They got *kasha*, the local barley porridge, or cabbage soup from the restaurant car and didn't venture near the windows of the train, though in truth there was little to see. Forest had given way to the vast plains of Siberia, with days of travel ahead and few stops except small refuelling halts in the middle of nowhere, with no road access for cars. Zofia was dimly aware of the sound of voices from the *Platzkart*, the students reciting their regular prayers, their voices rising and falling in sing-song. It was oddly comforting to be between places, in a no man's land, with only these ethereal voices for company.

Otto's gaze would drift to her when he thought she wasn't looking, so she was relieved that he sometimes went to join the yeshiva group to play cards or chess. Masha never did. She continued to just look blankly out of the window, and rarely insti-gated conversation. Because her company was dull, and Haru held a fascination for her, Zofia found herself making more excuses to go to the samovar in the hope of seeing him again. Simply to have a conversation with someone who was from the ordinary world; the world where men did business in peace instead of fighting like beasts over territory. To find sanity and normality.

Now back in her ordinary clothes and her blue coat, she staggered down the moving train towards the samovar compartment as if on a ship, her flask in her hand. She had the rucksack with her as usual but was thankful there'd been no stops yet, because the next one filled her with irrational dread, the fear that more Nazis might be waiting on the platform. They still had so far to go, and the thought of it was exhausting.

She hung around the samovar a little while with her flask, hearing the gentle bubble of the water boiling, feeling a little self-conscious, one eye always glancing up the train towards first class. She was about to give up, but all at once he was approaching, swaying down the corridor with his thermos held in one hand. He was tall for a Japanese person, and lithe, and moved confidently, one hand aloft for balance. Immediately she felt like a fool, waiting for him, and her face grew hot at the thought she might look so blatant.

Hurriedly she turned the tap on the spigot and began to siphon the boiling, spitting water out of the urn. She pretended to be surprised to see him. 'Oh! Are you needing more water? I won't be long,' she said in Polish. 'We drink a lot of tea.'

'Us too. My boss has a stash of Japanese tea in his luggage. Won't drink the black Russian stuff. And to make tea passes the time,' he said. 'Our *provodnitsa* still hasn't been replaced, and anyway, I like the walk. There is so little to do between stops, except to watch the view, and it hasn't changed for days.'

If only he knew. 'I find it quite restful,' she said.

'If you like bare trees.' He smiled.

She glanced out of the window to see the endless forest fading trunk by trunk beside them. Grey trees stretching over grey slush. 'I like the sameness of it,' she said. It was true, she liked the fact it held no surprises. She was tongue-tied now he was actually there, fiercely aware of him standing so close to her, leaning against the compartment door.

'To be honest, I was hoping to find someone interesting to talk to before I die of boredom. Oil field net yield and profit as a sole topic of conversation can get dull.' He smiled. 'Tell me something interesting instead.'

Her mind went blank. What could she tell him? He was from another world; one where you didn't have to run for your life. A world where you could dress in that suave manner, all pinstripes and shiny shoes, and assume your house would still be there when you woke up.

He saw her hesitation. 'Who are you travelling with?' he prompted.

She wanted to keep the conversation going. 'My brother's girlfriend, Masha, and another friend who worked for Mr Sugihara in the Japanese consulate in Kaunas.' She knew this might pique his interest.

'Yes, you mentioned his name. Sugihara-san, I mean. How come he's travelling with you?'

'Oh, not Sugihara. His aide. His name's Otto.' Of course he was interested, but she realized too late that she could tell him nothing else. She wasn't sure about the wisdom of confiding in anyone, let alone the fact that both Zeitel and the NKVD might be waiting for them at Vladivostok. She'd already said too much, and though she regretted it, she couldn't retract it. 'Forget it. I should never have mentioned him. He's a very private person.'

'But you are travelling together?'

'I'm sorry. I can't tell you more. Everything is too complicated.' She screwed the top on her flask.

He put a hand on her arm. 'Are you in trouble? Is he bothering you? Can I help?'

She looked up at him with anguished eyes. 'No. Nothing like that.' How could she explain? 'I'd better go. Please, don't tell anyone what I told you.'

'I won't.' But she could see the puzzlement in his expression. She put her flask under her arm and, red-faced, stumbled away down the train.

But she couldn't get his face out of her mind. The way he'd asked her so gently if he could help. She'd been strongly tempted to say yes, to try to unload the whole mess of her life onto him. But she knew that would be wrong. He was a stranger and he wouldn't understand about Jacek, about how she'd got into this. That she was completing something he'd started and couldn't do himself, and that she had to do it, so governments would recognize the terror of people like her in Nazi-occupied lands.

She couldn't explain the long straight line she was travelling on, the journey to the east that she felt in her bones. That as well as a physical destination, it was somehow her destiny.

When she got back, Masha stared at her. 'Where've you been? You were ages.'

'Just to get water.' She was aware her face was flaming.

Otto too seemed to sense something different. 'All right?' he asked, gazing at her with eyes that wouldn't leave her alone.

'I'm fine,' she said. 'Don't fuss, just a bit hot.'

'Hot?' Masha said. 'You must be kidding. It's about minus five outside.'

It was the middle of the night when they arrived at Irkutsk, one of the largest cities in Siberia. Masha had buttoned up her coat and was ready to brave the cold dark platform; she knew this would be the only chance she would get to contact Illeyvich. At first it had seemed like a game, but since those unwelcome visitors had got on to search the train, she had realized she needed help, or more instructions. It was sobering to know that the Nazis were intent on finding Zofia and the parcel she was carrying, and that Zofia, stubborn fool that she was, would never willingly give it up. She wished she could read Polish and understand exactly what was in there that was so damning, but it was clear it involved the Nazis' brutal treatment of the Jews.

She swung herself out of the bunk and onto the footholds to

the ground, but her movement disturbed Zofia.

'What's up?' Zofia sat up, instantly awake.

'It's Irkutsk. I'm just going to stretch my legs.'

'Be careful, we don't know who's out there.'

'No one's out there. They got the package they wanted, didn't they? Nobody could get here quicker than the train. Go back to sleep.'

By then Otto was awake too.

Masha was amused to see that Otto watched Zofia like she was a genie that might suddenly disappear, his eyes always drifting to her. Masha repeated what she had said but Otto was shrugging on his overcoat. 'Keep the compartment locked, I'm going to call my mother,' he said to Zofia.

There were few people about, only a few passengers being helped to board by the *provodnitsas* in each class. Masha had kept the uniform in her suitcase – you never knew when it might be useful. She strolled up and down, watching Otto head for one of the call boxes, hoping he'd be quick.

He seemed tense and frustrated as after only about five minutes, he passed her by. 'Line's dead,' he said.

Masha waited until Otto was back on the train before she hurried to cross the platform to the telephones in the main concourse, where she took a moment to tidy her hair before she dialled Illeyvich's number.

The telephone rang and rang. So it must only be Otto's mother's phone out of order. The time zone meant it was even later and Illeyvich would be sleeping, so of course he wouldn't answer. She put the phone down and redialled. Again the insistent ring shrilling in the distance. *Come on, come on.*

On the third ring he answered, and she pumped coins into the machine. 'Who is it?'

'Masha. I'm at Irkutsk.'

'Do you know the time?'

'I know. I had to call, something's happened.'

'At four in the morning? It had better be bloody important.'

She explained as briefly as she could. There was a slight hiatus when she'd finished before he said, 'Get her off at Birobidzhan like I said, but don't just dump her, make sure we have that package. If the Nazis are so keen to get what's in it, then we want it. Bring her in for questioning. The NKVD offices are just out of the main town on Karinsky Street, you can get a public troika from the station.'

'Not a car?'

'It's not that kind of place. And I've heard the weather there is appalling.'

'Who shall I ask for?'

'I'll call Arsenyev in the morning. Captain of State Security. Ask for him.'

'And after?'

'It's too damn early for me to think. Ask Arsenyev. I expect he'll arrange your return to Kovno.' A pause. 'Oh, and Masha? Good job.'

Masha said her goodbye and put the receiver down, cheeks glowing. She had to take a moment to press her cold hands to her cheeks to calm herself.

She had rarely had praise from anyone, but praise from Illeyvich felt like nectar, and she drank in the warming sensation of pride, before the seriousness of the situation hit her like a cold drench. She must show nothing untoward on her face. Through the hiss of steam and tang of smoke, she strolled back to their carriage with an air of blank hauteur. Zofia wouldn't want to leave the train at Birobidzhan, so it would need an iron will, or force, to make her.

Just after Irkutsk they stopped to refuel with coal, and there was some sort of hold-up because the weather had frozen the water system. After sitting in a stationary train for what seemed an age, they reached Lake Baikal at sunset the following evening.

The light shining on the expanse of the lake reminded Zofia of a painting her parents used to own in Poland, a picture of the Creation with light shining over the waters.

She turned to Otto. 'In Lithuania the Russians got rid of the churches and synagogues, just like the Nazis. Do you pray? Have you any kind of religion?'

'Not really,' Otto said. 'Lapsed at everything, I suppose. Why?'

'Just wondered, that's all.' She didn't tell him she prayed for Jacek and Tata every night, and doing it was the only thing that assuaged the ache in her heart.

'Being with Sugihara, well, I read everything I could about Japan. I've been swayed by Buddhism and Japanese thought. I couldn't see how there could be a Christian God if he didn't help my father. And also, the idea that He is omniscient and sees the past and the future ... well, if God's so great and He sees war and disaster coming, how can He bear to watch it go on?'

'You think there's a God?' Masha asked, looking back from staring out of the window.

'I'd like to think so, but my faith comes and goes. Having religion seems to make you rely on something else instead of yourself. But I think there must be something bigger than us.'

'There is something bigger than us,' Masha said. 'Society and community. Not the fear of some man in the sky.'

'Dostoevsky said, "God is the one being who can be loved eternally". Maybe that's it, we need to love more than be loved, and that's what God is for. It's hard to love other humans when we see the awful things they do.' He was looking to Zofia for a reaction, but she didn't want to talk about love with Otto.

'Huh.' Masha got up. 'I'm going to the toilet.' Her manner suggested that she was tired of their conversation.

'She's prickly these days, isn't she?' Otto said.

'I guess she's still grieving. Or maybe just bored with the journey. She doesn't read like you do, and there's not much else to do. The weather's been grim, and the view's been pretty uninspiring, especially in the evenings. And it feels like we're in a peculiar kind of limbo, caught between one world and the next.'

'She doesn't share much with us, though, does she?'

'I think she still feels like an outsider now Jacek's gone. You know, she looked more alive than I've ever seen her when she was robbing the stores and when those Germans were searching for us.'

'D'you reckon she had a criminal past?'

'A rough past maybe.'

Otto smiled and leant forward. 'Wouldn't surprise me. Look how keen she was to throw that man off the train.' He paused. 'Can I tell you something?' He didn't wait for an answer. 'The last few days has given me time to think. You know, make me take stock. I couldn't get through to Ma and it made me see how much I relied on her. Her say so before I did anything. And I realize I've just been too passive, drifting along, keeping my head down for a quiet life. I nearly died at Krasnoyarsk, and it really churned me up. Couldn't stop shaking for hours. Now the thought of losing my life has woken me up. Made want to squeeze every last drop of experience out of whatever's left of it.'

'You can't do much on this train, though.' She smiled.

'No. But listen ... I want to go with you to Tokyo and deliver Sugihara's message.'

'You don't need to help me. It's not your problem.'

'It's always been my problem, right from Moscow. Five thousand miles of a problem. But I was too scared to do the right thing.' He paused, swallowed and looked up at her, his expression serious. 'Sugihara didn't choose me to take his message because he didn't dare trust me. That's why he chose your brother. He chose well. But now Jacek can't do it, and he couldn't have wished for a better person to deliver his message than you.'

She brushed him away with a flap of her hand. 'Masha's much—'

He cut her off. 'I was thinking you'll need a translator when you get there. One who knows the consular etiquette and can speak Japanese.'

215

She immediately thought of Haru, but she had to dismiss his face from her mind.

Otto was waiting for her answer, and practically, it did seem to be a good idea. 'I hadn't thought of that,' she said. 'In that case, yes please. We'll go together.'

'You know that I care about you, that I hope … that I hope—'

The door banged open and Masha was back.

'It will be good to have a friend I can trust,' Zofia said with relief. She knew what Otto was trying to say and she was desperate that he shouldn't say it. For she didn't feel any inkling of romantic attachment to him.

She watched him bite his lip and look down at his shoes, and remembered Sugihara's words: *I hope you too find love.* But she knew it could never be with Otto.

Chapter 28

For the last few days Zofia had seen nothing of Haru, except a brief glimpse of him from the train window at Irkutsk, where, like Masha, he had obviously got off to buy a newspaper.

Zofia had made as many excuses to go back to the samovar as she dared. This time, her stomach gave a flip as she saw Haru was already there with his flask. 'More tea, or is it shaving water?' she asked in Polish.

'No. Just waiting for you to come along, that's all.' It was a flirtation; she could tell by the way he aimed his smile right at her. A pause, in which she found herself unable to meet his gaze. 'My boss sleeps much of the time,' he went on. 'When he does, I walk about. I'm not used to being so still, and the view hasn't changed for days. I can't decide if it's beautiful or ugly, the vastness of these uninhabited spaces. The going back seems so much longer than the outward journey.'

'Perhaps because you long to be home.'

'True. In Japan in the autumn the trees now are not like this ... they are like fires – their colours burn so bright. Red, orange, yellow. It is one of my favourite times of the year. And especially those cooler crisper nights when we go out for the festival of the full moon.'

'You have a special festival for the moon?'

'Please, get your water.'

She stepped towards the samovar and there was a moment's fumbling as they tried to change places.

He looked down at her and smiled again and there was a light dancing in his eyes that made something tighten in her chest.

'*Otsukimi* – the moon viewing, but I'll miss the festival this year, being here on the train. Shame. It makes us aware of how small we are – seeing the full moon at its biggest.'

'What happens at the festival?' she asked, determined to put herself back on an even keel.

'We eat these big rice dumplings, *tsukimi dango*, they're shaped like the moon. Actually, they're pretty bland. Or sweet potatoes. Sometimes chestnuts. But mainly we just look. Celebrate the beauty of the moon.'

'It sounds like a lovely idea. Can't you do it on the train? I mean, do you know when the next full moon is?'

'The day after tomorrow. I know because it's printed in my work diary with the other festivals. We could meet and I could—'

'Ah, I see we all want tea!' Dr Rabinowitz bustled in, a metal flask in each hand, his hat perched askew. 'Our urn's empty again.'

'It's all right, I've finished,' Zofia said, stepping back out of his way.

'Good, good,' he said. 'Oof, my students are like locusts – eat and drink everything in sight. But we're out of food until we get to the next big town, and can't afford the restaurant car, so tea it is.'

Haru continued to chat to the rabbi as he filled his flask and it seemed to take a long time, because she didn't know whether to wait and hope Haru would finish what he was saying about meeting or not. She clutched her own thermos to her chest, but Dr Rabinowitz had started to talk to him about what it might be like in Japan, and whether it was true there was a Jewish agency there that would help them when they arrived.

Haru said he was sure there was.

'You walking back, my dear?' Dr Rabinowitz asked her.

'Yes,' she said, unable to think of any reason why not. She glanced at Haru to find him looking at her out of the side of his eyes.

'Come on, then,' Dr Rabinowitz said, waving her ahead of him.

She wished she'd been bolder and waited to see if Haru really wanted to meet on the night of the full moon. But it was all so difficult. She wondered what Haru would have made of her if he'd seen her dressed in the *provodnitsa* uniform, and the thought made her smile. Maybe he would have demanded she bring him tea.

She returned to the carriage and to Otto and Masha.

'I just met a man from Japan at the samovar. He's travelling on business with his boss. They've been to a conference with the Russians.'

'I don't think I've seen him,' Otto said.

'They're travelling first class, that's why.'

'Oh.' He showed no interest in the other man, and she couldn't blame him. His face was still bruised and his fingers were scabbed, and he had the gaunt look of a man in shock.

She was sad she couldn't feel for him the way she felt for Haru. He looked like he needed love and yet she couldn't summon it to order.

Stations always made her nervous, even though nobody had harassed them at Irkutsk. Time had passed and they'd now been on the train for thirteen days and were drawing closer to Birobidzhan, a new settlement built in the 1930s close to the Chinese–Russian border. Sleet slammed against the windows.

Zofia wiped her damp palms down her skirt and looked at the map of the route. 'Nearly there,' she said to calm herself. 'We'll be able to get out, maybe buy food.'

'Where's Otto?' Masha asked. She'd been restless the last couple of hours.

219

'Chatting with the yeshiva students. He said if it looks okay, he'll get off here too, just to buy provisions. The dining car's got little left, and it's just a half-hour stop.'

'Uh huh.' Masha was distracted, and was getting down her suitcase. She'd changed, Zofia noticed, into a red skirt and silky blouse, and puffed up her hair.

'He was telling me before that Birobidzhan's a Jewish settlement. Created after the Bolshevik Revolution as a kind of state for Russian Jews. He says everyone there speaks Yiddish. Can you imagine! Building something like that, all the way out here?'

Masha didn't reply; she was rummaging in her handbag.

Zofia rubbed the steamy window. 'I can see rooftops now. And snow. There are horses with sleighs in the streets. How sweet.' She peered at the town, which seemed to be a conglomerate of brick buildings in the middle, surrounded by rough log cabins, smashed together any old how. 'Looks dismal, though, and very cold out there, like a place caught in a time-warp. I can't see any cars or trams. If we are going to get off for a few minutes we'd best put on our coats.'

She reached up to the net rack to get down her coat and after shrugging into its heavy warmth, slipped the rucksack with the precious parcel onto her shoulders. A scarf around her neck and her woollen cap to keep her head and neck warm. She combed her hair with her fingers where it stuck out from her hat, because last time she'd met Haru at the samovar, they'd managed a few quick moments before someone else came. He'd told her he was going to get off here too and try to find a decent cup of coffee, so she hoped he'd have escaped his boss and would be looking for her when the train stopped.

Masha was tying a headscarf around her neck, leaving her head bare. But she didn't put on her coat, instead it hung over her arm.

'Better put your coat on or you'll freeze,' Zofia said, but Masha ignored her.

Outside, the platform was full of women in badly worn clothes with blankets wrapped around their heads and shoulders to keep off the unseasonal cold. The engine seemed to exhale steam as it jerked to a halt, and Zofia, getting ready to leave the compartment, grabbed the door jamb for support.

'You will do exactly as I say.' The tone of Masha's voice was odd. Zofia looked over her shoulder, puzzled. Masha was pointing a gun directly at her.

'It's loaded,' Masha said.

She laughed. 'Don't play about, Masha.'

But Masha's face remained stony. 'You'll do as I say.'

'Wait, what's going on? Stop messing, it's not the time for jokes.'

'No. Not a joke. This isn't Otto's gun, it's mine. A revolver, complete with silencer. You are to get off the train and keep my arm linked in yours. Don't try to run because the gun will be under my coat and I shan't hesitate to pull the trigger.'

She was serious. Zofia felt her world tilt and a sudden sinking sensation in the pit of her stomach. 'Why? Are you German?'

'No.' A contemptuous laugh. 'NKVD.' She sounded proud. 'I'm to bring you to Birobidzhan to the NKVD offices. To take you and Sugihara's parcel to the Russians. So now you will do as I say.'

'But why? What do the Russians want with it?'

'For bargaining power. And if German war atrocities are investigated, it will be useful propaganda that the Nazi regime is inferior, lacking in what Stalin can offer the Russian people – safety, community, brotherly goodness.'

Zofia couldn't take it in. This wasn't the Masha she knew speaking; this articulate person was a stranger. Masha had always made out she barely understood politics. 'What about Jacek? If you work for them, why didn't you …? Oh.'

It had just dawned on her that Masha had probably been tailing Jacek from the beginning. That she was probably the reason why he'd been arrested. A million small things clicked into place. 'It was all lies, wasn't it?' she said bitterly. 'Your whole dumb blonde act. You never cared for Jacek at all.'

'Not true. I admired your brother. He was an intelligent man, except as far as women were concerned. And I'm good at what I do. The Russians use me for tailing important people, or when the person is too difficult to get close to.' She smiled a smile that didn't show her teeth and her eyes were hard as marble. 'You can call it a compliment. Jacek had a way of writing that could persuade people with words, so it made him dangerous to communism. He's no danger now, of course.'

'Where is he? Do you know where he is?'

'No.' The train was slowing but the gun hadn't moved. 'Now walk slowly out of the compartment, hold my arm.'

Zofia had no choice but to do it. Where was Otto? A quick glance along the corridor showed him bundled in his overcoat and, though he was making his way back towards them from third class, he'd stopped to chat to another passenger.

'Masha, please. We're friends, aren't we?'

'Feel that?' Masha asked. Zofia gasped as the hard nose of a gun pressed into her ribs.

'When we get there, climb down slowly.'

Otto was still talking. She willed him to stop and look her way. She kept close to the door as the train came into the platform.

'No nonsense now,' hissed Masha into her ear.

The station had taken on a nightmarish quality. How could all these people be waiting so calmly? The world had turned into a place she didn't understand and Masha's hard face was the thing that perplexed her most of all. Zofia wondered if she could run, but had no idea where to go. The crowd was too deep and she worried someone else might get hurt.

Too soon, the platform seemed to halt before them, and she opened the window to turn the door handle. It was awkward climbing down linked to Masha like that, and when she stumbled, she felt the gun stab into her side. She feared a bullet through her ribs. Zofia was still in shock. She'd trusted Masha. She wouldn't use the gun, would she?

Yet Zofia couldn't be sure.

A flash of her eyes to the side and she saw Otto glance her way.

A diversion. She needed to make a diversion, get more people involved.

Without warning she dropped. She flung herself down onto the hard platform as if in a dead faint. She felt Masha's fingernails in her wrist as she tried to haul her up.

Well-meaning people rushed to help. The yeshiva students turned gawping eyes on her and from the corner of one eye she saw Otto's long legs rushing down the platform.

'Little fool.' Masha was trying to drag her up, with eyes full of suppressed rage, but Zofia closed her eyes tight and remained on the ground, inert, a dead weight.

When she refused to move, Masha tried to shift her to pull the rucksack off her shoulders.

No. She wouldn't let her have it. Zofia let her body sink into the hard ground, made her limbs heavy like a corpse. The bag dug into her back.

'She's fainted. She needs a doctor.' Dr Rabinowitz's voice, and then he called out in Yiddish. A flutter of her eyes and she glimpsed an elderly woman gabbling to a large group in Yiddish as more people gathered round.

The hard nose of the gun was still pressing into her ribs as Masha attempted with one hand to turn her over, but Zofia lay still. Masha couldn't move her without letting go of the gun.

'I'm a doctor.' Otto's voice shouting in Russian. 'Give her room!' She blinked to see him push Masha roughly aside. He crouched to put one hand on Zofia's shoulder. 'What?' he asked her.

She groaned as if coming round and pulled him close so his ear was near her face. 'Not ill,' she whispered. 'Masha. NKVD. After the papers.'

Before she could resume the fainting act, Masha saw that she was whispering, and a dark fury flashed in her eyes. 'Get up.' She slapped Zofia hard on the face. Zofia didn't move. 'Get away from

223

her.' Masha's voice was hard as flint.

The gasp from the crowd made Zofia open her eyes. Otto backing off and Masha openly wielding the gun.

She was lying alone. Masha's coat had fallen in a heap beside her. Everyone else had fled backwards at the sight of the gun.

'Sit up!' Masha said, her voice low and threatening. She yanked the rucksack from Zofia's shoulder.

A piercing whistle. Everyone startled and turned to the noise. The stationmaster was marching over to see what the commotion was about.

By now Masha had hold of the bag. She twisted it away from Zofia and tried to run.

'Stop! Thief!' Otto made a sudden ungainly leap and knocked Masha to the ground, pinning her squirming body down with his long arms.

Masha cursed in Russian as the gun skittered from her hand but she was stronger than she looked and she wriggled free, still clinging to the rucksack. Within seconds she was dodging away, running awkwardly in her heeled shoes.

The stationmaster grabbed the weapon from the ground.

'Stop her!' Zofia yelled to the crowd as she sprang to her feet.

The crowd gawped, unable to understand what was happening and Zofia's sudden recovery. She glimpsed Haru and his boss staring from further up the platform as she sprinted after Masha, yelling 'Thief!'

A couple of the yeshiva students made an attempt to run after Masha but she dodged out of their way.

'Split up,' Zofia shouted to Otto, 'Don't lose her!'

Had she come halfway across Russia only to fail now?

Her eyes fixed on the flap of Masha's red skirt; a flag weaving in and out of the queues as she dodged across the ticket hall.

Zofia plunged after her, narrowly missing knocking over a woman and baby, and almost tripping over a man with a dog. She cursed. No turnstiles to hold Masha up.

Otto cut the corner, shouting apologies to outraged passengers as he leapt over their suitcases and tried to block Masha's escape.

Masha turned back to look, saw they were after her, and leapt down the stairs at the front of the station, the rucksack bouncing over one shoulder.

Zofia thought her lungs might collapse. 'Masha! Wait!' Her voice was a gasp.

Out of the main concourse and helter-skelter down the steps at the front of the station, Otto breathless by her side, as they wove past a group of passengers heading up the ramshackle street to meet the train. Zofia flailed, struggling to stay upright, skidding and floundering on the compacted snow of the road. Ahead, Masha almost fell but kept on running.

She was making towards a waiting queue of horse-drawn sleighs for hire.

If she got in one of those, they'd never catch her.

Beside her, Otto put on a spurt to try to gain ground. Despite the ice, horse-drawn traffic was trotting along the main road to collect and deliver passengers for the Trans-Siberian. A sleigh drawn by two chestnut horses was heading fast down the road, its passengers, a man and a woman muffled in heavy coats, craning their heads towards the station.

Masha looked over her shoulder, just once, as if to see how close Zofia was to catching her. But the look behind meant she missed the oncoming danger.

Zofia was already yelling her name as Masha dodged across the road, hurrying towards the waiting sleighs.

The oncoming sleigh didn't slow, the driver intent on making the train. Neither did the cantering horses see the blonde woman, running like a hare across the road.

Otto saw the contraption coming and pulled up short, yelling 'Look out!'

He dug in his heels to stop, but Masha kept on running, oblivious.

Zofia stopped dead, breath panting in clouds, eyes fixed on the horses, mouth open in a scream of warning.

But the sound that she let out into the frosty air hung there, too long and too late.

The horses couldn't slow, though their hooves churned up the hard-packed snow. At the last second, Masha held up her hands, and her mouth opened as if to shout 'stop!' as if that might prevent what was coming, powerless to get out of the way in time, feet fighting to get purchase on the slippery ice.

A squeal from a horse. A confusion of hooves, and tumbling limbs. A whirl of red in the spattering snow.

The horses rearing and jostling at the thing tangled between their feet. A sickening thud as the front of the sleigh connected and Masha was dragged bumping along. Zofia's bag flew off to the side and landed in the piled-up slush at the edge of road.

No! Oh no. Zofia started to run.

The driver was leaning back, pulling on the reins and the sleigh slewed to the side as Masha was towed face down along the ice, until finally the whole contraption stopped and the horses were side-stepping, throwing up their heads, panting hot breath into the chilly air. Over in seconds, though it felt as though the reverberation of the squealing of the horses went on forever.

Otto was already running, arms and legs flying, towards the sleigh. Zofia stood a moment gasping for breath, unable to take it in.

Masha's legs were under the horses' feet, and blood pooled around her head. She still didn't move.

The driver stumbled out, distraught, trying to calm the wild horses so he could get Masha out. 'She didn't look!' he cried to his passengers, who were white with shock and horror. 'I tried to stop!'

A gawping crowd had gathered, and Otto and two other bystanders crouched over Masha to pull her gently free of the horses' legs. But they stood up quickly and the driver shouted for help.

One of the bystanders, a man with a thick moustache, grabbed the distraught passenger by the sleeve and shook his head before taking off his coat to lay it over Masha's body. 'Broken neck. She's gone.'

The passengers were aghast; the woman pressed her face into her husband's shoulder.

The driver was still shouting, tears in his voice. 'Did anyone see? It wasn't my fault! I swear it. She just ran out.'

Zofia's heart constricted. Why were they covering her up? It couldn't be true.

She was about to go to her when Otto ran over and grabbed her shoulder. 'No.' The single word was full of authority. He picked up the rucksack from the side of the road. 'We can't do anything.'

'Is she …?'

Otto put an arm around her shoulders. He didn't say anything, because it was obvious from the people gathered around Masha's motionless form that she was dead.

Someone ran off towards the station to fetch help, and a moment later Russian soldiers were heading up the road towards them.

'Time to leave,' Otto said. He took Zofia firmly by the arm and walked purposefully back towards the station. 'Don't look at them. No arguments. We have a train to catch.'

Zofia leant into his tall frame. She was stumbling in some sort of other reality. The image and sound of the sleigh hitting Masha kept repeating.

As they approached the station again, she said, 'Can't we go back? What if she's still alive?'

'She wasn't alive,' Otto said. 'And if she was, she'd be pointing a gun at us.'

Chapter 29

At the station turnstiles, they had to stop while Russian soldiers examined their permits. Otto's cheek twitched as they scrutinized Zofia's forged permit, tension etched in the set of his shoulders.

She turned to see the party of yeshiva students coming back in ones and twos. She dreaded Dr Rabinowitz asking about the commotion at the station, or asking after Masha, so she hurried on ahead. The sight of the train's bulk waiting there made her unaccountably fearful and she had to stop and steel herself to approach it.

'Come on,' Otto said, and he helped push her up the steps.

He led the way back to compartment number two, and within five minutes the Trans-Siberian was moving again, sliding out of Birobidzhan and on towards Vladivostok.

Otto sat opposite her and placed the rucksack by her side, and only then did Zofia see the bloodstains on it and begin to shake. A trembling that filled her whole body.

'What would Jacek think?' she said. 'She was a spy for the NKVD. He loved her. But it was all an act. She used him.'

'Hush,' he said. 'We don't have to tell him. When you see him in Kobe you can tell him it was just a foolish accident.'

He was pretending that they'd see Jacek again. In her heart

she knew the chances were infinitesimally small. People didn't return from the gulags any more than they returned from Nazi camps. But the truth was always harder to bear than a comforting lie. The truth was, people were prepared to kill for some sort of ideology dreamt up by men in nameless offices somewhere. And now she was complicit in hiding the truth, in polishing it up so that it seemed acceptable. To protect people from the raw truth that humanity was still a bunch of wild animals fighting for power and territory, and they could turn on you at any minute.

She wasn't sure how she felt about Otto. But he'd changed since he first got on the train, when he'd been a man who was fading away behind his own facade. Now he was all too present. She supposed his gun was still with Masha. Too many guns. War had made holding a gun too easy to do.

Later that night she slept, exhausted. Her body needed to rest, but it still seemed odd not to hear Masha creaking in the bunk above her. She couldn't erase the sight of Masha's blonde hair, the crash of hooves, and the streak of blood staining the snow.

The next day, Zofia was woken by Otto bringing hot tea. Her initial fear at waking was soothed by the sight of the two steaming glasses on a tin tray, though nothing could soften the harsh fact of Masha's missing presence. Her suitcase was still on the rack. Otto locked the door even though the train was rattling sedately through the blur of frozen countryside and there were no more stops for days. They still had nearly six hundred miles to go, and she was weary and heartsore.

When she thought back on the journey, it seemed darker than even the fairy tales she heard as a child. Masha seemed a princess now, bound to a fate she had no control over, like Karen in the story of *The Red Shoes*. It seemed unsurprising to her that Masha would never grow old; that the owl of death had swooped down on her from the Lithuanian myth of Giltinė. She wondered if those stories too had been conceived in war.

'It was my fault,' she said to Otto. 'I persuaded her to come with us. I actually went to her house. If I hadn't, she'd still be at home in Kaunas.'

'You can't know that. Maybe you persuaded her in the beginning, but then she had her own agenda, one that suited her and her NKVD friends.'

'I keep seeing it, in my head. Hearing the horses.'

'Me too.'

They sipped their tea, both deep in their own remembrances. An hour passed as they let the landscape slip by.

'I'm nervous about the next stop,' Zofia said. 'Do you think the Nazis will have realized that the testimonies you gave them are fake and that there should be photographs?'

'Yes. They knew there were photographs. Zeitel told me. He's part of a bigger Nazi organization. Its aims are to suppress any evidence or bad press about what the Reich are actually doing. How they are annihilating the Jewish population. We are only two people, but they have a whole department and armies of men at their command.'

'You're not being very reassuring.'

'Better to be straightforward and know what we're up against. The danger will be more at Vladivostok, I should think. They will have had time to look into the package and discover it's fake, and maybe wire someone to meet us. Still, that's a way off yet.' He sighed. 'Before we get there, I need to write to my mother, her phone's dead, and just in case …' His mouth worked, but he didn't go on. He was thinking the worst, she could tell.

'It's hard, not knowing, isn't it?' Zofia looked at him wanly. 'It came to me last night, that now I have no one. Somehow, with Masha there, I could still believe Jacek would come back to me.'

'No parents?'

'My mother died when I was small, and my father – well, you know. He died in Poland. Shot in a Nazi round-up.'

He pointed to her rucksack. 'Those testimonies prove you're not the only one with these experiences. So much pain and heartache, because of what? Being born in the wrong place?'

'A year ago I would never have believed it, that both my brother and my uncle would be in Russian camps. We were only scared of Nazis, not Russians.' She paused a moment. 'I don't mean to offend you.'

He shook his head to dismiss it. 'The Russians have a long history. They faced the powerful forces of Napoleon, but drove the aggressors out by sheer will-power. They don't give up easily. Even if we get to Vladivostok safely, I can't go home to Kaunas. One word in someone's ear and they'd find me somehow and arrest me as an undesirable. I feel terrible that I'm abandoning my mother. She's ill and she relies on me. You know, she had a kind of breakdown after my father died. To be honest, I think we both did.'

'When did he die?'

'He took his own life in 1926, when I was fourteen. For years I blamed myself, not realizing my mother tortured herself with the same thoughts. It took us years to work out it was not our fault. And d'you know what? War makes it harder. Because other people are dying for a cause, and my father had no cause. No excuse or reason to die.' He paused. 'Except the demons in his own head.'

His face was so earnest that she could not help but warm to him. 'I'm sorry.'

'You know, when I went away to study, I wrote to my mother every day. Just a few lines sometimes. It was like me and her against the world. But it made us kind of insular. She never approved of anyone I brought home, they were always a threat. She was so scared I'd leave her like he did. And now I have. I can't bear to think of her sitting there, on our old worn-out sofa, waiting.'

'And Jacek will still think Masha is waiting for him. The person he thought Masha was, I mean, not the real Masha. I wonder what made her the way she was. I always thought there was something broken in her, but I didn't know what, and Jacek used to think I was just being jealous. I should have trusted my instincts.'

'You weren't to know. You couldn't have done anything differently.'

'The strange thing is, I still miss her.'

'I still miss my father.'

As they were still sipping their tea, there was a knock on the compartment door. Both of them froze. Otto exchanged a glance with her then opened it a small crack.

Haru was there, neatly dressed in suit and tie. 'Are you all right?' he asked in Russian. 'The rabbi told me which compartment you were in.'

'Oh, Otto,' Zofia said hastily, 'it's only Haru, my friend from the samovar. You can let him in.'

Otto opened the door but his mouth turned down in studied indifference.

Haru sat down on the opposite bunk. 'I saw something happened at the station yesterday. I asked Dr Rabinowitz what was going on, but he couldn't tell me anything.'

'He didn't want to be involved,' Otto said defensively, still standing holding the door. 'I spoke to him this morning. He has his students to think of.'

'Sit down, Otto,' Zofia said, 'you're blocking the light.'

Otto sat down reluctantly, next to Zofia.

Haru smiled at them both. 'I came to see if you needed anything. I saw you'd fallen over on the ground and then next thing you were chasing your friend, and then one of the students said someone had a gun—'

'We're all right,' Otto said firmly. 'Zofia just felt a bit faint, that's all.'

Zofia was uncomfortable. She didn't like him speaking for her, but for now it seemed best just to go along with it. 'I'm better now,' she said, though she still felt like an earthquake had gone on inside her chest.

'Did you stop the thief?' Haru asked.

'Yes,' Otto said, at exactly the same time as Zofia said, 'No, it was—' They exchanged glances.

'Sorry, Haru, like I told you before,' Zofia said. 'It's complicated.'

Otto stiffened, and she was sure Haru had noticed it because his gaze met hers in a question.

An awkward silence.

'We don't need anything,' Otto said in a clipped voice. 'But thank you for calling.'

'Well, as long as everything's all right,' Haru said, standing up again. 'It's just I was worried. And I hadn't seen you today so …'

Zofia just shook her head, unable to offer any further explanation.

'As long as everything's okay. But I was wondering what you would do when you got to the boat, whether or not you'd need a translator because—'

'Oh, I can do that,' Otto interrupted. 'I've agreed to help Zofia and take her to Tokyo. She has a message to deliver there.'

'Oh, of course, I'd forgotten,' Haru said. 'Zofia told me that you'd worked in the embassy with Sugihara-san. A very interesting job.' He nodded as if to expect more conversation.

Otto, though, was back on his feet and opening the door for him. 'Nice to meet you, but I expect you're busy,' he said.

Haru was obviously aware he was being hustled out, and turned to give Zofia a rueful look. 'No doubt we'll meet again at the samovar,' he said with a polite bow. 'They still haven't replaced the *provodnitsa* in our compartment.' And he was away down the corridor.

Heat rose to Zofia's face. What would Haru think of her?

As soon as he'd gone, Otto shut the door and rounded on her. 'How much did you tell him?'

'We had a pleasant conversation, that's all. It was nothing.'

'But you talked. What if he's some kind of spy?'

'No. He's just a translator on his way home from a business trip.'

233

'How often have you talked to him?'

'What is this? Some kind of interrogation? We just met a couple of times and had a chat while we waited for the water to boil.'

Otto sat down and his face was blotchy, as if he was upset. 'We're in enough trouble already. I don't think you should meet him again. We don't know enough about him.'

'For pity's sake! He's Japanese, like Sugihara. I think you should worry more about the Nazis and the NKVD, and less about random innocent passengers,' she said.

'He might not be an innocent passenger,' Otto insisted.

Zofia just ignored him and turned away.

Otto watched the sky darken and the landscape blur into a black and white movie. There were few lights out there now, and soon he found himself staring at his own reflection in the black glass.

He didn't like what he saw. He wasn't handsome, and there was no earthly chance of competing with that Japanese man. Why did Haru have to be on the train? His clothes were expensive-looking and he had that relaxed, confident air of a man who knew his own worth. And more, he seemed a nice person, genuinely concerned about Zofia.

Otto sighed. There was obviously more to these samovar meetings than Zofia was telling him. It made him feel left out, and a fool. And he dreaded that she might prefer Haru's company to his.

He was aware too that it must look odd now to other people, two single people sharing a compartment like this. Yet he was reluctant to move out. What if something else happened? He'd promised himself he'd protect her and stick with her while she delivered the parcel.

In his heart he knew he was jealous of Haru, a needle twisting in his gut. He'd have to engineer to keep them apart until they got off the boat. Once they got to Japan, Haru would have to accompany his boss and they'd be free of him. He had too much free time on this blasted train.

Maybe he should take courage and tell Zofia how he felt about her; maybe then he'd have a chance with her, but he knew he couldn't. The very thought of it made him sweat. He'd never been in love before, hadn't realized how it ate into your every thought, how when she looked at him it made his whole body flare like it was wired into the mains.

Chapter 30

Zeitel had been summoned to Brandt's office, behind a barber shop in Vilnius, and he dreaded another meeting where he'd be made to feel small and inadequate. The barber shop looked innocuous enough, but it gave perfect cover for Nazi sympathizers to come in and out.

He went through the shop, through the pong of hair oil and the awful 'burnt hoof' tang of singed hair, and up to the first floor. Up here three poky rooms were linked by a corridor, each crowded with filing cabinets and shelves of neatly stacked documents.

Brandt was busy dictating to his secretary and flapped Zeitel away with a dismissive hand. Disgruntled, Zeitel stood outside the door, leaning on the wall, knowing he was already on the back foot. Brandt's ample stomach hung over the top of his trousers as he barked out instructions to his secretary, Tilda. Zeitel liked Tilda; she rolled her eyes at him when Brandt wasn't looking, as if to say 'doesn't he go on?'. Brandt was a pain to work for. He kept close links to what he called the 'homeland' and was a fanatical Nazi. And by the size of his gut, it rewarded him well, being in the pay of two masters.

You must think I'm stupid, Zeitel thought, as Brandt ordered that papers giving away German tank positions were to be found and destroyed. War between the Russians and the Germans was coming, any fool could see that. They were calling it Operation Barbarossa. Once the Germans invaded, then he'd have to get out and fast, if he didn't want to be in a war zone, and the atmosphere was already uncomfortable in Kaunas. But until then, lip service had to be paid.

Brandt's voice droned on and Zeitel was bitter at being kept waiting. He shuffled from foot to foot, wishing he was back in engineering and had never agreed to be part of this Nazi anti-propaganda unit.

When he was an engineer, the Soviet–German pact enabled Germans to make armaments, something they'd been forbidden to do since the end of the Great War. Then, the Russians were happy to get his German military expertise and he'd made a packet. In those days German factories, weapons labs, and military training grounds were all relocated to the USSR. But since Germany had invaded Poland, demand for his skills had collapsed. He only used his skills at home now, in miniature.

He was left with this dog-end of a job. Russian patience was wearing thin, and every Russian was suspicious of him. They all knew the German Reich was powerful enough now to turn on its erstwhile neighbour. And he'd be the Russians' first target if war was declared.

The clatter and ping of the typewriter stopped, and Brandt dismissed Tilda to the outer office and beckoned Zeitel in. He was pretty sure Tilda overheard everything that went on, but he had no time to dwell on this.

The office had once been a bedroom and, because the weather had turned so damned cold, there was a coal stove glowing on a tiled hearth. Zeitel found himself sweating. He removed his gloves but kept on his coat despite the unaccustomed heat.

'It appears your men Fischer and Siegel intercepted the package that was on the train with Otto Wulfsson, but Wulfsson got away. At first I thought your man incompetent, but now it seems

Wulfsson is deliberately obstructing us.' He slapped down the package on the table. It looked battered and the brown paper was torn as if it had been opened in a hurry.

'Had it been opened?' Zeitel asked.

'No.' Brandt flapped a hand in impatient dismissal. 'It was sealed when we got it. But take a look inside.'

Zeitel drew the parcel towards him, his heart hammering. Brandt's expression was grim, and Zeitel didn't know what he was supposed to be looking for. He pulled out the contents onto the desk. At first he saw nothing, just a heap of papers, with scrawled writing in a language he didn't understand.

Brandt's fist landed on top of it with a bang. The whole desk shook. Zeitel startled and shot back in his chair.

'There are no photographs.' His face was so close to Zeitel's now that he could see the pores on his nose and the angry bloodshot whites of his eyes.

Zeitel didn't dare speak.

'What else do you notice, eh?' When he didn't get an answer, Brandt said, 'The whole thing is fake. These are not real testimonies. The paper is all the same. The writing doesn't vary enough. I had one of my forgery experts look at it and there's no doubt. Yet Wulfsson delivered this to my men at Krasnoyarsk.'

'So that's good, isn't it? We can just denounce it as a fake. They've been carrying fake documents all the way to Vladivostok.'

'Think, man. It means that someone's copied this on purpose. Look at the seal – it doesn't bear any kind of scrutiny. Sugihara would never have sealed it with crumbling candlewax. We got a native Japanese speaker to look at it, and some of the *kanji* are written wrong. Small but obvious differences.' He glared at Zeitel. 'Can you explain that?'

Zeitel blinked. 'I don't speak Japanese.'

A sigh. 'The real one is probably still with the Kowalski girl, and your man Wulfsson – far from helping us – is helping her.'

'How was I to know? I never even saw the documents or the

photographs.'

Just then a knock at the door. Brandt went to answer it and took delivery of a brown cardboard file from a motorcycle courier. He barked his thanks then put it down on the desk, where he undid the elastic ties to reveal a small collection of photographs. Brandt fanned them out on the desk with his sausage-shaped fingers. Grainy and blurred, the pictures were still clear enough to show a trench, and a group of German soldiers standing over it with rifles.

Zeitel squinted, his eyes following the gazes of the soldiers in the photograph to the pit below. Were these people? The pile of tangled grey limbs filled him with fascination and horror in equal measure.

Brandt picked one of the pictures up and waved it, unmoved. 'We get dozens of these daily. They come from wherever there is German-occupied land, but we search every Jew who comes through our system for evidence, so we can control any kind of photographic or written material. We don't want a single image to survive. We want total disappearance. That's what Hitler has asked for, and that is what I'm tasked to do.'

He picked up a photo and with a pair of tongs slid back the metal lid of the stove. With a flick, he dropped the photo into it, where it flared and shrivelled. Zeitel watched with fascination as Brandt crumpled up every document and photo and fed them to the flames.

The heat in the room increased, and Zeitel tried to inch his way back from the roar of the fire.

'You see,' Brandt said, 'Keeping records is very important to the Führer. But destroying records is equally so. We are removing the taint of Jewry from everything it touches, see? There can only be purity in the German race from now on.'

Zeitel stared in stupefied silence.

'Which is why we need those letters and photographs. Every last one. We can't allow them to exist.'

'I see. But what can we do now?'

'We? You will do nothing. Our SS operatives in Vladivostok will deal with it now. I've sent a wire to instruct them to stop the train before it reaches the station. Not at a proper stop, but at a fuel halt.'

'So am I released from the job?'

Silence except the spit of the stove.

Eventually the answer came. 'The office can't afford to keep dead wood.' Brandt took the last photograph, a picture of a cart bearing a mass of corpses and, seeing Zeitel staring at it, consigned it to the flames. 'Go home, Zeitel. Nazi Germany can't afford dead wood.'

Chapter 31

The train rattled on. Every time Zofia offered to fetch the tea, Otto jumped up to do it. She suspected he didn't want her to go to the samovar and meet Haru.

'Your Japanese friend was there today,' Otto said, with a slight edge to the word 'friend'. 'He seems to be at the beck and call of his boss.'

'His boss is difficult to deal with, I think,' she replied.

'Then he should leave and work for someone else. I wouldn't work for someone I despise.' Otto seemed determined to put Haru down.

Zofia changed the subject. 'Did you write to your mother?'

'Yes, I'll have to post it when we get to Vladivostok. She'll be worried to death that I haven't called, and she's not well. Cancer. I promised I'd take care of her.' Otto turned away to look out of the window; shadows of trees chased their way across his changing expression.

'She'll be okay. She has good neighbours, right? They will watch out for her. Is there no one else in your family? You haven't told me if you have any brothers or sisters,' she said.

'I wish. But no, I'm an only child.'

'Then you're lucky! You never had to fight for anything. I was

241

an only child for just two minutes, before Jacek was born and I became a twin,' she told him. 'We used to fight like cat and dog, but I'd never thought of myself existing without him.'

'You seem to manage quite well on your own,' Otto said. His gaze held hers with a kind of intimacy she didn't want to see. She felt heat rise to her cheeks, but looked away.

He had feelings for her, she knew that much. But she didn't want to get involved with him. Only someone who had been in Poland and seen it could know the deep level of distrust she held for Germans. Even the sound of his slight German accent through the Russian made her recoil. But she understood it was not his fault. He had been kind. There was no blaming him for the way she felt.

He did not press her further, but seemed to shrink back into himself, as if to hide from her embarrassment.

Vladivostok was now less than five hundred miles away and the landscape had changed to deep forests and steep ravines. The track went over wooden bridges with terrifying drops below, but the snow-line had changed and, though still cold, it was cloudy and damp with only occasional flurries of snow – perhaps because they were nearer the Sea of Japan, thought Zofia.

Otto had searched Masha's case for his gun, but it was nowhere to be found. Afterwards he'd carried the case away and given it to some refugees in third class. Neither of them could bear to see it sitting there day after day.

It was late in the afternoon when they came to a tunnel. The train slowed to pass through it, and shortly afterwards they were travelling alongside the Chinese border again, a twelve-foot wire fence with barbed wire scrolling on top. It went on for miles, winding ribbon-like alongside them. At half past three in the morning they passed the outlines of a few small, ragged settlements huddled in the dark, before the train came to an abrupt halt at the last-but-one stop before Vladivostok. Rain splattered the windows as the train slowed. She braced herself for the familiar clank as the carriages shunted together.

The train stopped briefly to let off some local passengers and take on some coal. Even at this time of night, there were more traders than at the Siberian stations. Their umbrellas jostled around the carriage windows and doors. 'Do you want to stretch your legs?' Otto asked, waking up from his doze.

She shook her head, barely awake. 'No. Keep the door locked. I just want to get there now. Get off this damn train and get on that boat. I never want to see another inch of Russia.'

Within five minutes they were rolling onwards, and the movement lulled her into a brief restless sleep. When she next awoke it was still dark, and she had no idea of the time. Her body clock was confused by all the different time zones. A slight snore from across the compartment told her that Otto was sleeping and, unable to sleep herself, she dressed in the dark, seizing an opportunity to do it away from his constant presence. She needed breathing space, to move her legs, to walk away from her thoughts of Russian soldiers with bayonets and Masha's limp form in the snow.

She unlatched the door and as usual she slipped the knapsack over her shoulders, always aware of the responsibility of those papers inside. She felt for her flask and walked down the dimly lit corridor to the samovar. She hoped to see Haru, though she pretended to herself she didn't care. Anyway, she guessed he would be asleep at this time of the night. So she filled her flask and then sipped at the hot water, watching the dark world flow by, and feeling the wheels' vibration under her feet.

She was there for half an hour, leaning against the corridor wall. 'Can't you sleep?'

Haru. She turned, startled, even though his voice was soft.

'The journey's nearly over. We'll soon be at Vladivostok.'

'I was thinking the same. I wanted to see you again, and to give you an address so we could write to each other. I would have come to your compartment, but I don't think your travelling companion likes the look of me.'

'He's just nervous. We've had quite a journey.'

'I must have been here twenty times. In fact, I've been hanging around this boiler so long I think I'm nearly cooked.'

She laughed. 'You don't look any different to me.'

'I know you have a story to tell because it's written in your eyes. And I'm curious what is in that bag you're carrying. You're never without it.'

'This is all my belongings, that's why. There is nothing else. I haven't a home, or anything else to my name, just what's in here.'

'Really? I dream of that. To have only a knapsack and be free.'

'Except it's not freedom, is it? Not when you haven't had the choice.' An image just behind her eyes, of Uncle Tata stumbling with his pack across frozen grass, his breath pumping out his fear.

Haru's eyes took on a soft look. 'Listen, there's a free compartment in first class, with seats where we can talk. Will you come? You can bring your friend with you.' He pointed to her bag.

She smiled, the image gone. 'For a little while. You need to tell me about life in Japan, so I can be prepared.'

'Oh dear. We could be there until Vladivostok.'

He led the way further down the train, through the silent empty restaurant car and into the wood-panelled carriage with only two compartment doors.

'Gosh, how the other half live!' she said as he opened the door to an empty suite. She put a tentative hand to the velvet curtains, marvelling at the tasselled pelmets and fine gas chandeliers.

Haru closed the door with a soft click. There were two tub chairs by a table near the window and they sat there, knees almost touching, feet on the soft carpet, while the steam from their hot flasks curled into the air. They didn't put on a light, but watched the dim shapes of trees pass them by in the dark. Haru's face was pale in the gloom of the carriage.

'So, Miss Kowalski,' he said, 'We missed the moon festival. But now you're here, tell me why you want to go to Japan.'

Something about this small square cabin hurtling through

space made it easy to talk. She began to tell him how they'd been driven from Poland to Lithuania, the terrifying tramp through frozen countryside with death always at their backs. How they'd been strafed by Allied planes and left the injured to groan in a ditch, because there was no doctor and no way to ease their pain; no way to carry anyone older than three years old. And then, as her confidence grew, how they'd seen the same thing coming in Lithuania, and feared it like animals fear a storm but are powerless to stop it coming.

All the time he was still, listening as she talked. When she got to the part about her brother being taken away, he reached out his hand. For the rest of the story his warm dry hand held hers. She told him the whole thing as their hands made their own conversation in small pressures of the fingers and palms.

'Otto wouldn't like me telling you,' she said at the end. 'He doesn't think we should trust anyone. Not after Masha.'

'I think he is right. But your secrets are safe with me. I am a professional secret keeper. Have to be, to work for Tanaka-san. Diplomacy is more about keeping secrets than doing business. Though I have to say, for secrets I usually charge extra.'

'How much will you charge for mine?' Their conversation had become a flirtation, and all of a sudden she was breathless.

He squeezed her hand and drew her closer where she could look into his eyes. 'How about a kiss?'

'Is that your usual charge?' His eyes were glittering in the half light.

He was about to answer when the carriage was plunged into blackness. A tunnel.

His arms reached around her neck and somehow they found each other. His lips were soft and it was a gentle, still pressure that left her wanting more.

The noise of the wheels changed to a deafening roar as they shot out of the tunnel. She found they were both smiling.

'Oh boy!' he said.

She laughed, clinging to his hands, reluctant to let go. 'Now you must keep my secrets forever.'

The noise of footsteps down the corridor. Footsteps in a hurry. She stiffened, listening.

'Don't go,' he said, tightening his grip.

'I must. If Otto wakes and I'm not there, he'll panic.'

'But we haven't stopped anywhere. It was just a tunnel. No one can have got on or off.'

She pulled away, filled with agitation. What was she thinking of? The real world was out there and she had gone into a kind of madness, having a liaison like this with a foreigner on a train.

'I'm sorry,' she blurted. 'I have to go. I can't … I mean, I'm sorry.' For a moment she struggled with the unfamiliar catch in the dark before it finally clicked open and she fled out of the door. Disorientated, she blundered the wrong way down the corridor before turning to go back the way she had come.

There was no sign of Haru but as she hurried back she saw Otto, gangling arms stabilizing himself on each side of the corridor as he made his way towards her.

'Where the hell have you been?' he said. 'I looked everywhere for you.'

'Just the toilet and then a walk.' She was glad he couldn't see the flush on her face.

'I thought something had happened.'

'No, nothing,' she lied. 'Go back to bed.'

'I got a Russian paper,' he said, 'from one of the yeshiva students. The NKVD are increasing their crackdown on people against the Soviet regime, especially Germans. The tank activity at the borders has increased and there's talk of a German invasion. In Moscow the Russians have started to detain all Germans.'

'Then thank heaven we're on our way out,' she said.

Chapter 32

When they got back, Otto felt like he couldn't sleep – that he had to be on watch all the time. He didn't like Zofia wandering about on the train without him. He'd been everywhere, the whole length of the train, before he found her looking dazed near the first-class carriages. That was where that Japanese man Haru had his compartment, and he feared she was hoping to see him again.

Zofia was hugging her bag to her chest now, as she lay down and closed her eyes. He tried not to watch her but couldn't help himself. She was pale and drawn and getting thinner, and it aroused all his protective instincts. His love for her, like a twist in the heart that he couldn't unwind, was a kind of revelation. The fact she showed no interest in him except as a friend merely made his yearning more intense. He couldn't believe they would soon be at the end of the journey, for it had felt like years, not weeks.

As the morning light came, he felt the train slow down and he went to the door of the compartment to look out of the window. The rain had stopped, though his breath steamed the glass, and he had to rub a hole to see out. A refuelling stop. Their *provodnitsa*, Tonya, brisk in her ill-fitting uniform and cap, was trying to keep hawkers, who'd appeared from nowhere, away from the carriages. Two men in German SS uniforms were waiting to get on the train, and the sight of them made him take a sharp breath. Alarm bells screamed in his head.

One of the men was youngish, carrying his *Totenkopf* cap under his arm as if to conceal it. He was smooth-skinned with very straight eyebrows, the other older and heavier with a jutting chin. Both wore heavy jackboots and long black leather coats of a type unusual in Russia, while the bigger one gripped an attaché case. They were restless to get on the train, their speech urgent.

He couldn't hear their words over the noise of the engine. Torn between the urge to flee and the necessity of watching them, Otto saw them ask Tonya a question, then show her something that looked like police permits. Tonya answered and gestured back towards their carriage.

Breathless, he hurtled back into the compartment, where Zofia was dozing.

'Quick. Look out of the window. Two SS men have just asked about us. I saw Tonya point out our carriage.'

'Shit.' She panicked and sat up, instantly alert and reaching for her bag, then poked her head out of the compartment door to glance to the window.

The two men were still waiting to board. 'Quick!' Zofia said, 'We'll go to first class. Haru will help us.'

'No,' Otto said, grasping her by the shoulder. 'We can't trust him.'

She let out an impatient breath, but there wasn't time to argue. 'The yeshiva carriage in the *Platzkart*, they won't dare try anything there, not with so many of us.'

They pushed their way down the corridor, but it was crowded with people trying to buy goods from the hawkers thrusting their hands through the windows. Since the last stop, a stack of luggage blocked the corridor.

'Back the other way,' Otto shouted to Zofia. He turned in the narrow space in time to see Tonya get back on the train and the first of the men clamber aboard.

Otto glanced into compartment four and saw it was empty except for the detritus of living on the train. The occupants must have got off. He grasped Zofia by the shoulders and pushed her inside. 'Shut the door. Act like you're still asleep. I'll deal with them.'

She began to protest about it being daylight, but he yanked down the blind and shut the door on her. 'Lock it. Pretend to sleep,' he hissed.

He ran back to compartment two and, pulse throbbing, jumped into his bunk and dragged the sheet up to his chin. He let out a snore, like a sleeping passenger. It was all he could think of, though he was pretty sure the bigger man had seen him as he climbed aboard.

Shit. I didn't lock it. Too late now.

The plod of heavy boots and scrape of the runners as the sliding door opened. He opened one eye to see the two men in leather coats, one crowding behind the other. By the greenish light of the corridor he saw they were both bigger than he imagined, built like bodyguards.

One of them threw off the covers and hauled him out by one arm.

'Hey! What is it?' he said in Russian. 'I think you're in the wrong compartment.'

'No,' the younger man said. 'This is the right one.'

'*Sind Sie Otto Wulfsson?*' The broader one with a growth of blue stubble spoke in German.

Otto summoned his courage. He'd have to brazen it out. '*Ja,*' he said, matching their German. '*Was ist los?*'

They had closed the door, and the taller one had thrown down his cap on the bunk opposite. He was smiling in a superior kind of way. 'I'm Gratz and this is my partner, Vering. We hope you will allow us to accompany you to Vladivostok.'

There was to be no choice, he saw that instantly. Vering, the one with a prominent chin, pushed Otto back down onto the bed, then Gratz sat too close, so now he was sandwiched between them, one on either side.

With one smooth motion Gratz drew a revolver from his pocket and clicked off the safety catch. His voice was urbane, the falsely polite voice of German authority, '*Kriminalkommissar* Brandt sent us.'

Otto's throat tightened at the name; Zeitel's boss.

'We're to relieve you of your weapon,' Gratz said.

'There must be a mistake,' he blustered. 'What is this? I haven't got a gun. I threw it off the train after I killed the girl.'

'Then you won't mind if we search,' Gratz said, nodding to Vering, his muscle-bound companion, who stood and thrust his palm under the mattresses and sheets and then, finding nothing, turned over any place he thought something could be hidden, including Otto's suitcase.

'I can't find it,' Vering said. 'The package Zeitel was after. No weapon either.'

A sigh of impatience. 'Here, let me look.' With one hand Gratz tipped up Otto's suitcase and shook it, scattering everything on the floor. He prodded Otto in the shoulder with the revolver. 'Where's the package Zeitel asked you to find?'

'You know damn well where it is. I handed it to his men at Krasnoyarsk.'

'Very clever. That package was a forgery. Where's the real one?'

Otto feigned ignorance. 'All this fuss over a pair of ladies' gloves. I don't know what Zeitel wanted it for. It's nothing important, just gloves for the Japanese consul's wife. I was in Sugihara's consulate in Kaunas when his wife packed it.'

'There was another woman,' Vering said. 'A blonde. Where is she? Has she got the gun?'

Otto remembered Masha pointing it at him, what seemed like centuries ago. When he didn't answer, Vering grabbed him by the collar and thrust him back against the wall as if he were made of tissue paper.

'She got off at Birobidzhan.' Otto's heart battered an uncomfortable tattoo.

'Very convenient. Two women disappearing like that. Except the *provodnitsa* informed us that Zofia Kowalski's still on the train. In this compartment,' Gratz said.

Vering stuck his big face towards Otto. 'And don't play dumb, we know you're a smart guy, so lies do you no credit. Save your breath, you'll need it later.'

Oh shit. The train was already moving again. Now he was trapped here with these two. They'd said they were taking him in. Where to? Nazi headquarters? Wherever it was, he was sure it wouldn't be anywhere good. His jaw was trembling now, from adrenaline or fear, he was not sure which. He pressed his hands onto his knees.

Gratz turned to his friend. 'Vering, go and ask the train attendant to point out where Zofia Kowalski is sitting; she and her friend Masha Romaska were both travelling on the Japanese visa.'

So they didn't know that Masha was dead. Was that good or bad?

Gratz was still giving Vering instructions. 'Tell the *provodnitsa* that Zofia Kowalski's an old friend we're looking to reconnect with.'

When Vering left the compartment, Gratz kept the attaché case beside him on the seat, and his revolver ready in his hand. 'We are all friends together, German men like us. There is no room in the Reich for unbelievers. You could be comfortable. Think about it.'

Otto swallowed to ease his dry mouth. Outside, the golden ball of sun was just rising over the trees, gilding the marsh with glittering light. A flock of geese flew overhead in a long V-shaped skein. Was this his last morning? Why had he wasted time, when there was a life to be lived?

He sat clamped to the seat, arms folded into himself, wondering if he could somehow make a run for it.

'Relax,' said Gratz. 'We'll be accompanying you to Ussuriysk, and then a car will collect us to take us to our offices in Vladivostok.'

Otto stayed still and silent, his mind whirring over possibilities, over what he could do. So far, nothing came to mind and there would be no more stops before Ussuriysk. Once there, he'd be at their mercy. 'What do they want me for?'

'Intelligence. They want to know more about Sugihara, and about why he's sending this package to General Sato in Japan. Rumour says it's anti-German material. If you've been harbouring that, it's an offence.'

'You have no right to detain me. I'm not getting off. My ticket's for Vladivostok.'

'Then there'll be a corpse in this compartment when we leave. And it won't be one of us. Your choice.'

Further up the carriage, in compartment four, Zofia was staring out into the passing landscape, barely seeing it, wondering what was happening. She could hear low voices from neighbouring compartments, but nothing she could make out.

Had those men found Otto? After another fifteen minutes, and still nothing from him, she could bear it no longer. She had to see what was going on, but she knew it would be risky to leave the compartment. They hadn't stopped again so those Nazis must still be on board, but so far no one had approached her. She was just thinking this when there was a sharp knock.

She startled, staring at the door where the black leatherette blind was down.

Another rap. '*Provodnitsa*. It's Tonya.'

Zofia got up and approached the door warily and lifted the blind a fraction until she could see Tonya's green uniform. She was alone. Zofia let out her breath. 'What do you want?'

'Miss Kowalski?' Tonya's voice held a distinct air of disapproval. 'You moved carriage, didn't you? I saw you come in here, and it needs to be cleaned. You must stay in the assigned seat. I

252

turned a blind eye before, but it's against regulations. Did your friends find you?'

Zofia shook her head, puzzled. She unlocked the door and slid it open a little. 'Two big Germans in leather coats.' Tonya was impatient, and the word Germans held a slight sneer. 'I told them you were in compartment two, not here. You shouldn't have moved. Didn't they find you?'

'Oh. Yes, yes.' Zofia said, playing along. 'Thank you.'

So the men definitely knew which compartment Otto was in.

For a fraction of a second, she wondered whether to enlist Tonya's help but she knew what would happen if she did. Trouble from the Soviets. She remembered Masha and it still stung that she could have been so taken in. Any allegiance was trouble, and she was sure Tonya was very much part of the whole Soviet regime.

The Germans had asked after her. This wasn't good news.

Tonya was still talking. 'Well, you'll need to go back to your original compartment now because from Ussuriysk we're very busy and all compartments are fully booked.'

'Thank you,' Zofia said. 'I'll move back before we arrive. Which one are my German friends staying in?'

'Second-class number six, just further up.' Tonya gestured to the front of the train.

'And how long will the stop be at Ussuriysk?'

'Fifteen minutes. Enough time to get your last refreshments. There's a shop on the concourse and a restaurant. We'll be loading many more commuters to Vladivostok, it's a busy stop.'

Zofia shut the door. So the two men were supposed to be further up in six, not in with Otto in number two.

If it hadn't been for Otto, the journey would have been easy, but these men were Nazis. She'd got to know him, and she couldn't just abandon him now. Would they take him off the train at the next stop?

She needed help. Otto wouldn't like it, but she'd go to first class and see if she could find Haru. She couldn't ask the rabbi, he had students with him, and she didn't want to put them at risk.

Gingerly, she risked sticking her head out of the door. She nipped into the corridor and set off at a pace, seeing the landscape whip by. She had the rucksack on her back; it was never off, as if she had grown an extra limb. On the way she shot past number six but, just like her own, the blinds were down and she couldn't see inside. Was it empty? Or were the Germans in there? Either way didn't bode well.

She didn't know what she'd say to Haru, or what he'd think of her bursting in on him. Through the other second-class carriages, hurrying towards the dining car, where already a few passengers were eating breakfast. No sign of Haru or Tanaka-san. The chink of cutlery on plates and a strong smell of frying sausage.

She was about to go through into first class when the *provodnitsa* for that part of the train, a narrow-eyed woman, stopped her at the door. 'Excuse me, this is first class.'

'I just want to talk to a friend.'

'Nobody in first class without a reservation.'

'But I'll only be a few minutes,' Zofia said.

'No. We have had some pilfering in our stores, so anyone without a first-class ticket is forbidden.' Just at that moment the green-uniformed conductor, bristling with disobliging efficiency, arrived behind the *provodnitsa*. The conductor was implacable and also insisted she should go back to her own carriage in second class.

What could she do? She couldn't make a fuss.

'I think my friend is unwell,' she said. 'Otto Wulfsson. Please would you send a doctor to carriage C in second class, compartment two?'

The first class *provodnitsa* looked at her with disdain. Obviously she had recovered from the flu. 'I'll tell Tonya. She can deal with it. Now please return to your seat.'

Would they send someone? She had to hope so. Perhaps it would give Otto some breathing space. It was so frustrating not knowing what was going on.

Deep in thought, she slid open the door to compartment four. And almost collided with the chest of a man who loomed towards her, his eyes shadowed by a Nazi cap.

There was no time to back out for he had her firmly by the arm and twisted her away. She smelled the leather of his coat and her own fear as it rippled up through her spine, dredging with it all the memories of Nazi men like him beating old men on the street.

He grasped her by the back of her hair to jerk her head back; yanked one arm so hard up her back it made her cry out. But he was too big and heavy to throw, and she was in a position where she couldn't use any of her wrestling skills.

Wait. Wait for the right moment.

He pushed her forward and up the short distance to number two, where he shoved open the door, and a push from behind and the movement of the train made her stumble inside. Otto was already under the guard of the other thick-set man.

At the sight of her, Otto tried to get up but was forced back down.

'Sit.' Guttural Russian. It was an order. The man in the cap pointed a gun at her.

'Leave her alone, she's done nothing.' Otto said. He was speaking German, but she understood the gist of it. After the Germans invaded Poland, they all had to make sure they understood the rudiments of German.

'No talk.' The taller man glanced at his watch, then in German, 'We should arrive in another three hours.'

She tried to smile at Otto, but he mouthed at her 'I'm sorry,' and she shook her head as if to indicate it was not his fault.

The heavier man tried to wrestle her rucksack from her and, when she refused to give it up, he hit her hard across the face.

'Stop!' Otto grabbed his arm.

'Shut up.' The man turned and smacked Otto in the jaw with

the butt of the gun. The brutality of it made her wince.

Cowed, her face throbbing, she let the man take the rucksack. She didn't want Otto to be hit again.

It was over. She'd have to give it up.

She prayed Tonya or a doctor would come.

The Nazi officer took out the package, turning it over. 'This is it,' he said. 'Can't believe this is what all the fuss is about.' He passed it to the other man. 'There's a Japanese seal and signature. But it's heavier than I thought.'

'Anything valuable?'

'Intelligence, they said. Paperwork, but they're tight-lipped about what it's about.'

'Shame. Shall I open it?'

'Hands off, Vering. Or Heydrich will do what he's planned for Zeitel. Arrange an AD.'

The other man looked blank.

'Accelerated demise. Taken to the woods and shot.'

Zofia made eye contact with Otto, who was listening and understanding this German conversation. She tried to convey to Otto that she'd understood enough of it, and the implications.

The man called Vering said, 'That important, eh?'

'Important enough that Heydrich will have a car and reinforcements waiting for us at Ussuriysk. We've to take them both to the Vladivostok office for interrogation.'

Zofia swallowed. She'd seen it in Poland; Nazi interrogation always meant the same. Torture and then transit to a camp if you were lucky.

The taller man, who she gathered from the men's conversation was called Gratz, had meanwhile put Sugihara's parcel in his attaché case. *At least,* Zofia thought, *I'll be going to the same place as the parcel. We will be at the end together.*

For the next three hours there was silence. The men sat close to the doors and smoked German cigarettes, so clouds of foul-smelling grey smoke filled the small space with a haze. Otto kept glancing at his watch. Every time they got near habitation she raised her eyebrows to him in question, and he'd give a slight shake of the head. Not there yet.

The hours passed slowly and the daylight was grey and wan outside the window. Zofia asked to go to the toilet but was refused. When they got nearer to the station, a few small factory buildings began to appear; dripping pylons and blocks of apartments stood isolated amongst scrubby fields.

She reckoned there was still an hour to go. She hoped Haru would come looking for her, but she knew this was a slim chance. Why would he? She'd practically run away from him. And Otto had never shown him any warmth.

Otto kept his eyes fixed on her as if he was trying to tell her something. He was fidgeting, his fingers tapping against his palm. Then she realized it wasn't fidgeting. He was drawing on his hand. A letter at a time. Then more gap, so as not to make the men suspicious. She watched his hands as they spelled out: AT STOP. I MAKE TROUBLE. YOU. GET BACK ON TRAIN. He repeated it and gave a slight nod.

She shook her head vehemently.

'Hey, what's going on?' Vering glared at Otto, who shrugged.

Having the message didn't help. Now she was even more nervous. What would Otto do? What did he mean by trouble?

The train crept slowly through the suburbs in the drizzled grey of the afternoon.

Chapter 33

Otto hoped Zofia had understood his message. He wasn't yet sure what he could do, but if he could give her a chance to get away he would. The pictures in the parcel had shocked him to the core. He couldn't let Zofia, beautiful, fragile Zofia, end up in a place like that. He'd read the testimonies about what the Nazis did to Jews.

The train rhythm slowed, *clickety clack, clickety clack*. Industrial suburbs bled by until the train slowed.

A pockmarked sign. Ussuriysk. They were only a few hours from the end of the journey. So near, yet so far. Vladivostok was the next stop.

Otto's stomach tightened to a fist. Gratz, now wearing his cap and carrying the attaché case, stood to leave and Vering, gun in hand, nosed them out into the corridor. Otto knew he'd have to do something before these men had help from their Nazi welcoming committee on the station. Their compartment was near the very end of the train, and theirs the last passenger door onto the platform. After their carriage there was only a goods van, and a wagon carrying spare parts.

In the corridor, even before they got to the door, loud consternation and men's shouts from outside made their captors stop to look out.

Otto shrank back. The platform was full of Russian soldiers, three deep and all armed.

'What's the hell's up?' Vering asked.

'Don't know. Russian troops. Shit, that's all we need. Quick, bring them back inside,' ordered Gratz.

But despite their orders they'd no time. The train door opened and Russian soldiers stormed aboard, bringing with them a harsh wind and the metallic smell of guns.

'All non-Russians to get off and line up on the platform,' came the shout. 'Papers ready for inspection.'

'What the hell?' The two Germans seemed nonplussed by this and began to feel their pockets for their papers.

Otto looked frantically to Zofia, but she could go nowhere; she was hemmed in, and her anxious eyes sought his. 'Some sort of Russian checkpoint,' he shouted to her. He tried to send her a reassuring look, but it was chaos and the soldiers were insistent they should all get off.

By the look of them, the Germans were as shocked as they were. Otto kept Gratz and the attaché case in view as they were ordered off the train.

A mass exodus. Hundreds of passengers had to disembark and line up along the platform. The soldiers harassed them to stand in line, even Vering and Gratz, whose faces had turned grey. Otto saw Gratz anxiously searching for an escape from the inspection, and from the wind which funnelled through the station. But everyone except Russians in the *Platzkart* had to get off. There were too many soldiers armed with rifles for them to do anything else.

Otto crept close to Zofia, because everyone was having their pockets searched. A man with a burlap sack was following down the line, and whenever they found something gold or valuable, it went into the sack. The two Germans began to look distinctly uncomfortable, and Gratz's face had gone a mottled shade of red.

They were armed, that was why, and there was nowhere to get rid of their guns.

Otto glanced at Zofia; she too was staring down the queue, her face anguished.

Haru was peering in their direction, obviously looking for Zofia, until the Russians yelled at him to stand up straight. They watched as Haru and his Japanese boss had their papers checked and then were made to empty their pockets. They bowed low to the Russians, their watches were confiscated, and then they were dismissed almost immediately and gestured back onto the train.

Those on board now stared out of the windows. Otto was sure he could see Haru staring at Zofia, and her answering glance, but she could show no other reaction. Everyone had dialled their body language down to zero. Everyone knew that compliance was the best defence.

Four of the eldest yeshiva students, German Jews, had been pulled out from the other end of the line, and were being herded towards a queue of waiting trucks.

Dr Rabinowitz tried to reason with the Russians but they refused to listen. 'Take me instead,' he kept saying.

The soldier spat at his feet. 'We've no use for an old man in the gulag,' he said. 'And all Germans are suspected enemies of the state.'

Otto blinked. So even here the Russians must be fearing Nazi invasion and had decided to clamp down on German nationals. It wasn't surprising, but it turned his legs to feathers.

Dr Rabinowitz hugged each student, one by one. 'Trust in the Torah, my boys,' he said. 'Remember what you've been taught.'

It made Otto's eyes water to see the disbelief in the eyes of Rabbi Nowak and the horrified students.

Some passengers, mostly elderly women of the poorer classes, were allowed to get back on the train. The richer ones had their furs and jewellery taken, plus their handbags and money.

The searchers were closer, and Otto caught Zofia's eye. 'Don't forget,' he whispered, touching his finger to his palm. He didn't know what he could do, but he knew that from now on she'd be alone, and his chest heaved with emotion.

She didn't respond, but he knew she'd heard him by the flicker of her eyes.

The main inspector, a Russian captain in a peaked cap and a chest full of medals, was now close enough for them to hear him. 'State name and nationality.'

'Sek Keong, Singapore,' said the terrified man in front of them in the queue, clinging to his wife's hand.

His entourage roughly separated them and searched the man and took his glasses, his books, and his pack of cigarettes, rudely calling him 'short-arse' in Russian. He was dragged off towards the trucks, leaving the woman on her knees on the platform, begging to go with him.

Two soldiers almost bodily lifted her and thrust her back onto the train at rifle-point.

Rage rose in Otto's throat. Despite their supposed communist ideals of everyone being equal, the NKVD were openly stealing people's valuables before they left Russia. It was clear they were arresting anyone they thought might cause a problem to communist Russia, anyone who looked like an intellectual or a teacher, probably for hard labour. Otto knew he'd not last two minutes breaking stones or digging roads.

He began to mentally go through what was in his pockets. A comb. Tolstoy's *The Road to Calvary*. A paper packet with a few nuts. Papers in the name of Otto Wulfsson. Yes, they would be the problem. They'd arrest him once they saw his passport.

He'd no doubt they'd want Gratz's attaché case too, with Sugihara's parcel.

Beside him, Gratz and Vering appeared to be frozen to the spot. Vering kept looking sideways to Gratz, but Gratz kept his head up and resolutely ignored him, the only sign of tension the deep scored lines around his lips. Served them right. It gave Otto deep pleasure to see the boot on the other foot, that now they were the ones to be intimidated.

The inspection squad was now two people away.

Vering was visibly shaking. His mouth worked and he had a wild look in his eyes as he glanced down the platform towards the end of the train, towards the rails drawn like pencil lines into the distance.

Abruptly Vering burst into movement. Otto startled, his heart thumping. Vering ran, veering like a rabbit, a sprint into an ungainly run, down the platform away from the train.

Beside him, Gratz stiffened as if a rod had been thrust up his back, but though his feet shuffled, he didn't follow. He simply gripped tight to his leather pocket flaps, his knuckles white.

The platform ran out, and Vering leapt down onto the tracks, stumbling over the sleepers, then off up the steep siding, making for a gap in the barbed wire fence. Two Russian soldiers, young fresh-faced boys, took aim, and opened fire. Vering scrambled on all fours but managed only a few more steps before he jerked and dropped, tumbling down the embankment.

He'd reached the bottom before the echo of the guns died away. He lay twitching on the track like a fish on a line.

Nobody else moved. No one dared.

The hush was intense. Otto ran his tongue around his dry mouth. The wind whistled, singing through the wire fence at the side of the track. So here they were, the last in the queue to be seen. Gratz, Zofia and him.

Gratz's face was hollow, his mouth now pressed together until it was bloodless.

The attaché case was still on the platform next to Gratz, close to where Vering had been standing. Otto sidled closer, inch by inch, until it was beside him.

A ghost of a plan began to form in his mind. He couldn't save himself. But perhaps he could do something for Zofia, and for the refugees who would follow her. A silence descended on him, like the calm eye of a storm.

The captain held out his hand to Gratz for his papers. Gratz, now red around the jowls, obeyed. The captain examined the passport with narrowed eyes. 'You want to join your friend?' he said. 'All Germans are to be detained.'

'Why? Germany and Russia allies, *ja*?' His Russian was heavily accented. 'I speak with your commander—'

'It's a matter of national security. Raise your arms.' He signalled for him to do so and Gratz complied. His assistant felt down his coat until he found the gun. He removed it and held it out for inspection.

Immediately the captain summoned more men, and Gratz was led away. He walked with dignity, and Otto felt a momentary flash of sympathy.

But only a flash, because they were shovelling coal into the tender and the engine was building up steam, ready to depart. Otto knew it would be Zofia next, and then his turn. His papers said he was German, and he knew by now what that would mean. The gulag like Gratz, or death like Vering.

By now the men were in front of Zofia. He ached for her more than for himself.

She stood meekly and brought out her papers. They examined them and made her turn out her pockets. Otto watched as she took out a pen and a brooch and a silver spoon, and a few other small objects.

'Hey, look at this.' The soldier snatched something and held it out on his palm. 'A little jade fox!' he said.

Otto blinked. It was his *netsuke*. Her neck flushed and she cast him an apologetic look, a look full of sorrow. It was over in milliseconds. The soldier pocketed the *netsuke* then they told her to put all her pathetic little treasures into the sack. She did so without demur. She showed them her passport and told them she was Polish, travelling from Lithuania.

There must have been an appeal in her eyes because they let

her go and gestured her to the train.

He wanted to sing. They were letting her go!

But she would have failed in her mission, and that he couldn't bear. The package was still in Gratz's attaché case. He'd do it. He could do this one grand thing.

She had never looked more beautiful than she did at that moment, her cheeks pale and her eyes glittering from fear and the wind. But he knew all at once that Zofia would be the last person to board the train here at Ussuriysk, and he would never see her again.

As she climbed the steps, he drank in every last detail of her, of her blue threadbare coat and her woollen cap over that dark shiny hair.

A soldier shut the door after her with a clang, but Zofia turned to wait for Otto, eyes hollow with anxiety. She had pulled down the window and was craning out.

He loved her even more at that moment.

But Otto knew what he had to do. The one thing that could make a difference. To get Sugihara's package to her. He was already a dead man walking.

'Your papers.'

'I am German,' he said pleasantly. 'Like him.' He pointed to where Gratz was being taken away.

'Another Kraut,' the soldier said in Russian. 'That's the last of them. Take him.' He waved an arm to the train guard to give him the signal to depart and the guard blew his whistle. No, it couldn't go yet!

Keep them talking. Just a few more inches towards the attaché case. A soldier took him by the arm. The train began to chug forwards.

'Excuse me, but have you a light?' Otto stopped dead in his tracks. The Russian looked at him as if he was crazy.

The man with the sack was about to pick up the attaché case. *Now.*

Otto twisted and ran. Scooped up the attaché case and sprinted towards the carriage door. He had to get it to Zofia before they had a chance to shoot. He was running into the wind, eyes streaming, close to the churning wheels, eyes fixed on her window.

Get a foot on the step. He'd done it before. He could do it. He had it in his sights, the criss-cross metal of the stair.

'Otto!' Zofia was shouting.

The noise of it, a hiss of escaping gas as it cranked under a head of steam, moving slowly away.

Zofia screamed his name but already he heard the thud of men chasing after him, swung out crazily with the attaché case, hitting at the arms trying to grab him.

A shot rang out and he jerked, feeling a pain searing into his shoulder. Still he kept on running. He thought his lungs would burst. But at the last moment he managed to get a foot up on the stair and grab for the edge of the open window.

All that mattered was that small gap. He'd have only a few seconds to post it through.

His fingers gripped the slippery glass and in an almighty effort he heaved the attaché case up through the window.

Zofia reached out her arms and fumbled to keep it against the wind, but she had it tight.

He began to fall, unable to keep his grip on the window. But it was sweet, the falling. He'd done it.

Sugihara would be proud. Another shot and pain riddled his back as his bones crashed down hard. But he tried to get up, to watch her go.

It was then that he felt the third shot. Just above the hips, like a blow with a spade.

Next moment he was on his back on the hard concrete, looking up at a sky where the clouds were just clearing. He turned his head. The train became a snake dwindling away into the steam.

'God speed, Zofia,' he whispered.

He hoped he would die quickly.

The image of Zofia's startled face as she grabbed the case from him floated before his closed eyes. He didn't open them when he felt the cold muzzle of a gun against his forehead, but hoped he'd meet his father on the other side because now he understood something about choosing how and when to die.

Chapter 34

Earlier in the day, in Kovno, Illeyvich lit a cigar and went to stand behind the big curved window of his art deco office. He'd just received the news from Arsenyev that Masha Romaska was dead, and he was surprised to find he actually cared. She'd been promising, that one, young and angry and alluring.

The manner of death made no sense, though. An accident with a sleigh?

And she'd been thoroughly searched and no package or parcel had been found with her, nothing except her NKVD intelligence and security card number, which was how they'd tracked her to him. One strange thing; at Birobidzhan station there'd apparently been a scuffle with a woman of her description and another woman. Was that Zofia Kowalski? They'd found Masha's coat, and in the pocket she had a German pistol, not the Russian revolver with the suppressor.

It was a mystery and Illeyvich didn't like mysteries.

He glanced at the wall clock as if it might help, and puffed out smoke before opening his desk drawer to take out the train timetable.

Flipping it open, he ran a long white finger along the column of stations. The train would arrive at Vladivostok later today. He uncapped his pen and wrote down the time on a pad.

When Masha rang him last week in the middle of the night, she'd told him the package was going to General Sato in Tokyo. So it was a diplomatic hot potato, and something important. He'd need to get someone onto it in Vladivostok. Undercover men, not uniformed. And some sort of ruse to get Zofia Kowalski to meet them.

He wanted to know what had really happened to Masha Romaska – and the Jew she was supposed to offload in Birobidzhan, Zofia Kowalski, must have the answer.

Ruminating, he stubbed out the cigar and picked up the telephone.

In Zeitel's apartment the toy train rocketed around the track, under the papier mâché bridge, and past the fire station built out of balsa wood. There was even a red tin fire engine in the double entrance with a ladder. Everything was running as it should, even the little lights in the traffic lights and the smoke wisping ingeniously from the factory chimneys. Zeitel sat on the bed, watching his breath and the smoke cloud in the air before him.

It couldn't be his fault that the NKVD had arrested Gratz. He'd had a call from Tilda, telling him they had taken all Germans off the Trans-Siberian and sent them to camps. He knew that this was a bad sign and he should get out of Russia while he could.

He thought idly of fleeing, but knew it was not possible. No transit papers would be issued to him. Brandt needed to blame someone, and now somehow it was all his fault Gratz had been arrested, and he had failed to get Sugihara's papers back. Brandt had been raging because there was no man he could trust in Vladivostok and there was no way he could find someone before he too had to get out of Russia. Unfinished business, something Brandt abhorred.

Tilda had borne the brunt of it, but Brandt himself would get out of Russia, Zeitel was sure. Men like him always did. Zeitel continued to stare into space, dimly aware of the trains' constant movement, two locos humming round and round the track with nowhere to go. He stared partly because it gave him pleasure and partly because there was nowhere to run. He might as well be here as anywhere.

Failure was not an option in Hitler's Germany. Those who failed, those who weren't the strongest and the fittest, were expendable. And now there were troops routing out German civilians. Rumour had finally made it to Kaunas about Operation Barbarossa, the planned invasion of Russia, so all Germans were suspected of spying and sending Soviet secrets back to Germany. They were to be arrested immediately and sent to gulags.

He knew it was only a matter of time.

It was cold, but he had no more cigarettes. He didn't hear the men coming into his apartment building until the harsh knock on the door.

So soon? Not even a few hours to prepare for it.

They broke down the door when he didn't answer it, and they found him sitting there in his overcoat, still sucking on his last cold tab end.

He was no trouble, he thought to himself as they thrust their rifles at him and ordered him to move. He'd go quietly, and at least have an hour or so of peace before the interrogation. He was sure there'd be one; didn't take a genius to work that out.

The Russians who came for him were young, with smooth unblemished skin and an exhausting air of good health along with the attitude that life owed them a favour. They would never be one of the hundreds of shivering, miserable men, the men with no names, who were digging the frozen ground by pickaxe to make a canal. The men in gulags gambling with their own fingers at cards because they had nothing left to give.

These young men wanted everything done yesterday; he couldn't move quick enough. They were so full of their own importance, so keen to dismiss the years of experience inside this old skull as worthless and meaningless. Had he been like them once?

To them, life was just a game. They had never had to witness their own diminishing, moment by moment. They had not yet been on the losing side. The young woman, Zofia Kowalski, she'd picked the wrong side too.

The wind scoured his face as the truck drove away, and he watched the familiar red-draped streets disappear and with it the life he'd known before. He was now to be sent to a 'corrective facility' as what the Russians called a 'special settler', slave labour. A place where survival was a lottery and where everyone had already drawn the short straw. So he was surprised when the truck stopped at the woods just outside Kaunas, and he was told to get out.

What struck him most was the green. The green of the pines after all that red, and the way they whispered in the breeze as if they were telling him something important. He listened hard, hearing the solitary song of a bird. When he saw the clearing, he realized he'd drawn the shortest straw of all, and tried to run.

After the shots, the train continued to run in his apartment for another three days.

When neighbours complained about the noise, soldiers came and, seeing a perfect replica of a German town, enjoyed smashing it to rubble and melting down the tin figures to make bullets.

Chapter 35

Aboard the train, Zofia had moved to sit with Dr Rabinowitz and the others from the yeshiva. There she felt like she at least belonged somewhere. She was unable to speak, one moment angry, the next just numb. But they accepted her as she lowered her head through their daily ritual of prayers. They had nowhere else to pray and she found their mumbled recitations and bobbing heads a comfort. They knew what had happened to Otto, and treated her with compassion. Their sadness and disbelief, and the fact they prayed for his soul, helped her feel less alone. Even so, she couldn't escape replaying the moment on the station over and over.

One moment Otto was at the window, the next he was gone. Like a leaf in autumn. His face, in that split second at the window, was like a child, full of elation.

But when the third bullet hit, and his fingers let go of the window, she knew there was no more hope for him. She'd craned her neck in the draught, hair whipping wildly around her face, looking back. Otto was surrounded by Russians in khaki uniform. The captain fired a bullet to his head, and the shock of that callous act was like a lightning strike.

'Stop!' she'd shouted. But though she'd willed the train to stop, the wheels kept on turning. In seconds they were away from the station and shooting through a wilderness of spindly trees, pale-trunked birches with no leaves, and the stark silhouettes of spiky bristled pines.

But, like a miracle, she had the attaché case in her arms. He'd done it for her. He could have gone to the camp quietly, but he'd chosen instead to give her this last gift.

Such bravery. It was unfathomable.

And now in the *Platzkart*, the engine was gaining speed and pushing Otto into her past. She pressed the attaché case into her stomach like a foetus. Yet hugging it did nothing to ease the tearing pain of her loss.

She cursed Sugihara, but hugged the leather case tighter, even though it could never bring Otto back. His journey was over. Outside, the sun shone weakly as if nothing had happened.

What Otto had done made her even more resolved to take the parcel to Tokyo, though the closer they got to the end of the line, the more she wondered how she would be able to find the Japanese general now Otto was gone. With no facility with the Japanese language, how could she possibly explain to the general why she had come?

Of course there was Haru, but she hadn't seen him, and now she didn't want to. That part of the journey seemed like a dream. And besides, it felt disrespectful to Otto, who she knew had been jealous of him. She felt she owed something to Otto, whereas Haru had done nothing to earn her love, so why did she still long to see him? She pushed thoughts of him away.

She had found Otto's letter to his mother tucked under his pillow. In it, Otto had called his mother 'dearest' and vowed he'd be home soon. He sounded like a small boy and to see that part of him had made her cry. Everyone was a child at heart, she realized, even those who thought they'd grown up. The letter was tucked into her bag, and she would post it for him in Vladivostok, though she didn't know how to tell Otto's mother that he was dead, shot by the Russians. Was it better to live in hope or know the truth?

She dreaded getting the letter telling her Jacek was dead. She'd rather think of him alive, long before the Germans came, eight years old and catapulting plum stones at a row of tin cans, like she remembered him.

The train did not stop again and their final arrival in Vladivostok was met with tearful relief from the students on the train, who had travelled halfway across Europe to escape the Nazis. The fact that the Russians were actually arresting Nazis now had given people tentative hope.

The party stuck together walking towards the station plaza, the tall ancient rabbi, Dr Rabinowitz, with his gaggle of eager young men. Zofia followed behind Rabbi Nowak, Rabinowitz's assistant, her rucksack on her back and the handle of the precious attaché case clenched in her hand.

As she approached the end of the platform she saw a familiar figure and her heart froze in her chest. At the turnstile where the conductor was collecting tickets, Haru was waiting, obviously looking out for her. A big leather suitcase was in one hand and a briefcase in the other and he was smiling at her expectantly under a Western-style trilby hat. She faltered. A shot of electricity whooshed up her spine. But she steeled herself. She didn't want to see him. Especially as he looked so neat and dapper, like an advertisement in a magazine. He made her feel shabby in her threadbare coat and scuffed shoes, and her eyes were red and prickly from crying.

Flustered, she handed over her ticket like the rest of the party and was waved through. Though she was dimly aware of the chatter of the students, there was no time to enjoy the moment of arrival, for Haru was hurrying to greet her.

She tried not to meet his eye, but it was impossible to avoid him.

'Zofia,' he said, stepping in front of her. 'I wanted to say I was sorry. To offer my condolences. Dr Rabinowitz told me about Otto. A terrible thing to happen.' He was speaking in his oddly accented Polish.

'Thank you,' she said, still looking deliberately over his shoulder.

'How are you doing?'

She just shook her head, unable to speak.

'I wanted to tell you that my offer still stands. For translation, I mean.'

'It's all right. I can manage.' She was trying to walk on, but he was hurrying beside her.

'I can show you around, help you get to know—'

'No, thank you. I'm going to stay with Dr Rabinowitz and his students.'

'But I—'

She stopped and gave him her full attention. 'Look, Haru, it's just never going to work, is it? We can pretend it might, but after Tokyo I'll be going on to America, and you'll be here in Japan. And let's be honest, your family won't like you associating with a poor Jewish refugee who owns nothing except the clothes on her back. Better to just save ourselves the heartache.'

He stopped, crestfallen. 'Can't we at least be friends?'

'Why?' she snapped, almost in tears. 'People I get close to, they all die. Or some catastrophe happens to them. Better to just say goodbye and good luck.'

'That's not true. It'll take time, time heals everything. And friends, friends who'll listen.'

'I'm sorry, Haru, but this is goodbye.'

He stared at her as if she might suddenly change her mind, but she took a deep breath in and tried not to look away.

Finally, it was Haru whose gaze dropped first. 'All right, Zofia. Have it your way. I wish you all the luck in the world. And I won't forget you.' He made a small polite bow, but she could see by the expression in his eyes that he was hurt.

She rushed on, to follow Dr Rabinowitz's group. There was a pain in her heart as if someone had punched her, and she felt lost as she strode through the station, a small soul in this vast pale building.

Ahead of her, the students were looking up to point out the vaulted roof and the chandeliers, the painted fresco on the ceiling, which was supported by frosted iron, like a palace from a picture book. Zofia glanced back, and saw Haru walking steadfastly towards one of the exits, his face closed off.

She saw him stop and speak to one of the students at the edge of their group, and exchange a few polite words. It made her feel worse, this feeling of wanting to call his name, to stop him walking away, but Dr Rabinowitz was already moving off and she was on his tail. Soon she was enveloped in a group of young men, all of whom were keen to escort her or help her with her rucksack, but she wouldn't let anyone touch the attaché case.

She missed Otto. She missed his pedantic explanations, his wide knowledge and his running commentary on anything and everything. Otto had told her Stalin would clamp down on any group he considered to be rebels, and that included Chinese, Chechens, Manchurians, and Armenians, as well as Jews and Ukrainians. He'd told her too that a camp for political prisoners had been recently opened in Vladivostok, the *Vladlag*, from where anti-communists were deported. Arrested prisoners arrived by goods train at the same station they'd just arrived at, and left on rain-rusted prison ships in terrible conditions. The thought of it made her shudder.

Dr Rabinowitz had purchased a map, because apparently in order to move on from Vladivostok and get a permit for their onward journey to Kobe in Japan, they had to pay a visit to Nei Saburo, the acting Japanese consul-general. Jews used Kobe as a staging post to go elsewhere in Japan or the rest of the world. Zofia still had no idea how to get from there to Tokyo, but she knew she must get out of Russia first and take one step at a time.

She kept with the knot of students as they threaded their way through the streets, which were wet with rain. The city was hilly, being built up from the harbour, and every street corner had hawkers with their wares.

'It's so much grander than I imagined,' she said to Dr Rabinowitz. 'And so many nationalities. I never thought it would be so busy.'

'Much of it was built before the Revolution, but it's always been a hub for people from all over the world, from East and West,' he said.

Zofia's legs were still getting used to solid ground, but she was amazed to see Russians queueing to buy newspapers from a street seller only to tear them up. They weren't avid for news, but used the paper to roll their cigarettes. Despite the city's impressive appearance, there were no cigarette papers to be had anywhere in Vladivostok.

The centre itself was busy, with sugared-almond coloured buildings towering over wide boulevards. She marvelled at their elaborate facades and colonnaded balconies and wished Otto could be here to see it all. Tears sprang in her eyes again. She hadn't understood the goodness of him until it was too late.

A few hawkers tried to sell them matches and gaudily wrapped sweets. After what happened to Jacek and Otto, Zofia regarded all Russian men as the enemy, and kept a wary distance from them all. These buildings gave the impression of civilization, but she knew it to be a veneer. Her visa was only just legal, and she was frighteningly aware that all it took was one over-zealous Russian busybody and she would end up in the *Vladlag*, the place where civilization ended.

Her apprehension increased when she noticed a man walking some way behind them, with his plaid scarf pulled up over his nose and mouth. It was warmer here on the coast, so it seemed odd. He was sticking to them, it seemed, and it made her anxious. She was seeing phantoms, she reassured herself.

She put herself in the midst of the students, and concentrated on Dr Rabinowitz as he led the way, pointing at the streets on the map in his carefully enunciated way. In the end they arrived at the consulate, and were able to see consul Saburo, a dry diplomat who treated them as if they were a nuisance he could do without. Zofia tucked her boat tickets and Kobe permissions into her passport, alongside her chrysanthemum visa from Sugihara.

When they came out of the consulate, the man in the scarf was still there. She got a glimpse of him, his plaid scarf, narrow trousers and strange lopsided gait before he hurried down a side road out of sight.

'Did you see that man?' she asked Dr Rabinowitz.

'What man?' He looked up and down the street, perplexed.

'A man watching us coming out of the consulate. He's gone now.'

'You think he's a pickpocket?'

'I don't know.'

'Well, whoever he was, he's gone. Let's get ourselves to the hotel. My feet are killing me.'

It was a two-day wait for the Japanese boat, the *Amakusa-maru*, to get them off Russian soil. The hotel was nothing like the luxurious one in Moscow, but a soulless functional chunk of concrete masonry. It was a cultural no man's land for those in transit. Because it was for refugees travelling to Japan on Japanese visas, there were Japanese soldiers at the hotel entrances to prevent trouble from the NKVD, and to check their papers, and this gave Zofia a measure of security, even though the workers at the hotel were all Russian. The Japanese soldiers themselves were military men, who rebuffed conversation but reminded her painfully of Haru.

Dr Rabinowitz relied on Zofia because they needed a translator for just about everything. He thought he could speak Russian, having studied his out-of-date guidebook, but his grasp of the language was quite rudimentary and he often had difficulty speaking, though he could make out most things well enough. Still, she had to ask the receptionist about who was to stay in which room, the boat timetable and if it would sail in bad weather.

When she signed the register and showed her passport, the receptionist, a small dark woman with her hair scraped back in a bun, looked up. 'Ah, Zofia Kowalski? There's a message for you.' Along with her room key, she handed Zofia an envelope with her name on in Cyrillic script.

Zofia frowned and took it to one side to open it.

It was written in Russian.

If you want news of your brother, Jacek Kowalski, meet me tomorrow, Friday, at the new People's Canteen at Yubilenyy Pier. I'll be there in the morning at nine o'clock. It was signed, *Your friend, Alina Merkova.*

Just the sight of her brother's name flooded her first with shock, then with hope.

'Who brought this note?' she asked the receptionist.

'I don't know, it came when I was off duty.'

'Do you know someone called Alina Merkova?'

A blank look and a shake of the head. So no clues there. Light-headed, she found her way to one of the chairs to sit down. Of course she wanted news of Jacek. But the lack of more information was concerning. And why didn't this Merkova woman just wait and speak to her at the hotel? The letter wasn't written on any kind of official paper, just ordinary notepaper. Though she called herself '*your friend*', it just didn't feel right. She'd be crazy to go there.

But the fact 'they' knew who she was, and the name of her brother, made her stomach churn. Was it a warning? The Cyrillic script smacked of the NKVD, not the Germans. She wondered how much Masha had been able to tell her superiors about her mission to Tokyo.

It was deeply disturbing.

'Is it bad news?' Dr Rabinowitz asked, his rheumy eyes kind.

'No. It's nothing.' She dragged her mind back to the hotel lobby, tore up the paper into small pieces and put them in the waste paper bin by the door. 'Let's go up.'

Had she made the right decision? She didn't know. Already she felt guilty, as if she was somehow letting Jacek down. The letter didn't say if he was still alive. A cold dread had settled on her shoulders. What if they were to tell her he was dead?

She was given a single room on the top floor. It was so small it could have been a closet, but even in this tiny room she was relieved to be alone for the first time in months. The hotel even had lifts. The yeshiva students went up and down in them like a ride, but the novelty soon wore off, for even in such surroundings they were all poor. Their clothes stank, their shoes leaked, they had no money to buy food, even if kosher food had been available.

Zofia was still wearing the same old coat she'd had in Kaunas, though now she sponged it down and it was sheer luxury to use the shared bathroom and have a proper bath, though she didn't dare let the Sugihara parcel out of her sight. She didn't go out of her door, except to the bathroom, let alone venture into the city, but looked uneasily out of the hotel window, watching. She wasn't sure what or who she was looking for, but the note had unnerved her, and she knew she wouldn't feel safe until she was out of Russia for good. Russia seemed to be one thing on the surface, all polite smiles, but hard, unforgiving ice was hidden underneath.

At nine o'clock the next day she was pacing back and forth in her tiny room, wondering who would be waiting for her at the café at Yubilenyy Pier. It was like torture, but she didn't dare go. It was best to stay indoors where it was safe, guarded by the Japanese, with the door locked and Dr Rabinowitz nearby.

Across the road was an arcade with shops, leading through to one of the main thoroughfares, and she and Dr Rabinowitz and his students had walked down it themselves only yesterday. At about ten o'clock a man appeared there, a man who didn't just walk on by like the other pedestrians, but remained leaning against the entrance, hanging around watching the hotel. Was he something to do with the mysterious Alina that she should have met at the pier?

She was convinced it was the same man who had followed them yesterday. It was hard to be sure, though. She kept watching him from the window. It was warm here for hats with ear flaps and scarves like his. And of course she hadn't seen his face and still couldn't. But the way he walked, one foot slightly turned out, the narrowness of his trousers, they were too familiar.

It was an hour before he slunk away, disappearing as mysteriously as he had come. She shivered. Just one more day and she'd be on that boat to Tsuruga, where nobody from the NKVD could reach her. She was not looking forward to the journey. There was a rumour that the boat would be a rough freighter, and Otto had told her that the sea around Vladivostok was protected by minefields and it took skilled navigators to steer the ships in and out of the ports. Tokyo and General Sato had never seemed further away.

Chapter 36

Finally the day of the crossing to Tsuruga arrived. The boat was leaving at noon and the coach to take them to the port would be arriving in a few hours' time. She had unpacked the Sugihara parcel from the attaché case because it looked an odd thing for a woman like her to be carrying and it drew attention to itself.

The package was scuffed and the fact it was ragged at the top and had obviously been repaired didn't help. The envelope with the photographs was still inside it. The fact that Jews, even women and little children, were being murdered by men like Gratz, and that it was still happening back in Poland, was too hard to contemplate.

She ran her finger over the nub of the broken seal, and the Japanese characters deftly painted in Sugihara's brushstrokes. Where was Sugihara now, she wondered? Would anyone tell him what had happened to Otto?

Carefully, she put the package to the bottom of her rucksack, and took another look out of the window. A movement in the shadows showed another man hanging around the arcade. So the first man had gone and another had taken his place. The building was definitely being watched. Other pedestrians passed him by, but this man lurked there in the mouth of the arcade, shifting from foot to foot. This spy was shorter, with a homburg hat pulled well down and his chin tucked into the collar of his overcoat. He was back in the shadows and so she couldn't see his face, but she was disturbed that the hotel was still being watched.

Were they watching for someone else or for her?

The sooner she could be on that boat, the better. Too restless to wait, she headed for the lobby where everyone would gather to go down to the port.

The woman at reception summoned her over and handed over another message. 'A newspaper boy brought it, just dumped it on the counter.'

She tore open the envelope to see the same writing.

Zofia. You didn't come, and this is a shame.

Your brother Jacek Kowalski is being held at a detention centre in Sverdlovsk, awaiting transit to a corrective labour camp.

He will be released in return for the package you are carrying.

Once I have the package in my possession, he'll be given immediate transit papers and a sea ticket to join you in Tsuruga.

But there is little time.

Before you leave Vladivostok, meet me at the People's Canteen at Yubilenyy Pier at ten o'clock to deliver the package. I'll be the one with red hair.

Come alone or the deal's off. I am the courier, and I too will be there alone.

If you deliver, then you have my word you and your brother can go free.

Alina Merkova

No. She didn't trust her. Or her word. But she clearly knew about Jacek, because Sverdlovsk was where he had been taken off the train.

Sugihara's package in exchange for Jacek's freedom.

It was a trick, she was sure of it. But what if it wasn't? What if it was the one chance for Jacek to be free, and she blew it? She agonized over it, her stomach in knots, her hands gripping the paper as she read it over and over. She was ninety per cent certain it was a ruse to get her out of the hotel with the package, but the other ten per cent? That was what got to her.

If she was to be caught and sent to a camp like Jacek, would she regret it? Would it be a fair price to pay to gamble for his freedom? She could almost taste their new life in America, both free, both away from this nightmare. She would give anything for it to be true.

Jacek would tell her to ignore it.

But if it was the other way around, and she was the one who was captive, what would Jacek do?

She pressed her forehead to her hands, because the answer was obvious. He'd have no hesitation – he'd risk it and go. There was her answer.

Yet the fear seemed to freeze her feet to the spot.

Could she ask someone to help? No, the woman had been clear; she had to do it alone.

Although she sat with it another ten minutes, her heart was already on the move, knowing that if she didn't take this one last sliver of a chance to free Jacek, she might regret it for the rest of her life. If she went to America without him, she would not be able to live with herself wondering if, after all, the woman was speaking the truth and she could have got him out.

Dr Rabinowitz had loaned her his map of Vladivostok and now she took it from her pocket. She spread it out on her lap, hands trembling, poring over the route, calculating the time it would take, and sensing it was less than a fifteen-minute walk. She'd have to be ultra-vigilant, and leave if it looked like the woman wasn't alone.

She was prepared for the risk, but it still terrified her as she walked past the Japanese guards and left the safety of the hotel.

The streets were busy with workers and trams squeaking past, and the smell of diesel and oil filled her nostrils as she navigated her way towards to the waterfront, keeping the open space of the sea in her eyeline. She was conscious of every footstep behind her, and whipped around several times to see unfamiliar Russian faces, sunk in their own thoughts as they hurried past. At one point she thought she saw the spy from outside the apartment, the man in the homburg hat, but when she looked round he was gone, and with so many office workers, all dressed in similar hats, it was impossible to tell.

On the waterfront there were steps leading down to a beach, now blocked off by barbed wire. It hadn't stopped the fishermen, who had gathered further around the concrete promenade and stood like statues, watching their lines in the grey grainy light. She wished she was as calm as they looked, but her stomach was already protesting.

She squinted at the signs above the shops by the pier. Most were boarded up or had their steel shutters down, but one had a light in the window. This had to be the place, but she was too much on edge to just go in. Instead, she walked past it, trying to see in through the window, but it was steamy and all she could see were dim silhouettes of two figures behind the notices that were taped to the windows.

She turned at the end of the row and the next time she stopped at the door. She glanced behind but could see nobody on the pavement behind her.

'People's Canteen,' the Russian sign read.

Posters were plastered on the glass. One showed two red flying flags and underneath, stylized women singing. *Listen country, the dream of the people is calling. Rejoice and sing!'* Another one showed men hammering on giant anvils. *'All power to the Soviet workers!'*

She couldn't see inside. She would have to go in. Even though it could be a trap. Mentally, she prepared herself, knowing the danger. She turned the handle and opened the door. An elderly couple in padded cotton jackets were hunched over bowls by the window, but a young woman with sleek auburn hair was sitting alone in a corner. She was wearing a beige raincoat and her hands were resting on the table beside her handbag and cup and saucer. She looked ordinary, like an office worker.

There were no men visible, and behind the counter only a serving woman in a tightly bound headscarf, rubbing vigorously at a cup with a cloth. Zofia stepped inside but left the door ajar.

'You are Alina?' she asked the woman in the corner.

'Zofia? Come and sit,' she said with a smile. 'Take off your coat. I'll order coffee.'

Zofia remained standing. Alina had a broad forehead and high cheekbones, her eyebrows heavily plucked. Her expression was inviting, but something about the way she was dressed reminded her of Masha.

'You have something for me,' she said, patting the space on the table. 'You can put the package down here.'

'Tell me what you know about my brother first.'

'Ah yes, Jacek Kowalski.' A pause. 'Your brother is already in a gulag in Vakhrusheva.' She smiled triumphantly and her eyes flicked sideways to the counter. At the same time Zofia heard the door behind her close.

Zofia swivelled on her feet and with a sickening jolt recognized the plaid scarf of the man from the alley.

'You bitch,' she said to Alina. 'You set me up.'

A man in a green uniform emerged from the kitchen. Her mind jangled a warning. *NKVD*. In an instant her hopes fled. She'd been a fool to come here, such a fool.

She lunged for the door but plaid scarf was blocking her path. He shoved her in the chest and pinned her by the shoulders, face to the side wall.

'Don't make a fuss.' Russian words in her ear. From the corner of her eye, she glimpsed the elderly couple staring idly at them as if this was an everyday occurrence.

'An enemy of the people,' the NKVD man announced to them. He reached to pull the rucksack off her shoulders but she had both arms in the straps and it wouldn't come loose. She inhaled and opened her mouth to scream for help, but the NKVD officer locked an arm around her neck, his sleeve clamped hard against her windpipe.

'You will come with us,' he said as she coughed and gasped, unable to grab a breath. 'Don't make trouble. We just want to ask you a few questions. About Masha Romaska.'

Masha. Just as she suspected. She kicked a heel backwards at his shin but it only made him redouble his grasp.

The officer holding her loosened his grip a fraction to shunt her towards the door. A small window of space. Zofia grabbed a fork from the nearest table and using all her strength stabbed it deep into his face. He let go immediately to clutch his cheek as she squirmed and grabbed the door handle to throw herself out.

She fell straight into another woman about to come in with a wheeled bag full of shopping. Zofia tumbled over it and her shoulder hit the ground with a crunch, but in a heartbeat she was up. She stumbled over the shopping trolley, and sprang into the road, powering away.

She'd been stupid. She'd nearly lost everything. They weren't going to let Jacek go. She could almost hear Jacek telling her how foolish she'd been.

Shouts in Russian and boots thumping just behind her as she careered away from the waterside, shoulder throbbing and legs straining to get up the hill.

Into a narrow passageway that ended in stone stairs – a curve of slippery flagstones. Lungs bursting, she hauled herself up them two at a time, hanging on the steel banister.

Still, they were gaining on her.

She darted down a side street, past two parked bicycles chained to a lamp post. Seeing the possibility, she paused a second too long to see if she could unhitch one, but the men closed in. The street was deserted, and a dead end. They were on her immediately.

The NKVD man's face was pouring blood onto his collar. 'That was a mistake. You are under arrest,' he said.

The other Russian in the plaid scarf was still cajoling her, his palms up in warning. Now he was closer she could see his pale face speckled with freckles, and his sandy eyelashes. 'We just need to talk to you about Masha Romaska,' he said, trying to quieten her. 'We wish you no harm.'

'You're lying,' she said, eyes darting sideways to look for a way out.

At the sound of someone coming, both men turned to look to the open end of the street.

Heading towards them was the other man she'd seen in the alley, the spy in the homburg hat. He was running, his feet slapping against the paving stones.

Shit. She hadn't a hope against three. She ignored him and made a last-ditch attempt to break away, but the NKVD man had already taken hold of her arm, and he was bigger and stronger. He twisted it viciously up her back. Zofia grunted as she tried to free herself. Then she went limp so they had to drag her. Meanwhile, every fibre of her being protested, gathering her strength like compressing a ball.

'Wait!' the approaching spy shouted.

At his voice she flicked her gaze up to meet his face. Haru. It was him under the hat.

She was too shocked to move.

'Where are you taking her?' Haru jumped before the two men, planting himself in their path.

'Out of my way.' The NKVD man paused to shout at him, but it was enough.

Zofia swung one knee sharp into the groin, which rocked her

captor on his feet. His grip loosened and she snatched herself away and ran.

She didn't look back because she had only one thought, to get out of their reach. And she didn't look back to see what Haru was doing there either, though the thought rattled in her head that he'd been the man she'd seen this morning, watching from the arcade.

No time to wonder why, now. She had out-run men before, she remembered. At the Polish crossing into Lithuania, when Jacek had told her, 'Go! Run and never stop running until you cross the line.' It had been dark and there were no lights, and she'd blundered through the inky black, dreading a sudden spotlight. Her feet were so frozen that every step over the icy tussocks was like daggers in her soles, while ahead of her, Tata was sprinting and stumbling, his arms flailing, his old raincoat flapping. He was going without her. She had forced every muscle into moving and her heart had beaten so hard she thought it might explode and kill her.

Here, the hard pavement throbbed through her thin soles, and she didn't know where to run. The Russians hadn't given up. She'd need to use her brains, and lose them somehow. She increased her pace, pumping her breath in time with her arms, searching for an exit.

A glance behind. The NKVD man was closest, the other man who was clearly less fit was lagging but still running, thudding after him. And after them, Haru, his hat flapping in one hand.

She shot around a corner and through an arch and within moments found herself in a maze of warren-like streets. She darted down the nearest passageway.

A pause to gulp air. A whole quarter of uninhabited buildings. Everything was sodden brick and wood and dripping with damp. Shutters were down or broken, trestles disintegrating against the bare brick walls. A dilapidated shop sign read, *Canary Birds, Millionka*. The place name was written both in Russian, and underneath in Chinese *kanji*, which she couldn't read.

One rotting bamboo birdcage dangled in the window.

She dodged sideways down another narrow alley and then slid to a halt, heart hammering.

She was trapped in a small courtyard, surrounded by a U-shaped first-floor balcony of rotting wood. It formed a bridge between two buildings, but there was no way out except back the way she'd come. Treacherous-looking steps led to the floor above. She had just decided not to risk the stairs when she heard running feet and then a few moments later, men's voices.

'Which way?' one of them said between gulps of air.

'You go this way and I'll try down here. Yell if you find her. She's a vicious little bitch.'

She needed to get out of sight. Grasping the damp wooden banister, she retreated up the mouldy wooden steps on tiptoe, her stomach dropping every time a stair threatened to give way.

Across disintegrating floorboards. Every shop had been looted, doors prised or jemmied open. Empty barrels lay on the ground. Display cabinets with unidentifiable objects decomposing under broken grimy glass. The peeling walls reeked of damp and mould, the stoves rusted. A glance showed more Chinese shop signs, or messages scratched into the wood in *kanji*.

Nobody here. No one to help. A sob escaped her as she wildly searched for a hiding place.

A curtain flapped against a broken window. She remembered Otto telling her Stalin had purged the port of Chinese people and sent them to gulags.

She flung open a cupboard but it was shelved. No room to hide there.

Into the next shop through the open door. A granary once, she guessed. A rotting barrel stood near the door, only its rusty iron bands holding it together. Another row of barrels stood near the wall. Her best chance. They had once held barley or rice for a few grains were stuck to the floor around them in a gelatinous mass. No lids, though.

The noise of someone moving below. Her pulse throbbed with fear.

There was no option but to wedge herself behind the barrels, crouching like a dog, pulling her coat in tight around her as she listened.

A creak on the stairs and a man's footsteps coming up. She tried to make herself smaller, but knew it was a bad place to hide. Her breath came fast and shallow as she weighed up whether to stay there or run; which would give her the best chance. And all the time she could hear the creak of the stairs.

She stood up again, priming her legs to run, but her knapsack hit against the wall. Only a small noise but it stopped the man outside.

Silence.

The footfalls came closer. She ducked back down, squatting, holding her breath and rigid with fear.

A whisper. 'Zofia? Are you there? It's me, Haru.'

She peeked out of the gap between the barrels. He was coming in slowly, as if approaching a wild deer. His hat had gone and his brow wet with sweat. He scanned the room as if he might have to run at any moment, but then his eyes fixed on the barrels and he came closer.

It was a useless hiding place. Reluctantly, she stood up. 'Why are you following me? You shouldn't be here.'

'They went into the next alley.'

'Is there another way out?' she whispered.

'No. I don't know.'

'What if they come up here?'

Her question was never answered because the scuff of boots in the yard below silenced them both.

It sounded like just one man. Haru beckoned her towards the door. She shook her head, not knowing what he meant. But then he pointed to the barrel by the door, mimed rolling it.

She nodded. They tipped it over and began to roll it towards the stairs. It was rotting and she wondered if it might disintegrate because of its own weight. Below them, the NKVD officer heard the noise and glanced up.

'Come out,' he said. 'We know you're up there.'

Over the rusted iron railing she caught a glimpse of a set jaw, the blood on his cheek. He grabbed the banister to stride up the stairs.

'Wait,' Haru said as the Russian began to climb. 'Now!'

A deep breath. Together they launched the barrel as hard as they could down the stairs. It hit the Russian right in the thighs and toppled him, the barrel crashing against the steps and bouncing over him as he was steamrollered to the bottom.

Zofia was motionless for a moment in shock. Then, 'Run!' she shouted.

Across the wooden bridge to where there were more slippery stairs on the other side of the courtyard. Down the steps as the Russian groaned but didn't get up. Perhaps he couldn't. The barrel was all around him in pieces of splintered wood and iron.

They shot out of the alley, Haru grabbing for Zofia's hand as they went. But he missed her hold by inches and she barged straight into plaid scarf man, who must have heard the commotion. Winded, she tried to veer past him but was brought up short. He had hold of the edge of her coat and wouldn't let go.

She looked into his freckled face, searching for something human, some sense of decency. 'Were you telling the truth? Do you know where my brother is? Is he in a gulag already?'

He laughed. 'What does it matter? He's nothing. One of thousands. Who knows where they sent him?'

A great surge of anger. She was in a perfect position now to use her wrestling skills and she rotated his forearm into an arm lock and with one sweep of the foot threw him to the ground. *For Jacek*, she thought.

He landed with a satisfying thud just as Haru arrived to help, and she shot out of the Russian's reach and bolted, with Haru's feet skidding after her. Haru was wiry and athletic under his coat and kept up with her easily.

A clock in the distance chimed the half-hour.

'Which way?' She was breathless. 'I need to get to the boat.'

'I guess downhill,' he said.

Zofia glanced back to see the Russian had stood up and was bent double, holding his knees. He raised his head to watch them go but didn't come after them. She guessed he wasn't keen on running.

'How did you find me?' she asked Haru as they wove their way out of the mishmash of abandoned houses, jogging past rusted braziers, rotting baskets and windows smeared white with pigeon droppings.

He didn't answer. Just turned to her and said, 'Where did you learn to fight like that? He must have been twice your weight and solid as a tree, yet you threw him over as if he weighed nothing.'

'My brother Jacek taught me wrestling. We used to practise a lot. When you practise a lot, you don't forget.'

They caught a tram down to the harbour. Zofia was agitated, wishing it would go quicker. Almost twelve, and they were still searching for the *Amakusa-maru*, the boat. Zofia was confused by the number of freighters lined up at the docks, at the crowds of men unloading crates and sacks of goods.

She turned to Haru in anguish. 'Where is it?'

'Is that it?' He pointed. He'd spotted the hotel's coach on the quay with the Japanese guard unloading a group of passengers.

She set off down the hill at a run, scooting past the cars and wagons towards the gangplank and the queue of dishevelled passengers, with Haru right on her tail. At the end of the queue, she turned to him, stricken, the unsaid goodbye stuck in her throat. She reached out a hand to him.

He covered it, where it rested on his shoulder. His gaze was steady, determined. 'If you will accept it, I will accompany you on the boat in third class.'

'Why? Aren't you travelling with your boss?'

'No. I gave in my notice.'

'What?'

'I was worried about you. I saw a man was following you, the one you just fought to the ground. He was tailing you right from the station at Vladivostok. I knew you were in some sort of trouble so I followed him to see what he did after you went to your hotel. He went to the offices of the NKVD in central Vladivostok. It didn't look like good news.'

She shook her head. 'They want the package I'm carrying.'

'I guessed it.'

'So why did you leave your job?'

'Because Tanaka-san wanted me to go straight back to work, and I couldn't do it. Because a young Polish woman in a blue coat had somehow got to my heart.'

She shook her head, pushing the compliment away.

'Zofia, I was scared for you.'

'I can take care of myself.'

'I know. I've seen it. But that's not all – these might be the last days, these days on the boat. Because I felt something for you and I was hoping it was not just on my side. I can get another job. But you only get one or two moments in life like this. *Koi No Yokan*, the Japanese say. It means "it is meant to be". The Japanese think of it as a blow to the heart from which you won't recover. It felt right to honour it.'

His words moved her. They were not how a Polish boy would speak. 'I did feel something. I mean, I do.' She looked up at him, at the light in his eyes.

He fished in his suit pocket and held something out on his palm. 'I got a third-class ticket for the boat. I thought if I couldn't get you to talk to me before you got on the coach, then I'd have more chance in the three days on the boat. I watched for you at the hotel, to ask you before you boarded the coach, but you

293

slipped away before I could talk to you. So I followed. I wasn't expecting to get into a fight, though.'

'I'm glad you were there, but I can't make any promises.' Her emotions were churned up.

She felt his warm hand pressing her palm just once before he let go. 'In Japan, we do not show our affection in public. It is always behind closed doors. This doesn't mean I don't care for you. I hope to show you in many other small ways. Excuse me if this is different from the Polish way.'

'It suits me. I need time to think. I have to finish what I started, and I won't be happy until the parcel Sugihara gave me is in the hands of his friend General Sato.'

The *Amakusa-maru* had once been a Russian cruise liner for tourists but was now an empty shell used to carry goods. The ship's echoing cargo space was already crammed with hundreds of men, women and children, and the noise of all the people talking was deafening. She realized that to have a conversation, she'd have to shout.

Dr Rabinowitz and his students were gathered in an excited knot in the centre of it all, getting out their shared blankets and beginning the *minchah*, the afternoon prayer. It was about as different from Haru's first-class compartment on the Trans-Siberian as it could be. There were no seats and people squatted on the metal floor with what little luggage they possessed.

To his credit, Haru didn't seem daunted, despite having no luggage with him either, only the tickets in his pockets and some small change.

'I can last a few days,' he said. 'I left my things in Tanaka-san's hotel. But I have plenty of clothes at home in Tokyo.'

Zofia couldn't bear the cramped conditions and went up on deck to try to breathe in some air. The shores of Russia receded, and the Sea of Japan was the colour of mackerel, shimmering shades of silver in the afternoon light.

But if it was goodbye to Russia, it was also goodbye to so many other things – to Otto, to Masha. She felt guilty for leaving them behind, though she knew they were nowhere to be found now, not even in Russia. She was saying farewell not only to her homeland in the West, but to Uncle Tata and Jacek, and she couldn't even bear to think of them somewhere out there in a gulag, in the whistling winds and snows of Siberia.

Tears slid from her eyes, but better here where no one could distinguish them from the salt spray. The ship tilted on the waves, and Zofia felt herself all at once stateless. Out here there was nothing to cling to; too much air. The shifting deck only made her feel more unstable, and she had a sudden, desperate urge to be back in the cramped belly of the boat with the rest of the human cargo.

When she made her way back down, Haru was waiting anxiously and spotted her immediately as she came off the stairs.

'I've been exploring,' he said. 'Found out where to buy food, the way to the ladies' room. The things you need to know to make it tolerable.'

She smiled her thanks at him, and his eyes lit up. And over the next few days Haru was invaluable. He translated the sheet of instructions for refugees given to them by Osako, the Japanese representative of the Japan Tourist Bureau. Otto's words came back to her, the quotation from Dostoevsky. *The mystery of human existence lies not in just staying alive, but in finding something to live for.*

Or someone, she thought.

The journey was never going to be luxury, but Haru was true to his word, and did his best to care for her. For Zofia, still feeling panic rising at every loud noise, his presence was like a lamp in the darkness. When she worried about mines and the Nazis torpedoing the boat, he even took her to show her the lifeboats.

At night, in the pitching gloom, he held her hand. He had found a blanket from one of the crew and they lay down side by side, gazing into each other's faces. She let him talk of Japan, its beauty and its culture, as the snores and grunts and cries of children went on around them. She told him of her twin brother, of their childhood together, and of how she felt Jacek was watching over her this whole journey.

'You will see him again,' Haru said.

'You can't know that,' she said.

'I can. Because you talk of him as if he were still alive, and if anyone should know it is you. Trust me, he will know when you deliver the parcel.'

She was silent a moment, hoping he was right.

'I will take you to the moon festival and to the *sakura*, the cherry blossom in the spring,' Haru whispered. 'It is so beautiful and yet so transient. It has a spiritual meaning for us in Japan. A reminder that life is fleeting.'

'I need no reminder of that,' she said.

He gripped her hand where he was holding it tight to his chest.

'I know. But I wish you could see it, all the same.'

Chapter 37

The first night in Tsuruga, Zofia fell asleep exhausted, barely aware of the itch of the tatami matting on the floor, or the milky paper and bamboo blinds at the windows. She slept clinging on to her belongings as usual, still frightened to let them go.

There had been so much to see in her first glimpse of Japan, the clusters of tiny blue-roofed houses, the sheer orderliness of the streets. She'd been amazed at how much writing there was on the shopfronts – all the vertical signs with the graceful *kanji* announcing what was for sale, picked out in gilding or with the touch of a brush. And at night, the ghostly glow of paper blinds at windows, of paper lanterns outside elegant gateways, of the moon like a half-bitten coin making the hostel roof shine silver. It reminded her of Haru's talk of the autumn festival, and the memory of it stirred up her longing for him.

Haru had gone to spend the night away from the refugees at a *ryokan*, a Japanese homestay with friends of his parents. When she awoke, she lay in bed wondering if he was thinking of her the way she was thinking of him. It seemed such slim odds that they should have met at all, and yet their rapport was instant, even amongst this mess of a war. She recalled her very first glimpse of him, back in Moscow, before they had even boarded the train, and how that moment, the picture of his slim, relaxed frame, had stuck fiercely in her mind, despite everything that followed.

She'd been lucky to pass through Tsuruga port control without incident – lucky because Sugihara had given her a transit visa stamped with Curaçao, and because Haru held on to her arm the whole time. And much luckier than two unfortunate souls, who after more than ten thousand miles and travel through eight time zones, were turned away at passport control and sent back to Vladivostok, where they were likely bound for the *Vladlag*.

Zofia threw off the rumpled sheets and dressed in the warm air. She said a silent prayer as always for Jacek's safety, knowing that now she was actually in Japan, she must do what he was tasked to do and deliver Sugihara's package to General Sato in Tokyo. She thought of all the men and women who had written their stories, through pain and grieving, and knew that they might as well have been written in their own blood. After all that had happened, the long journey from Kaunas to here, her stomach fluttered with nerves of a different kind. Would she be able to convince Sato of the parcel's importance?

She'd arranged to meet Haru at three that afternoon to discuss travel onwards to Kobe, and from there to Tokyo. The Hebrew Immigrant Aid Society was based in Kobe too, and they would provide them all with basic accommodation and Japanese Yen from the tourist board. Dr Rabinowitz and the yeshiva students were also bound for the town and had taken the early train, but she was waiting behind because Haru was telephoning the general's office to make their vital appointment.

During the day she watched the world go by, sitting on a pinewood bench in the garden of the hostel, admiring the women with their fashionable felt hats and neat little steps, and the men with their oiled black hair. Few kimonos or Japanese-style clothes were worn on the street here. After the confines of the train and the boat it felt good to be outside, breathing in fresh air and hearing the chittering of the birds. The maples in the garden glowed russet and gold in the sun.

From the garden she saw Haru arrive but he seemed agitated, and he kept glancing up towards the window where he expected to see her. Her heart gave a flip to see him and it was all she could do not to run to meet him.

'I'm here,' she called as she rushed over. 'Will he see us? What did he say?'

He shook his head. 'I've tried all morning and they wouldn't listen.'

'What?'

'First of all, I tried to tell them you had a gift of gloves from Sugihara for Sato's wife. They said he was too busy. Then, that they would enquire. Kept me waiting. Leave them at reception, they said. Then I told them you were a special diplomat from Lithuania. But they told me they don't want to receive a woman. It is not their way. They expect a woman to follow, not lead, and in their eyes you have no status as a woman, a foreigner, and a Jew.'

Zofia felt tears prick her eyes, but she held them back. 'So it's all been for nothing?'

Haru took her in his arms despite the conventions and hugged her tight. 'I'm so sorry. I kept insisting that you were a special envoy but they wouldn't budge.'

'I won't give up.'

'Even if you somehow managed to get an appointment, you will be the last.' He took hold of her by the shoulder and she could see it was going to be even more bad news. 'I'm sorry, but the general's aide was even less helpful when I told him you were Jewish. He regards Jewish refugees as a nuisance. He told me the Nazis are insisting Japan signs a paper, one that will ban all Jews from transiting through Japan. The foreign minister is inclined to agree and says there are too many Jews seeking asylum here and he intends to close the borders. Even now they are scheduling a meeting with the Reich officials to prepare the paperwork.'

'But that would be a disaster! What about all the people waiting to get out of Lithuania?'

'I know. Japan is under pressure because so few nations will take in Jews, and because when refugees don't leave straight away, we can't cope with the numbers. But I can't believe my government will agree to turn away people fleeing for their lives.'

'Even more reason for me to take this package to General Sato. If he reads it, he'd see why we need safe passage.'

'I don't think you'll even get through the door. His aide was dismissive. He just didn't understand. He told me to drop the gloves there in the lobby as if you were a simple delivery boy. So I had to explain about Consul Sugihara and how he had entrusted your brother with this package and about its importance. I told them they must hear your story.'

'And did it persuade them?'

A rueful shake of the head. 'Sato will not see you.'

'Then we go to Tokyo and sit on his doorstep until he agrees.'

Chapter 38

The journey to Tokyo on the small Japanese train was nothing like the Trans-Siberian. They rattled past the rice paddies and peak-roofed villages and, despite Haru's company, Zofia was too preoccupied to talk. They spent the night in a small hotel in separate rooms. Zofia fell into a sleep full of nightmares of running to catch up with Jacek, who was on a train that was always just disappearing out of view, so she slept fitfully, apprehensive about their reception at the naval offices.

After breakfast the next morning Haru handed her a cardboard carrier bag. 'Here. I went out yesterday and bought you this.'

'For me? What is it?'

'It's a kimono. A formal robe. A good-quality one with the symbols of good luck on the lining. Underneath it, you will wear the *nagajuban*, the cotton lining, and over it, the *obi* or wide belt. The kimono is rose-coloured and will suit your pale colouring and dark hair. Maybe it will help.'

Zofia went up and tried to put the unfamiliar garment on. It smelled new, and she realized she had owned nothing new for years. How like Haru to think of it. The edges of the sleeves were satiny and the main body of the gown was printed with a delicate pattern of flowers. She wrestled with it until she thought she had it right, wishing there was another Japanese woman there to show her. A robe fit for royalty. Zofia looked at herself in the wardrobe mirror. She suspected the kimono made her look even more like a fish out of water, but it was certainly less ugly than her old print dress underneath, and perhaps the fact she had made an effort might impress the men at the naval offices.

She looked at her reflection doubtfully. It made her heart beat faster that Haru had given her this expensive gift, and she wanted to please him, but she couldn't wear it. It hid her struggle, so she no longer looked like a Jewish refugee. It made her feel less like herself, less like Jacek's sister.

A honk of a horn outside. The cab must be here.

She took off the robe, put her old coat back on over her print dress, combed her hair and fastened it back from her face. This was it. She drew herself up and reminded herself of Jacek's promise to Sugihara.

Haru didn't mention the fact she wasn't wearing his gift, and opened the door for her to step into the cab. They didn't talk on the way, both of them deep in thought, both aware that this meeting would affect the lives of so many more.

The naval offices were constructed of yellow sandstone, four storeys presiding over immaculately kept lawns, so pristine they looked as if they couldn't possibly be real grass. It made Zofia's palms sticky just to see how perfect it all was. Maybe she should have worn the robe, she thought, just as Haru turned to her and said, 'You know, you were right not to wear the kimono. It would make them see you as a Japanese woman, to be seen and not heard. And you look quite beautiful, just as you are.'

Heat came to her face, but she knew she had to focus on her task ahead. A uniformed doorman escorted them to a long low reception desk, following them as if they were criminals, despite Haru's polite bow. Military men were stationed all along the corridor with bayoneted rifles. There was no chance they would get through without an appointment.

The man behind the counter, whose oiled hair was plastered to his scalp as if painted on, had the supercilious manner of the worst kind of hotel receptionist. When Haru began to ask him politely for an appointment, he became even more officious and barely listened to Haru's request that Zofia should be granted an audience with General Sato. Instead he shook his head and looked askance at Zofia, as if her very presence offended him. Haru persisted and finally after much persuasion the receptionist reluctantly picked up the internal telephone. After a moment, he handed the receiver to Haru.

Haru tried to reason with the man on the other end, but Zofia could see by Haru's body language that he was having trouble. The conversation went on in Japanese and she understood none of it, except she caught the word 'Rabinowitz' several times – the only word she recognized. When the conversation was over, Haru put down the heavy black receiver as if he had been cut off.

'What?' She was desperate to understand what was going on.

Haru drew her to one side. 'If we are to be seen he insists on having a delegation of high-up Jewish men to accompany you. Japan is like that, the status of the people doing the negotiations is paramount. I couldn't think of anyone else so I suggested Dr Rabinowitz from the train, and after a little persuasion, and my insistence that Dr Rabinowitz was of suitably high status, the General has agreed to receive him.'

'But he's only just gone to Kobe. And now he'll have to come back. How long will it take him to travel from Kobe?'

'Nine hours on the train.'

'And he's only a poor rabbi, not any kind of diplomat.'

'They don't know that. I told them he was an esteemed teacher of the leading yeshiva in Lithuania. And I suggested Dr Rabinowitz could bring his personal assistant and we will collect them from the station.'

'You mean Rabbi Nowak?'

'If he'll come. It made Dr Rabinowitz sound more important.

We'll have to persuade them both. It was the only thing I could think of.'

'Even if Dr Rabinowitz were to make such a long journey, I'm not sure he can be of much use. I told him nothing of Sugihara or what I was carrying.'

'It is the Japanese way. They refuse to negotiate with people they deem to be below them in rank. And if you do see anyone from the government, you must make sure to show due deference. Same to any dignitaries you will meet. Keep your eyes cast down. Bow, bow and bow again. The lower the better.'

'Do you think Dr Rabinowitz will come?'

'We'll wire him, and tell him—'

He turned, for just at that moment there was a crunch of gravel and another car drew up outside the entrance, a long sleek saloon. She turned to see the chauffeur open the door and to her horror, three German SS officers got out of the car, each impeccably dressed in all black with red swastika armbands, shiny boots and low-peaked caps.

They were coming in. Zofia was seized by emotion. Just the uniform itself was enough to intimidate her. She stood transfixed as they strode through the lobby as if they owned it, intent on casual conversation, completely ignoring Haru and Zofia, who were forced to step aside.

Behind the reception desk, the officious receptionist bowed low. A short smiling conversation ensued, and then the receptionist escorted the Germans personally down the linked corridor and out of sight as if they were honoured guests. Every soldier on guard bowed as they passed. Zofia felt the Nazis' power and it made her angry.

Haru had overheard their talk at the desk. 'They're the delegation from Germany meeting with Sato and other government ministers,' he whispered. 'I suspect they are the ones that want to ban Jews from coming in to Japan. They'll be here for preliminary talks to hammer out the details of the agreement.'

'You mean they might decide today?'

'No. I heard them say that von Ribbentrop, the Nazi foreign minister, will be here on Monday.'

The man behind the desk returned and glared at them with a look that clearly meant 'are you still here?'

Zofia grabbed Haru by the arm. 'Tell him Dr Rabinowitz will be here tomorrow. Tell him to schedule a meeting with Dr Rabinowitz and they mustn't decide anything until they've seen us.'

Haru tried, but the receptionist shooed him away and then went into a side room and shut the door.

COME TO NAVAL OFFICES TOKYO STOP MOST URGENT STOP AFFECTS ALL JEWS IN JAPAN STOP WILL COLLECT YOU AND COMPANION FROM STATION STOP ZOFIA FROM TRANS-SIB

When the wire was sent from their hotel, there was nothing they could do except bite their nails and await a reply. They sat in the small hotel bar and drank sake to bolster their courage, not daring to go out in case a reply came.

'I wouldn't blame him if he didn't come,' Zofia said. 'He's only just arrived in Kobe and we're asking him to turn straight around and get on another train.'

'I know, but we have to have trust. The sooner you can deliver that parcel, the sooner you'll be free. When it's out of your hands you'll be able to relax and enjoy Japan. You've come so far.'

'It will feel strange to let it go. It's the last link to my brother. Already I feel as if I have abandoned him.'

Haru took her hand and gave it a brief squeeze. 'No. You are so brave. You did everything possible. And you are just finishing what he started. He would be proud.'

'I hope I'm up to it.'

'You will be. Remember, they do things differently in Japan.

There is much more protocol, much more formality. Do not let it intimidate you. We have a saying in Japan, "fall down seven times, get up eight". It means we don't give up easily.'

'I'm not giving up. I'll never give up. I'm here for all the people whose lives are reflected in those papers.'

'Miss Kowalski?' The lift boy from the hotel held out a flimsy piece of paper.

It was the telegram.

LEAVING NOW STOP TRAIN ARRIVES TOKYO 10.37
TOMORROW STOP DR R

Zofia couldn't speak but just waved the paper at Haru, who read it and then swung her off her feet. Their lips met for only the second time, and then they grinned at each other, both tearful.

'Let's have a toast,' Haru said, tipping sake into two glasses, 'To Dr Rabinowitz.'

Chapter 39

Dr Rabinowitz and Rabbi Nowak approached them on the busy platform, looking grey-faced and worried. They were easy to spot, standing head and shoulders above the scurrying Japanese, but both rabbis seemed tired, their clothes crumpled and dusty, their shoes filthy. Zofia's jubilation waned. Japan was picture-postcard clean and these men were hardly going to impress anyone. But then, like her, their shoes had covered thousands of miles, and they had no sooner arrived in Kobe than they'd been asked to get back on a train.

She greeted them with affection – two familiar faces in a sea of foreign ones.

'Oh, it's so good to see you,' Dr Rabinowitz said.

'Thank you. And thank you for coming, I know it wasn't in your plans.'

'It is not me that makes the plans, is it now, but the one upstairs.' He gestured with his eyes to the sky and smiled.

They bowed to Haru warmly in the Japanese way. Haru telephoned the naval office to tell them of the imminent arrival of this great Jewish rabbi, then a taxi cab took them all straight there.

'What luxury,' Dr Rabinowitz marvelled to his friend, 'just to get in a cab.'

In the lobby their small delegation was greeted by a suited man in a brilliant white shirt who introduced himself in Russian as Fujisawa-san. His smile was fixed and his bow legs and over-intense gaze reminded Zofia of a bulging-eyed frog.

Haru introduced them all, then Fujisawa-san turned to Dr Rabinowitz and said in Russian he was to be their translator.

'But we already have a translator,' Zofia replied, dismayed. She indicated Haru. 'Kimura-san is to be my translator.'

'I am the best translator,' Fujisawa-san said in his heavily accented Russian, not even deigning to look at her, 'and have been with Miroyuki Sato for fifteen years. Kimura-san can wait for you outside.'

Haru stepped up to object and Zofia watched as the two men began to argue heatedly in Japanese. It wasn't a good start, but she didn't want to trust the translation to anyone else. Who knew how this Japanese stranger might twist her words?

Finally, Haru took her to one side. 'They won't see you unless Fujisawa-san translates. It's that simple. And not until this after-noon. There's nothing I can do. They will see only you and Dr Rabinowitz. But you must take this opportunity. You can do it. You can make sure they understand the truth. I'll wait for you outside, and I wish you all the luck in the world.'

She was angry that they'd effectively split their party in two and that Rabbi Nowak and Haru had to wait behind like second-class citizens. Finally, after what seemed like interminable waiting, the time came. Fujisawa-san's shoes clicked on the shiny wood floor as he led Zofia and Dr Rabinowitz down a panelled corridor past all the armed guards. Not one of them acknowledged the rabbi in the way they had the Nazis as they passed. Zofia's stomach twisted with nerves and her sticky palms only made her feel more apprehensive about their reception.

They were led into a small windowless antechamber. Fujisawa turned to her and said in Russian, 'Give the package to Dr Rabinowitz and General Sato will see him now.'

'No. I will give it to him myself. That is what Consul Sugihara asked my brother to do, and I am here in his place.'

'It is beneath the general to see a woman. Dr Rabinowitz is in your brother's place now.'

She held the package tighter, wrapping her arms in their threadbare sleeves around it. 'Either I see him myself or I do not deliver the package, and believe me, he will want to see what is in it.'

Fujisawa-san screwed up his face in a frown and disappeared through the double doors, beyond which she imagined the great man was waiting. Voices arguing from within – several gruff, guttural voices and the whining voice of Fujisawa-san.

He was gone about five minutes, during which time Zofia wished they had at least left a chair so poor old Dr Rabinowitz could sit. He was weary after the long journey, had been offered no refreshment, and was leaning against a wall now as if he could hardly hold himself up. When Fujisawa-san returned, he simply summoned them both with a sharp gesture and threw open the doors.

Across a polished expanse of wooden floor was a long table, at which a row of five men was sitting. Each one was in white naval uniform, clean shaven, with their black hair cut to within a millimetre, and every chest sported an array of medals. A glass of water and their peaked naval caps stood before each man in a ranked row. In the corners, two military guards with caps pressed almost to their noses stood to attention, with rifles at the ready.

The men said nothing but stared at her, unmoving, arms folded. It was the opposite of a welcome.

Zofia's mouth was dry. She did not know which was General Sato.

She stepped forward and made a bow from the waist. 'I bring greetings from the Japanese consulate in Kaunas, Lithuania. From Sugihara-san.' She looked to Fujisawa-san to translate.

After he'd finished, she stepped forward again and taking a deep breath, she lifted the parcel from her bag and placed it gently on the table before them. 'He asked me to deliver this important package in person.' She then bowed low again before stepping back.

That moment felt like letting go of her heart.

She saw all their eyes go to the battered package, before the man in the centre, the one with the most medals, reached out to pull it towards him. He examined it and then shook his head angrily. A rapid conversation with Fujisawa-san.

'He says the seal is broken, and to ask why,' Fujisawa-san translated. Zofia began to explain but she was interrupted. 'Not you. He is asking the rabbi. You may leave the room now.'

Furious that she should be so slighted, she dug in her heels. But by now Sato had pulled out the contents of the parcel. A ragged pile of papers and a message in Japanese *kanji*. A thin envelope bearing the photographs slid onto the desk in front of him.

General Sato read the message from Sugihara, prised open the envelope and withdrew the collection of small blackish-brown images. He brought his eyes close to the table, and she saw his expression change before he leant back away from them as if they might be contaminated.

Every eye at the table was fixed on the photographs.

'What are these?' The question was translated and addressed to Dr Rabinowitz.

The rabbi gestured to Zofia, 'The young lady will tell you.'

'The photographs,' she said, without being asked, 'show evidence of German atrocities in Poland. The documents are eye-witness accounts, including my own.'

Sato looked to Fujisawa-san for a translation. A further dialogue ensued, with Sato issuing some sort of order. Fujisawa looked disgruntled but bowed and retreated, banging the double doors behind him.

Zofia and the rabbi were alone in the room. She couldn't speak Japanese, so she was silent, detached from the others like an island. They stared at the pictures and then at her.

She could not bring herself to cast her eyes downward as instructed, but held her head high and stared back.

The men passed the photographs down the table. It was hard to think of these commanders in their immaculate white uniforms looking at those naked bodies piled on carts or riddled with bullets and thrown into a pit. She kept her head up and when one of them looked up at her, she met his gaze with her own challenging one until he was forced to look away.

Behind her, the noise of the door opening. And then, Haru's voice, greeting the men in Japanese.

She turned, surprised, and he came to her to explain in Polish. Apparently they needed someone who could translate Polish into Russian so the papers could be read to them. 'I can speak Polish, so I will translate them into Russian and then Fujisawa-san will translate the Russian into Japanese. That way, he is still the translator and doesn't lose face.'

All that fuss so a man could save face. It seemed a convoluted way of doing it, but a solution that produced nods from the implacable men on the other side of the table.

'But now's your chance,' Haru whispered to her in Polish. 'Speak now before they read, and I'll translate as best I can.'

She told them the story in her native Polish – right from when Sugihara had entrusted her brother with the parcel. And as the words spilled out, Haru translated them into Russian and then Fujisawa into Japanese. It was a low murmuring accompaniment as the story was being relayed in different tongues. She talked non-stop until she finally said, 'Please, honour these people by reading some of the testimonies.' She thought of Bronovski. 'A man died because he collected them. Do you want to be condoning these things? Ask Kimura-san to read some to you.'

Dr Rabinowitz, who had been standing silently all this time, began to sway on his feet.

Haru, seeing it, spoke swiftly in Japanese and Fujisawa-san rushed out of the door, returning with a chair.

Zofia hurried to help Dr Rabinowitz, who had turned pale and looked most unwell. He sank into the chair gratefully, and without thinking she grabbed a glass of water from in front of one of the naval captains and handed it to the rabbi.

He took it from her with shaking fingers and took a deep draught.

General Sato spoke and Haru translated. 'He asks where the elder travelled from.'

'Oh, just from Kobe,' Dr Rabinowitz replied. 'It is not so far. Not when you have walked from Warsaw to Kaunas.'

'Walked from Warsaw?' The word rippled around the table. 'The old man walked.'

'No need to make a fuss,' Dr Rabinowitz said.

This seemed to break the ice. A soldier was sent to fetch hot tea, and within moments, Haru was on the other side of the table, translating extracts from the documents into Polish, and Fujisawa-san was relaying the translation back to Sato and his officers.

Much shaking of heads and frowns of disbelief.

A sudden fist on the table. Sato had obviously heard enough. He gabbled angrily in Japanese.

Haru shook his head, obviously refusing to translate, but the general insisted.

More argument.

Finally, Haru wouldn't meet her eyes. 'He wants to know what the Jews have done that the German nation hates them so much,' he said.

'Not the German nation,' Zofia said, Otto's face immediately in the forefront of her mind. 'Only Nazis. The Nazis and their propaganda.'

The general seemed to have understood and waved away her objection, rattling another string of orders.

Haru shook his head, his expression torn. 'I can't translate this.'

Fujisawa-san had no such scruples and supplied the Russian.

312

'General Sato says the Germans have the impression Jews are born evil. What is the inherent evil they possess?'

Zofia looked to Dr Rabinowitz, whose colour had returned and who was sitting, fanning himself. It was a ridiculous question. Inherent evil? They hadn't done anything except live their lives. How could they answer? How could they explain? It was the one question they'd been asking themselves this whole war, and still they had no answer.

From his chair, Dr Rabinowitz, who had clearly understood, supplied an answer. 'It is because we come from the same roots as you.'

The translation passed across.

'What do you mean?' General Sato looked perplexed. 'You are Jews, not like us ...'

Dr Rabinowitz spoke again. 'They say one of the missing tribes of Israel came to Japan. And you are on the Nazis' list of undesirables too.'

Suddenly, Zofia saw what the rabbi was getting at and she spoke up to emphasize the point. 'If you read what the Nazis say in their original German you will see that they consider themselves to be what they call the master race. A master race of Aryans – tall, fair-haired, with certain athletic or Nordic characteristics. They consider other peoples to be inferior, those who are black or brown-skinned, Slavic, Chinese, Asian. I'm afraid to say, that includes the Japanese.'

Much consternation at the table. The simplistic translation came back. 'But Germany is our ally. That can't possibly be true.'

'They won't say it aloud to you while they want your armaments and your money. But have you ever seen a Nazi poster featuring anyone who isn't tall, fair and athletic? Have you ever seen any propaganda where the person is small and dark like me?' She paused. 'Or like you?'

When the translation was over, there was silence on the other side of the table. It was so obvious that they couldn't refute it.

Each of them was a short dark-haired man.

The five men at the table spoke in low voices amongst themselves. Their faces were serious and there seemed to be multiple stops and starts.

The papers were passed from one man to another before going back to General Sato.

Zofia gripped her fingers together tightly, unsure if they had really understood. Eventually they seemed to come to an agreement. Haru was asked to translate to her as Sato spoke rapidly, stuffing everything back inside the parcel.

Haru hesitated, his mouth working. Obviously he didn't want to translate, but felt duty bound to do it.

Sato shot out an order and gestured him to carry on.

'He says he has never seen these documents or these photographs. He has never set eyes on you, or heard anything about a message from Sugihara.' Haru's voice was so full of suppressed emotion he could barely speak.

Zofia pressed her hand to her mouth. She was still reeling at these words as Sato stood from the table and walked across the room towards the large open fireplace, before which stood a delicate arrangement of twigs and flowers.

Moving the vase aside, he thrust the parcel inside the grate and taking a zippo lighter from the stone slab on which it stood, flicked it open. Too late, Zofia saw what he was going to do. She dashed towards him as he flicked the flint and the flame leapt to the dry wrapping.

'No!' It was a shout of pure pain.

She tried to push past him to reach the papers but the wax seal had burst alight with a roaring whoosh and smoke billowed out into the room.

Sato was a heavy man, and he stood immoveable in front of the fireplace, one hand held out to prevent her getting by. She dropped to her knees and tried to reach past him into the flames until the two guards came to drag her away.

'You had no right!' she railed in Polish.

Haru came over to help her get up, and the big general spoke rapidly in Japanese to call his guards off.

The papers smouldered in the grate, charred into black tissue, disintegrating among flakes of ashes.

'How dare you.' Zofia spat out the words. 'Those memories cost men's lives, and now they are lost.' She turned to Haru. 'Tell him. Tell him most of those people are dead and will never again be able to tell their stories.'

Haru shook his head and looked at the ground to compose himself, but then he looked the general in the eye and translated it.

Words came back, addressed to Zofia, but she barely heard them. She had failed Jacek, and Bronovski. She had failed Otto, and all the unknown heroes like her father.

Haru was translating. 'He says they could not keep these papers. Not while they are allies of the Germans. It has already been agreed by President Hirohito that Japan's relationship with Germany will continue. It is out of his hands.'

More Japanese, but now General Sato was looking directly at her. The sudden murmur of surprise from the other men in the room made Zofia look up.

The general's eyes were warm and full of sympathy.

'He apologizes that he burned your papers and photographs, but he thanks you for bringing these things to his attention,' Haru translated.

The general kept his steady gaze fixed on hers. 'What has gone on in this room will not be forgotten. He has heard what you said and felt your passion and your heart. There will continue to be places for the Jews in Japan and he will see to it that refugees will always be welcome to travel through Japan. He says that though they cannot acknowledge the documents, your brother should be proud that you have fulfilled your duty.'

Tears had filled her eyes. Inside her, she felt Jacek smile. Perhaps the journey had not been a waste of time after all.

She bowed her thanks. A low bow right to the waist.

Through Haru's words, the general assured her that hospitality would await them all in fifteen minutes in another room.

In a larger reception room, a bright lobby with cream-coloured sofas around a large, low table, a banquet appeared. Japanese staff scurried in with plates of tempting dishes. Pains had obviously been taken to make sure the food was kosher, and two Shinto priests in tall black hats and white garb had been invited to join them.

Zofia took in the beautifully laid-out arrangements of rice balls with sesame, decoratively cut tangerines and chestnut paste sweetmeats. She had never seen such a feast.

'This is splendid,' Dr Rabinowitz said, forgetting the earlier frosty welcome. 'Such hospitality!'

He and his companion, Rabbi Nowak, were soon engaged with the priests in deep conversation about the missing tribes of Israel who had reputedly come to Japan, the translation aided by Fujisawa-san, who had lost his supercilious manner and now appeared to be equally fascinated by these strangers from the train.

All animosity had melted away, and the military presence had disappeared.

Zofia sank onto one of the sofas, exhausted. Her arms and her heart felt empty. She stared at the food and could not touch it.

Haru came to sit next to her. 'It's over,' he said in Polish. 'You did what you could and you spoke well. It was a conversation I will never forget. You spoke for the whole of humanity and I hope I did the translation justice.'

'Thank you for being here. I couldn't have done it without you.'

'Oh yes you could. You brought that package all the way from Kaunas with the NKVD and the SS both on your tail. You are incredible, do you know that? But now it's time for you to rest. Do you know what you will do?'

'I want to go on to America.'

'Oh.' She saw the disappointment in his face, and it made her both happy and hurt in a new way.

'There's no rush. Maybe you'd like to be still for a while. And you could do good work here,' he said, his eyes searching hers. 'I was thinking, I need a job and I might work for the Jewish Refugee Council, Jewcom, in Kobe.'

'Doing what? Translating?'

'Well, it would beat talking to Tanaka-san about oilfields. I can see how daunting it is, arriving here with nothing the way you did. And I like the idea of helping refugees when they arrive in Japan. I suppose I was hoping you might want to do the same.'

Unbidden, Sugihara's words came to her. *I hope you find love like your brother.*

She picked up a glass from the table and toyed with it. She hadn't really thought beyond this point. She'd focused on getting the parcel to General Sato. And she hadn't thought of falling in love, though clearly the way she felt now, that had happened, almost without her realizing it.

Haru was waiting with a hopeful look on his face. He clasped her hand between his. 'If you stay, there is so much we could do together,' he said, 'and I've so much to show you in the land of the rising sun.'

'You are too late,' she said, smiling. 'The sun's going down. Look.'

She pointed to the window where, behind the buildings, the sun was setting in a glow of pink and orange.

'Let's go outside,' Haru said. 'The air will do us good.'

He led her out through the double doors, past the waiting rickshaws on the street and around the corner to the formal garden behind the naval buildings. The air was warm, and it was an odd feeling to be in this open space with no one but themselves No one following them, no need to look over her shoulder.

His grip was warm as they walked, down past the ornamental flower beds, the heads of the chrysanthemums pale in the dusk, and out into an expanse of lawn surrounded by trees. There was

317

not a single other person in sight.

'It's getting dark,' he said. 'And I promised to take you to a moon festival. If we wait long enough, maybe the moon will come up for us.' He took off his jacket and lay it out on the grass before sitting down on it and stretching out his legs.

Laughing, she took off her old blue coat and shook it out.

'We might have a long wait,' she said, as she sat beside him, gazing up at the darkening sky. 'And I think the moon is waning.'

'Then we'll have to sit here until next month.'

'Sounds good to me.'

He lay back and she followed suit, looking out into infinite space.

'We're all under the same sky,' she said. 'It makes life so hard to understand.'

His hand reached for hers again and she felt the twine of his long fingers in hers, a gesture of understanding.

They lay there a few moments more before he rolled over to prop himself up on an elbow and look down into her face. His eyes were in shadow now under the fading light, but he brushed his fingers lightly over her forehead, a touch that made her hold her breath.

'Zofia,' he said. And her name had never sounded sweeter. Gently he lowered his lips to hers.

And she realized that now there would be time at last for all her unfinished things. Time for love to grow. Time for kindness, that most underrated of virtues. When before time had been her enemy, now it spread out before her, its hands full of wonders. And now her hands were empty, she was ready to grasp them all.

A Letter from Deborah Swift

Thank you for choosing *Last Train to Freedom*. If you enjoyed it, you can find out more about my books on my website www. deborahswift.com where you can also join my newsletter for news of my upcoming releases.

Operation Tulip

Holland, 1944: Undercover British agent Nancy Callaghan has been given her toughest case yet. A key member of the Dutch resistance has been captured, and Nancy must play the role of a wealthy Nazi to win over a notorious SS officer, Detlef Keller, and gain crucial information.

England: Coding expert Tom Lockwood is devastated that the Allies have failed to push back the Nazis, leaving Northern Holland completely cut off from the rest of Europe, and him from his beloved Nancy. Desperate to rescue the love of his life, Tom devises Operation Tulip, a plan to bring Nancy home.

But as Nancy infiltrates the Dutch SS, she finds herself catching the eye of an even more senior member of the Party. Is Nancy in too deep, or can Tom reach her before she gets caught?

Inspired by the true events of occupied Holland during WW2, don't miss this utterly gripping story of love, bravery and sacrifice.

The Silk Code

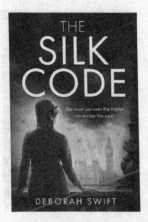

Based on the true story of 'Englandspiel', one woman must race against the clock to uncover a traitor, even if it means losing the man she loves.

England, 1943: Deciding to throw herself into war work, **Nancy Callaghan** joins the Special Operations Executive in Baker Street. There, she begins solving 'indecipherables' – scrambled messages from agents in the field.

Then Nancy meets **Tom Lockwood**, a quiet genius when it comes to coding. Together they come up with the idea of printing codes on silk, so agents can hide them in their clothing to avoid detection by the enemy. Nancy and Tom grow close, and soon she is hopelessly in love.

But there is a traitor in Baker Street, and suspicions turn towards Tom. When Nancy is asked to spy on Tom, she must make the ultimate sacrifice and complete a near impossible mission. Could the man she love be the enemy?

An utterly gripping and unputdownable WW2 historical fiction novel, perfect for fans of Ella Carey and Ellie Midwood!

The Shadow Network

One woman must sacrifice everything to uncover the truth in this enthralling historical novel, inspired by the true World War Two campaign Radio Aspidistra …

England, 1942: Having fled Germany after her father was captured by the Nazis, **Lilli Bergen** is desperate to do something proactive for the Allies. So when she's approached by the Political Warfare Executive, Lilli jumps at the chance. She's recruited as a singer for a radio station broadcasting propaganda to German soldiers – a shadow network.

But Lilli's world is flipped upside down when her ex-boyfriend, **Bren Murphy**, appears at her workplace; the very man she thinks betrayed her father to the Nazis. Lilli always thought Bren was a Nazi sympathiser – so what is he doing in England supposedly working against the Germans?

Lilli knows Bren is up to something, and must put aside a blossoming new relationship in order to discover the truth.

Can Lilli expose him, before it's too late?

Historical Note

About Sugihara Chiune and the 'visas for life'

Sugihara Chiune was a Japanese diplomat who really existed and saved the lives of thousands of Jewish refugees by issuing them with transit visas to Japan. There are several excellent biographies of Sugihara (including one by his wife) that tell his story, and how he and the Dutch consul became the lifeline for Jews escaping Nazi and Soviet persecution.

The Nazi invasion of Poland in 1939 trapped nearly three and a half million Jews in German and Soviet occupied territories, but before the Germans invaded the Soviet Union about two thousand Polish Jews found temporary safety in Lithuania, particularly in Kaunas, which had a large Jewish population.

However, the idea that Sugihara received any testimonies from these Jews before he left Lithuania, and that he gave them to a young man to deliver, is purely from my imagination. Zofia Kowalski and her brother Jacek are completely fictional, but I enjoyed thinking that this could have happened, and constructing a novel from my conjectures.

Sugihara really did have a German man working for him at the consulate, and I based the character of Otto Wulfsson on him. At that time, Germany and Japan were bound together through a political agreement, so it must have seemed a good idea at the time for the Japanese consulate in Kaunas to employ a young German with language skills. Little is known about the real man who worked for Sugihara, so I was free to make him a reluctant spy.

During the war, Nazi appeals to the Japanese government to adopt harsher policies towards the Jews were stalled by the Japanese, and the meeting and dialogue that took place at the naval offices in *Last Train to Freedom* is based on a rabbi's reports of a real conversation with Japanese officials. This meeting is detailed in the book *The Fugu Plan* by Marvin Tokaver.

On 31 December 1940, Japanese Foreign Minister Matsuoka stated, 'I am the man responsible for the alliance with Hitler, but nowhere have I promised that we would carry out his anti-Semitic policies in Japan. This is not simply my personal opinion, it is the opinion of Japan, and I have no compunction about announcing it to the world.' There were, however, many dissenting voices in Japan, who thought too many refugees were entering the country. When Sugihara gave out his 'visas for life' he knew he was acting without the permission of the Japanese government. He was forced to leave the foreign ministry after the Second World War for issuing the visas without authorization. However, his reputation was reassessed after the Israeli government bestowed upon him the honorific title 'the Righteous Among the Nations' in 1985, and since then he has become much better known for his deeds, which saved many lives.

The Tran-Siberian Railway is still in existence and is one of the most famous routes in the world. It is also the longest, at over 9,289 kilometres, or 5,772 miles, running from Moscow in the west to Vladivostok in the east. It was the only train route to traverse the whole of Russia during the Second World War. Several thousand Jewish refugees were able to make this trip thanks to the Curaçao visas issued by the Dutch consul Jan Zwartendijk and the Japanese visas issued by the Japanese consul, Sugihara.

All Trans-Siberian travel for private citizens ended on 21 June 1941 when the Nazis invaded the Soviet Union, so those who escaped Lithuania were the lucky ones.

About Kaunas, Lithuania, a place of divided loyalty

Lithuania has a centuries-long history of being governed by outside forces but declared independence at the close of the First World War, having been previously ruled by both Russia and Germany. As it was independent, many Jews fleeing the Nazis in Europe made their home there.

By the mid-1920s, dozens of foreign consulates had opened in Kaunas, Lithuania's then-provisional capital, but in June 1940 the Russians invaded again and by August all political ties were severed, and all consulates and embassies were forced to close.

After only a year of rule, the Soviets were ousted again by the Germans and for most Lithuanians this was a relief – all except the Jews who knew what Nazi rule would mean for them. Before the war, a quarter of the population in Kaunas was Jewish, but ninety per cent of them perished in the Holocaust. Some were confined to a ghetto from where they were transported to Dachau, where they met their fate, but many of them were murdered in Kaunas by Lithuanian Nazi collaborators.

The ghetto in which the Jewish population was confined was burned down by the Nazis as they retreated. Thousands were shot and thrown into mass graves at the Ninth Fort, a former Tsarist barracks on the outskirts of the city. There is now a museum there where you can find out more, and a memorial to the dead in the surrounding park.

About the 'mini ice age' of 1939–42

For three years during the Second World War there were unexpectedly long and severe winters. The year 1940 was part of a period of global climate anomaly that included a strong and long-lasting El Niño event from autumn 1939 to spring 1942. This event caused extreme climate conditions in the Northern Hemisphere, bringing low surface temperatures to Europe, Russia and the North Pacific Ocean, and conversely high temperatures to Alaska.

In 1939 the winter became so cold in Europe that Hitler was forced to postpone his attack on France and wait for an improvement in the weather. The rapid movement of ground forces and supply columns would be essential for keeping up the momentum of the attack, and poor weather and blizzards would make the logistics too difficult.

In 1940 temperatures were several degrees lower than average. Usually Moscow is warm in the summer, with rain in the autumn, and snow in the winter. However, the weather can bring surprises like extra-warm winter days followed by a freezing rain or snow even in June. The longest winters in Russia can be experienced in the northern part of Siberia and last from mid-September to the end of May.

After a hot summer, Siberia in the autumn of 1940 became much colder, with temperatures dropping as low as -10°F. I have used the idea of the lowest temperatures for this novel to emphasize the psychological emptiness of the refugees' journeys.

The fact that the winter 1940–41 also turned out abnormally cold in Europe and Russia caused Hitler to call for a climate workshop in Germany to evaluate the possible risk of a third cold winter 1941–42 in Russia, as he rightfully feared that this would affect his plans for a successful war against the USSR. The scientists assured him it was unlikely, with catastrophic results – over 186,000 German men were lost, mostly because of the severe weather.

Suggested Further Reading

Visas of Life and the Epic Journey by Akira Kitade

The Just – how six unlikely heroes saved thousands of Jews from the Holocaust by Jan Brokken

A Special Fate: Chiune Sugihara: Hero of the Holocaust by Alison Leslie Gold

In Search of Sugihara: The Elusive Japanese Diplomat Who Risked His Life to Rescue 10,000 Jews From the Holocaust by Hillel Levine

Official Secrets – What the Nazis planned, What the British and Americans Knew by Richard Breitman

The Fugu Plan: The untold story of the Japanese and the Jews in World War II by Marvin Tokayer

A Holocaust Memoir of Love & Resilience: Mama's Survival from Lithuania to America (Holocaust Survivor True Stories) by Ettie Zilber

To the Edge of the World: The Story of the Trans-Siberian Railway by Christian Wolmar

The Diary of a Gulag Prison Guard by Ivan Christyakov

Website: War Changes Climate www.warchangesclimate.com/b/Four_month_war.html

Acknowledgements

My thanks must go to my agent, Mark Gottlieb, and to all at Harper Collins for bringing this novel to publication. Special thanks to my excellent editors, Priyal Agrawal, Sophia Allistone and Cari Rosen, for their great editorial suggestions that have undoubtedly made this a better book. Writers often work alone and so I'm grateful for the daily friendship of the 'Coffee Pot' historical fiction gang, and as always, nothing would get done without the support of my husband, John.

Dear Reader,

We hope you enjoyed reading this book. If you did, we'd be so appreciative if you left a review. It really helps us and the author to bring more books like this to you.

Here at HQ Digital we are dedicated to publishing fiction that will keep you turning the pages into the early hours. Don't want to miss a thing? To find out more about our books, promotions, discover exclusive content and enter competitions you can keep in touch in the following ways: